SHIRL HENKE

in collaboration with

Jim Henke

CHOSEN WOMAN

LEISURE BOOKS NEW YORK CITY

For
Dale and Jan Harting
who opened their home to us
while we were in exile.

A LEISURE BOOK®

July 2009

Published by

Dorchester Publishing Co., Inc.
200 Madison Avenue
New York, NY 10016

ISBN 10: 0-8439-6248-8
ISBN 13: 978-0-8439-6248-2
E-ISBN: 978-1-4285-0696-1

The name "Leisure Books" and the stylized "L" with design are trademarks of Dorchester Publishing Co., Inc.

Printed in the United States of America.

10 9 8 7 6 5 4 3 2 1

Visit us on the web at www.dorchesterpub.com.

BESTSELLING AUTHORS PRAISE
AWARD WINNER SHIRL HENKE!

"Shirl Henke is one of the brightest stars in romance. Her engaging characters and talent for storytelling grip readers from first page to last!"

—Katherine Sutcliffe

"A riveting story about a fascinating period. I highly recommend *Paradise & More*."

—Karen Robards

"A grand and glorious novel....I couldn't stop reading."

—Bertrice Small on *Paradise & More*

"*Return to Paradise* swept me away!"

—Virginia Henley

"A romantic romp of a Western. I loved it!"

—Georgina Gentry on *Terms of Surrender*

"*White Apache's Woman* is a fascinating book...an absolute must read for anyone who loves American history."

—Heather Graham

"Fast paced, sizzling, adventurous...with a hot-blooded hero who will set your heart on fire."

—Rosanne Bittner on *A Fire in the Blood*

"A fascinating slice of history...with equally fascinating characters. Enjoy *Love a Rebel...Love a Rogue!*"

—Catherine Coulter

LAYING DOWN THE LAW

He grabbed her by her arms and fought the urge to shake some sense into her. Realizing what he was doing, he quickly released her.

Fawn almost lost her balance when he let her go. With one foot raised to kick him, she stumbled backwards. "Don't you ever touch me again!" she snarled.

"I'd sooner pet a tarantula. But your father hired me to keep you safe—I can see now why he paid so handsomely. You are a walking tornado, Miss Stanhope."

"And you are a coarse, vile-tempered, lower class... Irishman!"

"Guilty on all charges, but you're going to listen to me and do exactly what I say from now until I turn you over to the poor sons-of-bitches at your ranch. Then you're their responsibility. But as long as you're mine, no more getting off this train until we reach Hennessey. Don't you so much as wave at a sodbuster plowing a cornfield. Is that clear?"

"What will you do if I choose not to obey, Pasha Dillon?"

"Turn you over my knee and paddle your backside—something that your family, red and white, didn't do nearly enough of while you were growing up!"

Other *Leisure* books by Shirl Henke:

PALE MOON STALKER
THE RIVER NYMPH
TEXAS VISCOUNT
REBEL BARON
YANKEE EARL
WANTON ANGEL
WICKED ANGEL
WHITE APACHE'S WOMAN
RETURN TO PARADISE
LOVE A REBEL...LOVE A ROGUE
BROKEN VOWS
PARADISE & MORE
TERMS OF LOVE
McCRORY'S LADY
A FIRE IN THE BLOOD
TERMS OF SURRENDER
NIGHT WIND'S WOMAN

Authors' Note

Chosen Woman is probably the most difficult book I have worked on in over a decade. And it's all Jim's fault...well, maybe not entirely his fault. I'll get to that part later.

But he was the one who came up with the idea for an Irish-American lawman who would be hired to protect a now grown-up and educated Fawn from *Pale Moon Stalker*. I already knew she would be the heroine of our next story when I ended the last book with her vision gift. But I had no idea whom she would love or where her story would take place.

Jim persuaded me that Oklahoma Territory was the perfect setting. Okay, he was right about that—but he did so much research that I practically drowned in it! After reading his copious notes, I knew more than I ever wanted to know about the Oklahoma Land Rush of 1893. The only problem was, he had tons of historical detail and no plot. What...So... Ever. I'm used to taking his bare-bones story lines and developing them into coherence, but this was quite a challenge. I kept finding loose ends and continuity mistakes each time I resumed writing.

All right, I admit I had to stop work on Fawn and Jack's story to attend to other business, such as helping a friend recover from surgery. But if he had given me less history and more imagination, I wouldn't have felt so pressured when I returned to the computer. In spite of seemingly insurmountable obstacles, I fell in love with Fawn Stanhope and Jack Dillon, her Red Wolf. Oh, did I mention that Jim gave me the idea of making him her animal totem? He does get some things right...now and then.

After many false starts and revisions, I was finally satisfied that I had done justice to Fawn and Jack's story. And I did it without subjecting you, dear readers, to more than you ever want to know about land rushes!

Shirl

Second Author's Note

I think Shirl just accused me of lacking imagination. Nothing is ever enough for that woman. Listen, a while back I arranged a special wedding anniversary celebration.

I told Shirl we had reservations at one of her favorite eateries. Instead, I took her to the Stanley Courtel where, as impoverished grad students, we spent our honeymoon. To her complete astonishment, I pulled up to the very cabin where we had celebrated our nuptials, scooped her out of the car, carried her up the steps, and kneed open the door.

By prior arrangement with the Courtel owner the bed was strewn with dethorned long-stemmed roses, Champagne was icing, and a single candle burned on the nightstand.

Later, a sleepy Shirl murmured to me: "Honey, if you would learn to budget your time more effectively, we could have made those dinner reservations, too." Good grief!

Okay, so I got a bit carried away with the history, but there were actually three land rushes in the Oklahoma Territory and dozens of schemes to trick the Indians out of what small allotment lands they had left. So I went a little overboard. But I did give her a plot; she just didn't like it. And I even wrote the first chapter to get her started. But still she says I have no imagination! Well, I have enough imagination for this: the next time instead of red roses, the bed at the Courtel will be covered with cactus. And I am going to throw her right in the middle of it.

Jim

CHOSEN
WOMAN

Chapter One

"*Y*ou're a runt! Good grief, a veritable troll!"

Jack Dillon resisted the urge to turn around as the striking young Amazon circled him. He was half afraid that she'd pull a scalping knife from the folds of her elegant plum-colored day gown and slit his throat from behind.

She continued her insulting survey. "Why, I'm almost as tall as you!"

Nearly six feet in height, Jack felt that was her problem, certainly not his. He stared straight ahead, struggling mightily to keep his Irish temper in check. Lord, he needed this job to keep his newly established detective agency afloat.

As she walked around him, he could hear the click of high-heeled slippers. "Perhaps if I were wearing stilts . . ." he commented tightly, glancing pointedly at her shoes.

"You'd only appear more the escapee from Barnum & Bailey." She sniffed.

Dillon watched the expression in her exotic black eyes. She looked like a stock buyer who had expected to examine a blooded Arabian stallion but was confronted instead by a three-legged, one-eyed goat. He said nothing. Damned if he would furnish her with any more ammunition with which to insult him. She did not need the help. She was doing just fine on her own.

"Look at that nose! It's crooked. Broken in some brawl over a scarlet poppy, perhaps?" she inquired, her husky voice laden with ridicule. Oblivious to everything but her own temper, she missed the sudden flicker in his eyes. "How can you act as bodyguard to anyone? You apparently can't even guard yourself."

Jack resisted the urge to touch his offending anatomy. *Damned snotty brat! That beak of yours won't appear on any cameo brooch either.*

"Look at that hair," she went on. "It's . . . it's . . ."

Dillon's eyes turned translucent amber as his anger escalated. He stared at the girl, thrown off guard by her sudden silence. Now she seemed to be seeing him, really seeing him, for the first time. He cocked his head quizzically, then stood perfectly still. *What the hell will she do next?*

"Your hair is . . . red," she said, barely above a whisper.

"It was when I walked in here. Now it's probably gray!"

Dillon watched as the young woman, whom he prayed was not Fawn Stanhope, blanched, her golden complexion waxing a deathly pale. He thought she might be on the verge of fainting but fought the impulse to reach his hand out for her. If he did, he'd probably draw back a bloody stump. Besides, she deserved a fall from her high-heeled perch.

Perversely surprising him, she turned and fled down the long, polished marble hallway of the Stanhope mansion. Lord, she had acted as if a rabid wolf were about to devour her. "Ah, and sure the lad is never at a loss for charm. Great way to begin a job interview, Dillon," he muttered to himself.

"I do hope that you will forgive the lady."

The cultured, very British voice behind Jack made him turn. A frail, bald-headed man wrung his hands in embarrassment. "I assume, sir, you are Mr. Dillon?" he inquired.

Jack nodded, still fighting the urge to look down the hall where the Amazon had vanished.

"I am the Ruxtons' butler, Baldwin."

Of course you are, Jack thought dryly as the servant made a smart bow.

Ushering him across the wide foyer past a curving staircase, the elderly man explained, "That was Miss Fawn Stanhope."

Jack sighed. "I was afraid you were going to say that."

"She is really a kind and lovely young woman. Only sometimes a bit . . . ah . . . excitable."

"That's quite all right, Baldwin. I've encountered people suffering from the same condition. They were usually shooting at me."

The faintest touch of a smile passed fleetingly over the butler's face, but he suppressed it and gestured to a small, well-appointed room off the foyer.

"If you would wait for a moment in the receiving parlor, I shall inform m'lord and m'lady of your arrival."

Jack walked into the sitting room while the old man went to summon his employers. However, he was in no mood to sit. He paced, angry with himself and with the imperious Miss Stanhope . . . the brat! How could he have misinterpreted his information to conclude that the adopted Stanhope female was a pubescent girl instead of a full-grown woman? Then again, he'd had only a few days to conduct a hasty investigation of Stanhope after receiving the man's invitation. Still . . . *damn it!* Jack disliked sloppiness. He should have . . .

"Hullo, sir."

Dillon looked down at a young girl who could be no more than eight or nine, if that. A mane of thick, black, wildly curling hair framed an elfin face dominated by large eyes that were as green as fresh moss. She was the most beautiful child Jack had ever seen, with the possible exception of . . . *Not now!* His face hardened unconsciously as he thrust the memory back into the cellar of his mind.

Unperturbed by his expression, the child introduced herself. "My name is Delilah. I'm named after my Aunt Delilah, but everyone calls me Della. And this is Numbers," she said, gesturing to the small, untidy mutt that sat by her side, watching Jack with bright-eyed curiosity. "Please, sir, don't be mad with my sister!"

"My name is Jack, Miss Della, and I'm not mad . . . er, angry with your sister. She—"

"Well, you looked mad, Mr. Jack. But you see, Fawn gets fustated a lot when she has her sightings, 'cause she can't always understand what they mean. I think that scares her. I've heard that Great Grandpapa has sightings, too, but he is the oldest grandpa in the whole world, I think. He's so old that even Numbers can't count his age."

The scraggy old dog gave a wheezing woof in seeming agreement. *This ancient mutt can count?* Jack was absolutely confused but had no idea how to respond before Delilah broke into his thoughts.

"Great Grandpapa is very wise, Momma says. I bet he understands his sightings, and—"

"Pardon me, Miss Della, but what are 'sightings'?"

The girl pondered for a moment. "Well, Mr. Jack, I don't really know, but Fawn usually has them in dreams. She told me so." Little Delilah nodded for emphasis. "And when she can't understand them, she has fits."

"Fits! Your sister has 'fits'!"

"Mr. Jack, you shouldn't be rude. I was still 'splaining, and you keep interrupting me. Papa says civil . . . civilized people should never be rude. My brother Edmund is rude. But he's only six."

Numbers startled Jack by suddenly scratching the marble floor six times. Dillon decided not to ask. Instead, he agreed with her earlier remark. "Yes, Miss Della, civilized people should not be rude. I apologize, considering I'm no longer six." The mutt wheezed and pawed the floor six times again.

"Oh, Numbers was adopted by Fawn from a medicine show where he was teached to count. Even better than I can—yet, but I'm learning my multi . . . multi-pli-cation tables now," she said proudly.

A dog that counts? No! Forget about the dog. Concentrate on the 'fits'! "Would you forgive me and please tell me about Miss Fawn's fits?"

Della nodded with as much regal condescension as a child her age could muster.

"Well, Fawn has dreams and the sightings come to her in the dreams . . . mostly, anyway. But when she can't understand what the sightings are telling her, she sometimes gets real mad. You know what, Mr. Jack?"

The little girl charmed him. "What?" he asked.

The child looked about her to make certain nobody could overhear before proceeding. "I think Fawn gets mad 'cause she gets ascared, 'cause the sightings jumble up the inside of her head." Della titled her head from side to side rapidly. "Not knowing what you are supposed to do's frightening. You want to know what else I think, Mr. Jack?"

Digesting Della's opinion of Fawn, he prompted, "What else?"

"I think my sister is ascared of you, or she wouldn't have had a fit and been so rude." She beamed at her own cleverness.

Jack cleared his throat. "You might be mistaken. I doubt your sister is scared of anything."

The girl considered that for a moment. "That's true, sir. I'm ascared of lightning, but when it lightnings, Fawn comes to my room and cuddles with me in bed and sings to me. She's not ascared of lightning."

"That is brave," he agreed solemnly.

"Once a delivery man found me in the kitchen and touched my hair. He told me I was a pretty 'mite,' whatever that is. Then, Fawn came in and called him a pre-vert, which must be bad, cause she doubled up her fist and hit him. He was big, but she grabbed the cook's chopper and told him she'd cut his liver out if he ever showed up around here again. He ran! I've got the bravest sister in the whole world!" Della said proudly.

Jack thought of some brute touching this child and his old anger surged like fire in his blood.

"Mr. Jack, you've put on your mad face again. Please don't be mad with my big sister. I know she was only having a fit 'cause she's ascared of you. Else she would never have said all that dumb stuff. You have beautiful hair like our other dog Reddi . . . only Reddi got smashed flat by a beer wagon last year, and your nose is bent kinda like that—but not so much crooked that you aren't handsome. Just not as handsome as Papa. He's the most beautifullest human person in the world! He's even prettier than Momma, and she's even more pretty than Aunt Delilah."

Numbers woofed his agreement.

Jack stared at the dog, then at the floor, trying to appear as though he were pondering the child's wisdom. He absolutely would not laugh. He would not hurt this child's feelings. *I look almost as good as a dog smashed flat by a beer wagon! Daddy's even prettier than Momma!* Jack would bet that Max Stanhope, "the Limey," a former bounty hunter whom half the bad boys on the frontier had wanted to kill a decade earlier, probably often wished he were back living the quiet life again—just being shot at instead of being badgered by one daughter with 'fits' and another able to outtalk an auctioneer!

He was spared having to reply to Della by Baldwin's return. *Saved by the butler.*

"Would you please come this way, Mr. Dillon? Er, if you will excuse us, Miss Della?"

Jack looked down at the girl and bowed smartly. "It's been a pleasure meeting you, Miss Della. And Numbers." He turned to follow Baldwin but did not escape the child's helpful parting advice. "Oh, Mr. Jack, I just thought—remember to sleep on your right side and the pillow will goosh your nose straight!"

Dillon followed the butler down the wide hallway behind the staircase and was ushered into a room whose walls were lined with what he guessed were hundreds of books. Seated in a chair by a glossy mahogany table was one of the most beautiful women he had ever seen. Her black hair was swept up on top of her head, her complexion slightly dusky, features cameo perfect, and her eyes were the blue of a Montana sky. She rose gracefully to meet him in the center of the room, hand extended.

"Mr. Dillon, I'm Sky Stanhope. So glad you could come." Her voice was slightly husky.

"Lady Ruxton, I'm . . ."

"Please, Mr. Dillon, in these parts, I'm just Sky Stanhope. The 'Lady Ruxton' business usually is a prelude to hand kissing. I've never been able to get used to that, unless it's by a friendly hound licking my hand. Sometimes dogs slobber less than men." She chuckled lightly. "Except, of course, for our little old rascal Numbers."

Jack smiled. "Well then, by all means let's avoid the hand kissing, Mrs. Stanhope. Having just met Numbers, I suspect I'd suffer by comparison. I'd surely hate to cause a beautiful woman to wipe her hand on her gown to remove my drool."

At this, Sky laughed with genuine delight. "Come. Take a seat, Mr. Dillon. My husband—"

At that moment the door opened and a tall man with silver blond hair entered. Jack observed him with interest. *So this is the Limey.* Dillon rose from his chair next to Sky and the man strode forward to shake his hand. "Max Stanhope, Mr. Dillon. Sorry to be tardy, but I had to scribble a reply to a note sent 'round by our attorney. The man is constantly fretting over nothing. Like a chicken pecking bugs that aren't there. "

"Good lord, Max, couldn't you even put on a coat and tie? You're British! You're the one who's supposed to observe decorum," an exasperated Mrs. Stanhope admonished. "If I hadn't hired you that valet, you'd attend board meetings in buckskins!"

Jack studied the floor to hide his smile. *Lord, a third managing female. To survive these odds, Stanhope had better hope his lady provides him with a couple more sons to even the odds.*

"Darling, you know I can't stand those damned boiled collars," Max soothed, then grinned rakishly. "Besides, I'm sure you do not wish to embarrass Mr. Dillon by illustrating the degree to which I am henpecked."

Sky gave a most unladylike snort. "Henpecked! Every female in this house dotes on you. Good grief, when Fawn was an eleven-year-old child, she wanted to become your second wife. We all spoil you rotten."

In spite of his best efforts, Jack's eyes widened. The adopted daughter had wanted to be Stanhope's second wife? *This place is a damned asylum!*

"I may be spoiled, but not as spoiled as our elder daughter, love. According to what Baldwin just told me, Mr. Dillon can attest to that. Seems she, ah, introduced herself to him in the entry hall."

"Oh no," Sky muttered softly.

"Oh yes, and from the way Baldwin described it, she was . . . well, somewhat . . ."

" 'Excitable' was the term your butler used, sir," Jack offered dryly.

"I can imagine, Mr. Dillon. I'd wager she was so 'excitable' that you wanted to turn her over your knee and paddle her backside." Max sardonically arched a brow, waiting for the detective's reaction.

Jack shook his head. "I don't think that would have been advisable, sir. It might have provoked a shootout."

Max threw back his head and laughed. "Lord, you're probably right. I told my wife it was a bad idea to teach that girl how to handle weapons." Shaking his head, Stanhope sobered. "Let's get down to business. Have a seat, please, Mr. Dillon. I'll be blunt. Before I give a man a job involving my family, I always have him investigated."

Jack took a seat. "That seems reasonable," he replied in a noncommittal tone. "What did you learn?"

Max shrugged. "For a young man, you've had a most impressive career in law enforcement. You were a deputy town marshal for Bat Masterson both in Trinidad and Creede. Later, you spent three years as a U.S. deputy marshal for the court of Isaac Parker in what is now Oklahoma Territory and the Indian Nations."

"Not three years, sir. Approximately four and a half," Jack amended, then almost smiled at a fleeting thought. *How would their canine accountant handle fractions?*

Max nodded. "Quite so. Then, until the fiasco at Homestead Mill last year, you were with the Pinkertons. William Pinkerton speaks highly of you. So do Bat and Judge Parker."

"You were thorough, Mr. Stanhope."

"About as thorough as you, Mr. Dillon. I'm aware you've conducted your own research into my background. Commendable. First, I would like to employ you and your men to escort our daughter to our ranch in the Territory. Her grandfather wants her to return as soon as possible. Then I want you to stop some potential skullduggery."

"Excuse me, Mr. Stanhope. I'm not Tom Horn. I don't roust homesteaders or small ranchers," Jack said firmly.

"Touchy, aren't you? And more than a bit precipitous, Mr. Dillon." Max smiled, his green eyes devoid of humor.

"Max would never send anyone to attack homesteaders or small ranchers," Sky interjected. "He's only trying to protect our daughter's clan, our extended family."

Stanhope smiled at his wife's tactfulness. "She's stated the case for me. We fear the vultures are gathering to rip from them the paltry land allotments that Congress magnanimously granted to compensate for the hundreds of thousands of acres of reservation land it forced the Cheyenne to cede."

Stanhope began to pace, running his hand through his hair. "It's already started up north in the Territory in what used to be Pawnee land—swindling old people out of their one hundred sixty acres, gaining control of orphans' allotments and shipping the children off to orphanages."

"You can imagine what sort of care those children receive in white orphanages," Max's quarter-Sioux wife said softly.

"If that weren't monstrous enough, many of the old people have died under suspicious circumstances after deeding their lands to white speculators. I want you to prevent this from happening to our people."

Max snatched up a folder from the parson's table. "This contains preliminary information and a contract, which you can modify to suit yourself. Ruxton Enterprises finds itself in need of an investigative agency to replace the one we have formerly used. You see, I don't like strikebreaking either. The Homestead Steel Mills thing was handled barbarically. If you and I suit, I would like to retain your agency on a permanent basis. What do you say?"

Jack stared at the unopened folder. "I'd say that I'd like a day's time to examine the contents of this file outlining the 'skullduggery' you're worried about before I make any decision." His face was unreadable as he stood up.

"Fair enough, Mr. Dillon." Max strode forward to shake his hand. "I hope to have your answer tomorrow." He pulled the bell cord to summon the butler. "Baldwin will show you out. Actually, Baldwin will act as backup, should you encounter Fawn again," he added with a chuckle.

Dillon joined in. "I'll take all the help I can get. I came unarmed." He nodded to Stanhope and turned to Sky, who he was aware had been studying him intently throughout the conversation.

She rose from her chair, extending her hand. "When you examine the proposed contract, you'll see it contains a clause that permits you at any time, for any reason, to unilaterally sever all relations with Ruxton Enterprises. That's in case you should ever take issue with what is being asked of your agency and wish to tell the Stanhopes to go to blazes."

"My wife is an attorney. She drafted the contract." There was a look of pride in Max's eyes.

Jack returned her smile as he took her hand. "Ma'am, I might be foolish enough to tell your husband to 'go to blazes,' but I hope my manners are good enough never to say such to a lady." His smile widened. "Besides, I heard that some vicious rancher over in Clean Sweep, Colorado, made that mistake a few years back. He never made it again."

"My, you have done your homework," Max murmured, impressed.

Dillon only nodded, then said, "Good day, Mrs. Stanhope, Mr. Stanhope. I'll be in contact with you tomorrow."

After Baldwin had ushered Dillon out of the room, Max and Sky sat across from each other at the mahogany table. Sky reached out to take her husband's hand and give it an affectionate squeeze. "Did you see his face when you mentioned the orphans? That was rather devious of you."

"You added your part to it, don't forget. And you know it's the truth."

"Is Jack Dillon our man, then?" Sky asked.

Her husband laughed softly. "You read his file. I doubt Jack Dillon ever was or ever will be anybody's man. But he has the right background, and the old man insisted upon him by name. Dillon will take the job. He's the one. After all, love, have you ever known the old fellow to be wrong . . . about anything?"

"Never."

"And our young friend seems to be a decent enough chap. I wonder what the hell set Fawn off!"

Sky looked worried. "Yes, I wonder . . ."

At that moment in her upstairs bedroom, the object of the Stanhopes' speculation was rooting through her closet like a squirrel digging for a misplaced nut. Fawn cursed softly in a fluent mixture of Cheyenne and English. Ever since her first woman's flow, she had seen visions of the red prairie wolf. It had been her dream-world companion. She had come to look upon it as her protector, her animal totem.

As she had grown older, in her dreams the wolf, once a distant presence, had come ever closer. Two nights ago, she had dreamed that she slept by a campfire on the prairie and, in the dream, had awakened to discover the wolf stretched out beside her, his paw resting on her hip—protectively, possessively? In the dream world, she had not been the least bit alarmed. But in the morning, when the spring sun shining through her bedroom window had awakened her, she had felt strangely uneasy.

At the bottom of the old trunk filled with her art supplies, she found what she was searching for—the portfolio containing the pencil drawings, watercolors, and paintings that depicted many of her dreams and visions. Her hands were trembling as she riffled through the sketches, seeking the most recent. She snatched it out of the portfolio and dropped the rest back into the trunk.

No! This was all wrong. It wasn't supposed to happen this way. She was the Chosen Woman. The one the Powers had selected. They would not, could not play this jest on her! She stared at the watercolor. In it she had rendered herself as she was now: a woman, no longer a girl. She was dressed in a ceremonial tunic decorated with fringe and porcupine quills.

Her face stared back at her from the painting. A breeze

whipped strands of her thick black hair across it, but that did not obscure her solemn expression or the fierce dark light emanating from her eyes. In the foreground, in front of her, stood a wolf with its head cocked quizzically, staring out at the viewer. The animal's fur was a deep russet red. Its eyes were luminous amber.

Was he her protector? Her mate? Fawn's hand began to shake so violently that she dropped the canvas. It floated gently to the floor.

Chapter Two

*I*t's that lovely ye look, colleen. If only it was not for the likes of that fool Frenchie," Fiona Madigan said with a sniff as she placed a final jeweled hairpin in Fawn's elaborate coiffure.

"Monsieur Beaurivage is neither a fool nor a 'Frenchie,' Fee, but a Creole from New Orleans and a refined gentleman," Fawn replied to the pugnacious little Irishwoman who had been her maid and confidant since both had come to live with the Stanhope family.

Fiona was only three years Fawn's senior, but in terms of worldly experience, the impoverished immigrant had seen more of "refined gentlemen" in the New York slums than she cared to remember. After her da died during the voyage from Ireland, she had been sold by the ship's captain to a brothel madam. A plucky twelve-year-old, Fee had been willing to empty slop buckets and wash linens in return for food and shelter. But when she had begun to develop womanly curves, the madam had insisted she earn her keep on her back. That was when Fee had laced the old whore's whiskey with laudanum and fled into the night.

Lady Ruxton had rescued her and offered her honest work at the Stanhope mansion in faraway St. Louis. When Fee had met the shy young Indian girl, a bond instantly formed. Both had suffered adversity, but while Fawn had a Cheyenne and a white family to offer her succor, Fee was utterly alone in America. If she was less than an elder sister, she was far more than an outspoken servant. She had appointed herself as Fawn Stanhope's guardian.

And Fiona Madigan had had an instinctive dislike of Claude Beaurivage from the moment she had seen him bowing and scraping over the exotically beautiful Fawn at the family Christmas party last December. She had herself experienced enough prejudice simply being Irish. She knew that Fawn's Cheyenne heritage was a far greater barrier to social acceptance, even if her adopted parents were fabulously wealthy and possessed an English title. Any gentleman in polite society who courted Fawn did so for the Stanhope name and what it would bring as dowry.

"Why do you dislike Monsieur Beaurivage more than any of the others?" Fawn asked as she tilted her head, inspecting her golden skin and gleaming raven curls in the ivory-handled mirror. The black eyes that stared back at her were haunted by childhood memories, deeply buried.

"Nothin' except that he's a dandy without a penny to his name, too lazy to do an honest day's work—oh, and don't be forgettin' that he's vain as a peacock, always preening when he passes a lookin' glass," Fee replied cheerfully, taking the mirror from Fawn's hand.

The hint of a smile touched Fawn's lips. "He is exceedingly handsome. Men like that always know they are—even my father. Would you accuse him of preening in front of mirrors?"

Fee gave a snort of disgust. "Ye know better. Himself is a far finer figure of a man than any dandy from New Orleans and don't need no lookin' glass tellin' him so." She waited a beat, then could not resist adding, "But I did see another handsome fellow here yesterday afternoon—a russet-haired, gold-eyed divil he was . . ."

"You can't be serious! That—that broken-nosed crude bodyguard Father and Mother have hired. He's nothing but a gunman."

"If that's so, then why did ye run from him like the hounds of hell were snappin' at yer backside?"

Fawn felt her cheeks burn and swished her violet silk skirt nervously, turning her back on Fee. "I did not run from him. He was simply rude and I chose not to suffer his presence any longer."

"From the way I heard the tale, 'twas ye who was the rude one, yellin' at him loud enough to bring down the chandelier on yer heads." Fee moved closer to Fawn and placed one small hand on her much taller companion's shoulder. "Why did he frighten ye? Was it one of yer visions?" she asked gently.

Fawn stiffened. "No—I mean, yes . . . I'm not sure. He just reminded me of a picture I painted recently . . . It's silly. It was a wolf, not a man in the painting." She massaged her temples with her fingertips, trying to block out the disturbing image she could not interpret.

"A redheaded Irish wolf," Fee said, considering. "Maybe a good sign."

"I doubt it. Besides, you're only saying that because of Jack Dillon's Irish ancestry." She shook her head to drive away the vision of his eyes turning translucent amber . . . wolf's eyes, no doubt about it, in spite of her denial.

Fee sighed and patted her back. "Now, don't be mussing yer hair after I spent hours curling it. Be off with ye and have a good time at the Danielses' party. Just don't ye be takin' up with that Frenchie. I know he'll be sniffing 'round yer petticoats!"

While Fee helped Fawn prepare for the festivities at Clint and Delilah Daniels' lovely home on Lafayette Square, Claude Beaurivage was already en route, having secured an invitation through a crude riverboat pilot he'd cultivated. The lout was not the sort a gentleman such as he would befriend, but Andersen worked for the wealthy Daniels family . . . and was an unskilled enough card player to be easily fleeced. Beaurivage had collected the invitation in lieu of cash.

Personally, Beaurivage disdained the former bordello owner Daniels and his ex-professional gambler wife. How shocking that such lower-class ruffians—no matter their wealth—had been befriended by a titled Englishman, the Baron Ruxton. But, then again, Stanhope himself had married a mixed-blood woman and adopted the full-blooded red Indian girl Fawn, educating her as if she were white! At least she was an exotic beauty—he could never deny that fact—which was the only thing that swayed him to consider courting her as if she were a proper lady . . .

That and the vast wealth she would inherit upon her marriage.

If Papa could see me bowing and scraping after a dusky-skinned woman, he'd roll over in his grave. He strolled along the wide street, nearing Lafayette Square. He'd considered hiring a hack, but decided against the extravagance since the weather was favorable. How galling to have lost everything back in New Orleans. His family had been one of the wealthiest and most prestigious in the city. Here in this crude river town, he and Aunt Cee Cee lived on a pittance and were being dunned shamelessly by merchants for bills they owed.

Ah, but soon all that would change. His mind on a bright future, Claude did not see the old cur lifting its leg against a hitching post directly to his left. Half blind, the ancient dog missed his mark and instead soaked the Creole gentleman's boots. Beaurivage responded with a curse and a hard kick to the beast, sending it tumbling into the street. Sparing a swift glance down at his ruined footwear—the last pair of dress boots he owned—Claude planted another kick squarely in the whimpering dog's belly.

"I wouldn't try that again or you'll need crutches," a hard voice behind him stated quietly.

Beaurivage turned, red-faced with anger. He looked down his aristocratic nose at a shorter man dressed in a cheap suit. In spite of the fellow's attire, there was something in those hard eyes that made him bite back a challenge. He opted for disdainful dismissal. "Is the cur yours?" he asked haughtily.

"No, but it's an innocent creature and I don't take kindly to men abusing animals."

"That innocent creature just soiled a fifty-dollar pair of gentleman's boots," Claude replied, gesturing at his now dull and damp footwear. "The shine is quite gone," he added, noting the well-worn dusty boots on the coarse fellow's feet.

"You could always polish them up again . . . on the back of your trouser legs," the man dared to suggest with an impertinent grin, as the old dog limped down the street and disappeared into an alley.

Temper got the best of judgment. Claude snapped, "You doubtless would polish your own boots—if you cared enough about your appearance to bother, which quite apparently you do not!"

The stranger cocked his head and replied, "Oh, I polish my own when the mood strikes me . . . whose boots do *you* polish?" He stroked his jaw as he looked at the dandy. The skinny fellow had a good four or five inches on him.

Claude recoiled as if he'd been slapped across the face by a challenger's glove. "You, sir, are no gentleman and I have no wish to dirty my hands in a common brawl despite your insult!"

"Dirty hands . . . or bloody nose? Which are you afraid of?" The mockery in his voice was cold, deliberate.

His fists looked like sledgehammers to Beaurivage, who could ill afford to ruin his finest suit, or worse yet, have his aquiline nose broken as this pugilist's had been. Claude's face was all the fortune he had left! "I refuse to engage in fisticuffs as if I were a denizen of the levee." It galled him to back away, but he was saved from the humiliation by a woman calling out his name from an approaching carriage.

"Monsieur Beaurivage! Is Mr. Dillon trying to provoke a fight?" Fawn's husky voice was rife with anger as the carriage halted a few yards from the combatants.

"Monsieur Beaurivage has a longer reach, but I'd put my money on Dillon," Max Stanhope said as he jumped gracefully from the vehicle that held his wife and Fawn. Mrs. Stanhope looked amused but Fawn's furious black eyes continued to skewer Jack.

Although Max did not like the Frenchman, he knew his daughter was infatuated with him. It signified nothing, as she would be leaving St. Louis shortly. Stanhope could afford to endure Beaurivage for a few days more. "Just what's caused this, ah, misunderstanding?" he asked genially.

"A dog," Jack replied. "He kicked it for accidentally wetting his fine footgear. I offered him the chance to try kicking someone his own size."

Bolstered by the Stanhopes' arrival, Beaurivage gave a snort of derision. "You are scarcely my height."

"The taller the tree, the bigger the crash when it falls. Sister Mary Joseph used to say that back in the orphanage where I was raised." Jack turned to Max, ignoring the incensed Creole. "She taught me to box."

Max threw back his head and laughed heartily. "Now I'm sure I'd wager on you."

Fawn climbed down from the carriage and faced the trio of men. "Where is this supposed dog Monsieur Beaurivage abused? I think you've made the whole thing up as an excuse to fight," she accused Dillon. "The young men in Grandfather's village often did such foolish things."

"You're very perceptive as well as beautiful, my dear Miss

Stanhope," Claude put in smoothly, making a handsome bow to her. "I have no idea what led him to accost me."

"Look at his boots," Dillon said. Then he added, sotto voce, "If a dog didn't make that mess, then the man had better see a doctor . . . or a plumber."

Only Max heard the jibe. He choked back a chuckle as Dillon tipped his hat to Fawn and Mrs. Stanhope.

Jack turned to the baron. "I hope this won't interfere with our business agreement."

"So, you've decided to take our offer. Capital! Why don't you join us for the soiree at Clint and Delilah's? They'll want to meet Fawn's new protector and we'll have a chance to discuss the trip to the ranch . . . and other matters."

"Father, you can't invite this—this brawling ruffian into polite society!" Fawn pleaded.

Dillon was pleased to see the surprised chagrin on Pretty Boy's face at Stanhope's invitation. But when Fawn turned her flashing dark eyes on Jack, he knew the upcoming journey was going to be longer and far more difficult than he'd yet imagined. Better to begin the combat now and get matters settled. If he couldn't handle one spoiled young woman, he would never be able to untangle the land theft mess in Oklahoma Territory.

Smiling at Fawn, he replied to Max, "If you're certain Mr. and Mrs. Daniels wouldn't mind my horning in, I'd be honored to join you." He knew it was perverse pleasure at discomfiting both Fawn and her suitor that led him to blurt out his impulsive agreement. His clothes and manners were not equal to those of rich gentlemen. But he was proud of his heritage and knew he would one day make his mark in the world. Learning which fork to use and acquiring an expensive tailor would come in time, even if he did not consider such things important.

"Delilah will be quite pleased, Mr. Dillon. Fawn has always held a special place in her heart. I'm certain she'll approve of your escorting her to our Cheyenne friends," Sky said with a mischievous grin that set her daughter's teeth on edge.

"Mother," Fawn hissed, but was shushed with a serene squeeze from Sky's hand over hers. She could tell by the determined set of her mother's jaw that it was useless to argue. What was worse, she could see her father really liked the fellow. Traitors!

As Fawn fumed, both Jack and Claude climbed into the large open carriage bearing the Stanhope crest. Max was careful to place the two young men across from his wife and daughter. Seated between the women, he directed the terse conversation on the short ride, noting with amusement the looks Fawn gave Jack Dillon. *She's so furious with him, she's ignoring that bloody dandy.*

Delilah Daniels had been a professional gambler when she met her husband Clint and won his riverboat . . . and eventually his heart. Together they had forged a prosperous shipping business and expanded into railroads and other areas as the era of the big paddle wheelers drew slowly to a close. Shunned by the society ladies of St. Louis, she held the respect of bankers and industrialists for her shrewd business acumen—and striking beauty.

The Danielses' social ostracism was slightly offset in the conservative city by the friendship of Maxwell Stanhope, Baron Ruxton. Although wed to a woman who was one-quarter Sioux and—unthinkably—the only female member of the Missouri Bar, he was titled and even richer than the Danielses. Many of the men who had business dealings with both families forced their wives and daughters to socialize with the outsiders. In time a handful had grown to genuinely like and admire both Delilah and Sky in spite of their scandalous backgrounds. It was these friends who gathered in Lafayette Square that evening.

The slender brunette with burnished red highlights in

her hair held court in her elegant drawing room, but she rose when she saw the Stanhopes enter, excusing herself to welcome them. Delilah hid a sniff of dislike when she saw Claude Beaurivage's head above the crowd. She suspected Fawn's infatuation was based on his dwarfing her own considerable height. The girl would soon enough come to her senses, for she was perceptive and highly intelligent. Murmuring about the trials of youth, Delilah approached the newcomers, noting the rough-hewn handsome stranger engaged in conversation with Clint and Max.

My, he was a striking young man. The detective Max and Sky had hired? Beaming, Delilah joined them and was introduced by her husband to Jack Dillon. As they made small talk, she could not help noticing the visible tension simmering between Fawn and Jack. *This one should take her mind off the Beaurivage boy!*

"So, you are charged with protecting our Fawn as she returns to visit her grandfather and Cheyenne family," Delilah said with a smile.

"She's going to reclaim her birthright," Sky interjected with pride. "Max always intended that the lands we've accumulated in Oklahoma go to her and Grandfather's band."

"I'll see that she arrives safely," Jack replied. He watched Fawn smirk behind her mother and Mrs. Daniels's backs and raise her chin in a direct challenge to him. Whoever the hell her grandfather was, he pitied the poor sod.

Just then musicians began playing in the spacious courtyard at the side of the mansion. As if a puppeteer had pulled his strings, Claude bowed over Fawn's hand and said, "Would you permit me the honor of the first dance?"

"Ah, Monsieur Beaurivage, you must not be rude to your hostess. I insist on having you lead me out . . . that is, if my husband is as determined to discuss business with Max as I suspect?" She turned to the devilishly handsome man with straw-colored hair and cool blue eyes, as Claude stood frozen, struggling to hide his frustration. Both of them awaited Daniels's response.

Clint grinned, exchanging a conspiratorial wink with his wife. "As a matter of fact, the Stanhopes have a thing or two to discuss with me about English investors for the Great Northern. Mr. Dillon, would you be so kind as to lead Miss Stanhope out?"

Now Beaurivage's expression darkened but he bit back his protest, bowing over Delilah's hand. "I would be honored, Madame."

Fawn was not as well schooled at dissembling. She gasped and a look of horrified incredulity wreathed her face. "I'm certain Mr. Dillon would not—"

"They're playing a waltz and I might do the lady's slippers quite a bit of damage. I fear I'd tromp her feet," he added in all honesty.

"Balderdash," Max said, slapping Jack on the back. "There's nothing to it—and Fawn can take care of her own feet quite well." He gave her a steely-eyed look. "Do teach Mr. Dillon how to waltz, there's a love."

What the hell was he going to do? Stanhope had practically shoved her at him! Woodenly, he offered her his arm. Petulantly, she laid a slender gloved hand on it. It was clear she would have preferred petting a coiled rattler to touching his coat sleeve. They followed Beaurivage and Mrs. Daniels out the French doors onto the smooth stones beneath the wisteria twining around the pergola overhead.

"I wasn't joking about being unable to waltz," he said tightly as the dandy swept Mrs. Daniels into a graceful swooping movement.

"I imagine a good jig would be more to your liking," Fawn said dulcetly, offering her upraised arms, a gesture of ladylike politeness belied by the mocking expression on her face.

"And I would've thought you'd prefer something with drums and rattles."

Her eyes blazed but she bit her lip, probably to keep from slapping him silly. "And what would a white man from Chicago know about Cheyenne dance customs?"

He took her in his arms, saying, "You might be surprised."

In high-heeled slippers she was almost as tall as he. Amber and black eyes met, revealing the physical jolt each felt when his big hard body drew so near her tall willowy one. Her mass of gleaming ebony hair was curled and piled high on her head, giving off a heady perfume that made him dizzy. But it was wise not to look down at the lush curve of her breasts revealed by the low décolletage of her violet silk gown.

The slant of her large, thickly lashed eyes was the perfect foil for her high cheekbones and pale gold skin. *She must guard it from the sun to keep it so light.* Her nose was Roman, not conventionally feminine, yet it fit her strong face. He found her incredibly striking and was startled by the sudden attraction. It was all he could do to remind himself that she was the boss's daughter and far above him, even if she possessed the manners of a harpy and the screech of a banshee.

Fawn could feel the calluses on his hand even through her glove. She repressed the trembling elicited by her newly awakened awareness of his body. Was every part of him hard as flint? As flammable? Fawn pushed the image of the red wolf away. Bodyguard he might be for a short journey, but he would never be her protector . . . or her lover!

His thigh brushed against her skirts as he tried to emulate the other men's steps in the waltz. After a few stiff turns, he seemed to have it mastered. Until he stepped on her foot. "Uh, my apologies, Miss Stanhope! I warned you I was not a dancer."

"But you were a boxer?" Why had she asked a personal question of him? She intuited that it would be wise to know as little about the frightening stranger as possible.

"As I said, taught by Sister Mary Joseph," he replied with a fond grin as they resumed waltzing, albeit a bit more slowly.

"A nun taught fighting?" she couldn't resist asking, with incredulity in her voice. His laughter was warm and rich, washing over her like the honey stolen from a choice bee tree.

"Ah, but you didn't know Sister MJ. She was a big admirer of the Marquis of Queensberry. And a realist. She knew her boys would be forced to fight in the Chicago slums, especially considering we were orphans and Catholic ones at that. It was for our own protection—and to protect younger, weaker ones from bullies. Woe to any boy under her charge who started a fight."

"After all my years living and being educated among white people, I still find it strange that they turn on their own. Among Grandfather's people, children are all considered precious and the whole band cares for them. We even take in outsiders, no matter their race or beliefs."

"Then I should blame your low opinion of my poor Irish background on white prejudice, not Cheyenne?" he taunted.

"I may have been mistaken about you the first time we met," she said. "But not when I saw you menacing a gentleman like Monsieur Beaurivage," she added sweetly, this time tromping on his toes. He grunted in pain and concealed it by bowing as the music ended.

Fawn made the barest of curtsies and fled the dance floor, heading toward the refuge of Delilah and several of her friends. What was it about the bodyguard that made her so ill mannered . . . so unsettled . . . so . . . yes—she admitted it—frightened? She could feel those translucent amber gold wolf's eyes following her across the crowded courtyard.

And I have to travel over six hundred miles with him to reach Grandfather and safety!

Late that night at the Portland Place mansion, Fawn paced restlessly. Tomorrow would be her farewell to St. Louis for a long while. A pile of paintings she had done of herself and of the wolf lay scattered across her bed, taunting her. What did the Powers mean? Her visions had been no clearer about the duration of her time out West. In spite of her doubts, she had assured Claude that evening that she would return before the winter snows made rail travel impossible on the Great Plains. Why had she not told him the truth? She had no idea when she would return . . . or if the Powers ordained a future with him.

He was everything she had believed she wanted in a husband. He was handsome and charming, respectful of her Cheyenne heritage when many inferior men dismissed her as less than a lady merely because of the shade of her complexion. She had always scorned such prejudice as the refuge of fools. Then why did she have cause to doubt her tall knight now?

Claude made her feel delightfully dainty and feminine. He towered over her, yet was always solicitous and never disagreed with her opinions. Her slightest wish was his command, just like a prince in a fairy tale. But it disturbed her that shrewd Fee and even Aunt Deelie and Uncle Clint disapproved of him. From the first, she had sensed her parents did not like him, although they had never forbidden his calling on her.

For all meaningful purposes, Lord and Lady Ruxton were her parents, the ones Grandfather had led to that awful little town in Texas where she had been held captive as an eleven-year-old girl. They had rescued her from a sadistic evil man and brought her back to her Cheyenne family. When she reached her thirteenth year, they had returned as promised, adopting her and providing for her education in the white world. Her biological mother and father had perished in a cholera epidemic when she was three. Although no direct relation, Bright Leaf and Talks Much had been like loving aunts. The two old women had raised her but it was

Grandfather who had given her the greatest blessing . . . or curse. She was not certain which it was yet.

He had bequeathed the gift of visions to her.

A very mixed blessing indeed, to be the Chosen Woman. The Seer who would one day take his place, guiding their small band of Cheyenne. At first, she had felt honored. But then the disturbing dreams had begun. Visions of a red prairie wolf with strange gold eyes haunted her, driving her to capture his image on canvas. She stared down at the scattered paintings. "What do they mean?" she asked in a hoarse whisper. The last one, where she was in ceremonial garb with the wolf standing boldly in front of her, disturbed her most. She knew the elaborately beaded buckskins could be the ceremonial dress Cheyenne women used as wedding garb!

When she awakened from the dreams with her wolf, her heart always beat like a wild thing in her breast and her pulse raced. As she had danced tonight with Jack Dillon, her reaction had been frighteningly similar. Fawn suppressed the thought with a shudder.

Her mind clouded and her hands trembled whenever she painted the images of her totem. If she had hoped to exorcize them, it had never worked. Such spirit animals were supposed to provide guidance and comfort, but hers did quite the opposite. The wolf terrified her, for it seemed to possess her in some indefinable way.

Fawn Stanhope, the Chosen Woman, would not be owned by any man, red or white.

Chapter Three

ooks like one of them robber baron's mansions set on wheels," Hans Schmitt said, whistling low.

His boss, Jack Dillon, inspected the private car at the end of the train that would take Fawn to Oklahoma Territory. "Well, Smitty, the man who ordered it is the real thing, an honest-to-god English baron, and rich as most of the millionaires in New York to boot." He grinned at the swarthy little man. Smitty's complexion was pitted with smallpox scars but keen intelligence shone from his slitted gray eyes. His family had immigrated to America from Swabia in southwestern Germany before Hans was born. He and Jack had met in the orphanage in Chicago. Dillon had trusted Smitty with his life on more than one occasion.

"Ya, it sure is some fancy rolling stock," Lars Swensen said in his rolling Norwegian accent. Swen was the only other employee in Dillon's new detective agency. Although the strapping blond with shaggy yellow hair and hands the size of hay forks spoke in slow syllables, he, too, was shrewd and observant. In spite of his Minnesota farm background, he made an excellent investigator.

Jack had watched him take on three men in a bar room a year ago. When one of the toughs had called a dance hall girl a whore and slapped her, Swen had intervened. He'd trounced them handily and then calmly said he would fight any other fellow foolish enough to treat a woman disrespectfully. Dillon had hired him on the spot and had never had cause to regret it.

"The lady who'll be traveling in that car is used to nothing but the finest," Jack said dryly to his men.

"I heard she's Injun," Smitty said, scratching his head. "How'd she get to be a baron's daughter?"

"You just got off the train from Chicago or you'd have heard the St. Louis gossip. Baron Ruxton and his part-Sioux wife adopted her out West and brought her to St. Louis. She's had a fancy education and been trained to act like a lady in polite company. But she's not much of an actress," he added with a growl.

"Or you ain't polite company," Smitty retorted, with a grin that revealed several gold teeth of which he was very proud.

Swen chuckled. "Is she pretty?"

Jack shrugged as the Stanhope carriage pulled up to the railroad platform. "Judge for yourselves."

The trio watched a tall slim gentleman with pale silver blond hair step from the closed vehicle and assist down a short, voluptuous little pigeon of a woman with curly tan hair. "Not bad looking, but if she's got a drop of red Indian blood in her, so do I," Smitty said.

"That's not her," Jack replied, wondering if this was some chaperone or lady's traveling companion to further complicate his job.

"Too young to be her mother," Swen said, taking in the woman's youthful energy and generously curved body.

Next a tall, dark-haired woman dressed in an elegant blue suit alighted. "That's the mother," Jack said.

"She's part Sioux?" Smitty asked, clearly not believing the cameo features of Sky Stanhope indicated she was anything but white.

"Only a quarter. Now, here comes our assignment, gentlemen," Jack said grimly. He watched Fawn step down, resplendent in a deep green traveling suit of the finest linen. A jaunty little hat adorned with several green peacock feathers was fastened in her gleaming inky hair. She wore heeled slippers and stood staring up at them on the wooden railroad platform like a queen surveying her court jesters. Something deep in his gut tightened. What was it about the girl that bothered him so?

"She is a long one," Swen said in awe. "And where I come from, we are used to tall women."

"I've warned you about her temper. Just stay clear of her. When we get to Hennessey, it'll only be about a half day's ride to the Stanhope place. Then our job with her is finished," he said. Somehow, he doubted it would be that easy.

"After that we start snooping to see who's taking over Cheyenne land allotments and what they're doin' with 'em," Smitty said.

"Stanhope wants to know who's behind it. Apparently, it's quite a big operation. I've been doing some research. We'll have time to go over it on the train ride. The car in front of the princess's castle is where we'll have a couple of private compartments. You can stow your gear as soon as we finish with the meet and greet," Jack said, gesturing to another passenger car adjoining the last one. "Too bad she left the old mathematical dog home for her little sister. You'd have liked him. He doesn't bite."

Watching the party approach them, Swen said, "Our first job is to see the Cheyenne lady to her home—a ranch, ya?"

"Yes . . . and she's lucky to have a home," Jack replied softly. As one of Judge Isaac Parker's deputies, he'd seen dozens of Indian Nations crammed into the wild country which had become the government's dumping grounds for Native populations. Now even this last refuge was being stolen by greedy whites. "Once we reach the ranch, there'll be plenty of men to protect Miss Stanhope."

As his eyes met hers, he muttered beneath his breath, "Heaven protect those poor devils from *her*!"

Fawn inspected the two men standing beside Jack Dillon on the platform. One was almost as tall as Claude but far more heavily boned, a yellow-haired giant of a fellow with a ready, shy smile, which she returned warmly. The other barely came to Dillon's shoulder but there was an aura of quiet, almost lethal confidence about him. He studied her with narrowed gray eyes that she intuited missed nothing. He looked neither friendly nor unfriendly. His expression was unreadable. Yet she understood.

He doesn't like me. Dillon had poisoned his mind against her. She would win him over. When she wanted to, Fawn could charm birds from trees. It was a gift the Powers had given her, but one she reserved only for those she deemed worthy of befriending. Both of Dillon's men were worth having on her side.

"Sure and they're an odd lot, one tall as an oak tree, the other little as a leprechaun," Fee whispered to Fawn.

"I'd scarcely call the short man a leprechaun," Fawn replied with a snort. "More like a troll." The minute she said it, she remembered calling Dillon exactly that to his face. She vowed to keep her temper on this trip. Then at the ranch she'd bid him good-bye and good riddance. It would be done between them.

But her grandfather's voice whispered inside her head, *You know such is not to be.*

After introducing his family to Jack's detectives, Max Stanhope took Smitty and Swen's measure and seemed satisfied. Dillon noticed Sky's assessment of them as well. He would bet a year's wages that they had investigated his employees almost as thoroughly as they had him. Smitty had been a Pinkerton with him until they'd both quit the agency after the Homestead Steel strike. Swen had served as a police officer in St. Paul before the lure of the West took hold of him.

Fawn's feisty little companion seemed pleasant enough and if she occupied her mistress's time until they reached Hennessey, all the better. Jack sensed that she liked him, but he also had the disturbing feeling that she harbored romantic fantasies about him and Fawn. Now that was a frightening idea indeed! He watched, bemused, as a completely different Fawn hugged and kissed her mother and father in fond farewell. Her affection for them was obviously quite real.

"I'll tell Grandfather that you'll be out for a visit as soon as the baby's old enough to travel. You know he'll want to bless his newest grandchild," she said to them.

"We will treasure that gift," Sky said, patting Fawn's cheek with love as Max placed an arm around each woman's shoulders protectively.

Jack now had his answer as to why the fearful "Limey" was not personally escorting his daughter home and attending to the Cheyenne being swindled out of their land allotments. Stanhope was a devoted family man whose beloved wife was with child, although her pregnancy was certainly not apparent yet. But his research had indicated that although the couple had a son as well as the memorable little girl he had encountered that first day at their house, the baroness had suffered several miscarriages since then.

They could always adopt more hellions from among Fawn's cousins. But Jack knew that the exotic beauty standing so regally on the platform was one of a kind. His ruminations were interrupted by the baron, who ushered him aside for a private last-minute word as the steam engines up front began to hiss and belch in preparation for leaving the station.

They strolled a little away from the others before Stanhope spoke. "I am entrusting you with someone very precious to me and my family." He paused, as if considering his words very carefully. "I would not do this if I weren't certain you were capable . . . but there is something you should know about Fawn . . ."

Jack waited, thinking, *I already know she's spoiled rotten and has a lethal temper.* He held his peace.

"I know the two of you didn't have an exactly smooth introduction. For some reason I've yet to fathom, she's afraid of you—"

"She's afraid of me? I'm the one who's terrified of her!" Jack burst out, then subsided, red-faced, when Stanhope threw back his head and laughed.

The Englishman quickly sobered and replied, "It's true. I've never seen her react to any man the way she has to you. You can imagine the snubbing and the cruelty she's been subjected to by white society, but through it all, Fawn's always held herself above such attacks, believing—rightly so—that she was dealing with inferior people unworthy of her attention."

Jack nodded. "Being the son of Irish immigrants, I understand prejudice, and I know it's far worse for the Indians."

"I knew you were the right man for the job. But there's more . . ." Again, Stanhope seemed to choose his words carefully. "If she warns you about any danger . . . or tells you she knows something is about to happen, don't ignore her. Among the Cheyenne, she is called the Chosen Woman. Bizarre as this may sound to you, she can sometimes see into the future."

"My great grandmother on my father's side had what the Irish called the gift of the sight," Jack said dubiously. "I never had the opportunity to meet her or even know if the old stories had any basis in fact."

"Over the years she's lived with us, Sky and I have come to believe in Fawn's . . . gift. When we first met her grandfather, he, too, had an uncanny ability to see what was going to happen. It saved our lives many times."

"And you believe he's passed this down to her?"

Now it was Stanhope's turn to nod, very gravely. "Will you promise me you'll keep an open mind and heed her? This trip is dangerous and there are powerful men involved in stealing Cheyenne land. They'll stop at nothing. If she tells you to beware, better listen."

Jack could tell the Englishman was deadly serious. "Yes, sir, I will." *Even if I want to throttle the brat, I'll keep my word!*

Apparently satisfied, Stanhope offered his hand and they shook. Within moments, Fawn, Fee and their protectors were aboard the train and it pulled out of the station. Soon St. Louis was only a distant, sooty blur on the horizon. The rolling hills of eastern Missouri would soon enough give way to the vast open prairies and grasslands of Kansas and then Oklahoma.

"Are ye going to be hiding like a titmouse instead of takin' meals with the others in the dining room for the whole of the trip, then?" Fee asked as Fawn announced on the second day that she again would order dinner in their private car.

Fawn's eyes flashed. "I do not hide and you of all people should know I am no timid small creature," she said, biting off each word.

"Ah, then, it is himself yer avoiding, ain't it?"

Fawn knew to whom Fee was referring and it wasn't Swen or even Smitty. "I find Mr. Dillon to be odious and overbearing. Why should I choose to subject myself to his rudeness?"

"Ye know full well 'tis yerself who's been the rude one, ever since ye laid eyes on that Irish red wolf."

"Don't call him that!" Fawn blurted out. At Fee's knowing look, she added, "He's not the wolf in my drawings. I should never have shown you the paintings."

"Ye didn't. I just happened to be tidying up yer room when I saw them, lying out plain as ye please for any and all to see," Fee retorted, then offered Fawn a comforting squeeze. "Ah, don't fret, colleen, soon ye'll be with yer grand da and all will be well. He'll help ye understand where this Jack Dillon fits into your life."

"He doesn't!"

Fee fixed her with a level stare. "Then I dare ye to sit across from him at table and exchange a civil word or two."

Fawn stood up abruptly. "Done!" No way would she let Fee think she was afraid of the gunman . . . even if it were true.

Fee sent a note to Dillon requesting bodyguard duty while they dined. With any luck, Fawn hoped, he would send Swen or Smitty, choosing to avoid her as she preferred to avoid him. However, luck did not run her way. Swen knocked on the door a few moments later to say Mr. Dillon would be pleased to escort the ladies to dinner.

Fawn quickly selected a high-necked travel gown of rich brown trimmed with ecru lace and had Fee twist her long hair into a bun at the nape of her neck. Then she set to pacing back and forth across the carpet, waiting for their tardy bodyguard to make his appearance. "A person could starve to death while Jack Dillon dawdles," she said. "I know he's doing this just to show me he's in charge."

"Now, Mr. Swensen explained he was up front talkin' with the engineer about some trouble at the next water station. He'll be along, don't ye worry," Fee soothed.

After another quarter hour, Fawn's patience had run out. "To hell with Dillon. We'll collect one of his men on our way to dinner." With Fee sputtering protests behind her, Fawn stormed out of their car and crossed the platform to the public car ahead of them. Just as she opened the door, she called out over the rail's loud clacking, "Please, Fee, I forgot my reticule. I'll need a handkerchief to brave the smoke from the engines."

"Wait just inside the car for me," her companion instructed like a mother hen, then turned back.

Fawn was tired of waiting. She negotiated the narrow aisle, heading toward the detectives' compartment. When the train made a sudden lurch, she reached out to brace her arm against the wall, but instead touched a door—which swung inward abruptly. She was catapulted into Jack Dillon's arms.

It was difficult to tell which of them was the more startled, but his strong arms wrapped around her, steadying her as she wriggled and squirmed, trying to get her footing and pull away. The wretched train did not cooperate. It was traveling over hilly country with sharply curving tracks that only made her struggles more useless. Jack tried to keep his balance, but the tall woman's flailing made it impossible.

With an oath, he careened backward into his compartment, landing with a solid, painful thunk against the hard wooden floor. His body cushioned Fawn's fall but he took a savage blow to his head and backside. Still, he held her wrapped securely in his arms, protecting her from injury. Hell, he was the one injured!

But other matters diverted his attention. Jack inhaled the subtle perfume she wore and felt the pressure of her well rounded breasts against his chest. The warmth of her breath touched his cheek . . . and her lips were only an inch above his. Very plump, luscious lips they were, too. He felt the irresistible urge to kiss them and see if they would feel as soft as they looked.

Jack raised his head ever so slightly, seeking out the sweet taste of her mouth, but just as he brushed her lips, she jerked her head backward. The confusion in her dark eyes was unmistakable. "I didn't mean—oof!" A hiss of air exploded from his lungs. All the breath was knocked from his body when Fawn planted a fist squarely in his solar plexus and shoved herself up. Stars danced behind his eyelids. He squeezed them shut in pain, vaguely aware she was trying to disentangle herself from him in the cramped quarters of his sleeping compartment.

"You—you brute, you loathsome troll, you bastard!" Fawn tried to climb to her knees, clawing for the edge of the cabinet, but her fingers slipped when the treacherous train took another curve. She plopped unceremoniously down on the cushion of his hard body once more. "You are no gentleman!" she rasped.

"No, right now I seem to be a punching bag," he gritted out between grunts of breathless pain. As she scrambled backward on her hands and knees, trying to get out of the compartment, he felt his aching body being poked and kicked black and blue. "You weigh as much as a draft horse! Are your bones made of lead? Your fists must be!"

"If I weren't a lady, I would show you how a Cheyenne warrior woman treats a rapist!" she hissed.

Jack went deadly still, all his bruises and aches forgotten. Leaning up on his elbows, he stared at her with cold amber eyes. Silent. Unmoving.

Fawn could feel the fury radiating from him. His stillness only served to intensify the frightening vibrations humming between them. This was quite different from their clumsy encounter on the dance floor at the party. That had been some sort of crude animal attraction. This was . . . shock and anger . . . and pain.

Without warning, a vision swept over her eyes, while she knelt between his legs. She swayed with the rhythm of the train as the waking dream mesmerized her. She saw a girl, young and frightened, with carrot red hair and a pale, pinched face, thin and hungry. She was cowering until large male hands pulled her from the dark corner of a filthy room where she had been hiding. One meaty fist ripped the ragged dress from her body while the other fumbled with his breeches. A keening cry echoed in Fawn's mind, piteous and yet resigned.

Fawn gagged with the realization of what she was seeing. The rape of a girl who could have been no older than she had been when Johnny Deuce had captured her. Just as quickly as it had appeared, the ghastly vision vanished. She sat back, shivering, too stunned to move. What did this mean? Who was the girl? What connection—if any—did the vision have to Jack Dillon?

Dillon looked up at her, the red haze of his anger receding as he realized she was shaking like a leaf in a thunderstorm. Her eyes were unfocused, her expression a million miles away. She had her arms wrapped around herself like a child in the throes of a nightmare . . . or a vision? Recalling what Max Stanhope had told him about Fawn's ability to see the future, he suddenly wondered if it could be true.

"Are you all right?" Stupid question. Of course she wasn't. An idiot could see that. "Fawn—Miss Stanhope, don't be afraid. I'm not going to hurt you, just help you up," he said softly, all his anger over her foolish accusation forgotten.

"I—I'm all right," she managed to choke out as she seized hold of the cabinet and pulled herself to her feet while he rolled away from her and righted himself.

When she looked at him, her eyes were focused clearly. "I should not have said what I did. I apologize. It was just the train and my own clumsiness that caused me to fall on you."

If she had sprouted a second head or grown large white wings, Jack couldn't have been more amazed. Fawn Stanhope apologizing? "I didn't intend to frighten you," was all he could manage, but then he forced a wry grin and added, "I said some very ungentlemanly things. Having my head rattled like a gourd must have affected my judgment."

Fawn returned his smile hesitantly. "I thought Irishmen were noted for their hard heads." What was she doing—flirting with him? "I—I have to find Fee. She should've been right behind me," she blurted out, suddenly embarrassed when it dawned on her that he had seen her in a trance. She must have looked like a candidate for an asylum.

Hiding just outside his compartment, Fiona Madigan quickly slipped through the outside door of the car so Fawn and Jack would not know she had been eavesdropping. A sly smile wreathed her face. Yes, she'd had a feeling about that handsome Irish devil. Now Fawn would forget all about Claude Beaurivage!

"A clerk! You want me to become a common scribbler in that ugly wilderness filled with savages? Bad enough I must woo one of them and wed her to get her fortune," Claude said angrily to the man standing in the luxurious hotel suite where he had been summoned as if he were a livery servant.

"It is no mere clerking job. By calling in some political debts, I've gotten you the position as registrar at the Guthrie Land Office. Do you realize what that means, you young fool?" the older man asked.

Claude stiffened. "If you were not—"

"It means," he continued, his gravelly voice interrupting Beaurivage's petty rant, "that you will be able to accomplish two things for our mutual benefit, my dear boy. First of all, you will once again be near your lady fair," he said with a sneer. "You can't court Fawn Stanhope while she's six hundred miles away."

"She will return this fall. She promised—"

"The promises of any vaporing female, much less those of a redskin, are worthless as a milk bucket beneath a bull. You'll continue your courtship and marry her as quickly as possible. We've already discussed what that will mean in the grand scheme of things. Then," he went on, ignoring Claude's sullen frown, "there is the matter of being the man who keeps all the records of land transfers and ownership in the territory. In case it's escaped your notice, Guthrie is the capital of Oklahoma. You will be able to handle the paperwork for me as I acquire Indian allotments and deeds from white riffraff."

"If you have so much power, why can't you just take the Indian and homesteaders' lands by any means necessary? Why do you need me to sweat in the heat and dust? We agreed if I obtained the Stanhope ranch by marrying the squaw, your plans could go forward."

The St. Louis weather had taken a turn toward sticky heat since his arrival. The older man loosened his tie and felt the sweat trickle down his neck. Sighing, he looked at Claude, whom he was beginning to believe was an imbecile. "I can't just start gobbling up all the real estate between the Cimarron and Canadian Rivers and put my name on record. Questions would be asked. Competitors alerted."

"There must be a great deal of money to be made from that land," Claude said grudgingly. "I expect my fair share."

A sly smile crept across the older man's face but did not reach his small pale blue eyes. "Oh, the land is quite fertile in the river valleys, but that's not the half of it, my boy. You just leave the details to me and my associates. You will be well rewarded. After all, your ranch is situated right in the middle of the acquisitions we're making."

As he left the luxurious Planter's House Hotel, Claude Beaurivage thought of the hovel he and his aunt Cee Cee were forced to live in. But not for much longer. He considered how soon after he married Fawn Stanhope he could safely dispose of the bitch. Oh, he would enjoy her lush body until he tired of it, but to remain wed to a red Indian! Unthinkable. No, he would arrange an accident and then the whole ranch would be his. He could sell it or hire someone to run it for him while he returned to New Orleans and lived a civilized life with a proper white lady.

To hell with his grandiose schemes!

Inside the fine hotel, the object of Claude's bitter ruminations poured two hefty crystal glasses with fine aged bourbon and handed one to the man who'd hidden in the bedroom of the suite while he had instructed his young protégé. "You see how malleable he is. Young and stupid. All he thinks of are his fancy clothes and chasing skirts."

"He has no idea why we want all that land—you're sure?" his companion asked as he accepted the drink and swallowed deeply.

"None whatever . . . and neither he nor his redskin wife will live long enough to find out."

Chapter Four

Fawn sat gazing out at the passing landscape. Although flat and treeless, the grass was lush from spring rains, and wildflowers in a bright array of colors were sprinkled like gemstones across the fields. Of course, now cattle, not her people's buffalo, grazed peacefully in sight of the train.

"Ye look melancholy, colleen. Missin' yer family in St. Louis already?" Fee asked.

"I do miss them, but no, that's not what makes me sad. I know they'll be fine and come to visit as soon as they can." She paused thoughtfully. "It's the land that's changed forever . . . and the Cheyenne way of life. I only hope I'm worthy to carry on Grandfather's gift. It's such a big responsibility!"

"That it is, but yer strong and smart and . . . yer heart is good—isn't that how yer grand da would say it?" Fee asked with a smile.

Fawn gave a husky chuckle. "When he isn't upbraiding me for my impatience or some other infraction, yes. He would say my heart is good. I'm looking forward to seeing him and Bright Leaf and Talks Much, Snake, Bronc and Clyde, even Sergeant Major, all my friends at the ranch. I can hardly wait to get there."

"And escape that handsome divil Irishman?" Fee asked, chuckling herself now. "I was thinkin' the two of ye were gettin' on better the past few days."

"At least I haven't dumped my dinner plate in his lap or

stabbed him with a fork . . . not that the urge hasn't come upon me to do either—or both. Grandfather would be proud of my newfound patience."

As if to test that statement, a knock sounded at the door of their car and Dillon said, "Ladies, we're pulling into the supply station. If you want to get out and stretch your, er, limbs, get ready."

Fawn rolled her eyes. "My limbs are stretched quite adequately, Mr. Dillon. If they grow any longer, they'll resemble the stilts you mentioned when we met," she replied through the door.

"Coward," Fee whispered. Opening the door, she said, "I'd appreciate the chance for some fresh air, thank you kindly, Mr. D."

"I'll be at the rear of your car as soon as the train stops. Oh, Miss Stanhope, if you decide to brave the sun and breeze—and a possible case of stilt-itus, please join us . . . It seems like a shame to hide inside on such a beautiful day."

"I am not hiding," Fawn shot back. When she heard his mocking laughter, she realized she had fallen into his verbal trap. "Perhaps some fresh air would be good. Is there enough time for me to ride Remy?" She had brought her favorite gelding from her father's St. Louis stables, housed in a private stock car on the train, a beautiful paint pony Max and Sky had given her for her last birthday.

"There've been some reports of cattlemen and homesteaders feuding hereabouts. I don't think it'd be a good idea, even if we had enough time to unload your horse."

"Why don't we ask the engineer how long the stop will be?" Fawn asked. "Remy could use some exercise and fresh air, too."

"Afraid not," Jack replied. "One of my men would have to saddle up another horse and ride with you."

"Or you could ride with me," she dared. Her eyes widened when she looked past Fee and saw how he was dressed. The cheap suit was gone. Instead he wore twill trousers and a blue shirt with the sleeves rolled up to reveal tanned forearms lightly furred with hair. That same pale reddish brown hair peeked indecently from the open collar of his shirt. Sweeping her eyes away from his chest—which she remembered all too well from her tumble onto it several days ago—she looked down at his well-worn boots, obviously those of a horseman.

That was when she noticed the Colt Army Model 1873 .45 caliber revolver strapped around his narrow hips. An old Peacemaker. He shoved back the battered Stetson on his head and hooked his fingers in his gun belt, grinning in that way that always set her teeth on edge.

"Do I pass inspection?" he drawled.

She shrugged. "The detective business must not have been all that profitable for you before you met my father." She gestured to his weapon. "That gun looks almost as old as I am."

Dillon nodded. "You're right about that, but it's not as loud."

She huffed but bit her lip to keep from responding to the insult. "At least the clothes you have on are more appropriate than that awful suit you've been wearing."

His expression hardened. "I know I'm sadly lacking in sartorial splendor compared to Monsieur Beaurivage," he replied sarcastically. Sudden images flashed into his mind of the hand-me-down orphanage clothes that Megan had hated.

Fawn sniffed. "Wardrobe is the least thing you lack compared to Monsieur Beaurivage. Manners come to mind."

"You, an authority on fine manners? I never would've guessed," he muttered to himself. "Who would?"

"Let's be takin' that fresh air, colleen." Fee quickly interposed, seeing Fawn clench her fists at her sides, never a good sign. *Sure and Jack Dillon gets her temper up like no other man.* Fiona Madigan had a pretty good idea why.

She practically grabbed Fawn's arm and pulled her toward the rear of their private car, where the small platform had steps reaching near the ground. Moving with amazing speed, Jack must have jumped off the train and walked rapidly to the rear, where he waited politely to assist them down. Fee watched how quickly Fawn pulled away from his strong hands once she'd set foot on the ground. It was as if lightning had struck both of the young fools, but neither of them had any idea the attraction sizzling between them was apparent to others.

With her gift of sight, why did Fawn not realize how well she and Jack Dillon suited? Of course, Fee had often wondered why Fawn could not see how unworthy that Frenchie was. Love, as the poets said, must truly be blind, even to those gifted with special powers.

"How long before we'll be reaching Hennessey, Mr. D?" she asked Jack.

"Another day or so, depending on the train's engine and the weather."

"The weather's that lovely, it is."

"Out here it can change in minutes from sunshine to gray funnel clouds. You ever been in a tornado, Miss Fee?" he asked, enjoying the shrewd little Irishwoman's good humor, a refreshing change after dealing with her waspish employer.

"No, but I've heard of them. Fearful destructive things," she said, eyeing the western horizon uneasily.

"Nothing's going to happen now. Listen for the horses in the stock car. Animals can always sense when bad weather's coming," he assured her.

While they were engaged in conversation, Fawn set out walking toward the big wooden water tower near the front of the train, where the engineer was issuing orders to his men. The station was flanked by a hodgepodge of shanties—the usual saloon and bordello, a livery stable and several small cabins for the railroad employees. The cowhands and some more disreputable types from the surrounding area gathered at their "watering hole" when the day's labors were done. It was like hundreds of other small way stations along the tracks that crisscrossed the West—poor, harsh and desolate.

Ignoring the hard-looking men lounging at the front door of the saloon, Fawn fixed her attention on Mr. Whithers, the engineer. "How long will we be here, sir?" she asked.

Whit Whithers, a rotund red-faced man in striped coveralls, removed his billed cap and smoothed his thick white hair with one callused hand. "Depends. If I can hire some of them fellers to help us load up, a hour, if not, might be pret' near three."

Fawn nodded, looking at the rough bunch of drifters congregated around the saloon. "I should think it wiser to depend on your own men. That bunch doesn't look as if you'd get an honest hour's work from the lot of them."

"I tend to agree," Jack said, coming up behind her silently.

She turned to him with a surprised expression. "You agree with my assessment?"

"There been some rumors 'bout cowhands 'n sodbusters fighting 'round these parts," Whithers said to Dillon.

"That's why the lady should stay at the back of the train, well out of harm's way," Jack replied. Turning to her, he said, "I don't like the way that man in the plaid shirt is looking at you, Miss Stanhope. Let's get out of here."

She glanced at the man Dillon referred to and saw that he'd detached himself from the others and was walking deliberately toward them, his dark eyes narrowed on her. A nasty leer twisted his unshaven face. It was the face of hate. She'd seen it before, could even smell it when an Indian-hating white man was nearby. But she stood her ground in spite of the pressure of Dillon's hand on her arm.

"I'm not afraid of him," she said coldly.

"Hell, I am," Jack snapped, glancing pointedly at the well-tended Remington six-gun at the fellow's hip. "I'm responsible for your safety. Let's go."

"I can take care of myself. Cheyenne don't run." Fawn felt the stubby Smith & Wesson .32 caliber pocket revolver concealed in her skirt.

"I smell me the stink of Injun—a squaw playin' at bein' white," the man said, his eyes moving from Fawn to Jack. "And her squaw man trying to turn tail and run with her." His greasy hair was an indeterminate shade of brown and hung around a narrow face etched with cruelty. Deep creases bracketed his mouth when he opened it and spit through his missing teeth. A lob of noisome tobacco landed close to Jack's boots.

"Move away, Fawn," Jack said to her in a resigned voice. It was obvious the man's hatred ran deep and mean. He stepped in front of her and faced the gunman. "The only stink around here is coming from you. Look around. You're outnumbered. You don't want a fight with the railroad."

"Naw, I don't. I want a fight with a squaw man. She any good under all them fancy white-lady clothes?"

"I have one thing under my 'white-lady clothes' that might interest you," Fawn said calmly. She had the thirty-two pointed directly between his eyes before he could turn his startled gaze back her way. "I can't miss at this range. Actually, I never miss at any range."

"That a fact?" he asked, dismissing her to concentrate on Dillon.

Leave it to that damned brat to carry a hidden pop gun. "Forget Miss Stanhope. Your problem is me."

"Oh, Miss Stanhope, is it?" He made a mocking bow but never took his eyes off Dillon.

"My adopted father is Max Stanhope. You might know him by another name. Out West he's called 'the Limey.'" She was pleased to see that register on the vile fellow's face.

"He ain't been 'round lately. Heard he up an' got him a redskin bitch to share his blankets. Guess she's keepin' him real busy."

Fawn choked down bile at hearing her mother described in such a filthy manner. "You stable-mouthed pig, you aren't fit to utter Sky Stanhope's name," she said, her voice low and ice-cold.

"Get out of here, Fawn, before you get us both killed," Jack commanded her in an equally menacing tone.

"If you insist," she said, lowering her weapon.

Jack figured if he appeared to turn his back on the bastard, the gunman would do what cowards like him always did—try for a back shot. He'd taken down more than one opponent with the trick. He waited for her to walk away. As soon as she moved back a step, he turned slightly to draw the killer's attention.

As he had expected, his opponent reached for his gun, clearing his holster with considerable speed. Just as Dillon whirled and started to squeeze the trigger on his Peacemaker, a shot rang out from his left side. Whithers and the two firemen dove for cover as soon as Fawn fired her gun. She had done a variation on his old trick and shot the son of a bitch after lowering her weapon! He watched the gunman drop to his knees, cradling his forearm as blood gushed from it. His Remington lay on the ground where he'd dropped it when Fawn's shot hit him.

Dillon kicked the gun away, cursing furiously, drowning out the hissing oaths of the wounded man, whose face now resembled a shade of bleached bone. "You should've finished him," he said to her.

"You're welcome," she said sweetly. "He was going to back shoot you!"

"No, he wasn't. He just thought he was. I could hear him touch leather." He raised his Colt and showed her it was still cocked, ready to fire. "He was as good as dead."

"No need for that. He'll never back shoot anyone again unless he learns to fire left handed."

Jack shook his head. "Lady, you are a real piece of work, but you need to learn something quick—when you shoot, kill." He turned away from her. "Get this trash out of here, Whithers. The baron would take it real unkindly if anything happened to his daughter." He waited until the engineer seized the wounded man's gun and then dragged him toward the saloon.

By this time Smitty and Swen were approaching at a dead run, guns drawn. When they saw the outcome of the shooting, they stopped, assessing the situation silently, waiting for orders.

Uncocking his weapon and sliding it into his holster, Jack took a firm grip on Fawn's arm. "Let's get the hell out of here before we find out he has friends."

Fawn scoffed. "His kind doesn't make them."

"For all our sakes, let's hope you're right. Why the hell do you always dash directly into trouble? Couldn't you see those men ogling you? Any woman's fair game to animals like that."

"Are you speaking from experience?" she snapped back. When he stopped dead in his tracks, she wanted to call back the foolish words, remembering how she'd accused him of being a rapist and then had to apologize. When she looked at him, his eyes had turned that eerie shade of translucent amber again. *Wolf's eyes.*

"Yeah, I am. I've killed my share of men just like that one, but if he'd never seen you, the whole mess would've been avoided."

"I'm Cheyenne, not some frightened little white girl," she said angrily as an image of the little redhead from her vision flashed through her mind again.

He grabbed her by her arms and fought the urge to shake some sense into her. Realizing what he was doing, he quickly released her.

Fawn almost lost her balance when he let her go. With one foot raised to kick him, she stumbled backward. "Don't you ever touch me again!" she snarled.

"I'd sooner pet a tarantula. But your father hired me to keep you safe—I can see now why he was willing to pay so handsomely. You are a walking tornado, Miss Stanhope."

"And you are a coarse, vile-tempered, lower class . . . Irishman!"

"Guilty on all charges, but you're going to listen to me and do exactly what I say from now until I turn you over to the poor sons-of-bitches at your ranch. Then you're their responsibility. But as long as you're mine, no more getting off this train until we reach Hennessey. Don't you so much as wave at a sodbuster plowing a cornfield. Is that clear?"

"What will you do if I choose not to obey, Pasha Dillon?"

"Turn you over my knee and paddle your backside— something that your family, red and white, didn't do nearly enough of while you were growing up!" He turned and stalked away when he saw Fee and his men approaching, calling over his shoulder to them, "See that her royal highness climbs back on that train before anyone else gets shot!"

Fawn stood rooted to the spot, remembering the days she had been held captive by Johnny Deuce. Dillon was wrong. She'd had more than her share of beatings . . .

Hennessey was a small town composed of frame buildings hastily slapped together, the fancier ones even whitewashed. It looked like most of the white settlements that had sprung up or been expanded in the Territory since the first land rush of '89. Fawn glanced out the window as the train slowed, heading toward the makeshift station platform. "Why do white men have to turn everything green to dust or mud?" she murmured to herself.

Fee looked at the wide dirt streets where horses and wagons left billowing clouds of dry red dust in their wake as the sky filled with scudding gray clouds. Recalling what Jack had said about the weather, she noted that the horses and dogs on the street appeared calm. "We'll be gettin' muddy streets soon, but only rain, no tornadoes, thank the good Lord. I can imagine how that grand boulevard will look after a torrential downpour."

"With any luck, we'll be halfway to the ranch before the skies open up," Fawn replied, not relishing the prospect of five hours on horseback in Jack Dillon's company. Since their ugly encounter at the fuel stop, she had avoided him and he her.

"I do hope they have a wagon for me. Ye know how afeard I am of the great beastie horses," Fee said with a shiver.

Fawn chuckled. "Don't fret. Look at all the trunks we have to carry. My cousin knows I'd never return without gifts for the whole clan."

Fee watched as her mistress adjusted the brim of her hat carefully and also chuckled. "Ye think Mr. D will be surprised to see yer change of wardrobe?"

"I don't give a fig what Jack Dillon thinks about anything. In a few days I will never set eyes on him again," Fawn replied curtly, ignoring Fee's continued laughter.

"I wouldn't be bettin' on that, missy."

Fee had been correct in her assessment of Jack's reaction when he saw Fawn step down from the rear of the train. He had felt her enticing curves when she'd fallen on top of him, even seen her lush breasts in a low-cut ball gown, but now he could see a great deal more. She was dressed in a white cotton shirt laced up the front and buckskin breeches that revealed the curve of her hips and length of her splendid legs. She wore moccasins instead of boots and a plainsman's flat-crowned hat to shade her face from the sun. Her hair hung down her back in a thick, glistening plait with a silver ornament fastening the braid at the bottom.

She had a Navy Model .38 caliber Colt strapped to her slim waist and clutched a customized Yellow Boy Winchester rifle in her right hand. *Lord, don't let her start shooting.* He knew he'd be her first target and he knew she was a really good shot. Her outfit indicated how she stood between two worlds, red and white, choosing from each what would serve her best.

As soon as she saw him, her expression darkened. They hadn't crossed verbal swords for two days. Fine with him. Now all he had to do was reach her ranch and then escort her to her Cheyenne family. Jack assured himself he could hardly wait for this part of his assignment to be done, but something deep inside his gut called him a liar. His ruminations were interrupted when Swen and Smitty greeted him.

"We got our gear from the compartments, Jack," Smitty said.

"Ya, and doncha mean I carried most of it, little man," Swen said with a good natured chuckle.

"What else is a big Norse ox good for?" Smitty shot back, then asked Jack, "You and the lady still avoiding each other? Gonna be pretty hard riding for hours."

"She's avoided me. I'll just be glad once we can leave her behind. Why don't you bring out our horses and saddle them up . . . that is, if you think you can handle yours while Swen takes care of his and mine?"

"Oh, I can handle a horse or three. Better that than one long, tall lady's temper," Smitty replied with a knowing smirk.

They went to work while Jack cautiously drew near where Fawn stood. Instead of the verbal sally he expected, her face suddenly split into a wide grin and she emitted a squeal of positively girlish delight. It was not for him. She looked past him to a small group of cowhands who must have been the welcoming committee from her ranch.

"Mercurial as Kansas weather," he muttered, watching her dash to the end of the platform and jump into the arms of a tall cowhand. His shaggy, straight black hair and swarthy complexion indicated that he was a mixed blood. Jack approached them as the man swung her around in a circle. She jabbered in Cheyenne, holding on to his neck as if he were her own true love. Damn, did she have one in every port, like a sailor? The Creole in St. Louis, a cowboy at her ranch—who knew how many more? Perhaps a full blood with her grandfather's band?

He cursed himself for reacting like a jealous fool as the tall cowhand admonished her, saying, "Dammit, Hellcat, watch that rifle of yours or you'll crack my skull!"

As she slid to the ground, Fawn continued speaking to him in Cheyenne, but the mixed blood from the ranch looked over her head and nodded to Dillon. He shushed her with a grin, then extended his hand to Jack. "Howdy. You must be Jack Dillon. Been expectin' you. Folks call me Snake."

Jack exchanged a handshake with him. "I hope that moniker doesn't refer to your disposition," he said, liking the fellow in spite of himself.

"Only if you listen to my ex-wives. Got it at boarding school when the missionaries didn't figure Burning Snake was a fit Christian name. They changed it to Bernard Snake." He laughed and Jack joined him.

"Institutional logic. I was Jonathan Padric Aloysius Dillon to the good sisters at the orphanage in Chicago. The other children all called me Jack after I was lucky enough to beat the biggest bully in the place."

Snake grinned, then glanced at Fawn, who was glaring at Jack. "This Hellcat, much to my grief, is my cousin."

"My sympathies, Snake," Jack replied gravely. The fellow could grow on him.

Ignoring Dillon, she scolded Snake. "Two ex-wives ought to know all about your grief—and your disposition," she teased.

"Ah, darlin', it's three ex-wives now. Thelma Sweet Rain up and left me last month." Snake's sorrowful words were belied by the merry gleam in his eyes.

She replied in Cheyenne and Snake laughed. Jack recognized enough of the language to know she was cussing him for the way he loved and then drove off the tribe's womenfolk. Her tirade was cut short when Fee approached.

"Snake, this is my friend and traveling companion, Miss Fiona Madigan," Fawn said, introducing Snake in turn.

Fee craned her neck to look the tall stranger in the face as she curtsied. Snake doffed his hat and bowed. Jack suppressed a chuckle. The way the two of them stared in fascination at each other, it might be love at first sight.

"Sure, and aren't you the tallest man ever I've met," she said, her brogue thickening as she batted her lashes at Snake.

"And you're the loveliest little leprechaun I've ever laid eyes on. They guard their treasures well," he responded gallantly.

Fee blushed with pleasure.

"You'd best watch out for your companion's virtue, Miss Stanhope. I think she's smitten with your lothario cousin," Dillon whispered.

"Maybe Fee can pound some sense into his irresponsible head. Some women have more patience than others when it comes to men." She gave Jack a look that indicated he was beyond hope.

"Any woman on earth has more patience than you."

"And any man has more sense than you," she snapped back.

Seeing he was never going to best her in this particular war of words, Jack turned to Snake and his men, saying, "We'd better get the horses and baggage unloaded. Miss Stanhope's brought enough trunks to fill a wagon train."

Breaking off from his flirtation with his Lilliputian leprechaun, Snake nodded. "We should beat the rain coming in if we hurry. Bronc has probably worked himself into such a lather, his stomach ulcerations are rumbling like thunder. Besides, everyone at the ranch is waiting to greet my Hellcat . . . darlin' girl," he added to her with a wink.

The two buckboards the men had brought from the ranch were loaded so full, some of the excess trunks and bags had to be lashed to the sides. While the men worked efficiently under Snake's direction, Fawn led her paint, Remy, from the boxcar, whispering sweet words in his ear as she guided him by the hackamore she'd slipped over his head.

"Where's your saddle? I'll have him ready to ride in a few minutes."

"No, thank you," she said dismissively. " You'd best see to your own horse. I don't need any help with Remy." Ignoring him when he crossed his arms over his chest and watched, she tossed a handwoven blanket with a beautiful design over the horse's back and secured it. Then she grabbed a fistful of the black and white gelding's mane and leaped onto him in one fluid motion.

"Very impressive." Jack watched the way her long legs hugged the big horse's sides. Images of how they'd fit around a man's body flashed into his mind. He tamped down the base—and dangerous—instincts and tipped his hat. "I'll see if Swen and Smitty are ready to ride."

Fawn watched him join his friends, who had three fine horses saddled. Jack swung easily onto a big bay stallion like a natural-born rider. She had read her father's reports and knew Dillon had been one of Judge Parker's deputies, but somehow she'd never thought of him as anything but a Pinkerton detective . . . until she'd seen the way he almost killed that scum at the water station. No, he was a lot more than just a city boy from the wrong side of the tracks.

Fee's giggles interrupted her admiration of the way Jack Dillon sat a horse. Snake's big hands encircled the Irishwoman's waist as he lifted her up and placed her on the lead wagon's seat as if she weighed no more than a feather. "Fee, giggling? This might mean trouble," she muttered, watching her cousin climb onto the wagon to drive the team.

Trouble for Snake. If he broke her friend's heart, she'd turn his hide into a hatband!

Chapter Five

The sky turned from bright blue with smears of gray on the horizon to solid dense pewter. The travelers wended their way toward the east bank of the Cimarron, where the headquarters of the vast Stanhope lands were situated. Jack and Smitty rode ahead while Snake drove the first wagon, Fee by his side. Three other hands and Swen guarded the rear of the two-wagon cavalcade. Not wanting to be near Dillon, Fawn rode alongside the wagons, but Remy was restless and eager to run after days of confinement on the train.

She patted his neck and leaned low, saying, "You want to go for a good workout?" With that, she kicked him lightly with the soft heels of her moccasins. Remy picked up his pace, passing Dillon and Smitty, but Fawn abruptly reined him in, coming to a full stop. She cocked her head and stared into space, silently.

Ready to ride after the fool woman to keep her from breaking her neck, Jack looked at her frozen body as he drew near. *If she warns you about any danger . . . or tells you she knows something is about to happen, don't ignore her . . .* Jack recalled Max Stanhope's words.

"Is something wrong?" he asked, reining in beside her. The hair on the back of his neck stood up. There definitely *was* something wrong, he could sense it through her. Then he looked at her face and saw that same vacant faraway stare that had transfixed her when she'd fallen on him aboard the train. "What—"

Fawn shook her head and her eyes cleared. Suddenly she dived from Remy and launched herself at him. When they started to tumble off the opposite side of his horse, his hat went flying behind him and both horses nickered in alarm. Their riders landed in scratchy prairie grass with her on top of him.

"This is starting to become an annoying habit—"

"Look at your hat," she said, rising to her knees and cocking the rifle she had managed to hold on to when she leaped.

Jack glanced behind him and saw the bullet hole through the crown of his Stetson, now lying in a wagon rut. Another shot pinged into the dirt a couple of feet from them. He knocked her behind him and lay over her body protectively, whispering fiercely, "Stay down, dammit—someone's shooting at us." The moment he said the words, he realized she'd known it was going to happen before the shot was fired. *She can sometimes see into the future . . .*

Fawn gasped mockingly. "Someone's shooting at us," she echoed. "What a brilliant piece of detective work!"

Ignoring her jibe, he scanned the horizon. "Quiet, brat." With the noise of the horses and the force of his surprise landing, he had not heard the first shot, but Smitty and the others had. Both of his men rode quickly up to them and leaped from their horses, crouching with rifles drawn in front of Fawn and their downed boss.

"You're pulverizing me. Get off, you great ox." Fawn shoved him away so she could raise her Winchester again.

"I thought I was just a troll," he said, taking care to keep his body in front of hers.

"If they're all as heavy as you, small wonder they lurk under bridges, not on them," she snapped.

"You both all right?" Smitty asked.

"Can't you tell? The lady's tongue is still flapping . . . but then, it will be when they nail her coffin shut," Dillon replied.

"I figure those shots to be coming from them trees by the creek," Smitty said as Swen nodded agreement.

Snake had shoved Fee beneath the wagon seat and crouched with his rifle ready to fire. One of his men, leaning low in his saddle, led Snake's horse to the wagon and he jumped onto it.

"Fawn!" Fee yelled, starting to climb out of the wagon.

"She's all right. You stay down and don't move until I come back for you," Snake commanded.

"He's right, Fee," Fawn called out. "Stay down." She paused a moment, then said, "They're gone."

No more shots were fired.

After waiting for several minutes, Jack stood up and retrieved his hat. The bullet had made a neat hole just above the band, dead center. "Not bad shooting." He looked down at Fawn. "Guess I owe you one, Princess."

"Don't call me that. I'm not a cigar-store wooden Indian," she snapped, climbing to her feet. She picked bits of dry grass from her shirt and brushed the thick red dust off her clothes.

"You're wooden between the ears," he muttered quietly, but before she could retort, Snake rode up.

Looking at the hole in Jack's hat, her cousin inquired, "Some old friend come callin' on you?"

"Possible, I suppose," Jack said neutrally. "Or a new friend who doesn't want me to find out what's happening to your people's land allotments."

Snake grinned. "Max said you were a good detective. Let's see if our bushwhacker left any clues before he hightailed it back to Hennessey."

"He didn't go back to Hennessey," Fawn said. Before anyone realized what she was doing, she whistled for Remy, who came immediately. She made another agile leap onto his back and headed for the creek where the shots had originated. The men quickly caught up with her as she charged through a thick screen of brush. She stopped several feet short of a cottonwood and a large boulder. After pausing for a moment, she said, "He stood on that boulder and leaned his rifle against that tree limb to steady his aim. One man."

Perplexed, Smitty and Swen looked from her to their boss. "How does she know such things?" Swen asked.

Dillon shrugged as Snake and his men dismounted and began to examine the area, without questioning why she was so certain about what had happened. Jack followed suit, watching as Snake examined the dusty loose earth between the boulder and a small sapling at the creek's edge. "Here's where he tied his horse." Clear boot prints led from the muddy bank to the dry higher ground around the boulder and cottonwood.

Now Jack and his men joined them, checking the direction in which the rider had fled by following his muddy boot prints from the boulder back to his horse. Smitty tipped his hat back and looked up and down the twisting gulley lined with brush and scrub trees, enough cover and soft ground to muffle sounds of an escape. "He could be circling north to get around us and then ride for Hennessey."

Dillon watched Fawn, who had dismounted and walked around the large boulder. She stooped and picked up a spent cartridge casing as if it had been lying there waiting just for her. Her eyes again took on that unfocused expression as she rolled it around between her fingers. He started to walk over to her, but Snake placed a hand on his arm. "Ease up a minute," he said quietly.

Everyone remained silent until she spoke. "The man who tried to kill Dillon is headed south for Kingfisher."

Snake turned to a hand who appeared to be a full-blood Cheyenne and said, "Cloud, you and Teddy follow the creek south." Teddy was as white as Swen, only smaller, with a freckled face and wide innocent eyes. "See if you can find where the bushwhacker leaves the creek. If you can't find him before the skies open up, turn 'round and catch up with us."

Johnny Red Cloud and Teddy Barlow nodded and mounted up, heading south along the creek. Cloud watched the ground and Teddy held his rifle across his saddle horn like he meant business. As soon as they vanished into the brush, Snake turned to Dillon and his men. "Cloud can track fly crap in pepper and Teddy's the best shot at the ranch."

"Both Smitty and Swen are good with a gun. One of them could ride along," Dillon suggested.

"Suit yourself, but it's damn long odds they'll catch him," Snake replied.

Dillon nodded to Smitty, saying, "Try to take him alive if you get to him. I want to know who hired him." Smitty swung into the saddle and quickly took off after the two younger men.

Fawn approached then, still holding the spent cartridge in her hand. When Jack reached his open palm toward her, she gave it to him. "I can tell nothing else from it," she said simply.

Jack examined the casing. "It's a .38-40 caliber, from a Marlin, probably an '89 model. Not rare but not that common either." He studied it more carefully. "The rifle this came from has a weak firing pin. The pin stroke made only a light indentation in the brass."

Swen, who had climbed atop the boulder, jumped off and walked over to his boss. "There are scrapes on a branch in front of the boulder. Shoulder high for a short man. The gunman must have used it to steady his aim . . . like the lady said." The big Norwegian looked at Fawn uneasily. "Ma'am, how did you—"

Fawn cut him off quickly. "I saw him—I mean I saw the glint of his rifle barrel." The men from the ranch nodded agreement.

Jack knew it was too overcast for anyone to have seen the shiniest rifle barrel in Oklahoma, but he held his peace. "Like I said, I owe you one . . . Miss Stanhope," he added with a grin. "You plumb ruined that fancy white shirt rolling in the dirt."

As she looked down at the red dust on her clothes, he walked past her, whispering so only she could hear him, "Princess."

"Troll," she fired back, brushing ineffectually at her clothes as they all mounted up and returned to the wagons.

Fee was pacing back and forth so furiously her sensible dark blue skirt's hem was stained with dust. "Thank ye, Lord! Has anyone been hurt?" she asked, looking from Fawn to Jack, then letting her gaze linger on Snake. "Where are Mr. Schmitt and yer two young riders?" she asked him.

"Tracking the bushwhacker, but it's unlikely they'll catch up to him." Snake explained. "The trail will probably be swallowed up in one of the herds of cattle between here and Kingfisher."

"We'll find him . . . sooner or later," Jack said quietly. "And he'll lead us to whoever he works for."

The skies opened up, drenching wagons and riders in a warm summer rain that quickly blew past them. In two hours Smitty, Cloud and Teddy rejoined them to report they'd lost the trail, just as Snake had surmised they would. "Over two hundred head of allotment beef being trailed down to agency pens around Reno. He probably acted like a drover. Cut through the herd, 'n then we couldn't pick up a trace of 'im after the rain hit, the smart sumbitch—beggin' your pardon, ladies," Teddy said, his face red beneath his freckles for cussing in front of the women.

Fawn only smiled at him, nodding, but Fee spoke up. "Sure and I've heard worse . . . from yon fine young lady there. 'Tis a good thing most back East don't understand her native tongue."

The hands exchanged chuckles, knowing Fawn's penchant for swearing in Cheyenne. Dillon, who had heard her do a fair job in English, raised an eyebrow and gazed at her. She kicked her paint into a canter and rode past him, saying, "I know some French and Spanish, too."

"And all of it obscene, I bet," Dillon replied, catching up to her.

She did not say anything further or try to pull ahead of him. They rode in uneasy silence for nearly another hour, the hot sun drying their clothing so it stuck to their bodies, causing itchy misery. Fawn knew her breasts were outlined by the sheer fabric of her shirt, which had been loose and flowing before the rain. Why had she worn such an impractical garment?

Because the fabric would be cool on a muggy day, she told herself, trying not to look at Jack Dillon's upper body. His shoulders looked even broader than usual and the muscles knotting his upper arms were outlined beneath the damp shirt. He had unfastened several more buttons and rolled the sleeves up farther as a concession to the heat. He had discarded his ruined hat back at the ambush site. Sunlight glinted on the thick reddish brown hair of his head. Once again she was reminded of a red wolf . . . the one in her visions? She quashed the idea.

Jack noticed she was staring straight ahead rather than looking at him, which was fine because it allowed him to study her in profile. Her hat shaded her face from the sun but her complexion was still a rich tan shade, smooth and unblemished. She lowered those impossibly thick black eyelashes against the wind carrying bits of dust their way, shielding her luminous ebony eyes. Her nose was slim but curved and long, fitting her strong, striking face, but his attention returned again and again to her mouth, so lush and full.

He remembered brushing those tempting lips when she lay on top of him in the railcar. If she gave them willingly, they would be soft and sweet. Jack shook his head and shifted his gaze lower, trying to break the spell she had somehow spun around him. But the sight of her long legs wrapped around Remy didn't help him relax any more than did a glimpse of the way her breasts stretched the lacings of her shirt. They jiggled slightly. Damn! He shifted uncomfortably in the saddle and cursed himself for being seven kinds of a fool. She was off limits, an heiress, his employer's daughter, spoiled rotten. And she possessed a frightening gift of sight about which he had heard stories long ago.

Jack pushed that disquieting memory away when they crested a rise and Snake called out from behind him, "There she is. Quite some spread, ain't it?"

Dillon looked down on a small kingdom carved out of the wilderness. If he'd for a moment entertained any idea of a relationship with Fawn Stanhope, looking at the princess's castle and the fiefdom surrounding it quickly dispelled the notion. A pair of long bunkhouses sat with a big cookhouse between them. Two stables with large corrals behind them were nearby. Dozens of prime pieces of horseflesh munched hay or trotted around the paddocks, swishing their tails. Off to one side a cluster of trim cabins with neat little yards overlooked the corrals—private residences for family men? The ranch even had its own blacksmith and carpentry shops.

Everywhere people worked, calling out to one another as they passed by. The clang of the smith's hammer rang across the rolling hills. Cowboys saddled horses and repaired tack. A few in one corral busted newly acquired wild mustangs. In the distance the bawl of calves echoed from a branding fire where the spring chore was well underway.

Central to this whole beehive of activity was the ranch

house, a castle indeed—two stories of white frame with a double-tiered porch that stretched across the front and around both sides. Gingerbread trim was painted a rusty red, providing an eye-catching accent. A half dozen big cottonwoods rustled a welcome and offered cooling shade from the afternoon sun. In the yard enclosed by a white picket fence, beds of hollyhocks and roses bloomed in profuse colors.

The porches were set with big, comfortable rockers and small tables scattered around on both levels, as if inviting visitors to sit and enjoy cool lemonade and freshly baked cookies. Inside the long windows, opened to let in the air, Dillon could see fancy lace curtains hanging from ceiling to floor, swaying in the breeze. He imagined the big house had at least a dozen bedrooms, judging by the number of French doors leading out onto the top porch.

There was a separate summer kitchen with a trellised pathway linking it to the back of the house. "All the key men who oversee the ranch take dinner with the family in the dining room," Fawn said as she reined in beside him.

"Your father must have brought over King Arthur's Round Table," he replied.

"He just hired a fine cabinetmaker," she said offhandedly.

Snake pulled up his wagon team and let Fee take in the view. "Every time I return, it still impresses me," he said to her.

"'Tis far more grand than ever I imagined," she breathed, looking over at Fawn. "Even yer paintings could not do it justice," she said. "Now I wish I'd been brave enough to come with ye for a visit afore." She looked from Fawn to Snake, then quickly back to her friend.

"Well, you're here now and I'm glad," Fawn said fondly, noting the interplay.

"So am I," Snake added, with a wink at Fee. Then he observed Dillon's careful scrutiny and announced, "Welcome to Red Wolf Ranch."

Jack fought to keep his expression neutral, but he knew that Snake and Fawn sensed his surprise. She was uneasy, her cousin amused as he added, "The little Hellcat named it herself when she was just a tadpole. Mr. Stanhope let her since he intended it to be hers when she grew up."

"Got some time to wait then," Dillon quietly murmured to her.

"I'm in charge now," she gritted out, shifting uneasily on her horse.

"How many people work here?" It was all Dillon could think to ask as Fawn kicked her horse and moved ahead. Everyone else followed suit.

"Over a hundred last count," Snake replied. "Since Mr. Stanhope was a British officer, it's run like a military post. He even hired his old sergeant major from the army to take charge of the arsenal and keep order. A real stickler for rules, ole Higgins is, but considerin' how dangerous it can get out here, that ain't a bad idea."

Remembering his brush with the bushwhacker, Dillon nodded.

As the cavalcade approached the ranch house to unload the wagons, everyone along the way greeted them. It was obvious to Jack that they all were overjoyed to see Fawn return. How could the snotty hellion inspire loyalty, much less such open delight? He realized that there must be far more to her personality than he had as yet seen. Maybe she was a witch and had put them all under a spell. That he, too, was falling beneath it, Jack refused to consider.

By the time they'd reached the big house, most of the hands had peeled off, heading to the stables to unsaddle and rub down their horses. Only Snake, Teddy and an older fellow named Butte Jackson, who had driven the second wagon, remained. The front door swung open and a pair of elderly men began to climb down the steps. One had a thick head of snow white hair and a decided paunch. His taller companion sported a handlebar mustache of heroic proportions and curly salt and pepper hair that reached his stooped shoulders.

Fawn's eyes lit up as she jumped from her horse and raced up to greet them. "Bronc, Good Heart, I've been waiting for nearly a year to see if you old goats would make it through another winter," she teased as she hugged them.

"The feller with snow on the roof's Bronc Bodie. He's foreman of Red Wolf. The other is Clyde Campbell. Used to be our people's Indian Agent afore he give up on the Great White Father's broken promises and put his stake in with Max Stanhope. My people named him Good Heart," Snake explained as he helped Fee from the wagon.

"Yore a sight fer these ole eyes, gal. I ain't give up yet. Ain't fixin' to neither 'til I see yew settled," Bronc said, as he held Fawn at arm's length to inspect her.

"Ah, lass, I dinna ken how ye keep getting lovelier every year," Good Heart said in a thick Scot's burr.

Dillon dismounted and was watching the fond reunion when he heard the unmistakable sound behind him of a weapon being unsheathed from leather. He whirled, drawing his Peacemaker, only to realize that it was young Teddy holding his rifle, butt end extended outward. The kid froze, his freckles bright as stars against the sudden pallor of his skin. The whole crowd stood utterly still, everyone but Smitty and Swen amazed at Dillon's incredible speed.

Teddy recovered enough to stammer, "M-Mr. Dillon, I wuz just shucking this here rifle to g-give to S-Sergeant Major H-Higgins. I didn't mean no harm. It's th' rules here."

"None of the hands are allowed to carry guns around the headquarters," Snake explained. "Sergeant Major collects 'em when they come in off the range."

Jack was still frozen in a crouch, carefully easing down the hammer of his Colt. From behind Teddy, a tall, sinewy man, improbably wearing a brown tweed coat in the heat, took the rifle from the still-quaking cowhand. "Thank you, lad. Now then, Mr. Jackson, your weapons, if you please." As the second wagon driver handed over his rifle and sidearm, the man with the clipped British accent turned his attention to Dillon, who had straightened and slid his gun into his holster, red-faced with a combination of horror and embarrassment.

"Damn, I could've killed you, kid!" he said to Teddy. "An apology isn't enough, but I am sorry for scaring you. Now, let me give you some advice. Never, never pull a gun out of leather behind a man's back unless you intend to shoot him—all right?"

Teddy's Adam's apple bobbed as he nodded. "Y-yessir, you bet, M-Mr. Dillon."

"Capital advice, sir," Higgins said to Jack. "But while you are a guest here, sir, would you please refrain from shooting any of our men—unless circumstances warrant?"

Jack nodded, still feeling his cheeks burn. "I'll do my best, Sergeant Major."

"There's a good gentleman. Lieutenant Stanhope would be extremely distressed to lose a good lad such as Teddy." The sergeant major pronounced lieutenant "leftenant" in the English manner.

Snake explained to Higgins, "Dillon was almost killed on the trail. Some bushwhacker shot his hat clean off his head. Makes a man a tad touchy."

Fawn observed the whole thing, stunned by how fast Dillon's draw had been—and how great his control. He could have killed the boy, but his reflexes were so good that he had not fired in the split second he realized his mistake. Not even her father, known as the Pale Moon Stalker among the Cheyenne and the Limey among whites, had been any better. She could see Jack was badly shaken, in spite of Snake's attempt to smooth the matter over.

She approached Dillon and said, "You might have killed him, but you didn't. No need to torment yourself."

"Thanks. I'll leave that to you," he replied, with a half-hearted smile.

Bronc approached Jack and pumped his hand vigorously. "We heerd Max wuz sendin' a detective to pertect our gal, here, 'n see about them land grabbers. Looks ta me like we got us a good 'un fer the job o' work."

"Aye, that we have. Welcome, Mr. Dillon," Campbell seconded as Fawn made introductions all around.

"Where should I put the bags, Miss Stanhope?" Jackson asked as he and Teddy waited for orders about unloading the wagons.

"Fee's things will go in the room to the left of mine." Fawn paused, considering where to put Dillon and his men.

"Doncha be .frettin' 'bout where folks should sleep," a thick drawling voice interrupted. "I'll take keer o' room arrangements 'n sech. Got me chickens fryin' and beaten biscuit batter all ready fer the oven."

A great stocky block of a woman, almost as tall as Swen, came trundling around the side of the house from the summer kitchen, wiping her red, meaty hands on her apron before she flung wide her arms and Fawn rushed into her embrace.

"Oh, Lula, I've missed you so!" Fawn said, returning the hug.

The giantess had pink hair, an odd blend of red streaked with white, kinky and frizzing around her face where strands had escaped from the tight knot at the nape of her neck. Her round face was browned by the sun and well lined, and her eyes were a light greenish gray. As she looked over Fawn's shoulder, her shrewd gaze fixed on Dillon.

After a brief exchange, Fawn turned to Fee, Jack and his men, saying, "This is our housekeeper and the best cook west of the Mississippi, Mrs. Lulabelle Jones. Just wait until you taste her biscuits! Lula, meet the woman I've told you so much about, Fiona Madigan. And this is Mr. Dillon and his detectives, Mr. Schmitt and Mr. Swensen."

"Yew are an itty-bitty thang," Lula said to Fee. "But jest yew wait. I'll fatten yew up good."

As she and Fee smiled at each other, Snake murmured to Swen, who was standing closest to him, "Miss Fee looks to have plenty enough meat on her bones for any man's likin'."

Swen only smiled as he and Smitty doffed their hats to the housekeeper. Jack, being hatless, made a polite bow. Smitty had to crane his neck to see her smiling face. She quickly commenced barking orders at Teddy and Butte, who jumped to obey. Much to Fawn's distress, Lula put Jack in the room next to hers. She wanted to protest, but if she did, she knew Dillon would smirk and give her one of his insufferable grins, as if she were actually afraid of getting too close to him.

She held her peace, as the housekeeper shooed them all inside to rest and clean up before dinner. All Fawn would have to do was endure a few meals with him before he escorted her to Grandfather's band. Then he and his men would leave to investigate the land fraud. But something kept nagging at her, a gut-deep feeling that she had not seen the last of Jack Dillon or that damnable red wolf . . .

As if echoing her uneasy thoughts, Fee whispered to her, "Sure and it's an odd coincidence, yer ranch bein' named Red Wolf and himself lookin' sorta like one."

Fawn gritted her teeth and stomped into the cool front hall. This was certainly not the way she'd envisioned her homecoming. How was she going to sleep tonight, knowing Jack Dillon was just beyond the next wall?

Chapter Six

$\mathcal{D}$illon lay back in the big tub, letting the warm, sudsy water refresh him. He had not enjoyed a real bath since they'd boarded the train in St. Louis, although he had seen a hip bath tucked discreetly away in Fawn's private car once when Fee had opened the door. Visions of Fawn's golden tan skin glistening with soap bubbles rose in his mind. He snapped his eyes open and sat up. Damnation, he had to stop mooning over the brat as if she were his—or he were hers. There wasn't much that frightened Jack Dillon. But this growing sense of oneness was beginning to rattle him.

I've just been too long without a woman, that's all. But he knew his strange link to Fawn was far more complicated. Why in hell had she named her ranch Red Wolf? He climbed from the tub and seized a fluffy towel, drying off with more vigor than necessary, as if he could rub away the bond he felt growing between them.

Dinner, according to the formidable Lula, would be served at seven. He had more than an hour to kill. Getting the lay of the land around the princess's little kingdom would be a good way to spend the time. He'd start by checking out her palace. The porch that he'd seen when they rode up wrapped around the house on all four sides. He slipped on a fresh white shirt and clean pair of brown trousers. Like Fawn's Creole suitor back in St. Louis, Jack also had only one pair of boots, but they weren't the fancy custom-made kind Beaurivage wore. Dillon had wiped his share of road apples and cow manure off of his.

Recalling Fawn's snide remarks about how the detective business must not have been lucrative until he was hired by the Stanhopes, he grimaced, suppressing the idiotic urge to sniff his boots. One day he'd own fine clothing and wear hand-tooled boots. He would, by God, be rich as the Pinkerton brothers—and he wouldn't beat desperate striking workers with a billy to do it. He glanced at his reflection in the bathing room mirror. He'd shaved before sinking into the tub of hot water. The dampness made his thick russet hair slightly curly around the nape of his neck. More things he couldn't afford yet . . . a good barber or frequent haircuts. He ran a brush over his head one final time and decided he looked presentable . . . for a troll.

Whistling, he let himself out of the bathing room by the door leading to the porch. Jack stopped and gazed around, watching the beehive of activity at the summer kitchen. He started walking the upper tier of the porch. It always paid in his line of work to know where entries and exits were positioned. He spied a narrow flight of stairs at the far corner of the porch, after making the second turn. It led down to the backyard, where a huge vegetable garden stretched on for a hundred feet or more, overflowing with ripening produce and even an orchard at the far end of the well-tilled plot.

When he'd lived at the orphanage, Sister MJ had had a small garden that gave her young charges a few fresh vegetables during the summer. Recalling a childhood with scant happy memories, he smiled. When a boy was hungry enough, even a fresh turnip tasted good. He could only imagine how delicious the bounty of this garden and orchard were. Holding his dirty trail clothes in one hand so they wouldn't soil his clean shirt, he continued around the opposite side of the house. His room should be just past the corner. He'd drop off his old clothes, then take the outside stairs down and circle the lower porch.

Unknown to Jack, Fee stood just around that corner. She had been stationed outside Fawn's private bathing room, where her mistress was enjoying a leisurely soak. Her job was to make certain none of the men wandered by and inadvertently peered inside, while the door was standing open to let in a cooling breeze. She had seen no one . . . until Jack Dillon approached, gazing out at the front gate of the ranch.

Some devilish impulse made her dart silently into Fawn's bedroom before he noticed her. She stood very still, pressing her hands to her mouth to hold back a wicked giggle of pure delight. Fee waited as he approached. *Sure and he'll hear her . . .*

Jack did indeed hear a rich feminine voice humming softly. There was no way he could mistake that low, husky tone. Even when she was boiling mad, her voice never became high or shrill as so many women's did. Had he passed his room? Become turned around because he was paying more attention to the grounds than to the house . . . or was he unconsciously scenting her? Then he heard water splashing . . . bathwater.

Fawn's bathwater.

Every fiber of his being ached to see her body stretched out in one of those big tubs. She'd probably had one made specially to fit her long legs. But he was not a Peeping Tom, blast it! No gentleman would spy on a lady that way. He started to turn around but then remembered her taunts about his lack of breeding and fine manners. She had accused him of being no gentleman on more than one occasion. He had told her she was no lady. Why not live down to her low expectations? The door to the room was standing open, moving ever so slightly with the breeze.

It was as if she'd issued an engraved invitation for anyone to barge in. He should give her a good dressing-down for being so careless, if not of her decency, at the very least of her safety. Like a man mesmerized, he walked slowly toward the sounds of splashing water. This was insane. He should stop, backtrack all the way around the big house and find his damnable room, which he now realized must be right next to hers. Was she expecting him to catch her in her bath? It sure looked that way to Jack. The least she could have done was post Fee to shoo away intruders. Where was the little leprechaun?

Probably off mooning over Snake.

He decided he would give Fawn a good lecture. Then the subtle essence of lilac bath oil wafted out of the room and his mouth went so dry he could not have uttered a word if the house had just caught fire. Like moth to flame, he took those last few steps and looked in the doorway. His imagination had not done her justice. She sat in profile, facing the wall with her eyes closed. Her whole body was slick with bubbles, glistening like pale polished bronze. He fought the urge to walk in and run his hands over that satin-smooth skin.

Fawn obliviously raised one incredibly long leg and applied a sponge to the sweet curve of a calf, then lowered the leg and raised the other. Her feet were slender and narrow with high arches. He followed the progress of the sponge eagerly when she leaned forward and arched her back, squeezing soapy water between her shoulder blades. As she washed her back, her breasts stood at attention, high and taut, the nipples small nubby buds of rose brown in the cool air.

His hand curved unconsciously as if fitting around one of those perfect globes. Jack had large hands, just the right size to cup them. An ache began deep in his gut until his erection grew dangerously hard. This was wrong. He had to get the hell out of there before she saw him! Jack had never felt so guilty in his life. What would Sister MJ say! *She'd give me the caning of my life.*

Jack started to move, but then Fawn ducked her head into

the water. He stood rooted to the porch floorboards. With her eyes tightly squeezed shut, she poured some golden liquid from a small bottle into her hand, then worked it vigorously through her long black hair. His fingertips tingled just thinking about feeling her luxuriant hair, massaging her scalp . . . But when she called out for Fee to fetch the rinse water, the spell shattered.

He turned and retraced his steps around the corner of the porch as if all the demons of hell were pursuing him. But he feared only one. A tall, lithe hellion named Fawn Stanhope. How in the name of all that was holy could he face her across the dinner table in another hour? Then he recalled how many people would be sitting at that big table. Surely as mistress of the house, she would make certain he was placed as far away from her as possible.

Jack slipped guiltily away, unaware of Fee, who was grinning like a Cheshire cat. She carried a large pitcher of clean water into Fawn's bath. Would it not be lovely to have him watch Fawn standing in the tub while the little Irishwoman dumped the water over her head? Humming merrily, Fee climbed on the step stool beside the tub and slowly emptied the pitcher. She could hardly wait for dinner. As soon as she finished assisting Fawn with her bath, she would change into her best dress and then make a discreet alteration of the place cards at the table.

Dillon studied the place cards glumly. Luck was certainly not running his way tonight. Hell, ever since the first time he'd laid eyes on Fawn Stanhope, she had been trouble. He'd been out of his mind to spy on her in her bath, no matter how foolish the brat had been to leave that door standing wide open. Now he had to sit directly at her right hand and pretend nothing had happened. *How the hell will I explain the bulge in my pants the minute she walks into the room?* He could hold his hat in a strategic position—if he still had one.

The diners began filling the large room, which was dominated by a massive oak table and high-backed cane chairs. Snake squired an enraptured Fee while Bronc and his old pal Campbell argued politics. Smitty and Swen looked as nervous as choirboys caught cussing. They peered unhappily at what seemed like acres of white linen set with fine crystal and china, and a daunting array of silverware. Truth be told, Jack wasn't a lot more certain than they about which fork to use first.

"Just watch the others and do what they do," he whispered to them. Sergeant Major Higgins, still wearing his tweed jacket without breaking a sweat, strolled in with three other men who worked in supervisory capacities. Except for Higgins, everyone was dressed in clean but regular ranch duds, not suits. Mrs. Jones had informed the guests that dinners at the Red Wolf were not dress-up affairs except for holidays, but she had not warned them about the table setting.

Jack would have bet his last dollar that Fawn had instructed the housekeeper to fancy things up. Of course, considering that it was her mistress's first night home, perhaps Lula had made the decision. Either way, he'd managed in the train dining car and he would manage now. Smiling grimly, he considered that this challenge might be a blessing in disguise, since watching Sergeant Major Higgins handle the cutlery would keep his mind away from memories of Fawn's glistening wet body.

Their hostess made her grand entrance, dressed in a simple brown cotton gown that showed off her rich coloring to excellent advantage. She wore her gleaming raven hair in a sleek bun. *Cool and refreshed from her breezy bath, no doubt,* Jack thought sourly as she laughed and teased with Bronc and Good Heart. Apparently they were surrogate uncles. Like a tongue worrying a sore tooth, his mind kept wandering back to earlier questions about the identity of her mysterious Cheyenne grandfather.

I'll settle that tomorrow. After I deliver her, I can get to the real job I'm here to do.

Fawn was all smiles, giving him only a perfunctory nod before turning to Higgins to inquire about one of his men who was ill. Then she noticed the rearrangement of the place cards. She glared at Fee, who ignored her and kept giggling at Snake's tall tales. Jack studied the little Irishwoman, who gave him a quick, conspiratorial wink before returning her attention to her swain. So she had seated him next to Fawn. Then another very disturbing thought occurred to him. What else might she have manipulated? He'd expected her to be guarding Fawn's bath and she had been nowhere in sight. Could she have . . . ? He dismissed the idea. No lady's maid would permit such an unthinkable lapse in decorum. She was Fawn's older chaperone, her friend, for heaven's sake!

When Lula signaled Fawn from the kitchen door, the hostess said, "Please be seated, Miss Madigan, gentlemen." She moved to her place at the table, waiting for Dillon to hold out her chair.

Lilacs! Who would ever believe his composure could be undone by the faint smell of lilac perfume? Damn the brat, all he could think of was her in that big tub. The erotic image would not abate. "Lilac bath oil?" he murmured softly in her ear as he slid her chair closer to the table. What in hell had made him blurt that out?

"Your nose for fragrance is keen, Mr. Detective. A surprise, considering its battered appearance." She kept her voice as soft as his. A disturbing thought flashed into her mind. He's said bath oil, not perfume. She'd used both. Could he have . . . ? No, it was beyond consideration.

"When it comes to noses, Princess, I'd be careful about commenting on others' if I were you," he whispered back. He walked around and took his seat, watching her stiffen in outrage. Good. Their usual hostile exchanges would keep his mind off his trespass.

Lula burst through the kitchen door, carrying a huge platter piled high with fried chicken, which she offered to Fawn, who carefully took a piece. Then Lula moved around the table. Two young kitchen helpers trailed behind her, one girl with a bowl of mashed potatoes and the other a boat of gravy.

Fawn gave Jack an arch look. Leaning toward him, she said with a smile, "Keep irritating me and you'll be wearing spuds and gravy."

"Truce?" he asked, raising his water glass in a salute to her.

"Only pretend to be a gentleman until we reach my village tomorrow. Then we'll be quit of each other, Dillon."

The men quickly depleted the supply of chicken, and like magic yet another server appeared with a second platter. "No body ever gits 'nough o' my fried chicken," Lula said, beaming as Snake piled four pieces on his plate.

Halfway down the table, Bronc noted the fierce whispers between Fawn and the good-looking young detective Max had hired. He grinned. "Kindy reminds me o' Sky and Max, don't it you?" he asked Campbell.

"Aye, that it does," the Scot averred. "The lass needs a firm hand to guide her . . . but a gentle one as well."

Watching Dillon carefully handle his crystal water glass, the foreman replied, "I reckon he might fit the bill. After whut that little gal's been through, she deserves nothin' but th' best."

As everyone at the table chatted and ate heartily of Lula's heavenly repast, Snake observed his cousin and Dillon. Smiling inwardly, he thought about what tomorrow would bring. *Just wait until we reach the old one's lodge . . .*

Fee watched Jack and Fawn as everyone else dug into the food. After their little set-to, neither said a word, nor did they even look at each other. Both made it a point to talk with everyone else up and down the big table. Perhaps she could liven things up a bit. After all, tomorrow they were leaving the ranch. Since no self-respecting city girl such as Fee would ride a wild horse across trackless prairie or sleep in a tepee, it was agreed she would remain behind. If she wanted the relationship between Fawn and Dillon to heat up in her absence, this was her last opportunity to do something.

Leaning slightly toward Jack, she asked him, "Did ye get a good look around before dinner, Mr. D?"

Dillon dropped his fork with a loud clank against his plate. He looked down in horror, but the china had not been cracked. Not so his composure. Damn, had the little leprechaun deliberately deserted her post? He could feel Fawn's eyes on him and knew he had to say something. "Yes, the grounds are quite ... remarkable. Well tended," he added, hoping to God she was not implying what he'd first thought.

"I know ye didn't have much time, but did ye see all ye wanted?" Fee persevered.

Jack could feel his face begin to burn as if he'd been scorched by a blast furnace. She'd caught him just as he bit into a chunk of chicken breast. He chewed manfully. Knowing he could not spit it out under Lula's watchful gaze, he swallowed. But it did not go down. Instead the barely chewed meat lodged like a cannonball in his throat.

"Oh, my, watch ye don't choke," Fee said, pounding on Dillon's back. "Have a care. My da used to say, 'the tastier the dish, the slower it should be eaten.'"

Lula, who had rushed forward, nodded in agreement, shoving Fee's small hand away and giving Dillon a hearty slap with one huge paw. "Yer pappy wuz right," she said to Fee. "A man with a big appetite like this 'un, gotta be keerful."

Jack threw up his hands, surrendering in consternation as the two women fussed over him. "I'm all right. Just bit off more than I could chew." Damn! Wrong thing to say!

Both of them backed off, Fee nodding in seeming earnestness while Lula trundled toward the open doorway, calling out for one of the cooks to fetch more chicken and green beans from the summer kitchen.

Fawn observed the episode, noting the odd expression on Snake's face as he watched Fee. Of course, he was besotted, but now he looked puzzled. Fee had been tweaking Dillon about something, but what? She studied her companion and saw a cat-in-the-cream expression flash across her face. Fawn knew Fiona Madigan well enough to realize it meant mischief. She lowered her lashes and looked to her right at Jack. He sat staring down at his plate as if it were a nest of rattlers, but he ate methodically, cutting every bite into tiny pieces.

Did ye get a good look around? Did ye see all ye wanted? Now Fawn nearly dropped her fork. No! Fee would not have dared . . . Yes, she would. With sinking certainty, Fawn remembered that she'd waited while Fee fetched the rinse water and her companion had come from the bedroom, not the porch! It was after Fee had asked that first question that Dillon had dropped his fork. Then when she persisted, he'd choked. Were they in this together? Had Jack been tricked just as she had been . . . or, like a wily lobo, had he just seized an opportunity?

Fawn said to Fee, "How do you like the ranch so far?"

Fee looked at her with round, innocent eyes. "'Tis that grand, it is. I positively love it here." She quickly turned her attention to Snake and asked him some inane question about roping steers, trying to make Fawn think she was so taken with her cousin that she had eyes only for him.

That might be true, but Fawn knew as surely as her face burned with embarrassment that Fee had deserted her post. *While I was in my bath, she let that—that lecherous troll spy on me!* Forcing her rage under control, she swore she would scalp Fiona Madigan with a rusty skinning knife! And as for Jack Dillon, that perverted troll, he was about to meet up with Billy Goat Gruff!

Lula served peach pie and fresh-churned ice cream after

her helpers cleared the plates and a mountain of chicken bones. Fawn observed Dillon take a bit of rich ice cream and combine it with a forkful of pie. A grin spread across her lips. She waited as he swallowed and then took a drink of coffee. Miss Billy Goat Gruff lowered her head to butt. Holding a piece of pie on her fork, she said, "Shame on you, Mr. Dillon."

Jack dared a wary glance at her for the first time since they'd commenced eating. "What?" he asked, peering over the rim of his cup.

She gestured with a forkful of pie that contained no ice cream. "You strike me as a man who'd prefer it naked . . . so to speak." When she popped the pie into her mouth, she was rewarded by a gargling sound as Jack sprayed coffee across the white linen tablecloth.

With a slightly worried look, Fee again pounded on Jack's back.

This time Jack recovered quickly from his choking fit, apologizing for his inexcusable gaffe. "I am so sorry. This seems to be my night for making a fool of myself. Please forgive me."

"Ain't no harm done," Lula said. "Lookee at all the chicken grease 'n gravy stains 'round this here table. Red Wolf men, ain't none o' 'em neat eaters."

Snake took the whole scene in, watching Jack, Fee and especially Fawn, now that she'd joined in the bizarre conversation. Those two women were deviling the detective, but damned if he knew what it was about.

After chancing one last bite of pie, Jack scooted back his chair. "Mrs. Jones, I do thank you for a delicious dinner, but I seem to be a bit indisposed." With as much dignity as he could muster, he stood up and forced himself to bow politely to Fawn and her devilish Irish henchwoman, then left the room, fighting the urge to run.

Fawn struggled to keep her expression neutral and her

hands concealed beneath the table while he walked away. Her fists were tightly clenched, itching to punch the rotter! She glanced down at Fee, wondering again if they were conspiring together. She knew her visions would not tell her. Grandfather had always said the Powers revealed things in their own good time, not according to human will. And the gift was not intended so that the recipient could see his or her own future.

Why had she been chosen? Surely there were others among her people better suited for the arduous task. But she knew that when she saw Grandfather, he would calm her fears and reassure her. *All I have to do is to keep from killing Jack Dillon in the meanwhile.*

Lula waited until Jack's footsteps echoed out the front door and down the porch stairs, then shook her head. "Jee-hosaphat! How'd that boy know whut the food tasted like? He spewed half 'n choked on t'other. Don't 'pear ta have the knack o' swallerin' real good."

"Well, Lula, mebee his eyes is bigger 'n his stomach," Bronc offered, scratching his head in perplexity. Dillon surely had acted oddly for a man handpicked by Max Stanhope.

Glancing menacingly at Fee, Fawn then turned to Bronc and said, "Yes, I suspect that Mr. Dillon's problem is definitely big eyes."

Smitty and Swen had taken in their boss's fit of spewing and choking from the opposite end of the table. "Somethin' ain't right," the little German murmured to his companion.

"You think we should see to him?" Swen asked reluctantly, eyeing the peach pies on the sideboard where Lula was serving second helpings to the other men. He had hoped for more himself, but realized that Dillon might be unwell. "Miss Stanhope, we better see if the boss has orders for us before we leave in the morning. If you will excuse us, please?" he asked Fawn.

As the pair rose politely, she smiled. "Have a good evening and don't let Mr. Dillon keep you up too late."

"You better get your beauty rest, too, Hellcat," Snake said with a gleam in his eyes. "You're in for quite a day tomorrow." With that cryptic remark, he stood up and bowed to Fee. "Miss Madigan, if you'd do me the honor of taking a stroll around the veranda, I'd be pleased."

Fee bobbed her head, curls flying as she replied, "I'd love to stroll on the veranda." Not only did she want to enjoy Snake's charming company, but also to escape, for the moment, Fawn's wrath.

While the rest of the dinner guests complimented Lula and bid Fawn good night, Smitty and Swen caught up to Jack out by the blacksmith's forge. "You all right, Jack?" Smitty asked.

"You did not look so good in there," Swen chimed in gravely.

"With a badgering woman on each side of me, how could I look like anything but a chewed-on steer?" Jack asked crossly. "Now, we have business to discuss," he said, quickly changing the subject. "I have assignments for each of you." Jack handed Smitty an official-looking document. "This says you're an auditor from the Department of the Interior. Show it to the registrar at the main land office in Guthrie and tell him you need to conduct a routine audit of his records."

"I'm looking for Cheyenne who done give long-term leases of their land allotments to whites, or whites who got guardianship of orphan kids," Smitty said, reiterating the information the Stanhopes wanted, from what Jack had explained aboard the train.

"That's right, and don't forget death claims. Lots of old people will sign over anything under duress or be hoodwinked into it if they can't read," Jack said.

"They sign and then they die. Some white man ends up with the land," Swen said. "And where do I go?"

"You head to Kingfisher, Swen. There's a land office there, too. Nose around and see what you can find. Since many of the townspeople are Negroes, I expect they'll be cautious about talking with a stranger, but you have a way with folks."

"My young, innocent face, ya?" Swen said with a grin. He was good at getting people to trust him.

"Remember, both of you are looking for any evidence about who's behind this. Names, dates, suspicious activities. If a guardian has control of a Cheyenne orphan's allotment, what happened to the child? What were the terms of the lease—how much money, if any, changed hands and how long is the lease supposed to last?"

As both men nodded, Jack said, "When you've found out as much as you can, head back to the ranch. The baron has his own telegraph line here, so we can send word back to St. Louis about what we learn. I'll do some snooping of my own once I get shut of the princess. With any luck, she'll stay with her grandfather's people for long enough that we can finish the investigation."

"After we gather all the facts, what then?" Smitty asked.

Jack shrugged. "If the baron's hunch is right—and I'll bet it is—he'll have to get directly involved, because these men are politically powerful."

Smitty grinned in the moonlight. "Aw, shit. And here I was hopin' we'd get to shoot us some varmints."

"We might, but I wouldn't want to go after some rich politician without the Ruxton name backing us up," Dillon said. "This runs deeper than land theft from helpless Indians. I have a gut feeling there's more to it. Just wish I knew what these men, whoever the hell they are, really want."

Fawn stood on the porch, looking down at the moon-drenched ranch. In the distance she could see Dillon and his men talking as they stood outside the smithy's shed. She wondered what they would learn about the thieving of her people's land allotments. Her father believed Jack Dillon was the man for the job. Fawn knew Max Stanhope only hired competent men. He was also a keen judge of character and would never have entrusted her safety to anyone who would do her harm. If Dillon had spied on her in her bath, surely it must have been accidental—precipitated by Fee's foolish matchmaking.

Foolish indeed! The detective had made it clear he regarded her as nothing more than a spoiled child pretending to be a lady. He did not like her sharp tongue or ready wit. He did not like her. "And I detest him." Saying the words aloud did not convince her they were true.

There was some strange bond between them. Her gift of sight had not explained what it was, but she was confident that Grandfather would know. He could explain everything to her. With that consoling thought, she headed to bed. Morning would come early and she could not wait to be reunited with her Cheyenne family.

Just as she reached her door, she heard Fee giggling on the lower level of the veranda, then Snake's voice. Lovebirds. Fee had always been so levelheaded. Why would the Irishwoman fall for a womanizing charmer like her cousin, a man who'd driven three wives to leave him? In spite of her anger over Fee's probable dereliction of duty, she knew she would have to warn the Irishwoman to be wary of Burning Snake, lest she be burned herself.

Then Fawn remembered his strange words to her when dinner had ended, as if he knew a secret that she did not. What had he meant when he'd said she would be in for quite a day tomorrow?

Chapter Seven

As Fawn walked to the corral where Snake was overseeing the loading of wagons filled with gifts for her Cheyenne band, she mulled over her early-morning talk with Fee. She had held her temper last night and slept on her anger before confronting her companion. Fee simply said that she'd gone into the bedroom to fetch the water pitcher before Fawn had called for her to do so. By the time she realized Dillon was looking into the bathing room, she felt too embarrassed to run him off.

"Ye should've seen his face, that dumbstruck he was. He didn't stay long. But he did admire what he saw," Fee had insisted.

Fawn let out a snort. "Nothing about me suits Jack Dillon in the least. He has nothing but contempt for me—or have you been too blind to see the obvious?"

"Ask him, why don't ye then?" Fee had planted her fists on her hips and replied with a dare in her eyes. "Ye have no idea of his feelin's for ye . . . nor yers for him."

That had led to more verbal sparring. Fee was certain Dillon was smitten with her mistress—and even more foolishly, the Irishwoman insisted Fawn was more than passing interested in him!

"Who is the Chosen Woman, the seer? The one burdened with visions? Don't you think I would know if Jack Dillon were anything but an arrogant, annoying . . . troll?" Fawn had demanded. Without waiting for an answer, she'd stormed out of the ranch house, slamming the door. So much for holding her temper. But mixed with her anger was that insistent trickle of fear, the fear she'd tried to suppress from the first day she'd met him. His coloring, his eyes . . . *the wolf!* And from the first, she had sensed in him a . . . a darkness. Its presence unsettled her, angered her, and certainly brought out the worst in her.

Why could not the Powers grant her the ability to understand what those disturbing dreams about the red wolf meant? What her own paintings meant? She had brought one of them, the last one, with her to show Grandfather. Surely he would know.

But for now, she decided to take Fee up on her dare. Some deeply buried part of her feminine vanity—or was it insecurity?—wanted to know what Jack Dillon had thought when he'd seen her naked in that tub. "No true gentleman such as Claude Beaurivage would ever spy on me in such a despicable way!" she muttered, kicking a stone in her path. Suddenly, Fawn realized that she had not given her suitor a thought since leaving St. Louis. What did that mean?

Before she could pursue that worrisome question, Bronc hailed her from the corral. "Yew look purty as a wagonload of speckled puppies, gal." He grinned and gestured to the work going on behind him. "Speaking o' wagons, reckon yew got 'nough presents fer ever'one?"

"I hope so, Bronc. Especially the children." Her big smile faded when she saw Dillon emerge from the stable, leading his blood bay. Even his horse had to have red hair! She swallowed nervously when he tipped his hat.

"Good morning, Princess," he said, knowing the pet name irritated her but unable to resist using it.

"I see you've acquired a hat to replace the one that was shot yesterday. It looks just as disreputable as the other."

Jack grinned at her. "As you pointed out, it matches my

boots . . . and my Peacemaker. Sometimes older is better, but you have a lot of growing up to do before you learn that."

Fawn wanted to slap the condescending look off his face. Did he think she was a child . . . even after seeing her in that tub? Her body was long-boned and slender, but she had womanly curves . . . didn't she? "Let's ride ahead of the wagon. I have something I want to discuss with you," she said to him.

Snake, who was climbing into the wagon seat, said, "Now you're in hot water."

Her cousin did not notice the way Jack's face reddened at the remark, but Fawn did. *So, Mr. Dillon, time for a little inquisition.*

The small cavalcade headed southwest toward the banks of the Little Canadian River and the lodges of her grandfather's band, which were strung out along the edge of Stanhope land. Teddy and half a dozen of Higgins's best men accompanied them. Jack directed two of them to ride point and positioned the rest around the wagons. There was little danger but he kept his eyes on the countryside, ever watchful for possible ambush sites . . . and to avoid looking at Fawn. What in hell did she want to torment him with now?

When they had ridden in tense silence for ten minutes or so, she finally spoke. "You spied on me in my bath yesterday, didn't you?" She managed to get out the words without any overt display of nerves, but watched Dillon from the corner of her eye to gauge his reaction.

Jack flushed and licked his lips. Damn! He'd been afraid she was going to chew on him some more for his incredibly stupid, unprofessional mistake. His throat closed up, but he swallowed determinedly and replied in a raspy voice, "I don't spy on ladies in their baths."

"I believe you've mentioned on occasion that I'm not a lady," she shot back without missing a beat.

So much for diversionary tactics. His mind went blank.

Before he realized it, he was saying, "I don't spy on beautiful women in their baths either." *I'm only digging myself a deeper hole!*

Fawn whipped her head around to look openly at him now. He was staring intently at the horizon, his face hidden from her. She quickly turned back before he caught her gawking like the immature girl he'd so often accused her of being. But he'd just called her . . . beautiful . . . a woman, not a brat. Then why did he act so embarrassed and uncomfortable? Because he'd blurted out what he really thought of her! The faintest hint of a smile teased her lips. She felt in control, perhaps for the first time since she'd met Jack Dillon. And she liked it very much.

"Fee admitted to me that she saw you look in the door. If you weren't spying, then what were you doing?" she asked.

Dillon couldn't tell by the tone of her voice if she was embarrassed or infuriated. She sounded calm, but he did not want to look at her to read her expression. Would she ask her father to dismiss him? Somehow that mattered less than her opinion of him. He gathered his thoughts and replied, "I was getting the lay of the land, er, I mean checking points of entry—to the house," he quickly added. Talk about digging a deeper hole! "It's what I always do at a new location." He paused and swallowed audibly. "So . . . I was walking around the porch when I saw an open door and heard water splashing. Nobody was around." He tugged on the battered hat he'd borrowed from Snake. This was not going well. She was giving him enough rope to hang himself. He cleared his throat and finished. "I thought I would . . . I mean, I should . . . investigate."

"Of course, that's what you do . . . investigate." Beneath the calm reasonableness of her words there was a hint of gleeful sarcasm.

"Okay, I walked over to the door and looked in," he admitted.

"And you saw . . . ?" she prompted.

The woman was relentless. "You know I saw you taking a bath," he snapped.

"And how *long* did you see me taking that bath?"

Unable to take the badgering any longer, his temper frayed. He turned to her with narrowed eyes. "Goddammit! It was a mistake. When I realized that, I got the hell out of there . . . fast! I apologize. Does that satisfy you?"

Fawn looked into his amber wolf's eyes for a long moment, almost mesmerized by the depths of them. He was dangerous, but he desired her. He'd run from that desire, from her, but he had very much liked what he had seen. A burst of pleasure washed over her with the realization. She was a desirable woman, not the spoiled brat he had tried to dismiss earlier. *Fee, perhaps you've done me a favor . . . now I can control him!*

"Well, I accept your apology, Mr. Dillon. Mistakes do happen. You were a stranger in a very large house . . . and I'm sure it won't happen again. After all, now you've seen all there is to see."

Was she smirking? So much for the offended feminine sensibilities of the princess! "I didn't see it all. I didn't see nearly enough!" He kicked his horse into a swift gallop and lit out toward Teddy, who was riding point.

Fawn's face heated as she watched Dillon ride. So much for control, unless she used a whip and a chair! *You're prodding a lobo wolf, you fool.* Was that her destiny? Was *he*? She shivered, whether in fear or pleasure, she could not say.

The old man seemed to stare out into thin air. But he knew his granddaughter would appear soon . . . along with the man. Silently, he thanked the Powers for their gift. He had waited patiently to see the course her life would take. Fawn had been chosen . . . and the one bringing her safely home had been chosen as well. He turned and gazed at the two old women emerging from the lodge adjacent to his. A small string of lodges followed the twisting banks of the stream. The women looked expectantly at him.

"Yes, they will be here before the sun touches the trees," he said, in reply to their unspoken question. He gestured to where the glowing golden ball hovered, just above a stand of cottonwoods that grew along the river.

In the distance, they could hear the sound of shod horse hooves clicking against stones on the trail. The old man crossed his arms and waited serenely. In a moment, the first rider crested the hill, followed closely by a second. Fawn. And the man who protected her. The old Cheyenne stood motionless but for the smile softening his austere face.

As Jack approached the small fork of the river, his feeling of wariness grew stronger. Something was about to happen. *Hell, I'm acting like Fawn!* Then they crested the hill and he looked down on a cluster of lodges strung along the river. One in particular drew his attention. A prickle of premonition swept up his spine, tingling until the hair at his nape stood on end. When he saw the tall figure calmly waiting to greet them, it was as if the breath were punched out of his body by an invisible fist. *It can't be . . . but it is!*

Fawn kicked Remy into a swift gallop and rode past Dillon, hell-bent to reach her grandfather and the two old women who scuttled quickly to his side. Their faces were wreathed in smiles, as was hers. She vaulted from her horse and rushed to him. "Grandfather! How I have missed you!" she said in Cheyenne, throwing her arms around him.

Bright Leaf and Talks Much joined in. The old women had raised her after her Cheyenne mother had died. They exchanged hugs with her while all three spoke excitedly. None of them noticed Jack Dillon sitting frozen on his horse just a few yards away. But the old man did. He took Fawn and held her at arm's length, as if inspecting her, then shook his head in fond exasperation.

"I see your mother has not yet taught you manners, child," he said in clear, well-modulated English. "It would seem even a Sioux warrior woman cannot make you into a proper female, red or white. Look at these man clothes."

Fawn laughed joyously as she replied in English, "You're right, Grandfather. Mother says I am incorrigible."

"What is this in . . . corrigible?"

"It means wild and unteachable."

He nodded. "Sky Eyes of the Ehanktonwon has said well." Then he turned to Dillon, who sat still as a statue on his big red horse. "But from you, my young friend, I would expect proper respect. Why do you not come down from your pony to greet old friends?" By this time others of the small band had begun to trickle from their lodges, drawn by the commotion of Fawn's homecoming. Adults smiled and children jumped up and down in excitement.

Fawn gasped audibly, turning to watch Jack slide off his mount. What did Grandfather mean? *He knows Jack Dillon? It can't be!* Then Snake's cryptic words came rushing back to her. *You're in for quite a day tomorrow . . .*

"Forgive my bad manners, True Dreamer. I did not know Fawn was your granddaughter." Dillon walked forward and clasped arms with the surprisingly sturdy old medicine man.

True Dreamer replied to his young white friend, "You are forgiven, my son. A day's ride with this one would spin the brain of any man like the twisting winds."

Jack nodded in agreement. "She is a tornado, all right." He turned to the two old women. "It makes my heart glad to see you again, Bright Leaf, Talks Much." He doffed his hat and gave them a courtly bow as they tittered happily. Several of the children approached and he tousled their hair with genuine affection, greeting the older ones by name.

Fawn was speechless.

"You look much better than the last time I saw you, Red

Wolf," True Dreamer said. His keen gaze swept up and down the younger man with approval and he nodded.

Red Wolf! No, the Powers could not play such a trick on her! This was all wrong. *The red wolf is my totem, my protector . . .* She started to sway, biting her lip to keep from crying out in frustration . . . and apprehension.

Seeing her distress, Bright Leaf and Talks Much placed their arms around her shoulders. Talks Much said to her in Cheyenne, "You have brought the Red Wolf back to us. This is good. We will feast tonight to celebrate."

True Dreamer turned to them and said, "Take Chosen Woman to your lodge. She is . . . not well, I think. But she will recover quickly."

Jack watched as they led the unresisting Fawn into their lodge. He had never seen her so quiet, so pale and at a loss for words. "You called her Chosen Woman. Is that the name she earned when she grew up?" As far as he could see, Fawn Stanhope was a long way from being grown up!

"Yes, that is her name among our people, Red Wolf. She has been chosen by the Powers to receive a great gift."

Max Stanhope's words about his daughter's ability came back to Jack again. "You mean she can see the future, or tell when danger lurks?"

True Dreamer nodded solemnly. "In time, that and more will be true. But her gift is veiled now . . ." He turned abruptly and walked toward his lodge, expecting Jack Dillon, the man he had named the Red Wolf, to follow.

Numbly, Jack did so. Once they were inside, True Dreamer hospitably offered his friend a seat on a soft old elk hide robe, then nimbly took his place across from him. "Bright Leaf will bring us cool water in a few moments, but now we must smoke and speak of matters of importance to the son of my heart, Pale Moon Stalker."

"You mean Max Stanhope." Jack had heard Fawn refer to her adopted father by that name, as had Snake.

The old man nodded as he lit a long-stemmed pipe. He took a puff, then offered it to his guest for a ceremonial exchange. When the formalities were over, he said, "The Pale Moon Stalker believes the Cheyenne allotment land is threatened. That is why he sent you here."

"What do you know about the men who're stealing it?" Jack asked, knowing the old man always seemed to find out what was going on before anyone else.

"You must widen your vision. The vultures looking down on us seek to feed not only on the People. They soar in ever-widening circles."

"You speak in riddles," Jack said, knowing True Dreamer would explain in his own good time. "Remember, I am only a poor, foolish white man."

The old man grunted. "Poor, perhaps. White, yes. Foolish, no. Just young, but you will grow in wisdom . . . and patience, I hope." The medicine man shook his head and sighed. "You will need it to fulfill your part in the great design the Powers are weaving . . . but now is not the time to speak of that."

An uneasy feeling swept over Dillon as Fawn suddenly appeared in his mind's eye. He blinked and focused on the land issue again. "I have felt there is more to this land grab than appears on the surface." He waited.

"I have said well. You are not foolish, Red Wolf. Go seek out a widow named Cook. Her small farm is at the edge of our lands. Two hours' ride from here. The sheriff says her husband was killed by robbers . . ." His voice trailed off.

"But you think otherwise?" Dillon interjected.

The old man sighed again. "The young are so impatient. Only give me time to gather my thoughts and I will tell you." When Jack looked appropriately chastened for interrupting, True Dreamer continued his story. "The widow is named Elsa Cook. Her man was leader of a . . . clan of farmers who are white and black white men. All of them have a good heart for us. The widow and her sons will make my words clear to you. I will give you my best pony to ride tomorrow when you visit them."

"I have a fine bay—"

True Dreamer shook his head, quieting Dillon. "They know my pony. They will understand you come with my blessing and speak true to you. But your journey will be tomorrow. Tonight we feast to honor the return of the Chosen Woman and the Red Wolf. Our young men have killed a fine big elk such as we seldom see anymore. Your visit and the fresh meat are both rare gifts from the Powers."

Jack was not certain he liked being linked to Fawn, even if it was only for a welcome-home feast.

"How did the one you call the Red Wolf become a friend of the People?" Fawn asked Talks Much, who, as her name indicated, loved to gossip and would know all the juicy details about Dillon's time with the Cheyenne.

"He is a brave warrior and performed a deed of great valor," Bright Leaf interjected, knowing her garrulous sister would fill in all the details.

"Oh, yes!" Talks Much said excitedly. "There was a young woman—she came to us from the Crow People as an orphan and we took her in. This was a moon after you left to live in the white man city with the Pale Moon Stalker and Sky Eyes of the Ehanktonwon. We lived on the White Father's reservation lands then." Her face suddenly darkened. "Evil men did to this young woman even worse than was done to you."

"They kidnapped and raped her?" Fawn asked, her stomach clenching as ugly memories, so deeply buried, bubbled to the surface again.

Both old women nodded, but it was Bright Leaf who spoke now. "They treated her with great cruelty."

Fawn digested this information. She knew it was why no

one had ever spoken of this Crow girl in her presence. "What happened to her?" *And how is Jack Dillon involved?*

"She was rescued by the Red Wolf. True Dreamer summoned him in a vision. He was one of Law Chief Parker's hunting wolves then," Talks Much replied. "He was badly wounded when he and True Dreamer returned with her . . . but the three men who did this evil thing died! He took vengeance for what had been done to that girl. To reach us, True Dreamer had to tie him to his pony to keep him from falling off. We nursed him back to health and sang his praises around our campfires.

"Then we were separated when the White Father gave us these little pieces of land and moved us from the reservation. Crow Woman, as she became known, recovered and married a white trader. His heart is good. They live in a faraway place now, to the south across what the whites call the Red River," Talks Much recounted.

"Once two winters ago they came for a visit—with four fine children," her sister said with quiet pride. "We feasted that night—and we will feast again tonight. Come, let us speak of happy things. You are returned safely to us and so is the Red Wolf."

"Did . . . did Grandfather give him his name?" Fawn asked hesitantly.

Both women nodded. Then Bright Leaf stood up. "Now, if you are recovered from your faintness—"

"I never faint!" Fawn said indignantly, then immediately lowered her head in shame for her rudeness to an elder. "Please forgive me."

Bright Leaf snorted. "Your Sioux mother must have been very patient . . . and frustrated," she added with a shake of her head. "We have a feast to prepare and serve. Have you forgotten how to chop roots and cut up meat while in the white man city?" she asked with what looked like a smirk.

Fawn knew it was the custom for the women to serve the

men and children before sitting down to eat themselves. Wives and older daughters prepared and dished out food to their families, and anyone who was asked to serve an outside guest considered it an honor. *I'll have to wait on that insufferable Dillon!* She could not face his leering grin when he saw her in a subservient role. The hell with tradition! She would go to Grandfather and wheedle her way out of it.

But luck was not with her when she tried to speak with the old man. He was sequestered with Dillon and there was no way she could interrupt without being unforgivably rude. Fawn knew her grandfather well. Rudeness was not the Cheyenne way, and any lapse in decorum would only strengthen his resolve that she learn manners by waiting on his precious Red Wolf!

Abandoning her quest for the moment, she joined Snake at the wagons while he and the other men made quick work of unloading the gifts she'd brought from her white family in St. Louis. There were items for everyone—fine cloth in bright colors for the women; toys of all sorts for the children; and hunting rifles, ammunition and other tools for the men. Everyone bowed politely before the Chosen Woman and asked her to convey their gratitude to the Pale Moon Stalker and Sky Eyes of the Ehanktonwon. Fawn knew she would be laden with return gifts to take back to her white family. The People did not accept charity.

Too shy to speak, one small girl, clutching a doll, hugged her. Fawn's eyes misted over and she swallowed back tears. Without the Stanhopes, what would have become of her people? She knew life in Oklahoma Territory was harsh and dangerous. Her adoptive father might have literally saved them from extinction . . . like the buffalo, which no longer roamed across a land now dissected by railroad tracks.

Dismissing her gloomy reverie, she did as her aunt had instructed and joined the women who were busy chopping fresh chunks of elk and gathering wild onions. These and foraged roots, as well as other vegetables the Cheyenne had learned to grow, were placed in a huge iron kettle simmering over a fire while Bright Leaf oversaw the proceedings. The feast would take place near the riverbank, where an open area of level ground had been fashioned into the band's central gathering place.

While she sliced carrots and onions, Fawn bided her time, watching as a steady stream of tribal elders entered Grandfather's lodge to greet and smoke with Dillon. As the meal preparations drew near completion, her frustration grew. How was she going to get out of this humiliation? Then an idea occurred to her. Perhaps there was more than one way to outsmart a cunning and arrogant wolf.

Jack sat by the dancing flames of the big bonfire, listening to the steady drumbeat and songs of celebration, recalling his months living with these people back on their reservation. They had saved his life. Young warriors danced in the twilight; women bustled around while children chased each other, giggling and happy with new toys. The wagonloads of gifts Fawn had brought were greatly appreciated. He'd watched her as she interacted with her people and was struck with how regal and genuinely kind she appeared. And she obviously had a soft spot for children. Was he the only one who brought out the worst in her?

When it was time to eat, the men took their places around the campfire with the young children sitting politely behind them. The women served bowls of fragrant elk stew accompanied by a flat crumbly bread they had learned to fry in iron skillets. As a guest of honor, Dillon was seated next to True Dreamer, their leader. Then he saw Fawn emerge from her aunt's lodge.

She wore an elaborately beaded buckskin tunic and leggings with matching moccasins. He was struck by how incredibly right the clothing looked on her. She was every bit as comfortable in the soft leather as she'd been decked out in a silk ball gown and high-heeled slippers. But now instead of fancy curls piled on top of her head, she had her hair done up in two elegant coils of braids, one at each side of her slim face. The shining jet black tresses were decorated with feathers. Large gold hoops hung from her ears, gleaming in the firelight as brightly as her eyes.

He was amazed when she smiled at him, then disconcerted. *She's planning some deviltry. I can feel it in my bones.* He sat watching as she ladled a bowl of stew and brought it to him, kneeling before him and raising her offering with downcast eyes. Jack was dumbfounded. This was not the Fawn he knew. He recovered his voice as he took the stew, whispering, "Did you put poison in it, Princess?"

Fawn merely shrugged and said, "The thought has appeal, but you're our guest. That wouldn't be polite. My grandfather has taught me better manners. Women serve warriors. It is the Cheyenne way."

He sat stunned as she rose and walked away, her stately bearing making him feel petty and rude for his teasing comment. Then she returned a moment later with a hunk of the crisp bread and a mug of coffee, the latter a treat she'd brought from St. Louis. When she again knelt and held out the offerings, he accepted uncomfortably, managing to choke out, "Thank you, Miss Stanhope."

Damn, she had been raised as a lady of quality in a wealthy family with servants to wait on her! This wasn't right. He glanced over at True Dreamer, who appeared unconcerned but watchful. Something was going to happen—something bad. He'd bet his boots on it, but when he asked the old man about the premonition, he received only an enigmatic smile in return.

Then True Dreamer said, "All will be well . . . in time."

That did not reassure Dillon. *All will be well, all right . . . if she doesn't kill me first!*

Chapter Eight

$\mathcal{F}$awn kept her face expressionless, but inside a sly smile warmed her. It was working. He was nervous as a deer that had just caught the scent of a mountain lion. She had made him feel guilty and uncomfortable. Well, it served him right. Eyeing the sugar and tinned milk she'd brought, she recalled that he took a bit of both in his coffee. Might as well heap coals of fire upon his head . . . the rotter!

When she picked up the items, Bright Leaf said, "You have served our guest as befits the mighty deeds he has done for the People. Now it is your turn to feast. You are the Chosen Woman, returned to her people, and you should be honored, too. I will serve the Red Wolf."

But when she reached for the sugar bowl and tin of milk, Fawn shook her head. "No, er . . . I mean, it is all right. I wish to serve such a great warrior." Bright Leaf gave her a skeptical look, but, undaunted, Fawn walked demurely toward the campfire with her offerings.

When he saw Fawn refuse the old woman's obvious attempt to take over, Jack suddenly realized what was going on. Each time she had knelt before him, he'd felt like hell. And she'd fed on it, damn the little witch! Well, two could play at this game. He waited until she knelt with the sugar and milk.

"I know you like your coffee sweetened with these. Please

forgive me for not remembering when I brought it to you earlier," she said.

He looked down at her and grinned. "Yeah, kind of thoughtless, wasn't it, Princess?" he said softly. "But then, you're young. You'll learn. Oh, about half a spoon of sugar, just a dash of milk. There's a good girl."

If he'd patted her on the head, she could not have been more furious. What had given her away? And more importantly, how could she regain the upper hand? Taking a deep, calming breath, she did as he instructed, then stirred the coffee until it was blended. "Is this to your liking?" she inquired, demure as a debutante, with lashes lowered so he could not read the fire in her eyes.

Yes, she was playing him. If he'd ever had a doubt, her posture gave it away. She was boiling mad now. Dare he risk more? Dillon could not resist. He glanced at his host, who sipped his coffee contemplatively, utterly unconcerned by the exchange going on between the two of them. *He's waiting to see if I can best her, the old devil!*

"Fetch me another knife . . . Miss Stanhope, if you would. This one's a bit on the dull side," he said, daring her as he handed the blade, handle first, to her.

"Careful I don't sharpen it and cut your heart out," she hissed ever so softly, before snatching it from him and flouncing over to the old women. "Our guest requests a sharper knife," she said.

Talks Much quickly reached for a fresh knife and gave it to her, saying, "I remember once when I was a girl and my father tried to cut his buffalo meat with a dull knife—"

"I believe it would be wise for me to take it to Red Wolf," Bright Leaf said calmly, extending her hand for the implement.

"No, I will do it—and I promise not to gut him with it,"

Fawn added through gritted teeth. *But that red hair would make a dandy scalp for a lodge pole!*

Grinning from ear to ear, Jack watched her return. "I think your granddaughter intends to kill me," he said conversationally to True Dreamer.

The old man shook his head. "That is not the will of the Powers."

Wondering just what the devil the Powers did intend, Dillon carefully took the knife from Fawn. Once he had it safely in his hand, he let her rise and take a step away. Then he called out, "I'm still hungry. Would you refill this stew bowl for me . . . please?"

Fawn snatched it from him and stalked toward the big kettle. This was not working out the way she'd planned, but then . . .

Jack watched her return with a steaming bowl of elk stew. She was really playing this to the hilt. Did she intend to impress her grandfather? His ruminations ended abruptly when she ignored his outreached hands and dumped the bowl all over his head. "Ow! Damn, that's hot, brat!"

As Dillon wiped the gravy from his burning eyes, Fawn stomped to the old women's lodge and disappeared inside. True Dreamer stabbed a hunk of meat from his bowl and popped it into his mouth. Chewing thoughtfully, he said, "Elk makes good stew." Then looking at Jack and the upturned bowl still perched on his head, he added, "But bad hat."

At dawn Dillon emerged from the lodge where he'd spent the night, braced for what lay ahead. He tried not to notice the women's titters, hidden behind their hands, or the sly grins of the younger men. Damn the hellion, she had outsmarted him again! Would he ever learn not to cross swords with her? It was as if some irresistible force drew them together—and yet brought out the worst in both of them!

Grimly, he forced a smile and walked toward the old

medicine man's lodge, greeting friends along the way. Just as he had expected, True Dreamer sat in front of the open door, facing the rising sun with his back ramrod straight. He chanted softly, a morning ritual that Dillon would never interrupt. He stood respectfully at the side of the lodge, waiting silently until the prayers were complete.

Without turning his head, the old man said, "Please, come join me, Red Wolf."

Jack took a seat beside him, still faintly disconcerted by the way True Dreamer always seemed to have eyes in the back of his head. Dillon had not made a sound when he'd approached. "I am going to meet Mrs. Cook as you told me to do. Will your young men see Fawn returned safely to her ranch?"

"Yes, to Red Wolf Ranch, hmmm," True Dreamer said with a hint of amusement in his usually enigmatic expression. "I do not think she will require our young men to accompany her."

More riddles. Jack tamped down his irritation at the mention of his link to Fawn and wondered what the medicine man meant by that last remark. Better not to ask. "Just so she is safe. I thank you for your hospitality but it is time—"

True Dreamer raised his hand to silence Dillon. "Do not forget to ride my pony on this journey. Go south until the sun clears the treetops." He pointed to indicate the direction. "There will be a small creek and a poor farmhouse nearby. The widow woman Cook lives there."

Suddenly Dillon knew what the old man had alluded to earlier. "These land grabbers are after her farm, too? They're stealing from whites as well as taking red people's allotments." It made sense. There were lots of hardscrabble homesteads sprinkled between the one-hundred-sixty-acre allotments given to each Indian under the current treaty. "If all the land owned by red and white is gathered up by one powerful group, it'll be worth a lot more."

"There is hope for you yet, Red Wolf. Now, go to Burning Snake. He has put your saddle upon my pony while we talked." With that dismissal, True Dreamer continued his prayers. As Dillon rose and walked away, the old man smiled to himself and thanked the Powers. There would be no reason for his young men to return the Chosen Woman to Red Wolf Ranch. The Red Wolf himself would do so.

Within a quarter hour Fawn watched from Bright Leaf's lodge while Dillon rode out of the camp on her grandfather's finest buckskin pony. "Where is he going?" she murmured to herself—and why was he not riding that great red beast of his? There was only one way to find out. True Dreamer must have some very important reason for giving him the buckskin and dispatching him on a mission. Now she had a mission of her own—to find out what the Powers had revealed to her grandfather about this man he called the Red Wolf.

She went to the cook fire and dished up two bowls of the elk stew from last night's debacle. As she ladled thick gravy filled with chunks of meat, Fawn could not stop herself from smiling. She would always treasure the look of astonishment on Dillon's arrogant face the instant before the steaming stew covered his head. *Play games with me, White Eyes, will you?*

Fawn arrived at her grandfather's lodge just after he finished his morning prayers. "I have brought food. May I eat with you?" she asked politely in Cheyenne, knowing that he was aware of her presence even though she had not made a sound.

"It is my wish, Granddaughter," he replied, accepting the bowl she offered. "Please be seated and we will enjoy the elk . . . I do not think you tasted much of it last night."

Fawn felt her face heat. Only her grandfather could make her feel embarrassment for giving Jack Dillon what she considered a well-deserved lesson in manners. Making no reply, she sat down across from the old man. They enjoyed the stew in companionable silence. She could hear the sound of water trickling over rocks in the riverbed and smell the sharp tang of prairie grass beneath the late-spring sun. Life was always good in camp with her Cheyenne family, far simpler than her other role as the eldest Stanhope child. She would always be grateful to her adoptive father and mother for all they had done for her. She loved them with her whole heart. But they understood, just as she did, that her place would ultimately be here as the Chosen Woman.

Her thoughts were interrupted when the old man placed his empty bowl on the ground and said, "Now, we have important matters to discuss."

"Yes, I wish to know—" Fawn stopped short when he gave her a look of gentle rebuke. She knew it was rude for anyone to interrupt an elder. Casting her eyes down, she waited for him to continue.

"What we wish to know and what we must do are not always the same, child," he replied enigmatically.

Fawn waited as he closed his eyes and gathered his thoughts. *He's going to explain where he sent Dillon.*

Then he opened them and said, "We will speak of the Red Wolf . . . as you already know." He allowed himself a gentle smile before continuing. "For this, it is best, I think, that we use the white man's tongue," he said in English. "Some things I must explain have no words in our language."

Fawn sat back quietly, expecting to hear about where Dillon was going. Instead, the old medicine man surprised her.

"I first met Jack Dillon, who is called the Red Wolf by the People, six summers ago. He was a hunting wolf for the great Law Chief Parker."

She remained quiet as he paused. Bright Leaf and Talks Much had already told her the story about what Red Wolf had done to earn his name, but now Grandfather would tell her what had happened while he'd accompanied Dillon on that quest.

"Red Wolf's task was to take evil ones back to his chief so they could taste justice. He came into our camp looking for two white men who were horse stealers. They had killed a Cherokee horse guard. Only Chief Parker gave justice to red and white alike," he said thoughtfully, then continued, "I could not help Deputy Dillon. We had seen no sign of the stolen ponies or the stealers. But we did have a trouble of our own that required one of Chief Parker's hunting wolves.

"A Crow woman had been staying with us for a few moons since her band had all died of the spotted throat. She was young and pretty. Three white men stole her away while she was out digging roots with a small group of older women. Our warriors could not rescue her."

Fawn nodded. She knew if they had, the red men, not the whites, would have ended up in trouble with reservation authorities. Little matter that those kidnappers had raped an innocent girl. She waited until True Dreamer continued.

"I had been shown by the Powers that a white man would come to our aid, as the Pale Moon Stalker once did. I told Parker's hunting wolf of our trouble . . ." He paused, searching for words. "Have you ever seen his eyes turn the color of . . ."

"Amber? Like the glow of a prairie wolf's eyes?" she responded.

He nodded. "You have said true. When I told him what had happened to the Crow girl, his eyes gave off that light. That was when I knew what his name would be among the People."

"The Red Wolf because of his eyes and his hair . . . and because he is a fierce hunter."

True Dreamer nodded once more. "He agreed to search for the girl and her captors. I accompanied him. For three days he followed their tracks. They stopped several times to . . . use her," he said uneasily, studying Fawn's face.

"They raped her," she said bitterly, remembering a man named Johnny Deuce so many years ago.

"It is an ugly word. An ugly deed. We found them at a campfire. They did not hear us approach. The Red Wolf killed all three of them when they pulled out their guns and shot at us. Then he did a strange thing . . . for a white man . . ."

By this time Fawn was engrossed in the mystery of who Jack Dillon was, but she remained silent, waiting for her grandfather to continue the story. *What is the strange connection between us? Why do I fear this one called the Red Wolf?* She intuited she would not like the answer . . . when she finally found out what it was.

"The girl looked at the dead men, then stared at the knife in the Red Wolf's belt. He handed her the blade and watched as she took their scalps . . . and more. Then he turned and walked back to his pony. The left side of his shirt was covered with blood. One of the evil ones had shot him in the fight. The girl wrapped his wound with a shirt he had in his saddle pouch while I buried the dead ones—their guns, saddles, everything, so no white men could accuse us.

"The Red Wolf lost much blood. I tied him to his pony so that I could lead him back to our camp. There, the wound poisoned and he raged with fever. As I made medicine over him, he had dreams. I was pulled into them. This was not the first time he had killed . . . men who force women. They seem to be his natural enemies—even more than others who break the white man's laws. When their law councils failed to avenge such women, he gave them justice."

Fawn digested his words. "Now I understand why he has always made me feel so . . . uneasy. He smells of guilt. I thought it was some evil thing he had done."

"Do you consider avenging wronged women evil, child?"

She shook her head. "No, of course not. I know many white men consider it no dishonor to force a woman—especially a red woman."

"They why did you speak as you did?" he prodded.

"He was a peace officer who took the law into his own hands. This is considered a great evil among whites. Now he feels remorse for his deeds." She was startled when she looked at her grandfather and saw him shaking his head. "How am I wrong?" The question seemed to ask itself.

"The Red Wolf feels no remorse for killing evil men. His guilt is for not being able to stop such men before they harm women."

She sat, stunned, then blurted out, "Does he think he's God?"

"Not at all. Only a man," he replied.

"But if juries and the law failed, he acted honorably as a warrior. It is foolish to feel guilt over what no human could control."

The old man nodded. "You have said true, Granddaughter. Though the Red Wolf is no fool, his thinking in this matter is foolish." He sighed deeply, studying her with wise eyes. "The workings of a white man's mind are often difficult to understand. This you know after living among them for so long. I was not able to discover the cause of his guilt . . . but you will."

Fawn sat frozen, terrified. *I don't want to know the inner workings of Dillon's mind!* Then suddenly an unbidden image formed before her eyes. She could see exactly where Dillon was and what he was doing. When she tried to shake off the vision, her body trembled and she knew that it was useless to fight the will of the Powers. The Chosen Woman's duty was clear. She must go to him . . . aid him in his quest. *It is for our people . . .* But that assurance rang hollow. *No, it is for him,* an inner voice whispered.

Somehow she would untangle the mystery of their intertwined lives—but not today! Fawn leaped to her feet and rushed away, leaving her grandfather alone. As she fled, she called back to him, "I know exactly where he is. He's in danger!"

Fawn's failure to ask permission to leave was a dreadful breach of decorum. But as he watched her run toward the place where her pony awaited, True Dreamer sighed and smiled. "Patience, Red Wolf, patience."

Jack found the pitiful shack after riding for two hours. It was situated a short distance from a twisting stream that had already dried to a muddy trickle in the hot, thirsty soil. Scrub cottonwoods and thistle bushes grew beside it, but the shanty sat baking in the morning sun without a hint of shade. He reined in the buckskin and approached the place slowly. He'd always had a good sense about when someone was waiting nearby.

The windows had no glass in them. Nothing stirred inside except the low drone of horseflies. He dismounted around fifty feet from the front door and called out, "Howdy," being careful to keep his hands elevated, nowhere near the Peacemaker at his hip.

A woman whom the years had ravaged stepped through the doorway. Her thinning hair, a dull yellow-white, was knotted in a small bun at the back of her neck. She wore a calico dress so faded neither pattern nor color was distinct. When she opened her mouth to speak, he could see she had more gums than teeth, but it was the single-barrel shotgun held skillfully in her gnarled hands that he considered more significant.

True Dreamer had been wise to offer him the horse. Judging from the extra shells laced between her fingers, she was ready to fight if need be. Although the shotgun barrel did not point at him, Dillon was sure she could swing it up and fire quite quickly. He removed his hat with his right hand and inquired, "Are you Mrs. Cook?"

She took her time answering, squinting at him with pale eyes that were as faded as her dress. "I'm her. Who be yew?" She eyed his mount, then added, "'N how'd you come by Dreamer's pony?"

"Name's Jack Dillon, but True Dreamer calls me Red Wolf. He loaned the buckskin to me so you would know you could trust me. I've been hired by the one he calls the Pale Moon Stalker, Max Stanhope, to find out who's trying to get control of the land around here. True Dreamer only says the buzzards circle wider and wider, not who they are."

Mrs. Cook digested his words for a moment, nodding. "Yup, that's Dreamer. Ole man's a caution, he shore is." She gave a rusty chuckle and lowered her weapon. "I done met the Stanhopes once't. Good neighbors. So's Dreamer an' his'n, even if they air Injuns. Come inside and set a spell. I got some coffee left from breakfast, a hunk of bread 'n sech. Yer welcome ta share."

"Much obliged for the offer, but just a bit of water would serve." Dillon followed her inside the tiny two-room cabin. The shade it afforded offered little relief from the blistering sun. She poured two mugs of water from a chipped pitcher. They sat across a scarred oak table on cane-back chairs badly in need of reweaving. The furniture had probably been brought from back East.

"How's that granddaughter o' Dreamer's? Two years sinc't I seen her. Wilder' n a Texas longhorn with terpintine on its bung, that 'un."

Jack grinned, liking the old woman. "She hasn't changed much. Part of my job was to fetch her back to her Cheyenne kin here before I set after the land grabbers."

"Whut's thet child's name agin? Trouble with gittin' old. Memory fails."

"Fawn, ma'am."

Mrs. Cook snorted. "Don't fit. Should be called She-wolf er Wildcat."

Dillon grinned. "You know her, all right."

The widow nodded, making a snort of disgust. "Gal wears breeches! Like I said, met her white folks. Mother's a real proper lady and daddy's some lordy kinda feller, a Britisher. 'Pears ta me they shouldda taught her better. Breeches!" She shook her head. "Gawdalmighty, breeches 'n a pistol strapped ta her hip like'n as if she wuz a Texas road agent."

Although he agreed with the old woman's assessment, Jack felt as if he were drowning in a torrent of words. He realized she must not have many visitors in this desolate place. *Talk to her, True Dreamer? How the hell do I have a conversation with her when I can barely get a word in edgewise? Woman could talk a mad dog off a meat wagon.* Then her words conjured up an image of Fawn in her deliciously tight breeches. How he'd love to get into them!

Forcing himself to focus instead on Fawn's proficiency with the thirty-eight strapped to her hip, he seized the opportunity when the widow took a gulp of water to ask, "What can you tell me about any men trying to steal land hereabouts?"

She placed her mug on the table with a solid thunk. "They kilt my man, Charlie. County Sheriff Buddy Tillman tole me robbers done it. Charlie wuz on his way back from Kingfisher. 'Bout ten miles southwest o' hyar. My boys found they father layin' cross the wagon seat. Horse jest a standin' there. Killers didn't take Charlie's Spencer rifle, neither. Not even the gold watch whut belonged ta his grandpa. Had pret' near ten dollars in his poke, too. Thet sound like robbers ta yew?"

Dillon shook his head. "No, it doesn't." He waited for her to continue, giving her time.

"Bout four, five days after we put Charlie to rest in the back, this hyar feller showed up. Greasy 'nough ta fill up a barrel with lard. Wouldn't have ta squeeze him hard ta do it neither. Called hisself Josiah Ledbetter. Said he worked fer the Big Oak Land Company. Had him a sneaky way o' talkin'. Said whut a shame it ware 'bout Charlie 'n 'bout how me 'n my boys needed protecshun from wild outlaws roamin' 'round hyar." She fixed Dillon with narrowed eyes. "Ain't never been no outlaws . . .'til now."

"He threatened you." It was not a question.

"Said it'd be a shame if'n my boys ended up same as they pa." She took a deep ragged breath. "I was afeared, Mr. Dillon."

"What did he want?" Jack expected one answer but received another.

"Ta sign a paper givin' mineral rights ta this hyar Big Oak Land Company. Ever' farmer hyarbouts signed, too."

"What kind of mineral rights?" Dillon asked. *I knew there was more to this than just a land grab!*

"Got no idee, none t'all, Mr. Dillon."

He vowed to find out. "Could you give me directions to where this supposed robbery took place? I'd like to look around."

"Ain't hard ta find. Take the farm road southwest 'bout ten miles. Yew'll find a hickory cross markin' the spot ware they found Charlie."

"Very sorry for your loss, ma'am. I used to be one of Judge Parker's deputies. Maybe I can give you the justice your county sheriff couldn't." As he stood up, she nodded and rose, too.

"We'd all be much obliged if yew could, sir. Much obliged."

As they approached his horse, he asked, "Where are your boys now?"

"They's down at the crik bottom. Tulip—that's our stupid ole cow—she's fixin' ta drop a calf any time now. Always picks the dangdest places ta do it. If Jimmy 'n Joey don't find her quick, she'll drop thet calf in a brake or thicket where varmints'll git it. Cain't afford ta lose thet calf . . ." She swallowed hard. "Lord God, cain't afford ta lose my boys neither. They's all I got left o' Charlie."

"Are they armed?"

"Jimmy's totin' his pa's Spencer and Joey's got the twenty-two. They's both good shots. I tole 'em ta always stay tagether an' pack they guns ever'where."

"You told them right, ma'am. I'd be obliged if you'd warn the other folks who sold mineral rights to this Ledbetter to keep their guns ready and watch their backs."

"Yew 'spect he'll come back ta kill us?"

Dillon shook his head. "It sounds as if they got what they wanted for now, but just in case, I wouldn't take any chances with bushwhackers. Someone shot at us on the road from Henessey to Fawn's ranch."

"This hyar territory is purely goin' ta hell in a handbasket," she said, shaking her head.

"When I get back to the ranch, I'm going to wire what you've told me to Max Stanhope. We just might turn this Big Oak into kindling wood before we're through. Meanwhile, if Ledbetter or anyone else stirs up more misery, you get word to Red Wolf Ranch. They have around a hundred men there trained to guns."

As he swung up on the buckskin, Mrs. Cook nodded, then said, "We'll do thet. Yew watch yer back, too, Mr. Dillon."

Chapter Nine

Fawn galloped out of camp, riding Remy bareback. She kicked the big paint's sides, urging him to go faster. Her rifle was clutched in one fist as she leaned over the horse's neck. Snake watched her fly past and muttered, "Now, what's put a bee in her breeches?" Then he grinned. Dillon had ridden out earlier and she was headed in the same direction. "Hope she doesn't shoot him," he said to his companion, Red Feather.

The full blood merely shrugged. "With her, who knows? Do you think we should ride after her?"

Snake glanced over to where True Dreamer stood, his arms crossed over his chest, gazing serenely at Fawn as she vanished beyond the trees. "No. He'd send us if we were needed."

Fawn rode swiftly, as the vision of Dillon being stalked by a killer unspooled in her mind. Would she be in time? Why did the Powers not grant her the ability to see more so she could understand what she was supposed to do? All she knew was that she was meant to go to his aid. Pushing aside her brooding thoughts about what that signified, she focused on getting to Dillon as quickly as possible.

In less than two hours, she recognized the small winding stream and a formation of scrub cottonwoods. This was the road to Kingfisher. Then she saw Dillon on foot, his rifle in his hand, quartering the ground near where a crude wooden cross had been placed.

Relief washed over her in waves. *He's alive!* Scanning the horizon, she concentrated on the concealment afforded by the brushy undergrowth along the river. There! The killer was there. She could not see him. His image was shadowy yet embedded in her mind . . . oddly familiar. Certainly evil.

Dillon caught sight of her and stopped his search. His eyes narrowed. He started walking toward her, out in the clear.

"Get down," she yelled, riding directly between him and the cover of the riverbank. She leaped from her horse just as a bullet whined past, missing them by inches. Jack grabbed her and they went down in a tangle of arms and legs. She managed to keep hold of her rifle and raise it, scanning the brush from where the bushwhacker had fired, but Dillon pulled her down and rolled over her protectively.

Her horse galloped off after his, both animals terrified by the sudden noise. "Stay put," he whispered, while she wriggled beneath him.

"I know where he is. Let me take a shot," she hissed softly, struggling to get free of his cumbersome weight. "Get off me, you clumsy oaf!"

Another shot pinged in the dust a foot from them. Dillon seized her arm and rolled to his feet, crouched and running for the scant cover of buffalo grass across the road. He pushed her ahead of him as a third shot grazed his left arm.

Fawn jerked free of his grip and knelt, aiming her rifle into a brushy area to fire. She still could not see their attacker . . . but she could sense him hidden behind the chokecherry. Dillon spoiled her aim, grabbing her by the wrist and rolling them into the grass.

"You ruined my shot," she said furiously, feeling her chance to stop the man slipping away. But she had finally seen his face, mottled by leaves and sunlight. She knew who he was.

"Are you crazy! You can't see where he's hiding!"

"I know exactly where he *was* hiding. He's gone now." Just as she spoke they could hear the sound of hoofbeats pounding away, less than fifty yards across the stream.

Dillon cursed, looking around for their horses, which had stopped their headlong dash a good two hundred yards in the opposite direction. No chance of catching up to the bushwhacker. He looked down into blazing night-dark eyes and suddenly became aware of the pressure of her breasts against his chest. She was breathing as if she'd just run a race. He could smell her scent, a blend of horse and woman. Lord, he was practically melded to her. One of her long legs rested between his thighs in a most intimate place. And his body responded, hardening instantly.

Fawn could feel his reaction. A swift blur of fear enveloped her. She forced herself to focus on anger so it would pass. "You idiot, you imbecile, you . . . you broken-nosed buffoon! I would've had him if you hadn't spoiled everything," she said, panting with fury now . . . or, at least, she told herself that was what she felt. "You turd-brained troll! I ought to butt you into that creek and stomp a mud hole in your chest. I had him in my sights. He could've killed you!"

Dillon rolled off of her, sitting up with his leg bent to conceal his erection. He looked into her eyes and read a mixture of fury and fear. The fury was certainly directed at him . . . but the fear? "How could you know . . ." His voice trailed away as he remembered the ambush on the road to the ranch.

"I just knew, that's all." Her voice was flat now.

He pulled her to her feet and watched as she brushed dust and dried leaves from her buckskins. His mouth went dry when her thick satiny braid slid over her shoulder and lay against her breast. He fought the urge to reach out and tug her to him for a kiss by pulling on that braid. *She'd use that knife at her belt to scalp me. Or would she?*

Fawn tried to ignore the way he was watching her and focus on the killer in her vision. He was the man she had shot when they'd stopped for water on the train. For some strange reason, when she was near Dillon, her visions became clearer. That both puzzled and angered her. It also fit with what Grandfather had told her. She didn't like it. Her jumbled thoughts were interrupted when Dillon made an involuntary grunt. She could see he was in pain. Blood seeped from his shirtsleeve.

"You've been hit. Let me look at it."

"I've had worse," he said, moving the arm to assess the damage. "It's just a scratch." He started walking toward the peacefully grazing horses.

She followed. "In this heat and dust, it would be foolish to let it fester. Come down to the creek and wash it. Do you have any clean cloth in your saddlebags that we can use to bind it up?"

"Just the change of clothes I brought to the village," he said as he picked up the reins of the horse True Dreamer had lent him. "You could tear up this shirt. It's ruined anyway."

Fawn recalled her grandfather's story about how the Crow girl had bound up Dillon's far more serious wound after he'd rescued her. "As long as you have another," she said neutrally.

He pulled a blue cotton shirt from the saddlebag and held it up. "Yep." Fawn turned and strode toward the water as her paint followed to drink. "First you'd better wash that arm."

They knelt upstream from the horses in the shade of the tallest cottonwood. She watched as he stripped off his bloody shirt and then sluiced cool water over the slash, washing away the blood. His chest was thickly furred with russet hair that narrowed at his waistband. He really was a red wolf. She watched the play of sinuous muscles rippling as he moved, and knew a deep, unfamiliar stirring in her belly. When he felt her eyes on him, he stopped and glanced up.

"Maybe you could do this better," he suggested with a crooked grin, daring her.

"Maybe I could," she replied, hiding her trepidation. She positively would not back down from this impossible, disturbing man. After all, he did find her desirable and that always gave a woman power over a man. She moved closer and placed one hand around the hard muscles in his left arm, holding it out over the stream.

The jolt was like a direct hit by lightning. Shimmering heat danced between them. The earth held its breath . . . and so did they. Everything seemed to move with incredible slowness. Dillon felt her long slender fingers curl around his arm. His heart hammered suddenly in his chest. She had cool, soft lady's hands, even if they were light tan in color. In her haste to reach him, she had forgotten the wide-brimmed hat and leather gloves that protected her from the sun's rays. Fawn would always be beautiful to him, no matter the shade of her skin.

She felt the tension in his muscles, the way his chest rose and fell with growing rapidity. She fought to calm her own breathing. The water was cool when she dipped her other hand into it and cupped the clear liquid, bringing it up to the bright red slash. She repeated the process with slow, deliberate care. He stared straight ahead, making no sound.

"That's deep. You'll require stitches for it to heal properly," she said when the water finally washed away the blood running down his arm.

His pain and the cold water combined to break the spell that held them in thrall. He turned toward her and said, "Let me guess. One of the things you learned in school was embroidery and now you want to practice on me."

"I received a meaningful education, not silly finishing school fluff," she replied with a huff of insult.

"I imagine you did." Jack realized that few white "gentlemen" would ever consider marrying an Indian woman, no matter what her education. The image of Claude Beaurivage flashed in his mind. Fawn Stanhope deserved better than that fortune hunter. *But she's not for the likes of you.* He shifted the subject to cover his disconcerting thoughts. "Your mother read law, didn't she?"

"Yes, but I was more interested in history and the sciences." She picked up his discarded bloody shirt and used the knife at her belt to slice a clean strip from the bottom. "Hold still." She bit her lip in concentration, struggling mightily to keep from trembling as she wound the cloth securely around his arm.

She had to lean close to him to work and her breast accidentally brushed against his shoulder as she tied off the binding. A tingle of pleasure tightened her nipple, startling her anew.

Dillon heard the tiny gasp and willed her to look at his face. The silence thickened around them. Although he uttered not a word, she understood. Irresistibly, she raised her head and met his level, penetrating eyes, those predatory amber wolf's eyes. Did her black ones reveal the compelling communication she had just felt?

Jack sensed her reaction. He knew he should not take advantage. She was young, an innocent . . . an heiress . . . and the Chosen Woman destined to lead her people. He had no part in that life. But he could not stop himself. He reached up with his good arm and touched the very tip of her chin, tilting her head up with two fingertips. Her eyes were huge and gleaming, like pools of ink, deep and mysterious. He could drown in them. Her thick black lashes fanned down, but she did not pull away when his mouth lowered toward hers.

It was luxuriously wide and warm. His lips brushed hers, butterfly soft, and he wondered if that dandy back in St. Louis had ever kissed her. But when he increased the gentle pressure against her mouth, the thought fled. He reached out with both hands and cupped her shoulders, pulling her closer to deepen the kiss.

The moment she felt his callused fingers gliding over her flesh, drawing her to that muscular chest covered with russet hair—his wolf's pelt—Fawn raised her hands and laid them on his hard slab muscles, feeling the pounding of his heart beneath. Without realizing what she was doing, she curled her fingertips and raked them through his chest hair, over the hard nubs of his male nipples until a deep growl of masculine pleasure rumbled against her hands.

His kiss was both soft and incredibly intense as his lips moved over hers, making her mouth pliant and sensitive. She followed his lead, learning from his guidance. *This is wrong! I never allowed Claude more than a brief peck.*

When his tongue teased the seam of her lips, she gasped softly and felt it dance just inside, teasing, cajoling, then withdrawing. Unsure of what to do, she hesitantly let the tip of her tongue touch his. It was scalding hot, yet so pleasurable that she dared to repeat the exercise, not quite so timidly this time.

Her action was irresistible, so shy and innocent, yet as old as Eve. He drew her tongue into his mouth, letting her feel the delicate delight. When she hummed with startled pleasure, he followed her retreat. His tongue sought hers, brushing the sensitive insides of her mouth, twining with her tongue. The world spun around them, picking up speed.

Jack was lost. This was what he'd wanted since the day he'd seen her sleek, wet body in that bathtub. All thoughts of who she was, how wrong this was, how stupid and irresponsible he was, all of it fled. His left arm encircled her waist and he pulled her against him, rocking his pelvis against hers. "You are incredibly beautiful," he murmured against the silk of her hair, nuzzling her neck.

But the sudden shift from delicate kissing to feeling a hard male body pressed against her broke the magical spell.

Fawn did not hear his tender words. Suddenly, she was a little girl again with a man's hands on her, tearing off her clothing and . . . her mind shut down and she pushed against him with all her strength. Her eyes were unfocused, blank with terror. She could not see Jack Dillon, only Johnny Deuce.

Johnny Deuce and his whip . . .

When she screamed and shoved against him, Jack released her instantly. Their shattered passion ended with such sudden force that he felt himself tumbling in a void. He knelt back on his heels, fists clenched on his thighs, helpless, stunned. He looked at her as she scrambled to her feet. It was as if she were having another one of her visions. She seemed somewhere miles away, just standing still now, hugging herself, staring out into space. She looked so lost, so frightened and vulnerable that it made his heart ache.

"I'm sorry, Fawn. I didn't intend to frighten you. I thought—damn, I wasn't thinking." He combed his fingers through his hair, frustrated and angry with himself for acting like a besotted animal. "Please, don't be afraid. I won't hurt you."

She did not reply as he slowly stood up, making no attempt to come closer to her. "Fawn? Can you hear me?" he asked softly.

Then suddenly her eyes cleared and her whole body jerked as if she'd been instantly transported from a hellish nightmare back to the present. She blinked and stared at Dillon. "Put on that clean shirt," she commanded with as much composure as she could muster, pointing to the blue garment he'd taken from his saddlebags. He turned his back and picked up the shirt, slipping it on. She watched as the muscles of his broad shoulders bunched with the effort. He had scars everywhere on his body. Visible scars.

Her own were hidden. Deep inside of her.

"It would be best if we forget this ever happened," she

said, proud of the level tone of her voice, dreading having to look him in the eye but knowing she must.

After buttoning his shirt with fumbling fingers and tucking it into his denims, Jack turned and faced her. His arm throbbed wretchedly now. The pain allowed him to regain control of his body. But his mind was in turmoil. "I would never force a woman. I despise men who do. I've killed . . ." He broke off raggedly.

"You did nothing to force me. We merely made a mistake," she replied, turning away, but she remembered Grandfather's story about rapists being the Red Wolf's natural enemies. She knew she was not the only one with dark secrets. Why did Dillon feel constrained to protect all women from that terrible evil? She desperately wanted to know . . . but she would never ask.

"I've given you ill repayment for saving my life. Thank you. This could've been a lot worse," he said, holding out his left arm. "You had a vision about that bushwhacker, didn't you?"

Fawn nodded. Without saying another word, she started walking, rifle in hand, into the chokecherry bushes downstream. Puzzled, Dillon waited. She emerged a few moments later holding something in her hand.

"What is it?"

She opened her palm and revealed several spent shell casings. Two were fresh. One was dulled by heat and rain. All three were .38-40 caliber. She dropped them into his palm, careful not to touch him.

His fingers closed over the shells, then opened so he could examine them. "These are all the same caliber used by the bushwhacker on the road from Hennessey."

She held out her hand silently. He did as she had, dropping the shells into it without touching, then watched as she rolled them between her palms. "The new ones were fired at you today by the same man. The old shell killed Charlie

Cook. Right there." She pointed to the cross by the side of the road.

"It's not a real common caliber, but . . ." He felt that eerie prickling creeping down his spine again as he examined the casings more carefully. "Those both have the marks of a weak firing pin. Just like the first ones on the road from Hennessey."

"Yes. Remember the man at the water stop by the train?"

"It was him? But you shot his right arm," he said, not wanting to believe her.

"You were right. I should've killed him. Apparently he's ambidextrous."

With that, she spun on her heel and walked over to her horse. Jack watched as she effortlessly leaped onto it and rode toward True Dreamer's village. He quickly retrieved the buckskin and followed, wondering for the hundredth time what in hell he had gotten himself into. When he'd heard as a child that his Grandmother Moira back in Ireland had "the sight," he'd always dismissed it as a fable.

Now Jack Dillon was not so certain.

When they neared True Dreamer's lodge that evening, both of them were tense and weary. They had ridden slowly on the return trip, resting their spent horses, each lost in private thoughts, neither willing to reveal anything to the other. Even before they could see the visitors, they heard loud voices arguing in Cheyenne.

Three warriors circled the old man, who stood impassively, listening to them with his arms crossed over his chest. The fellow doing most of the talking was a veritable giant, even among the tallest tribe of horse Indians on the plains. He had to be over six and a half feet and he was obviously quite angry.

Jack gestured to the big fellow. "Who is he?"

As she reined in Remy, Fawn wrinkled her nose in distaste.

"Thunder Mouth. The other two I don't know. Probably from his band. They live to the north above Cantonment. Thunder Mouth is a troublemaker."

"With a name like that, what else could he be?" Jack said dryly. "A better name might be Loud Mouth, though."

Fawn smiled in spite of the tension that had been simmering between them. "He's a bully."

"He might hurt your grandfather." Jack dismounted some distance from them.

Following suit, Fawn replied, "No. He would not dare."

Jack could hear the uncertainty in her voice and saw her raise her rifle ever so slowly. "Let me handle it," he said.

"It's best if you don't interfere. You already have one fresh bullet hole in you."

"I don't like the way they're acting," he replied, ignoring her jibe in spite of the throbbing misery in his left arm. He started to walk up behind the giant, noting with some relief that Snake and a number of other men from True Dreamer's band had heard the commotion and were also approaching.

"You will receive many presents for letting them use this land. We are not like the white eyes who rip our mother earth with their plows or herd spotted buffalo. We do not need this place. Only agree to make your mark on a piece of paper and you will be a warrior once more! You will have honor returned to you," Thunder Mouth said.

"I have kept my honor all along. I do not need it returned to me," True Dreamer replied calmly, when the big man had finished his tirade.

Thunder Mouth emitted a hiss of breath, clearly furious at the implication. He stepped toward the old man, raising his fist, but True Dreamer did not move.

"I wouldn't do that," Jack advised, standing close behind the much taller man. His hand rested lightly on the butt of his pistol as he watched the other two Cheyenne glaring angrily at him.

Thunder Mouth whirled around with his raised arm out-stretched, smashing Jack hard in the face. Dillon stumbled back as a blinding pain lanced up his nose into his forehead. Damn, this day was ending every bit as rotten as it had be-gun. He was fed up! He shook his head, blood flying from his rebroken nose, as he considered how to deal with his adversary.

Snake and Red Feather reached the fracas along with several other men, quickly quelling any impulse Thunder Mouth's companions might have entertained about joining in the fight. Fawn stood to one side, her expression unread-able, her rifle at the ready. Dillon knew he had to take down a man who had better than half a foot and forty pounds on him. How to do it?

Grinning like a big gorilla Jack had seen in a traveling circus in Chicago, Thunder Mouth advanced. Dillon looked up to maintain eye contact with his foe while snapping his right foot on target. The toe of his boot connected wickedly with the Cheyenne's crotch. Thunder Mouth gave a yelp of amazed pain, starting to go down to his knees in front of Dil-lon. He twisted in agony as his left hand cradled his private parts, but his right grabbed for the knife at his waist.

Sliding to his right, Jack drove his right fist into the side of Thunder Mouth's neck just below his ear. The big man spun sideways, dropping face forward, out cold. Blood streamed down Jack's chest as he stood over his fallen adversary. He looked at his second ruined shirt of the day and cursed. "By the time I finish this job, I'll be mother naked," he mut-tered.

"I think you two should take your companion and ride north," Snake said to Thunder Mouth's two friends in Chey-enne.

"Cut-Hair," one of them muttered at him. "You . . ."

The other one put his hand on his friend's arm, urging caution as Red Feather and several other warriors from True

Dreamer's band encircled the intruders. Snake's face hardened at the insult but he said nothing as they dragged the unconscious Thunder Mouth away and struggled to lift him across the back of his horse. In moments they were gone.

While Jack was watching the retreat, Bright Leaf handed him a cloth to staunch the bleeding from his aching nose. His voice was muffled as he asked True Dreamer, "Why were they here?"

"They wanted me to convince my band to sign leases giving away our allotment lands in exchange for gifts from Ledbetter. I know Thunder Mouth has been paid to do this evil thing. He despises his own people as much as he does the whites."

"Ledbetter. That's the man who forced the farmers to sign away the mineral rights on their homesteads," Dillon said, wondering again about Fawn's assertion that the gunman they'd tangled with en route to Hennessey had killed Charlie Cook.

The old man nodded. "He was an agent for the Great White Father many years ago, before Good Heart came, before the reservation was taken from us and allotments were given. He stole our supplies and sold them to white traders."

"So this Ledbetter's a former agent and a thief," Dillon said, considering. "He may be the key to unraveling the whole scheme."

Standing behind him, Fawn listened. "You need to let my father know about Ledbetter and that other man immediately." She turned to True Dreamer and gave him a brief explanation about the attempt on Dillon's life earlier that day.

The old man nodded. "That evil one works for this Ledbetter."

"Yes, I'm sure of it, too," she replied. "My father has many sources inside the government in Washington. There's a telegraph line at the ranch. If Dillon leaves at dawn, he can get word quickly to St. Louis." She turned back to Jack and, eyeing his nose, added wickedly, "That is, if you don't bleed to death during the night."

True Dreamer's face remained impassive at her barbed comment. *So, they strike sparks like a flint on a rock. Good.* "It would be best if you went with the Red Wolf to your ranch."

"But Grandfather, I just arrived. We have not had time—"

"You will return here after the evil ones are punished. There will be sufficient time then, child."

Jack watched the exchange, wondering if the old man was attempting to be a matchmaker. God forbid! "Old One, I don't want to endanger Fawn any more," he replied uneasily.

True Dreamer just smiled serenely. "When we finished our meal this morning, Chosen Woman had a vision. She knew that someone would shoot at you. She saved your life. Now you two must join together to stop the coming evil." He turned from Jack to Fawn, his eyebrows raised.

Jack wondered just how much of what had happened that day had been revealed to True Dreamer in his visions. Did the old man know about the kiss . . . ? He tried to shrug the thought away. There was no reading that enigmatic expression. Grudgingly he nodded.

Fawn, too, wondered just how much her grandfather knew about the strange attraction that had flared to life with such calamitous results that afternoon. She desperately wanted to understand what part Jack Dillon would play in her life, but the Powers—and her grandfather—gave her no answers . . . yet. *Why does he send me with his Red Wolf?*

Or is he your Red Wolf? an inner voice asked.

She would not consider the disturbing question for now. Instead, she looked at Dillon's bloody nose, from which he had just removed the cloth. "You must have Bright Leaf straighten it. Perhaps she will do a better job than the white bonesetter after it was broken the first time."

"I was just a kid. No one set it," he said, wincing at the sharp ache when he touched it.

The old woman stepped forward. "Yes, I can make it straight and perfect to match the rest of your face, Red Wolf. You will be even more handsome than before."

Fawn's nose wrinkled at Bright Leaf's effusive praise. "He also has a slash on his arm you must stitch."

"Come, come," the old woman said, shooing Dillon and Fawn ahead of her as she gave orders to several young girls to fetch both cold and hot water, clean cloth and other items.

True Dreamer stood outside his lodge watching as Fawn and her Red Wolf rode away. A subtle smile touched his face. When they had returned yesterday, he knew some awakening had passed between the two stubborn and proud young people who were so dear to his heart. They had survived death and danger by relying upon one another. That was good and he thanked the Powers for it. But there had been more.

The bond of mind and heart grows stronger as each day passes. Not only their bodies but their spirits call out to each other. This was the knowledge the Powers had imparted to him. He was old. Soon it would be time for him to journey on the great Hanging Road to the Sky. Now he could do so in peace. With the Red Wolf beside her, the Chosen Woman would be able to understand her visions and use them to guide the People.

Chapter Ten

When they arrived at the ranch, Jack could see a fancy rig pulling up in front of the big house. Two well-armed men rode beside it, obviously guards. "Well, looks like you aren't the only one who requires a bodyguard," he said to Fawn.

"Considering how the past couple of days have gone, it seems to me that I'm the one doing the guarding," she replied in dulcet tones.

When a tall, distinguished man with thinning gray hair and a pronounced paunch climbed down from the rig, Jack watched her face light up in recognition. Whoever the dude was, he was wealthy, judging by the matched team pulling his buggy and the fancy luggage strapped to the back of it. As efficient as always, the sergeant major marched up to the two guards. After a brief exchange, they dismounted, handed over their weapons and followed him across the yard to his office in one of the cabins.

Before Jack could ask Fawn about the visitor, she kicked her paint into a canter, calling out, "Uncle Steven!" as she raced the last stretch and slid off her horse in front of him.

Was Uncle Steven some kin of the Stanhopes? Dillon watched as she hugged the visitor and he returned the gesture in a fatherly way. Jack listened attentively to their conversation as he reined in, waiting silently to be introduced, always the hired help, the outsider. He tamped down his frustration.

"And how is my girl?" the stranger asked Fawn, inspecting her with a fond smile. "You must have come from visiting your grandfather's band. Are they well?"

"Everyone is fine, thank you. I'm so happy to see you, but I know how busy you are. Surely you've not taken time just to visit me," Fawn replied.

"Fishing for compliments, my dear?" he teased. "As a matter of fact, nothing gives me more pleasure than seeing you, but it's merely a fortunate coincidence to find you here. I have just returned from the Outlet, en route to catch a train in Hennessy. It's been a long and arduous journey. The lure of a soft bed and Mrs. Jones's superb cooking induced me to stop by."

"How long can you stay?" she asked eagerly.

"Unfortunately, I must be in Washington as soon as possible. This is just an overnight visit," he said regretfully.

"Well then, we'll have to see you have a fine feast tonight. I'm so happy we returned today or else I would've missed you." As soon as she spoke, Fawn realized that Jack had remained on his bay, glowering down at them in silence. She had not intended to be rude. "Oh, Uncle Steven, this is Jack Dillon. He works for my father. Mr. Dillon, may I present Steven Peters, the assistant to the territorial governor and a very dear friend of the Stanhope family."

Mr. Dillon, indeed. Butter wouldn't melt in her mouth. He dismounted as the tall stranger looked at him, obviously startled by his poor abused face. His nose was indeed now straight, but overnight both eyes had blackened from the force of Thunder Mouth's blow.

"So good to meet you, Mr. Dillon," the older man said formally. "If I may ask, in what capacity does Max employ you?" he inquired as his eyes swept over Jack's ravaged face.

Jack offered his hand and Peters shook it gingerly. *I have a broken nose. It isn't contagious.* He didn't have time to waste answering inane questions from dear family friends, he thought sourly, then realized his foul humor had less to do with Peters than it did with Fawn. "Among other things, I've been hired to keep Miss Stanhope out of trouble. It's quite a challenge," he could not resist adding.

"But not as difficult as keeping yourself out of trouble. Anyone could tell that at a glance," she could not resist firing back.

"I came out of the fight with a straight nose this time." He grinned at Peters. "The other fellow wasn't quite as lucky." Glancing at the wires that stretched from the rear of the house, he said to Fawn, "I'll need to send a telegram to your father."

"Do you know code?"

"Yes."

"Then you won't require help. The office is at the end of the downstairs hallway. Anyone inside can direct you."

Jack nodded curtly. "Fine."

Just as he turned toward the house, Smitty hailed him from the corral. "Hello, boss. Glad you're back. Swen and I rode in a few minutes ago. Right in time for lunch. Sergeant Major told us Miss Lula's fixing ham sandwiches and potato salad. Made Swen real happy." Smitty eyed the fancy stranger curiously. Then he got a good look at Jack's face, but only the slight hitch in his stride indicated his surprise.

Jack made introductions and then turned to Fawn. "If you'll excuse us, Miss Stanhope, I have business to discuss with my men. I'm certain you'll want time to visit with Mr. Peters." He could see that she was torn between wanting to be in on his discussion with his detectives and wanting to spend time with her "uncle."

"We'll see you at lunch," she replied. Taking Peters's proffered arm, Fawn walked as grandly as a duchess toward the house, no matter that she was dressed in buckskins and sporting a six-shooter on her hip.

"She sure is something, ain't she, boss?" Smitty said as Jack stared after her.

"Yeah, but I'm not sure what," he replied grimly. "Where's Swen? I want to know what you've learned."

"She give you those shiners and the swollen nose?" Smitty asked with a grin.

Jack could see his childhood friend was overcome with curiosity. "She's tough, but not as tough as a guy named Thunder Mouth. I only want to tell the story once, so you'll have to wait till Swen joins us."

They headed for the large barn, where Swen's blond head gleamed as he stepped into the sunlight. Like Smitty, the big Norwegian was taken aback by the condition of his boss's face, but he did not ask, only waited patiently to see if Dillon would enlighten them. They strolled around the outside of the corral where no one could overhear what they discussed. He quickly filled them in on what he'd learned from the Widow Cook and subsequent events, including his fight with the Cheyenne giant, and ending with Fawn's assertion that the man at the water station was their shooter.

"So she some kind of Indian fortune-teller?" Smitty asked dubiously.

"She knew someone was going to take another shot at me and she found these," Dillon replied, still uncertain of what to make of Fawn's visionary abilities. He dug the shells out of his pocket and showed them to his men.

"Same caliber as the ones from that bushwhacker on the road, same weak firing pin. But she shot that guy in his right arm," Smitty said, shaking his head.

"Yeah, but we need to see if she's right. I want both of you to ride back to that water station and nose around the saloons. See what you can find out about him." Then he asked Swen, "What did you find out in Kingfisher?"

"The registrar at the land office was so lazy and incompetent, he never even asked to see any identification. No one from True Dreamer's band has lost an allotment, but up north, near the border of the Cherokee Outlet, it's a different story for the Cheyenne. There were several of those so-called death claims filed and leasing agreements signed by wards of Indian orphans."

Dillon grimaced. "Thunder Mouth's people. Big Oak Land Company acquire the land?"

Swen nodded. "Yes, and this Josiah Ledbetter is the company's agent."

"What about mineral rights?"

"No mention of that. But considering how messed up the office was, it is hard to say if anything was recorded properly."

"Or recorded at all . . . at least yet," Jack said, rubbing his jaw as he turned to Smitty.

"I had to show my fake credentials to some fancy fella in Guthrie. Guy was brand-new as registrar at the land office, a slick, pretty dude. He gave 'em a quick look, apologized 'cause the guy who had the job before him quit real sudden and headed north, fixin' to get a prime piece of Outlet land in the big rush this fall. The new fella asked me if he could have a week to try to straighten up the mess he'd been stuck with." Smitty shrugged. "No way to say no without gettin' this Beaurivage suspicious."

"Beaurivage. A slick, pretty dude. Was his first name Claude?" Jack asked.

"Yeah. You know him?" Now Smitty's eyes narrowed.

"He's from St. Louis. An old beau of Miss Stanhope's. Interesting that a city slicker like him would turn up here, isn't it?" he asked.

"You think he's part of this Big Oak Land Company deal?" Smitty asked shrewdly.

"Could be." Or it could be he had simply taken the job to follow Fawn and lure her into marriage so he could get his hands on her fortune. There was no way in hell Jack Dillon would let that happen. He knew he was jealous and that his reaction was stupid and useless. But the greedy young fool might just be the key to nailing Ledbetter. "I have to compose a wire and send it to the Stanhopes. They have resources we don't," he said to the men.

"Time for lunch after that?" Swen asked hopefully.

"Who is that old guy in the fancy rig?" Smitty asked Jack. "Some kin of Mr. Stanhope's?"

"Maybe we'll find out at lunch," Jack replied.

The midday meal at Red Wolf Ranch was never fancy, but the food was always tasty and plentiful and the atmosphere warm and relaxed. Lula spread the long sideboard with platters of ham, freshly baked bread, sliced tomatoes, chilled bowls of potato salad and fresh garden greens. Swen eyed the triple-layer chocolate cake at the end of the line and smiled. Everyone heaped his plate with food and took his accustomed seat.

Their guest Steven Peters chatted with Fawn and Fee and complimented Lula lavishly as he pulled up his chair at the head of the table, the place of honor for an old family friend. Dillon watched as the cook beamed with pleasure. Peters charmed Fawn and Fee with a mixture of teasing and compliments that brought Fee out of the crestfallen mood that had gripped her since she'd learned Snake had not returned with his cousin.

Having a perfect excuse in her uncle's unexpected visit, Fawn studiously ignored Jack, who chose a seat at the opposite end of the table. Fee cast several curious glances his way, as if wondering what had occurred while they were away. He only hoped Fawn confided nothing to her companion. The last thing he needed was more of Fee's meddling. If the brat wanted to pretend nothing had happened between them, that was for the best. For once, she'd made an intelligent decision.

But his eyes kept returning to her in spite of his resolve. She'd changed into a simple summer frock of yellow dimity with a rounded neckline that revealed the slight swell of her lush breasts. The color set off her deep golden skin as if it were bronzed silk. How well he remembered the feel of it . . . of her. Even from this distance he was certain he could smell the faint essence of lilacs. And Fee had twisted Fawn's hair atop her head in a fancy topknot that gleamed like ebony. His eyes traced the slender column of her neck. Damn the witch, he ought to wrap his hands around it and choke her for making him want what he could never have!

"Are the old medicine feller's folks doin' all right?" Bronc asked Jack, rescuing him from his lustful memories. "Rumors 'bout land grabbers is thicker 'n Miz Lula's rice puddin'."

"They're fine, so far, but there's trouble brewing with the Cheyenne bands up north," Jack replied, glad for a distraction.

"Is that where ye got those grand circles beneath yer eyes, then?" Fee asked innocently.

"Aye, I've seen Scots tartans with na half so much color," Clyde chimed in.

Dillon flushed, feeling Fawn's smug gaze on him. "I had a little set-to with a charming fellow from one of the northern bands. He wanted True Dreamer and his people to sign over their allotments for a pittance."

Peters cocked his head, swallowing a bite of ham. "The governor is concerned about possible land grabs and violence with the opening of the Outlet this fall. If you can shed any light on the matter, his Excellency would be most grateful."

"We know a man named Ledbetter is threatening homesteaders and various bands of Indians," Dillon said.

"Is there anything you can do, Uncle Steven?" Fawn asked.

He frowned. "I'm familiar with Ledbetter," he said. "I'm

on my way to Washington on behalf of the governor, to discuss the land rush with the Secretary of the Interior. His agents will have resources to check on Ledbetter's recent activities."

"You might also want to have them look into the situation in the registrar's offices in Guthrie and Kingfisher. The political appointees who hold the positions don't seem to be very good bookkeepers," Jack said.

Peters nodded, frowning. "The governor and I agree. Unfortunately, the system is so entrenched that it is most difficult to correct. But Guthrie is our capital. Who is mishandling records there? Perhaps we can at least take action on that."

Jack paused a beat as Fawn raised her coffee cup to take a drink, then replied, "A fellow from St. Louis. Claude Beaurivage."

Fawn choked, narrowly avoiding spewing the hot liquid across the table as Jack had. Fee pounded her on the back. "Are ye all right, then?" she asked, exchanging a smirk with Dillon. "If that Frenchie's the one mindin' the land office, 'tis small wonder the records—"

"Fee," Fawn said immediately, cutting off her friend's tart opinion of Claude with a quelling look. "I know Mr. Beaurivage." She turned to Peters and said earnestly, "He's an honest man, but new to the position. If he inherited a mess, it would take a while to straighten it out."

"If you vouch for him, child, I have no reason to place his name in an unfavorable light."

Jack looked down the table. Fawn's flashing black eyes told him that he had gotten even for at least one embarrassing moment she had caused him. But in spite of his admittedly petty satisfaction, he had no desire to have Peters oust the lazy dandy from the registrar's office. With the vain and inept Claude in charge, Smitty's job would be that much easier next week.

"I'd be interested in learning more about this land rush,

Mr. Peters," Jack said. "Will any of the Indian allotments be endangered by so many white settlers coming into the territory?"

Peters shrugged apologetically at Fawn before replying to Dillon. "I'm afraid whenever white settlers pour into an area, there are incidents with the original inhabitants, but the governor is determined to keep the peace."

"You indicated you were familiar with Josiah Ledbetter. What can you tell me about him?" Dillon asked.

Now Peters frowned. "He was an Indian agent until forced to resign for corruption."

"Uncle Steven's too modest," Fawn interjected. "He's spent his career removing corrupt appointees from government office."

Peters patted her hand affectionately, shrugging off the compliment. "He's greedy and unprincipled, precisely the kind of man we don't want involved in the rush."

"My father has asked Mr. Dillon and his detectives to find out who's trying to gain control of Cheyenne land allotments," Fawn explained. "Now Ledbetter's part of a group called the Big Oak Land Company. Have you ever heard of it?"

Peters shook his head. "I have not, but I will make inquiries." He looked at Jack. "Mr. Stanhope has given you a most difficult challenge. I fear there is no legal way to keep Ledbetter out of the territory unless he's caught breaking the law. Do you possess information about him that might enable the governor to take action against him?" the older man asked with a hopeful expression on his face.

"Not yet, but we're working on it," Dillon replied.

"If there is anything the governor's office can do, please send word. I shall return from Washington within a fortnight."

"Uncle Steven has a great deal of influence here and in Washington," Fawn explained, then turned back to her guest.

"My father and I would be very grateful for any help you could give us . . . and Mr. Dillon, too, of course."

"Of course," Jack muttered beneath his breath.

Wiping his mouth with his napkin, Steven Peters said to Jack, "When we finish our repast, I shall give you and your men personal notes of introduction written on the governor's stationary. That should clear the way for your investigation."

"Thank you, sir. I'm sure that will be very helpful," Dillon replied.

Swen nodded in agreement, but Smitty said very quietly, murmuring for his companion's ears only, "The only thing a politician'll give ya is the sleeves off his vest."

Swen coughed to hide his snicker.

But Steven Peters was as good as his word. He penned letters on the territorial governor's embossed stationary in beautiful, florid script, instructing all government officials to render to Mr. Jonathan Padric Aloysius Dillon and his designated operatives Hans Schmitt and Lars Swensen any aid or information requested. When Jack showed the letters to his men, Swen's eyes widened. "Aloysius?" he blurted out, then turned beet red.

Dillon's eyes narrowed. "The last time someone made fun of my unfortunate name, I beat the hell out of him—and he was twice my size, too."

"Remember what he done to Lightnin' Mouth, or Thunder Head, whatever?" Smitty chimed in with a smirk.

"That epic battle was quite impressive, I will admit," Fawn said, gliding silently up to where the three men were talking on the porch.

"I expected you to be entertaining your uncle," Dillon said.

"He's resting. His trip has taxed him greatly. You were lucky that he stopped by before catching that train to Washington."

"Would your father call on him for help?"

"He always has." Fawn noticed the haggard look on Jack's face. The beginnings of a reddish-brown beard and the harsh slash of his mouth indicated his mood. *He's exhausted . . . and angry with me.* But why should she care? He had only been hired to find the men responsible for threatening the People's safety and land. Once his job was done, he and these men would leave. She would never lay eyes on Jack Dillon again. That was what she wished . . . wasn't it?

Forcing aside her confused feelings, Fawn said to Smitty and Swen, "Tell me what you've learned."

Both men looked to Jack first. Dillon took charge, as they figured he would. He quickly outlined the information they'd gathered from Kingfisher and Guthrie, then added, "I imagine you're overjoyed to hear your beau is so close by."

Fawn smiled. "Of course. I expect he'll be paying a visit as soon as his new position allows him free time." Why didn't that make her more excited? Since leaving St. Louis, she had scarcely spared poor Claude a thought. He loved the amenities of large cities and hated roughing it. Even though Guthrie was the largest city in the territory, Claude would consider it a provincial backwater. Surely he'd taken the position of registrar to be near her. There could be no other reason . . . unless he was a part of this Big Oak Land Company they'd just learned about.

If so, he was nothing more than a fortune hunter who cared not at all for her, just like so many of the men she'd met in the East. A disturbing thought, but one that did not make her feel even a twinge of heartbreak. She must not be in love with him. But she had to find out if he was part of the conspiracy to steal from the People. Looking at Jack, she said, "Perhaps I won't wait until Monsieur Beaurivage has time to call. I may ride to Guthrie to visit him myself." Dillon gave her the expected angry reply.

"Not without me, you won't. Look, Miss Stanhope, I don't have time—"

Before he could complete his sentence, an approaching rider was hailed galloping toward the ranch house. It was Snake, whom the guards immediately waved past.

He swung down from his lathered horse and ate up the distance between the gate and Fawn, who had bolted from the porch with Jack and his men following behind her.

"What's happened? Is Grandfather all right?" she asked in Cheyenne.

Chapter Eleven

He's fine. That's why I'm here. He's made camp at his old place, down by the Cimarron. Wants to palaver about something real important. We have to ride north. He'll explain," Snake replied. He did not look happy.

Fawn knew if Grandfather had wanted her cousin to give her any information, Snake would have done so. No, this was a matter to be discussed only between her and True Dreamer. Nodding in understanding, she said, "I'll change and be ready to ride in a few minutes."

When Fawn grabbed her skirts and began to dash up the stairs, Fee, who wanted desperately to go outside and welcome Snake back, felt compelled to follow. She was paid to be Fawn's maid and confidant. "And what has that handsome divil said to put a bee in yer britches?" she called after Fawn.

Barely sparing a brief turn of her head, Fawn replied, "I've been summoned by Grandfather. I have to change and ride at once."

"I'll help ye," Fee said, as they entered Fawn's room. Then she dared to ask, "Will Mr. Snake be stayin' here then?"

"No, he's going with me." As she reached back to unfasten the buttons on her dress, she could see the look of disappointment sweep across Fee's face, but her friend made no comment, only stepped behind her and took over the buttons. In short order, Fawn had slipped out of her gown and petticoats, and into her buckskins. She strapped her gun belt to her hips.

Seizing the Yellow Boy from its place beside her bed, she said to Fee, "I'm sorry Snake can't stay, but maybe it's for the best. Fee . . ." She hesitated, wanting to warn the headstrong little Irishwoman about Snake's wandering ways, but knowing Fee would not listen. *When you're in love you never take advice.*

How the dickens would she know that? She had already decided she had not been in love with Claude, only infatuated by a tall, handsome man of whom her parents did not approve.

"Will the other handsome divil be goin' with ye?" Fee asked, with a gleam restored to her eyes. If she couldn't enjoy Snake's company, maybe at least Fawn and Jack Dillon might do some courting.

Fawn knew perfectly well whom Fee meant, but could not resist asking, "And who would that be?"

"Ye know Jack Dillon is a fine figure of a man," Fee replied.

"Yes, and those black and yellow circles beneath his eyes set off his red hair perfectly."

Ignoring the sarcastic remark, Fee persisted, "Is Mr. Dillon goin' with ye?"

Sighing, Fawn replied, "This is between Grandfather and me. No hired guns required." Fawn devoutly hoped that was the case.

"A pity." Fee sighed.

"Let him do his job from here while I'm gone."

Fee snorted in aggravation. "Yer a fool if ye let 'im go."

"He's not mine to let go," Fawn snapped, heading out the door into the hall. Then another thought occurred to her. "Oh, Fee, when he wakes up from his nap, please explain to my Uncle Steven why I had to leave without saying good-bye and tell him I'm ever so sorry we didn't have tonight to visit more."

"He'll be that disappointed, he will, but there's no helpin' it. Mr. Peters seems a nice gent," Fee said. "He'll understand."

Nodding, Fawn rushed past her and down the stairs. When she strode into the yard, she was pleased to see Snake had fetched Remy from the barn, ready to ride. Then she saw Dillon mounted on his big red horse, following her cousin. "Where's he going?" she asked Snake as he handed her Remy's reins.

Snake gave her a sly grin. "As if you didn't know. With us." Before she could protest, he added, "Grandfather's orders," knowing that would settle the matter . . . for now.

Fawn angrily leaped onto the paint's back without saying another word. She could feel Dillon's angry eyes on her as he reined in and rested both arms on the pommel of his saddle. "Let's ride," was all she said, then kicked Remy and took off.

Shrugging sympathetically at Dillon, Snake followed. The three of them rode in silence for a quarter hour until they reached the old campgrounds where True Dreamer always bedded down when he visited the ranch. As soon as word spread to Bronc and Good Heart, they would come to see him. Even Sergeant Major Higgins had been admitted to the old medicine man's inner circle. Whenever he visited, the four old men would sit and tell stories about their varied and interesting lives.

Seeing a thin wisp of smoke rising between a stand of cottonwoods by the river's edge, Fawn smiled. She had many fond memories of spending time here as a girl, when the Stanhopes had first begun building the ranch property. Then her expression changed. Grandfather would not have come if something important—and probably bad—had not happened today.

When Fawn slid from her paint and headed into the trees, Dillon started to follow suit. Snake said quietly, "Wait with me. The old one has to speak to her alone first." With that, the half blood clucked to his horse, which headed downstream into the shade of a big willow. Dillon went after him and they let their mounts drink as they took shelter from the sun.

Fawn followed the path to True Dreamer's camp, pleased to see her cousin divert Dillon, doubtless on the old man's orders. She found him sitting by the small fire he had built, staring into the flickering flames. His back was as straight as a man less than half his years and his body amazingly fit. Yet for the first time in her life, she sensed that he was aging.

Swallowing a lump that threatened to close her throat, she walked up to him and smiled. "Good afternoon, Grandfather." She waited respectfully for him to speak.

"Things have almost come full cycle now," he said softly in Cheyenne, motioning for her to take a seat across from him. They faced each other across the sweet-smelling fire, which gave off the scent of white sage. "Now my time on Mother Earth nears its end . . ."

He raised his hand when she started to protest, silencing her. Serenely, he continued, "This is the beginning of your time. And we must speak of it." He inhaled the white sage and smiled at her, pleased that she listened attentively, although he knew she would not wish to hear all the information he must impart to her. He let out the deep breath he had been holding and implored the Powers, *Please give me patience and strength to do your will. Let me say well.*

"Your gift grows stronger now, do you not know this?"

She nodded. "Yes, I see visions more clearly . . ." The memory of the man lying in wait for Dillon flashed through her mind. "I have acted on them and it has been well." She did not wish to consider that her powers had grown stronger since Jack Dillon had come into her life.

True Dreamer watched her expressive face and knew what she was thinking. He smiled. "You must soon use your gift to serve the People. You will ride two days from here to the old agency school building. A large council will be held near there three suns from now. Even as I speak of this many clans are gathering. I see the lodges being set up, the fires being lit. They come from far away . . . and near."

Fawn cocked her head, trying to intuit what he was seeing. A faint outline of cook fires and a long line of lodges strung like a spilled necklace around the bleak, bare grounds of the old reservation school shimmered behind her eyelids. "Yes, I can see them," she said softly, feeling a strange chill settling around her shoulders in spite of the warm afternoon air. "For what purpose do they gather, Grandfather?"

"I have not been given to know that, child, only that you must be present at that council as the Chosen Woman. You must arrive just as the council begins, when none expect you. This will be what Sergeant Major calls . . . 'strategic advantage.'" He pronounced the last two words carefully in English, then continued in his native tongue. "The Toad will not be prepared to face your challenge."

"Who is the Toad?" she asked uneasily, knowing that he had rightly called Johnny Deuce a weasel.

"You know him as Ledbetter." He heard Fawn suck in her breath.

"The agent who stole from us, who works for this Big Oak Land Company now!"

"Yes, he is the Toad, fat, cold and slimy, poisonous to touch."

An image of Josiah Ledbetter with a bloated red face and fat body appeared in her mind. She shuddered in revulsion. "How am I to deal with him—to stop him from doing more harm to us?"

"You will receive help from your cousin Burning Snake . . . and from the Red Wolf."

Fawn had guessed that this summons would involve Dillon, but hated that she had been right. "He is a white man. How can he help?" she argued.

"The Toad also is a white man. One is evil. The other good. Do you say you cannot tell the difference?" It was a rhetorical question and she did not reply. He continued, "The time for my talk is over. The Powers favor you. They also favor the Red Wolf. He has earned his place as one of the People . . . and without him your gift will fade. You will no longer be the Chosen Woman. With him by your side, you will make strong medicine."

Fawn digested this pronouncement. She had known deep in her heart, even in her mind, that this was true, yet she had fought the knowledge. She felt anger and confusion . . . and fear. *Because he is white . . . or because he is a man?* The question hovered, unanswered. Seeing that Grandfather waited for her response, she moistened her dry lips and spoke in an anguished voice. "Sometimes I feel unworthy . . . unable to accept what has been given me," she began hesitantly.

He nodded. "Because of the evil you endured at the hands of the weasel. That was a trial. One not yet complete. But with the help of the Red Wolf, you will finish victorious . . . and whole." True Dreamer studied the warring emotions on her face. "Your heart is good. You are stronger than you yet know."

"To prevail at this council, I will need the Red Wolf," she said in resignation, still unsure of what she and Dillon were supposed to do about Ledbetter. Was Jack going to kill him? Her head ached with the possibilities as visions of the assembling bands of Indians blurred together with the sweating, ugly image of Josiah Ledbetter's face. Her stomach churned and she felt dizzy. Then Grandfather's words pulled her back from the abyss and she listened to his calm voice.

"I have said Jack Dillon was once the hunting wolf for the

Law Chief Parker. Now he is the hunting wolf for the Pale Moon Stalker. His task is the same—to find evil and destroy it. You will lead him to this council, where there is much evil. Together you will vanquish it."

Fawn nodded. "I will obey you, Grandfather."

He grunted in approval. "My child, for this time, you will wear ceremonial garments that mark you as the Chosen Woman. The gathered men will not dismiss you as a mere female. They will know you have been touched by the Powers."

Fawn looked down at her buckskin trail clothes, worn and dusty. "I do not have—"

"The Powers . . ." He paused and smiled, "and Bright Leaf have provided." He gestured to his pack, which lay in the shadows of the cottonwood, gesturing for her to go to it and open it.

She did so, her lips forming an "O" of wonder as she pulled out an incredibly beautiful beaded tunic and leggings, then elaborately quilled high moccasins. The fringe on the tunic was long, the doe skin bleached pure white, soft as satin to her touch. She almost dropped the heavy garment when she realized she had seen it before—she had painted it long ago back in St. Louis. This was what she had worn as she stood with a red prairie wolf at her side, the wind whipping her hair around her shoulders, boldly facing the unknown. The future was still unknown . . . but the identity of that wolf was certain. Wordlessly, she looked at Grandfather.

"Take it with you. When you put it on, you will speak as a maker of strong medicine. Those present will hear my voice, and the Pale Moon Stalker's voice, even though he is far away and cannot be there."

Her heart squeezed painfully as she asked, "And you, Grandfather? Why can you not be there beside us?"

He smiled compassionately at her. "I am too tired for such

a journey . . . too old. Besides, Sergeant Major has not finished the retelling of his tale of the great fight between the Pale Moon Stalker and the dark warriors, the Zulu." He chuckled. "The English, he is a fine storyteller. With each telling the battle grows fiercer."

"I will spend time with you when I return." The moment she spoke the words, Fawn knew they were true. They had time left yet. The realization comforted her, but the image of her and the prairie wolf did not.

The old medicine man nodded, smiling gently to reassure her. "Go now. Use the gift you have been given to aid the People. You will be guided."

Dazed, Fawn collected the big medicine pouch containing the ceremonial clothes and left True Dreamer staring into the flames. When she heard Jack's and Snake's voices, she walked downstream to where they sat by the side of the river in the shade of a big willow. Her eyes were drawn to Dillon's. For a moment, she could not break the hypnotic hold of his gaze. When both men rose expectantly, she realized that he and Snake were waiting for her to explain why True Dreamer had summoned them.

Taking a deep breath, she began. "There will be a council of many bands in three days, near the old agency school house. We must arrive just as it opens and speak against the white man who has called it, Josiah Ledbetter. Grandfather calls him the Toad."

Dillon frowned in perplexity. "Sounds like a good name for the bastard. Did your grandfather explain what he's doing at a Cheyenne council?"

"No. But we will find out when we see him," she said with quiet certainty. Had not Grandfather always said true? She felt deep inside of her that they would accomplish the task given them. As to the rest . . . her gift and its connection to Dillon, she would sort that out later.

Snake started walking to where their three horses were grazing peacefully. "If Grandfather says go there, he must have a good reason. Let's ride. We're burning daylight."

Shrugging, Dillon gestured for her to step ahead of him, saying, "I reckon this is as good a time as any to meet Ledbetter. I sent Smitty and Swen to find that bushwhacker he hired."

"You will not do anything rash," she said, not quite a question.

"If you mean shoot him before I know what's going on, no. I don't act rashly." *Except when I think of you naked and wet or smell your perfume . . . or feel your skin.*

Fawn gave him a disbelieving look, then marched to her horse, still clutching the heavy bag. She was glad Snake had put a saddle on Remy so she did not have to carry the bundle on a two-day ride.

"What's in the bag? A present from your grandfather?" Jack asked as she swung up on her paint and tied the drawstrings around her pommel.

"More like powerful medicine," she replied, kicking the horse into a trot after her cousin.

"What in hell is that crafty old man up to now?" Dillon muttered as he followed them. He glanced at the heavy pouch, wondering what was inside. *A wedding dress.* The thought came out of nowhere. He almost fell off his horse. The big bay skittered until he brought it under control, patting the shiny red neck and crooning, "Sorry, boy. Sorrier than you'll ever know."

Snake and Fawn knew the way north to the old reservation. She said little during the afternoon ride. Neither did Dillon. Snake, noting the tension between them, did most of the talking. Loquacious and charming, he recounted anecdotes about his various wives and explained to Jack how he'd received the name of Burning Snake. "When I was a boy, I was bitten by a rattler. I was pretty little and the snake was pretty big, but it made me mad. So, I grabbed the ornery critter by its head and held it over my mother's cook fire.

"Damned thing wriggled like crazy but I never let go until enough of it charred to kill it. Then I dropped the carcass into the flames. My father cut open my leg. Whew, that hurt. He cleaned out the venom but my mother and most of our band were afraid I'd die of poisoning. Our grandfather applied a poultice to the wound and sang a medicine song to the Powers while my fever raged. When I woke up three days later, I'd earned the name Burning Snake. At least until I got to the white man's reservation school," he added dryly.

That elicited a grim chuckle from Jack, but Fawn, who had heard the tale many times before, said, "You wasted good food. Grandfather should've punished you for it."

Snake looked over at Dillon. "There's just no pleasing a woman, is there?"

Dillon turned his head to Fawn and replied, "Not this one, that's for certain."

She did not deign to reply, only stared straight ahead and rode silently.

Jagged streaks of red, gold and orange colored the sky as the sun set in the west. Snake reined in and said, "This is as good a place as any to stop. Last water for miles."

"Our canteens are getting low." Jack nodded. "Besides, I hate making dry camps."

Fawn simply dismounted in silence and set to work unpacking her bedroll while Snake used boxed matches to start a fire. "Kind of cheating, using those, isn't it?" Dillon asked his friend.

"Hey, my father was a white eyes," he replied good-naturedly. "'Sides, it's a hell of a lot easier than fooling with flints and punk. I never did get the hang of that very well."

While Snake worked at building up the fire, he was aware of Jack's eyes following Fawn as she walked to the stream to fill the canteens. Knowing they needed time in private,

Snake finished his task and stood up, brushing his hands on his denims. He grabbed his rifle and announced, "I'm going to meander down a ways and see if I can shoot us a couple of fat cottontails for dinner. Oh, there's beans and other supplies in my saddlebags in case I don't have any luck."

"Did True Dreamer tell you we were going on a trip before he sent you to fetch us?"

"Not in so many words. He just gave me a pouch of jerky and a few other things and sent me on my way." Snake meandered off, saying, "Yep, some rabbit roasted over that fire would taste mighty good. And maybe a skillet of beans. I'll be gone for a while . . ."

Could he have been more obvious about leaving her alone with Dillon? Fawn fumed as she yanked the foodstuffs from her cousin's saddlebags. She could feel Jack's eyes on her, those frightening amber eyes that seemed to pierce through her very soul. Damn the man!

Jack watched her lay out the pouches of food, a cook pan and a coffeepot. She scooped out the beans and dumped them into the water with enough force to make a loud splash. "Unlike the serpent in the Garden of Eden, our Snake isn't exactly subtle, is he?" he asked, leaning back against a rock with a scowl on his face.

"Oh, he's a snake, all right, but he can't trick me into doing something stupid," she snapped, making herself meet his eyes.

"Just what stupid thing do you suppose he expects you to do, Princess?" His tone was as tense as his body. "Or," he paused, leaning forward, "am I the one who's supposed to do something stupid . . . again. You can rest at ease. I'm not coming near you." The minute he said the words, he knew they sounded angry and . . . hurt. Her rejection, the way he'd lost control . . . he had never felt this way . . . until now, until her.

"I'm not afraid of you, Dillon." She knew her voice betrayed the lie. Oh, my yes, she was afraid, very afraid! But not in the way he thought. She felt her hands tremble as she performed simple camp chores. *The only way you can triumph over the evil tormenting you is to face it. Rid yourself of the poison by speaking out.*

Grandfather's long-ago words echoed in her mind. But she had done so. Over the years as she grew up, she had described her horrible time with Johnny Deuce, first to True Dreamer, then to her mother. She could never bare her soul to this man in such a way. After telling them, she had believed that she was healed. Yet her fear of physical contact—beyond chaste kisses with Claude—had never abated. The Creole had not pressed her, nor had she felt the slightest desire to touch him . . . to watch him . . . Yes, she admitted to herself, to want him the way she wanted Jack Dillon.

Fawn remembered every moment of that encounter when he'd been shot. She would never forget his hard, muscular body with all its scars, the crisp feel of the hair on his chest, the way his tongue entwined with hers, drawing her into far more than dry, tight-lipped kisses. She had been on fire, her fear replaced by hunger and a longing so sweet and powerful that it continued to haunt her.

But when he'd taken their passion to the next step, the old memories had torn through her, abruptly breaking the magical spell and casting her back into the black abyss. Fawn, like all Cheyenne maidens, had been taught about the way of a man and a woman, that it was good and natural, a blessing given by the Powers. She had called their passionate encounter a mistake, but she had been wrong. The compelling force that kept pulling them together was ordained by the Powers.

Her fear had made him remorseful, guilty. *I have never forced a woman in my life . . .* His stricken words came back to her. No, she was quite certain he had not, but he singled out men who did and killed them. What impelled him to do this? Someday he would tell her. Now, it was time for her to share her own memory of the face of evil.

Jack was surprised when Fawn turned and stared at him as if seeing him for the first time. "What is it, Princess?" Something was eating at her. She had been uneasy around him ever since he'd lost control yesterday by that stream. Now he could see that she had something to say. He waited patiently as she swallowed for courage, sensing that if he interrupted, she might not have the nerve to try again. She fixed her eyes on the far horizon, where the sun was going down in a blaze of crimson glory. But when she started speaking, what she said was anything but what he had expected.

"When I was ten years old, I was kidnapped from the reservation by an Englishman named Jonathan Framme," she said in an eerily calm voice. "He was a remittance man who'd been banished because of what he did to young girls."

Jack sat up, unable to keep an expression of horror from twisting his face. Ten years old . . . the same as Megan! The odds of such a thing happening to them both were impossible. "He raped you." It was not a question.

Fawn shook her head. "No, he . . . he could not be with a woman that way. That was what made him evil, perhaps." She shrugged, still unable to meet his eyes, although she could hear the shock and pain in his voice. "After he tore off my clothes, he used a whip on me . . . a riding quirt that cut and burned."

Jack sucked in his breath. It was as if the world stood still.

"Seeing my blood made him able to achieve . . . sexual arousal. Then . . . he made me do things . . . horrible, ugly things. When he could not gain satisfaction, he used the whip again."

He'd heard of men who could only respond by inflicting pain on children, but never would he have imagined that such a horrid thing had happened to this proud, beautiful woman. *Ten years old!*

"Out West everyone called him Johnny Deuce. He kept me prisoner, traveling from our land down into Texas. The Pale Moon Stalker killed him in Fort Worth after True Dreamer led him there to find me. Grandfather made strong medicine so that I would heal."

"But still, the evil follows in your nightmares, doesn't it?" Jack asked softly, knowing that his own restless, guilty sleep never gave him peace.

"At first it left me. But as I grew older and went to live in the white world, the long-buried fears returned. I think Grandfather always knew this would happen . . . that I would have to find my own way past them so they would die just as Johnny Deuce died." She looked at Jack now, her dark gaze direct and revealing as he slowly stood up and walked over to her.

Jack knelt in front of her and extended his hand, palm open. She placed her slender hand in it and he closed his fingers over hers, raising them to his lips. He bestowed a soft kiss on the back of her hand. "Fawn, I know that wasn't easy for you . . . I'm honored that you shared your story with me. If there is any way I could take away your pain, erase the terrible nightmares—"

"There is," she said quietly. Accepting what she now knew the Powers had ordained, Fawn leaned forward and placed her free hand around his neck, pulling him closer.

Chapter Twelve

$\mathcal{F}$inish what we started yesterday," she commanded, as her long, slender fingers dug into his thick russet hair and pulled his mouth closer to hers.

"This is crazy—you're the heiress to a great fortune, the Chosen Woman of the Cheyenne. I'm just a penniless detective your father hired to protect you, not seduce you." His mouth was inches from hers, his breathing ragged as he struggled to retain his dwindling hold on reality when all he wanted to do was pull her into his arms and make love to her.

Fawn could feel the heat of his body, the desire pulsing through it as he shuddered, trying to hold back. But understanding what she must do, she would not be denied. Her breasts arched forward, pressing against his chest, and he groaned. She raised her lips and brushed them against his mouth. When she felt that male part of him grow as her hips rocked against his, she knew she had won.

"Ah, Fawn, dammit to hell," he muttered as he pulled her into his arms while they knelt by the fire. He lowered his mouth to hers in earnest now and she opened for him, just as she had yesterday, but this time when his body pressed so intimately against hers, she did not panic or push him away. Instead, his mercurial princess melted into him, every delicious curve molding to him as her tongue dueled with his.

Hot and sweet and hungry, his kiss robbed her of breath.

Fawn returned it with every bit of the passion newly blossoming within her. He slanted his mouth, turning so their lips met at yet another angle. She followed where he led. Liquid fire flashed through her veins. She wanted desperately to know the mystery of man and woman, to feed the hunger burning so deep inside of her, like a flame consuming her.

His hands were everywhere, sliding down her back to the curve of her buttocks, lifting and holding them against his aching shaft. She rolled her hips against his until he growled deep in his throat. He unlaced the front of her shirt and reached inside to cup one breast, then the other, as his fingers teased her nipples. Already sensitized by pressing against his chest, they puckered into hard, needy nubs. When his mouth moved down her throat, trailing wet kisses to the wildly beating pulse point at her collarbone, she knew what she must have.

Fawn dug her nails into his impossibly broad shoulders and arched higher, urging his mouth lower, but her buckskin shirt was in the way. She slid her hands down the hard biceps of his arms, then reached for the bottom of her shirt, tugging it free of her belt and pulling it up over her head. Just as she tossed it aside, a shot rang out in the distance. Breathlessly, she murmured, "That's the first rabbit. We'll need at least two . . . or three."

"Your cousin will be a while . . ."

"I think he understands what's required," she replied as she continued to strip away her clothes. Grandfather most probably had instructed him to leave them alone like this!

Jack watched as she began unbuckling her belt, unable to take his eyes from her splendid upthrust breasts with their tight dusky nipples begging for his mouth on them. Her skin was golden all over, like lush satin. His hands, burnished deeply by the hot western sun, were barely darker as they cupped her breasts, holding one up so he could suckle it. Her gasp of pleasure sent a bolt of heat coursing through him. For whatever reason, he had been the one chosen by her—by fate or some mysterious power beyond his comprehension—to show her that all men were not like the one who had hurt her.

Her thick braid hung down her back. "I want your hair free, like a cloak around your shoulders, long, silky, night-dark," he murmured, grasping the plait in his hand. But when he swung it over her shoulder, trying to unfasten the tie that held it, his fingers shook.

Fawn smiled and placed her hands over his. "Let me do it," she said, quickly removing the tie and shaking her head so her hair spilled like ink around her. When he seized a fistful of it and brought it to his lips, she felt a thrill. She watched as he wrapped it around his fist and then brushed the straight ends across her breasts. Her legs felt weak and she trembled with the tingling pleasure. "I, too, would see more of you," she said, swaying as he teased her breasts, while her fingers kneaded against his chest.

"Whatever you want, anything," he said harshly. His hands still trembled as he unbuckled his gun belt and dropped it, then pulled his shirt off. Fawn stared at the broad expanse of muscle, so pale where the sun had not darkened it. She touched a scar running across his narrow waist and felt a thrill when he sucked in his breath.

"If you touch me that way, this is going to end much too fast," he said raggedly. "Let me finish undressing you."

"Yes," she murmured as he scooped her up in his arms. He was incredibly strong. She was a tall woman, no dainty St. Louis belle, yet he carried her over to a soft patch of grass and placed her on it as if she weighed no more than thistle-down.

Jack slipped off her moccasins and tossed them, then moved to her britches, peeling them with delicious care over her hips and down her long legs. She was even more perfect than he'd been able to imagine when she'd been partially concealed in that bathtub. He looked down at her naked flesh and feasted, letting his hand gently graze her cheek, run down her throat and over her breasts to the concave perfection of her belly, then lower to the black curls at the apex of her thighs. Skipping that ultimate treasure, he glided his hand down her thigh, marveling at the firm, lush flesh, the sweet curve of her calf, the slenderness of her ankle. He could encircle it easily.

"I want to look at you," she said boldly, her eyes meeting his, which were a hot amber color that matched the flames of the campfire.

"Anything to oblige a lady," he said in a choked voice. He felt her study every inch of his body as he yanked off his boots and shucked away his denims. "I'm more than a little the worse for wear."

"Worn moccasins fit the best," Fawn murmured. She sat up and grazed his face with her fingertips, then let her nails glide down his arms, his chest, feeling his hard, scarred flesh, admiring the contrast of pale and dark skin, glistening muscles and that cunning pattern of russet hair that veed down to where his very imposing sex jutted out. It was beautiful . . . *he* was beautiful, her wild red wolf. Dare she touch him there? How could she not?

When Jack saw her hand reaching toward his shaft, he could not believe she would do it. He held his breath as her soft fingers closed around its thickness, then let out a groan of bliss. "Ah, Fawn, sweet Fawn," he whispered hoarsely.

She changed her grip on him ever so slightly, experimentally, uncertain of what she should do. Placing his hand gently over hers, he showed her the motion and she eagerly complied. When he threw back his head and bucked his hips, she felt her power over him. *He belongs to me now.* But when he took her, would she then belong to him, as well?

The thought should have frightened her, but she was too hungry to consider it.

Jack dared not let her blissful ministrations continue. His hand covered hers, pulling it away as his mouth lowered to her lips in another kiss, long, slow, breathtaking. He gathered up fistfuls of her hair and framed her face with it, nuzzling her throat as he pressed her back on the grass. He trailed wet soft kisses down to her breasts, cupping and suckling them as she cried out and arched restlessly beneath him. His hand glided over the curve of her hip while she encircled his shoulders, holding tightly to him. Jack could feel her nails digging into his skin. All signs that a woman was ready—but Fawn Stanhope was not like any woman he'd ever had before.

I have to be certain. She's been through so much . . . Thoughts of Megan flashed into his mind, freezing him for an instant. He pushed them away and looked down into Fawn's fathomless black eyes as he raised his upper body, pausing at the brink of consummation. "Are you sure?" he forced out.

His breath was labored and Fawn could feel his body trembling as he waited for her response. There would be no turning back once she said yes. But she realized that it was the only answer possible. It had been decreed. "Yes, Jack, I'm sure," she whispered, pulling him back into her embrace.

His knee nudged her thighs apart and he positioned himself, then ever so slowly allowed the smooth, hard tip of his phallus to graze the soft, wet core of her. Her body was untried, yet ready. He caressed her without penetrating, letting her get used to the feel of him. Did she know that it might hurt the first time? *A hell of a time to think of that, Dillon!* But she had been raised Cheyenne. In spite of her later education in the white world, Fawn would have been taught what to expect.

"Now, Jack, now," she pleaded, arching up beneath him.

That was all the encouragement he required. "Wrap your legs around me," he commanded. When she complied, he gritted his teeth to hold on, to go slow. She was wet and tight, achingly delicious. "I don't want to hurt you, Princess," he whispered.

"I don't care," she said, tightening her grip on his hips, her heels digging into the small of his back.

He pressed in deeper, feeling her stretch to accommodate him, waiting for any sign she was in distress. But Fawn gave none, only little ragged moans that drove him mad with wanting. When he felt the slight barrier, he kissed her hard and pressed against it until it gave way, then slowly buried himself to the hilt deep within her. And held perfectly still, praying he had not hurt her.

She felt a twinge, not at all what she'd expected, after some of the stories women had told around the campfires when she was a child. There was little pain, only a sense of fullness and of wonder. And a restless craving for more—oh so much more. *He's waiting for me, to be certain he hasn't hurt me.* She twisted her hips and kissed him fiercely, signaling that she was indeed ready to continue.

Then the ride began. He withdrew and plunged in again, feeling a blinding rush of intense pleasure that drove him onward. Fawn quickly caught the rhythm and arched her body to meet his with each stroke. She was a hungry little wildcat, his princess! But she was new at this and he knew he had to last, to make it good for her. He slowed their wild pace, exerting iron will to hold on.

His face was beaded with sweat in the cool evening air. She could see the glistening sheen in the campfire's flickering light. Looking at the hard planes and angles of his rugged features only intensified her craving for her Red Wolf. She framed his face with her hands, caressing it, urging him to continue. The pressure and pleasure built and built until she thought she would grow mad from it. And then she understood why he sweated and knew she did, too. He was waiting for her.

But how could she reach for what was unknown? Especially considering that she never wanted this sweet agony to end? Then the stars and all the planets seemed to explode behind her eyelids as her body convulsed. The completion took her by surprise, robbed her of breath and seemed to go on until she had no sense of day or night, only the man moving deep inside of her. She clutched his shoulders and dug her nails in, riding as if her life depended upon it.

Jack heard her gasp, felt her flesh tighten around him and was almost lost. By sheer force of concentration he held back as Fawn trembled and cried out his name breathlessly, over and over for what seemed like an eternity. Her last shuddering contraction shattered his willpower and he let go. He thought the top of his head would explode with the force of his climax. Never in his life had he felt such an intense release.

As he gasped for breath, a second rifle shot rang out in the distance. It would not be long before Snake returned to camp. He supported his weight on his elbows and gazed down at Fawn's face, trying to read her thoughts. Never easy with any woman. Impossible with this one. In spite of every warning bell of self-preservation, Dillon dipped his head and planted a kiss on the tip of her nose.

Her eyes fluttered open and she met his assessing amber gaze. Was there a look of male possession in it? No, it was she who owned him, she reminded herself. He was her hunting wolf. Still, the warm satiation of making love drugged her senses, slowing down her thoughts. *I can't just lie here looking at him like a mooncalf!* She turned her head away and lowered her lashes as she said in what she hoped was a calm voice, "You'd better get off of me or my cousin will skin you along with those rabbits."

He sighed. "Why am I not surprised that you'd say

something like that, even after what we just shared?" Shaking his head, Dillon pulled out of her and rolled to his side, sitting up.

Fawn felt a keen sense of loss when he did so. She refused to think about it. When she sat up he placed his hand gently on her shoulder.

"Wait a moment," he said.

Fawn watched as he plucked a handkerchief from his denims and strode mother naked to the nearby stream. She was unable to tear her eyes away from his sinuous movements. The firelight gilded him, accenting the contrast between tanned and white skin. Red Wolf—white man? Either way, his scarred, muscular body made her desire him again. This was not the way it was supposed to be! He was a means to an end—the way for her to heal, to rid her memory of Johnny Deuce. Oh, he'd made her forget her fears all right. She knew she would never have those nightmares again . . . or be terrified of a man's touch.

But she wasn't supposed to need Jack Dillon! He was supposed to need her! How would she, the Chosen Woman, control an arrogant Irishman like him? Her troubling thoughts were interrupted when he returned with the wet cloth. He extended it to her and she took it. As he turned his back, she managed to choke out, "Thank you." Her virginal body required a bit of tending. There was only a tiny spot of blood. She could not help wondering if she owed that to his skill or to her own body's resilience.

Ignoring her, he pulled on his clothing and boots. She followed suit. As she sat, slipping on her moccasins, he asked warily, "Are you sorry, Princess?"

She looked at him with cool eyes. "I've asked you not to call me that."

"You didn't mind just a few minutes ago. Stop changing the subject. Just answer my question." She looked so damn regal sitting there. So far above a man like him. He cursed himself for seven kinds of a fool.

Had he called her "Princess" while they were making love? Fawn could not remember . . . but she could remember the way she'd called out his name and urged him on. Her cheeks started to burn but she forced herself to meet his accusing gaze. "What happened between us was ordained by the Powers. I needed to heal myself, I—"

"You mean you needed a man to heal you and I happened to be the only one handy. Glad to be of service. A pity your Creole dandy's in Guthrie," he said bitterly, grabbing the coffeepot and dumping the inky brew into a tin cup. When he took a swallow it burned all the way down his throat.

Fawn could see that she had hurt his pride. "No," she said quietly. "You are the Red Wolf. It was supposed to be you, never Claude."

"I suppose I should be grateful for the backhanded compliment," he snapped, throwing the remains of the coffee into the fire and stalking into the growing darkness.

Fawn heard Snake crashing through the brush a hundred yards or so away. Never in his life had her cousin been so clumsy. Grandfather *had* told him what he was to do. Would there be no end to her humiliation? She walked over to the fire and poured a cup of coffee, lacing it with sugar the way Snake liked. As he drew closer, she composed her features. "Do we feast or eat beans tonight?" she asked when his face appeared at the outer circle of light.

He held up two fat rabbits, skinned and cleaned. "Feast. They're young and tender." He ignored her unbound hair and flushed face as he glanced around the campfire, then asked innocently, "Where's Jack?"

"Attending to nature's call," she replied, exchanging the cup for the rabbits. With a forced smile, she said, "You'd make some woman a good husband—oh, but that's right, you've already tried that . . . several times."

He grinned back, raising the cup in a salute. "Practice makes perfect. I just might give it another go."

"Leave Fee alone. She's a city girl and you'll break her heart."

"Better watch out, you might hurt my feelings, Hellcat. I don't make a habit of breaking innocent hearts, just trying to please difficult women." He studied her with troubled eyes over the rim of the cup.

They both knew they weren't speaking of him and Fee but of her and Dillon.

Fawn turned and laid the rabbits on a rock, then walked down to the stream where she cut two green branches and peeled off the bark. She was proud that her hands were steady. It was a wonder she did not cut herself. Dillon strolled back into camp as she worked the rabbits onto the skewers and set them between two rocks so they sizzled over the fire.

"You'll need salt," he said, digging through the possibles sack Snake had brought until he found a small pouch. Shaking out a bit of salt, he sprinkled it over the meat while she watched. He tried to read her expression in the flickering light. She turned away.

So that's how it's going to be. I'm back to being the troll, the three-legged, one-eyed goat. Rather than look like a lovelorn fool in front of Snake, Jack said, "Good job. I'm starving."

"Oh, I imagine you'll get your fill," Snake replied. He waited a beat and grinned. "Both of you . . . eventually."

They broke camp in the morning with Snake once more carrying the brunt of the conversation. They stopped for a brief rest when the sun was directly overhead and ate some of the chewy jerky, washing it down with water from their canteens, then pushed on. By the time the western sky was etched with brilliant colors, they had reached the banks of the North Fork of the Canadian.

"We can't be far from the council gathering now," Snake said when Fawn reined in and dismounted.

"Then shouldn't there be enough daylight left to reach it tonight?" Jack asked, stopping his bay when Snake also dismounted.

Fawn shook her head. "No, Grandfather told me we must arrive just as the council starts in the morning. We'll ride in at sunrise."

Snake shrugged at Dillon. "She's the Chosen Woman."

"Yeah, I keep forgetting my place," Jack said.

Her heart squeezed and she swallowed hard, but said nothing. All day she'd felt the force of Jack's anger. She had not intended to hurt his pride. But before she could examine her feelings for him, or understand their relationship, she had to follow where the Powers led and obey. Now they wanted her to guide her people away from the evil Josiah Ledbetter represented.

Never before had the burden of her gift felt so heavy as it did at that moment.

They made camp for the night but Snake did not absent himself, sensing that whatever had transpired between Fawn and Jack had left both of them jumpy as jackrabbits and mad as poked rattlers. He attempted to oil the waters by making conversation while they fixed supper. After several attempts to elicit more than monosyllabic replies, he threw up his hands in aggravation.

"Might as well have a palaver with those horses. They'd have more to say."

"You could always tell them why Thelma Sweet Rain evicted you from her lodge," Fawn said tartly.

He gave her a dark look and stirred the beans. They ate in silence until Jack said, "I don't understand how Ledbetter hopes to cheat the bands assembling at this council. If they know he was a crooked agent, why would they listen to him now?"

"Probably because he has Thunder Mouth and others to speak for him," Fawn replied, glad to have something other than her feelings to discuss with Dillon. She had no idea what she felt toward Jack Dillon, or what—if any—his place would be in her life. "Many don't like this land."

Dillon looked around. "Seems to me, around here it's fertile, good for graze, even farming."

"That's just the problem, you see," Snake said. "Cheyenne warriors make lousy sodbusters, not much better stockmen on the whole. They used to range all across the high plains, from Texas up to the Canadian border."

"The buffalo have been slaughtered. Their old way of life is gone. To survive, they have to hold on to this land and learn to use it, not give it away. True Dreamer understands this," Jack said.

Fawn nodded. "Grandfather is a very wise man. He knows what's coming for the People and how they must adapt, but many are blind to the truth. They're angry because the allotment system is even worse than the reservation. It's broken up clans and forced them onto small plots of land."

"Anyone who's not white should be unhappy about the allotment system," Dillon said.

"Indian happiness doesn't count worth a bucket of warm spit, one way or the other," Snake interjected. "We have to play the hand we've been dealt by the Great White Father in Washington. If we don't, we'll lose what little we have left."

On that somber note, they retired to their bedrolls. Fawn made hers a distance from the fire in the opposite direction from where Dillon had laid out his. She felt his eyes on her as she crawled beneath the blankets. *What would it feel like if we curled together like two spoons, if I slept with his arms around me?* The night gave her no answer.

Across the campfire, Jack lay staring up at the canopy of stars overhead, trying to focus on what they would find at the council in the morning. How would he deal with Ledbetter? His thoughts kept straying back to the woman he had made love to last night. He had been the first . . . but would he be the last? *I was crazy to think a spoiled brat like her would settle for a man like me.*

But now she was his, by damn! And Jack Dillon never gave up anything that was his without a fight.

The sun hung like a huge ball of reddish gold in the east when they rose. While the men quickly packed up their meager camp, Fawn retired to the cover afforded by dense brush at the river. There she carefully donned the ceremonial clothing Grandfather had sent with her. It was quite splendid. She recognized the exquisite beadwork of Bright Leaf and Talks Much.

After securing the calf-high moccasins with doeskin thongs, she plaited her hair into two braids and wound them at the sides of her head, securing the heavy circlets with feathers and pins. Then she removed a glass from the pouch and inspected her appearance. Did she look like a medicine woman? To gain acceptance at a council, a woman must look the part and possess strong gifts. Unfortunately, most such women were quite old. Would her voice be heard?

"Grandfather has said," she murmured. That settled the matter. She would trust the Powers and do her duty.

When she stepped out of the bushes, both men turned and Snake grinned. "Whoowee. Grandfather sure intended for you to look like the Chosen Woman."

Dillon said nothing. His amber eyes glowed with an unholy light as they swept from her head to her feet. Then he turned and mounted up.

Fawn ignored him. "I only hope our words will influence the council," she said to her cousin as they followed suit.

They reached the old schoolhouse grounds after a couple of hours' ride. Strung along the twisting banks of the river, lodges stretched into the distance. The trio surveyed the scene as women finished camp chores and men assembled in an open circle around a large fire.

Snake whistled low. "There must be over a hundred lodges. Look, there's Whirlwind's. Last I heard, he and his band were camped down on the Washita, along with some Comanche and Kiowa. The Toad must be brewing some powerful medicine to bring him here."

"More like arsenic," Jack said sourly. "I take it this Whirlwind is one of the unhappy ones."

Fawn chewed her lip. "It's a bad sign that he's traveled so far to hear Ledbetter. As Snake said, he refuses to live on his allotment."

Dillon studied the men assembling around the main fire. He could see a corpulent white man dressed in a dusty black suit and improbable bowler hat, seated on a crude wooden chair that looked none too sturdy to support his weight. "That must be our friend Ledbetter," he said.

"I reckon," Snake agreed grimly. "Imposin'-looking gent, isn't he?" As Jack grunted, the half blood looked toward his cousin. "Are you ready to ride in, Hellcat?"

Fawn sat on Remy with her back ramrod straight. Her face was set, her eyes hard as obsidian. "Ready as I'll ever be."

Chapter Thirteen

*F*awn nudged her paint and the gelding started walking toward the assembly, with Snake and Dillon flanking her. People stared as they drew nearer. Some were merely curious, but others were openly hostile. The inner circle of the assembly was composed exclusively of men. A few woman, most of them old, sat around the outer edges. Fawn knew she must prove herself worthy to be heard. *The Powers will show you the way.* It was Grandfather's voice. She dismounted, feeling assured.

The men draped their gun belts over their saddles under the suspicious eyes of a group of young men guarding the horses in a rope corral. "We come to listen . . . and to speak at your council," Snake said in Cheyenne.

One of them nodded but a second muttered with a sneer, "Who listens to a cut-hair riding with a woman and a white eyes?"

Snake ignored him and stripped off his buckskin shirt, throwing it, too, across his saddle. Several of the others began murmuring when everyone saw the two jagged scars on his pectoral muscles. "He has swung to the pole," one said in awe.

"The sacred Sun Dance has been banned for many years," added another, his eyes wide. Judging by their smooth chests, none of them had performed the ancient ritual of purification and vision quest.

Jack raised his eyebrows in surprise. "You are a walking contradiction."

Snake shrugged. "You can take the boy away from the Cheyenne but you can't take the Cheyenne out of the boy . . . even if he had a white-eyes father. Take off your shirt, too. You have battle scars enough to impress the assembly."

"I trust I may keep my clothing on," Fawn said, trying not to look as Dillon stripped off his shirt. She was all too familiar with every scar on his body.

"I reckon you're decked out just the way Grandfather wanted," Snake replied dryly.

As they made their way through the crowd, Fawn looked around her, as if searching for something. Then her eyes clouded for a moment and she stopped. When focus returned, she pointed her finger at a skinny young man talking with a companion. "You!" He turned to her with an amazed expression on his face. "You have a small son who now plays on a boulder at the side of the river. In a minute he will slip and fall into the water. If you are not there to pull him out, the current will carry him away and he will begin his journey on the Hanging Road to the Sky this very day."

The man stood frozen in uncertainty as a chorus of murmurs rose.

Dillon could understand only a tiny bit of what she said in Cheyenne, but when she commanded, "Go, fool!" he was startled to see the skinny warrior take off at a run, heading toward the river.

"True Dreamer's granddaughter."

"It is said she has visions like his."

"The Chosen Woman."

Those words he understood. He looked at Fawn, whose expression was unreadable. She watched impassively as the young father ran away. Had she known he would do whatever it was she had asked? After Snake translated her words for him, Dillon looked at her. "Did you see that little boy?"

"Yes, but not the way you think," she replied, then continued walking toward the front of the circle.

Snake, who preceded them, whispered something to the men sitting directly in front of them. Everyone moved to make room. Fawn took a seat on the ground with Snake at one side. Jack sat on the other side, watching Ledbetter's reaction to the commotion. If the fat old man was bothered, he did not show it. He did fix his malevolent watery blue eyes on Dillon for a moment. *Yeah, he's the one who sent that bushwhacker after me.*

Jack's consideration of Ledbetter was interrupted when a loud, familiar voice called out in English, "What right do a cut-hair, a white eyes and a woman have to attend the council of the People? They were not invited!" Thunder Mouth's private parts and ear might still be hurting, but his vocal chords were unscathed. He stood scowling in fury, pointing at them.

"Let me make the introductions," Snake whispered to Dillon. He stood up, ignoring Thunder Mouth and Ledbetter, who sat red-faced, glaring with piggy little eyes at the intruders.

Snake turned, looking at all the elders and young warriors seated around the circle. He pounded on his scarred chest and received nods of approval before he spoke. "Many of you know me. I am the grandson of True Dreamer. This"—he paused and made a grand gesture to Fawn—"is his granddaughter, the Chosen Woman."

Many in the assembly murmured low among themselves. Dillon could make out such words as "strong medicine," "True Dreamer" and "his granddaughter."

Snake then pointed to Jack. "This man has been adopted into my clan. He was named the Red Wolf by True Dreamer. The Red Wolf received the scar on his side defending the honor of one of our women—defending it from other white men. My grandfather has sent him with us to listen and to make his thoughts known to you."

Thunder Mouth watched the way the crowd took in Burning Snake's words with seeming approval. Angrily, he spat on the ground. "That old man chooses foolishly." He pointed at Dillon's still slightly discolored eyes and swollen nose. "See my marks on the white eyes's face."

Snake laughed at the huge man as if he were inconsequential as a horsefly. "I have marks on my leg where a rattlesnake bit me when I was a boy. That snake gave warning before he struck. You," he sneered at Thunder Mouth, "struck the Red Wolf without warning. In return, my brother kicked your balls so hard they lodged in your throat. I am surprised you can still speak at all. We would be better spared such loud yapping."

Some in the assembly turned their heads politely or covered their mouths to hide their chuckles. Thunder Mouth was a bully whom few liked. He did not bear the badge of honor of Sun Dance scars, as did the half-blood Burning Snake, nor did he have the scars of honorable combat, as did the white man named Red Wolf. Ledbetter and those standing around him looked on grimly, waiting to see what would happen next.

Snake did not stop. "The Red Wolf gave such a blow to that empty head of yours that you fell senseless to the dirt. Blue Jay and Black White Man threw you over your pony like a sack of corn and saved you then. It would be wise now if you speak no more, Thunder Mouth. The Chosen Woman has a spell that bends a warrior's manroot so no woman can lie with him. She is very angry that you have dared to call Grandfather foolish. She can use the spell to turn your manroot upward. Every time you make water, it will splash into your loud mouth. You will have a new name—Fountain Mouth."

This time the chuckles spread around the council fire. Some erupted into sniggers of open laughter. Thunder Mouth's face burned like an overheated iron cookstove. He clenched his fists, taking a step toward Snake. Jack prepared to jump up as the ugly brute bellowed, "You lie! This squaw has no spells or power at all! Her medicine is bad. She—"

His tirade was interrupted when the thin young man who had run to the river returned. He was dripping wet as he walked through the crowd. Two women followed him. One carried a small boy who was also soaked. "Chosen Woman," the young man cried, "my lodge owes you a life debt!"

Fawn rose and stood before the assembly as the boy's father said, "I am Winter Bear and this is my son Little Turtle. He had slipped from the boulder and fallen in the river just as you said. If I had not caught him, we would be singing the death song in our lodge this night!"

Fawn smiled at the boy, then inclined her head at his father. She knew everyone here understood what this meant. Silently, she thanked the Powers.

"I have a fine paint pony—not so fine as yours," Winter Bear said. "Please take him with the gratitude of my family."

She nodded, regal as a queen. Although she knew this young family could ill spare the horse, it would be rude in the extreme to refuse the gift in return for what she had done. "Thanks be to the Powers, Winter Bear. I am only their poor servant, but I gladly accept the pony. I will give it to True Dreamer. He will be pleased that I was able to serve the People as he has bid me do."

Women and children crowded around her now, murmuring thanks and touching her magical clothing with awe. She was beautiful as a goddess, Dillon thought as he observed the spectacle. As the commotion subsided and the women returned to their seats with their young charges, Snake leaned over and whispered in English to Jack, "I see Fountain Mouth has fled. You think he's become a believer?"

Dillon replied, "She saved Little Turtle from swallowing too much river water. I reckon the bully tucked his tail between his legs and ran off to keep her from making him swallow another kind of water."

Snake laughed heartily, then translated Dillon's remarks into Cheyenne. Now almost everyone laughed openly and hard. One warrior slapped Jack on the back in a gesture of approval. Ledbetter glared helplessly, as Whirlwind translated everything for him. It was obvious that the council was not going the way he had intended.

Fawn whispered to Snake. "Ledbetter looks mad enough to chew a fence post. I think it's time to let him have his say."

"Why has Ledbetter, this 'friend of the People,' called a council?" Snake asked, emphasizing the irony of calling him the Cheyenne's friend. "Do those among us old enough to remember not recall how he stole from us when he was our reservation agent?" he asked scornfully. There were nods of agreement and murmurs rippled softly through the assembly.

Whirlwind, who was seated beside the corpulent white man on the chair, leaped to his feet as Snake sat down. "All things have changed now. Ledbetter is no longer an agent of the white eyes government. But he has strong medicine in their councils. He is here to help us. I will let him say in his tongue, then translate so all may understand why he has come."

With that Whirlwind stood aside as Ledbetter struggled to hoist his fat body from the rickety chair. Sweating profusely, he removed his dusty bowler and mopped his bald head and face, then replaced the hat and began to speak, as his watery blue eyes swept around the assembly. "It is true that I did as the Great White Father bid me when I was your agent. But I am no longer an agent for him. I now see that what I did was wrong—that the allotment system is wrong as well. These small plots of land are not good for the Cheyenne."

Many, including Whirlwind, murmured agreement when his words were translated. Ledbetter continued, "So I have thought much. And talked much with the Great White Father's big council in Washington. This big council has power that is far greater than that of the Great White Father."

He let that sink in before laying out his scheme. "You have been told that you are not allowed to sell your allotments for twenty-five years. But I have persuaded the big council that this is unjust. If the land is yours, I said, why cannot my red friends sell it as they wish? White settlers are allowed to do this."

As many murmured agreement with Ledbetter's words, Fawn whispered in English to her companions, "He is not the one who convinced the politicians in Congress to do anything."

"Yeah, I wonder who he's working for," Snake said.

"This Big Oak Land Company, but who are they?" she asked, looking at Dillon now.

His eyes narrowed on Ledbetter. "Before Smitty, Swen and I are done, we'll find out."

Hitting his stride, Ledbetter smiled and went on. "After many pipes and much talk, I convinced the big council to change its mind. Now, if a group of Cheyenne wish to sell their allotments, they need only make their marks on a piece of paper and send it to Washington." He held up a sheaf of crumpled papers in one meaty fist. "Then they may sell and have money to spend, just as the white man does."

Out of breath and sweating in his wrinkled, hot black suit, Ledbetter waved the papers and then plopped back on the chair, which groaned in protest but miraculously held his weight. The crowd grew excited and many chorused agreement that it was only just if the Cheyenne could sell their land and be paid just as white settlers could.

"Will you give me one of these pieces of paper to make my mark on?" one young man asked.

Another inquired, "How much will my family be paid for our lands?"

Snake stood up and his voice carried over the cacophony. As True Dreamer's grandson and a Sundancer, even though half-blooded, he possessed considerable influence. "Who will buy these allotments so many would sell?" His eyes bored into Ledbetter's.

Grunting as he stood up, the red-faced man spread his hands in a placating gesture. "I searched long in many places for buyers. There is only one who is willing to risk the money. This group of white men will pay twenty-five cents an acre." When some angry rumbles spread around the circle, he said, "That will make many dollars for the Cheyenne, for altogether your great nation has much land."

Now it was Fawn who stood up. She waited until the rumbling arguments around her subsided. When every eye was fixed upon her gleaming white garments and determined face, she spoke. "What will happen after we sell our lands?"

"We will go back to living in our villages as we used to do before the reservation land was taken from us!" Whirlwind said, barely concealing his contempt that a woman was allowed to speak at council.

As the Chosen Woman, she made no attempt to conceal her own contempt for his stupidity. "If the white man's government would not let us live on reservation land before, why would they let us return now? No, all we have are the allotment lands. They are much less than we had, but all we have left. By force and treachery"—she paused and stared at Ledbetter—"agents of the government have stolen our vast reservation lands. We will never get them back."

"We will fight for what is ours!" one young hothead cried out, but even among the younger warriors, there was a sad shaking of heads. Everyone knew they had no chance against the blue-coat armies.

Ignoring the outburst, Fawn said, "If we sell the allotments, or if we sign papers letting white men use them, yes, we will be given a small bit of the white man's money. But how long will that last? Our land will be lost . . . and so will the People. My grandfather has said that if we give up our land, we will follow the path of the buffalo."

When she sat down there was complete silence until Ledbetter whispered something to Whirlwind. The angry warrior said, "The money will last long! It is much. We are not meant to herd spotted buffalo or sow seeds like women! This little bit of land does us no good."

Snake and Jack exchanged a few whispered words as Whirlwind spoke. When the warrior had finished, Snake said, "I ask this council to allow my brother Red Wolf to speak. He knows the white man's world and he has lived among us long enough to understand our ways and respect us. What say you?"

"No!" The bellowing refusal came from the back of the crowd. Thunder Mouth had licked his wounds and returned. Several other malcontents nodded their heads. Some voiced agreement, if not as loudly as the giant. But then one young man across the circle jumped to his feet. "This Red Wolf avenged a Cheyenne woman. He killed white men to restore her honor. I say let him speak!"

"If True Dreamer has named him, he must be worthy," another older man said.

A general murmur of agreement followed as Snake looked around to see if any others would object. "A lukewarm endorsement, but it's good enough," he whispered to Dillon.

Fawn stood up and said, "My grandfather would have the Red Wolf speak. I will translate for him." That settled the matter. Most everyone now nodded.

Jack stood up and combed his fingers through his hair. She could see his nervousness. In a soft voice, she said, "Well, Troll, any white eyes should be able to do better than that fat old thief. You're Irish, for heaven's sake. Where's your silver tongue?"

He raised an eyebrow at her and mouthed the word, "Brat." Then he looked around the circle, studying the faces of the men, young and old. Some were curious, some hostile, most simply . . . unreadable. Many wore traditional buckskin loincloths and leggings but others sported odd assortments of white men's clothing—faded cotton shirts, ragged old denims, even battered Stetsons that were aged and greasy. These were men who had survived great hardship but knew little of the mysterious white world. Few had been educated beyond basic literacy.

How could he convey what he wanted them to understand? "After all they have stolen from you, no white man has the right to tell you what to do with the little bits of land that you have left. I have no words for that." He paused as she translated, seeing the assembly agreed with him. Then he plunged ahead. "But I do have words to say that twenty-five cents an acre for your land is as bad as stealing it from you. Any white man who offers so little is not your friend. He is a thief!"

A murmur went around the crowd and Ledbetter sputtered, mopping his red, sweaty face with a limp gray handkerchief. He tried to get to his feet to interrupt, but Dillon's voice cut him off before he made it. "At twenty-five cents an acre, the sale of one allotment would barely be enough to buy one good pony." He held up one finger on his right hand.

His audience began to see the point he was trying to make. Ledbetter sat back, shoulders slumped, as he, too, read the response of the assembly. Dillon persisted. "Many white settlers get five *dollars* an acre when they sell their land." He neglected to mention that an allotment would have to be improved farmland to command that price. "For five dollars an acre, a settler can buy *twenty* good ponies!"

As Fawn translated, she used all ten digits on both her

hands, opening them, closing them and then opening them again so the audience understood the number. Angry muttering now spread like a prairie fire around the circle, and grew louder. Hostile glares fixed on Ledbetter. Even Whirlwind stepped away from the man he had championed, a look of chagrin and betrayal on his face. Thunder Mouth was nowhere to be seen—or heard.

Dillon waited for the noise to abate. The people were now riveted on the white man whose scarred body bore witness to his willingness to fight for the Cheyenne. True Dreamer had named him. They would heed the Red Wolf. He watched as they seemed to lean forward to catch his every word. "I speak to you as a man who has struggled all his life to obtain money for the power it brings . . . for the respect it brings, just as many of you have hungered after a large pony herd for the same reasons. But I tell you this. Not all the money—not all the ponies in the world are worth your honor. Do not let anyone rob you of that. Do not let yourselves be cheated by white men like this one." He pointed at Ledbetter.

The fat man struggled to his feet, intent on escape, but the crowd now erupted with angry cries and surged forward. His red face blanched with pure terror. Ledbetter started to back away but several men reached him, fists raised. One punched him in his fat gut, doubling him over. He whimpered and rocked, starting to lose his balance.

"Do not kill him! That will only bring the blue coats to avenge his worthless hide," Snake yelled as he joined Jack, pushing through the melee. When they reached Ledbetter, each seized an arm. Snake led the way as they practically dragged the blubbering man toward his horse and buggy beside the old schoolhouse.

Fawn stood in front of them, facing down what had quickly become a mob. She lifted her hands high above her head and began to chant the old familiar peace chant Grandfather had taught her many years ago. Everyone stopped, suddenly silent, mesmerized by her strong, clear voice.

While Snake shoved Ledbetter into the buggy and tossed him the reins, Jack slapped the horse on its rump. The horse took off like a shot. The two men turned back to watch Fawn. An eerie prickling made the hairs on Jack's arms stand up. "She does have her grandfather's power."

"She's the Chosen Woman," Snake said simply, as if that explained everything.

Dillon knew damn well it didn't, but he made no reply.

When she had finished the chant, she motioned for everyone to sit down and the crowd complied. She then nodded to Whirlwind. "Who called this council for Ledbetter?" she asked.

"Thunder Mouth and Black White Man came to our band on the Washita and spoke of it," he replied grudgingly.

She nodded and looked around the assembly. "Where is the loud one now?" She waited until it was apparent that he and his followers had fled. "Who is the most senior of those who have come?"

Looking around him, a wizened old man wearing traditional dress and displaying Sundance scars stood up. "I am Broken Hand, an elder of the People, although not as wise or as powerful as True Dreamer," he said. "What would his granddaughter have us do?"

"Disband this council and leave this place. Ledbetter has evil friends who could send blue coats. They will say you attacked Ledbetter and use that as an excuse to kill you and take your land," she replied. "Return to your allotments. If any white men try to make you sell, refuse. Then come to True Dreamer and tell him."

"It will be as you say," the old man replied, looking around the circle. The Cheyenne nodded and began to get to their feet once more. In a few moments the grassy area around the fire was deserted. Women disassembled their lodges and packed up their cook pots while men rounded up their horses and prepared to travel home.

True to his word, Winter Bear returned, leading a paint pony. "From this day, my clan will heed your words as we have those of True Dreamer." He handed the reins to her.

"You honor me. This is a fine paint mare. She will make strong and beautiful colts for my grandfather's herd."

After the young man had left, Fawn led the mare over to where Jack and Snake were waiting. Along the way, she stopped and spoke with numerous men and women, all of whom echoed Winter Bear's sentiments. When she reached her companions, she noticed that both of them had put their shirts on and armed themselves once more.

Snake grinned at her. "You did Grandfather proud, Hellcat . . . or should I call you Chosen Woman now?"

She smiled at him. "Since I'll always call you womanizer, I guess Hellcat's only fair."

"I don't want any young hotheads to kill Ledbetter," Jack said. "We need him alive so we can find out who he's working for. Damn, I never intended to rile everybody up so much."

"You just told the truth," Snake replied. "No one followed him. He'll get away, but you're right, he's gonna run to his boss and blubber excuses for botchin' his job here."

"He'll meet someone from this Big Oak Land Company," Fawn said.

Jack stared off in the distance where Ledbetter had vanished. "I'm going to trail him and find out."

Snake swung up on his horse and tossed the new mare's reins to Jack, saying, "You were hired to bodyguard the Hellcat. You stay with her. I'll track Ledbetter. Seems to me you need to palaver with your men and see what they've found out while we were bustin' up this powwow."

Without waiting for either of them to respond, he kicked

his horse into a gallop. They did not see his grin. *You need to palaver with your "Princess" too . . . and maybe do something more.*

As Snake rode away, Jack looked at Fawn, his expression unreadable. "You did good, Princess."

His quiet voice made the simple compliment seem intimate, but he was provoking her with that hated name again. Still, he had risked his life to help her stop Ledbetter's scheme. She felt compelled to return the compliment. "You were quite an orator yourself, Mr. Dillon."

He felt her intense black eyes studying him and wondered what she was really thinking. She was back to calling him "Mr. Dillon" again, he thought dispiritedly. "Must be that Irish blarney you summoned up for me," he said dryly.

She cocked her head and looked into his amber wolf's eyes. Then curiosity got the better of judgment. "Does money mean so much to you as you said?"

Dillon stiffened, damning his stupidity. He'd revealed more than he'd intended to this rich woman with her eerie spells and keen wits. "Money is only a means to an end . . . to power—freedom, really . . . to respect."

"From what I've observed, men already respect you."

Dillon laughed harshly. "You're confusing fear with respect. Your father understands the difference. As the Limey, he was feared. When he became Baron Ruxton, he gained respect."

"You're the one confusing the two. Whether Limey or Ruxton, my father is feared by many, but respected by many more. He's earned the respect because of his decency, integrity, honor. You're too young to understand that you don't have to be rich to possess those qualities."

Before she blurted out anything else that revealed too much, Fawn spun around and grabbed the reins of her horse from Dillon. She swung into the saddle, saying, "I'm heading back to the ranch."

Dillon wanted to snarl at the sheer gall of the brat. *He* was too young! "You're a spoiled rich girl, Princess!" he yelled at her back.

She was the most infuriating female he had ever met in his life! He fought the urge to throw his hat on the ground and stomp on it. Instead, he settled for a good long cuss before mounting up to follow her royal highness back to her castle . . . leading the restive Indian pony like a damned stable boy.

Chapter Fourteen

Josiah Ledbetter had never been so terrified in his life. When his buggy nearly overturned as he rounded a sharp turn on the trail to Cantonment, his horse shied and reared up. He struggled to bring the thrashing animal under control until a rider loped up and grabbed the harness with his left hand. The beast shivered but stilled as the man cruelly twisted the bit in its mouth.

"Why the hell weren't you at the council to back me?" Ledbetter demanded. "I was nearly torn to pieces by a mob of red trash, thanks to Jack Dillon and that Stanhope bitch."

"Horse went lame back in Cantonment," the gunman replied. His gap-toothed grin was nasty as he released his grip on the harness. "So you got into trouble with Dillon and his squaw, huh?"

Ledbetter pulled the damp handkerchief from his pants pocket and mopped his face as he scowled at the homely gunman with the bandaged arm. "I wouldn't have had to run for my life if you'd done your job and killed him, dammit! You missed twice. I'm not in the business of paying men who don't do their jobs."

Mordecai Waters's eyes narrowed angrily. "You ain't the one payin' me, fat man."

Ledbetter's red face grew redder still but he dared not

push Waters. "You were told to kill Dillon and you haven't done it," he said defensively.

"I can shoot a six-gun with my left hand as good as my right, but case you ain't noticed, shootin' a rifle takes two hands. Would've had him clean anyways that last time— if'n his squaw hadn't spoiled my shot. You want, I'll kill 'em both. Won't even charge extry," he said, flexing his arm where Fawn's bullet had torn through flesh, barely missing bone.

"No! The last thing we need is for the Limey to come out of retirement to avenge his adopted daughter. Just kill Dillon. Don't touch the girl."

Waters shoved his hat back on his head and a chunk of greasy hair fell across his forehead. "Oh, I got me a score to settle with him. I'll kill him right 'nough." *And then I'll take that uppity squaw of his'n and make her squeal 'til she knows she ain't never gonna be white. Makes no never mind what you 'n your boss want.*

Ledbetter almost told Waters that Dillon and Fawn Stanhope were on the way back to Red Wolf Ranch but then he thought better of it. He didn't trust Waters not to rape the girl after he finished the detective. The vile little gunman was a mad dog they would have to put down . . . once he'd served his purpose and killed Jack Dillon.

Fawn and Jack rode for several hours without speaking. They both dreaded making camp on the trail without Snake as intermediary. Thoughts of what had happened between them two nights earlier filled their minds and added to the tension building with every passing mile. Around noon, they stopped to water their mounts and the horse Winter Bear had given her. Fawn looked at the thick brush and tall grass near the stream.

She took the heavy pouch containing her trail gear and

headed for the cover, saying, "I'm going to change out of these ceremonial clothes. They've served their purpose."

Jack shrugged. "I reckon they impressed the council." As she started toward the bushes, some unchecked impulse made him add, "When I first saw that outfit, I thought it was a wedding dress."

Her head snapped around. "You were mistaken." Her tone was level and cool but she had to force herself to walk slowly and not run from him. Damn the man, why did he spook her this way? It was blasphemy to question the will of the Powers who had decreed that their lives intertwine. But she need not like it . . . even if she had enjoyed his lovemaking.

Jack was leaning up against a tree when she stepped out of the brush in her old clothes with the gun strapped to her hip once more. He tossed aside the stem of grass he'd been chewing and said, "I liked the fancy duds better." In fact, she would look delectable in a nun's habit, but he wasn't going to feed her vanity by saying so.

When she swung up on Remy, Fawn could feel his amber eyes on her. Hungry wolf's eyes. Deep in her belly an answering hunger stirred. She fished out the sack of jerky from the provisions Snake had given her, as if the clenching in her stomach was caused by hunger. After taking a piece she tossed the bag to Dillon.

They chewed jerky and drank from their canteens without talking. After he had finished, Jack asked, "Did you know before we walked into the council that Winter Bear's son was in danger?"

Fawn stared straight ahead. "No. It . . . it just came to me unbidden. Suddenly I knew what I had to do."

"Like the urge to take me to your blanket—or was that planned?"

He'd laid a neat trap. She felt her face burn. "I did not seduce you, or intend for it to happen. The Powers—" She cut herself off abruptly, unwilling to reveal more. "What happened . . . happened," she finished haltingly.

She was holding something back. He could sense it. "You needed a lover to help you overcome the memory of that bastard who hurt you. I was handy. That about it?" he asked, unable to suppress his bitterness . . . and hurt.

"Something like that." She kicked Remy's sides and rode ahead of him. *Liar. You know you'll pay for misleading him.* But there was no way Fawn could bear to tell him the truth. She did not fully comprehend it herself. Or perhaps she simply did not wish to know.

"A good thing that wasn't a wedding dress, then, isn't it?" he muttered. Damn the man who had abused her as a child. If Max hadn't already killed the bastard, *he* would. He wondered if one night of mutual passion and pleasure had erased all her fears. If so, what that would mean? Would she fly into the arms of her callow fortune hunter in Guthrie? Dillon shouldn't care . . . but he knew he was deceiving himself. There was no possibility that he'd allow Claude Beaurivage to touch his princess.

A crooked grin spread over his face. How she'd hate the idea of being any man's princess, least of all, *his!* He urged his big bay on and caught up with her. "No use trying to run away from me," he said when he pulled abreast of her. "I'll be leaving as soon as I deposit you safely at the ranch."

"I'm not running away from you, Mr. Dillon. We have another day's ride together, much as both of us would prefer it otherwise. Or, you could ride directly to Guthrie from here and catch up with your men," she suggested.

"I'm still supposed to be your bodyguard whenever you leave the ranch. If I left you alone out here, Max Stanhope would skin me—and I'd deserve it. I hope he's wired me by the time we get back. He might have dug up some useful information about Ledbetter's associates or Big Oak Land Company."

Glad of a topic they could discuss without personal undertones, Fawn responded, "My uncle Steven may be able to find out something as well."

Dillon considered the older man. "He seems to have tangled with land grabbers and corrupt officials, but as he said, we have to prove Ledbetter's broken the law. What he tried to do at the council was immoral but, unfortunately, not illegal."

"Do you think Claude Beaurivage is involved?" she asked. The idea had been in the back of her mind ever since she'd learned he had taken the registrar's job in Guthrie.

Dillon looked at her, trying to read her face, but it remained impassive. "I don't know yet. He might be. Smitty may have dug up some information by now." He paused a beat, then asked, "Will it upset you if he's guilty?"

Fawn shrugged. "Not anymore. Once . . . I was infatuated by his charm, but if he's part of Big Oak, then he's going to jail. I won't shed a tear."

Jack noted that she did not say whether she'd be hurt to learn that Beaurivage had deceived her and was only after her land. But he decided it best to let that go. "He's a greenhorn. That should make Smitty's job easier."

She nodded. "I may pay my old suitor a surprise visit."

"Stay away from him," Dillon shot back before he could stop himself. Immediately he realized giving her an order was a mistake.

Fawn stiffened, then smiled coldly at him. "Oh, and what will you do if I don't? Lock me in my room—on my own ranch?"

Jack sighed. "Okay, you win. Fly to your swain like a lovesick calf."

If he hoped to deter her with that nasty remark, he greatly underestimated her resolve. "Perhaps I could be a decoy while Smitty scours his office," she mused aloud.

"Too dangerous. We don't know who his friends are. You

could be hurt," Jack replied, kicking himself for starting an argument he could not win.

"We'll see," she replied serenely.

They rode through the afternoon, making good time, stopping only to rest their horses and water them. But as the sun slipped low on the horizon, the usually brilliantly colored sky appeared only an ominous grayish yellow.

Dillon stared at it, then looked over to Fawn, with whom he had not exchanged more than a dozen words since their earlier argument. "Good thing Snake packed a rain slicker on your saddle. Looks as if you'll be needing it—unless you've had a vision about clear weather."

"Any fool can see a storm's coming in," she replied, unwilling to admit to an unsettling prickling on the back of her neck. "It may be a bad one. We'd best find shelter for the night."

They both scanned the trail ahead. The gentle swell of hills undulated, with no place offering protection from the elements. "You traveled this area a lot when you were living with your grandfather. Any ideas about a hidey-hole?" he asked.

Fawn chewed her lip, trying to recall. Then the perfect place flashed into her mind, clear as crystal. "This way," she said urgently, turning Remy westward and veering off the trail down into a shallow swale.

Dillon trailed behind her with the paint mare in tow. They crossed lush grass that surrounded a clear, trickling creek. The horses splashed through the shallow water as they followed its twisting course down a rise. Within half an hour fat droplets of rain pelted them and they quickly unfastened the slickers from their saddles and donned the hot, stiff, tent-like coverings.

The treated canvas was scratchy on her skin but Fawn was grateful it offered some protection when the rain turned to tiny pellets of hail that stung her hands and face as she rode. "There," she said at last, pointing up the slope to an overhang of rock jutting out over the stream. Beneath it a rocky ledge afforded space enough for them and the horses. "We won't be dry, but it's protection from lightning and high enough to avoid flash floods."

Dillon dismounted just as a deep roll of thunder echoed across the prairie grass, followed by a jagged flash of lightning. "Get the hell out of this weather!" he yelled over the din of the storm.

Fawn slid from Remy and led him under the overhang. It was barely tall enough for the three horses. "We won't have a fire," she said, looking around for dry twigs. The restless prairie winds had scoured the rocks bare. Outside the rain whipped furiously, interspersed with icy pellets of hail. "It's going to be a long, cold night."

Dillon grinned, his teeth flashing white in the dim light. "There's always body heat," he suggested, knowing she'd turn him down.

She did not disappoint him. "I don't cuddle with my horses," she scoffed.

"If you catch pneumonia and die, I'll have to explain it to your father."

"Use that Irish blarney. It's worked so far."

"Not that I've noticed," he muttered, as he hunkered down at the back of the overhang and stretched his legs out in front of him. His boots were soaked and he could feel a cold spot where the sole of the right one had come unsewn. He grimaced, thinking about Claude Beaurivage's fury when that hound had pissed on his boots. *I'd like to tie the bastard to a wire fence during a storm like this.*

Fawn had no choice except to join him at the wall. The horses offered a slight bit of extra protection from the wind-driven rain but not much. She'd endured far more discomfort as a child and thought nothing of it. Life back East had made her soft. She sat with her head resting on her knees, pulling the stiff slicker down to cover as much of herself as possible. Still she shivered.

They huddled there for over an hour as the storm raged. Finally, Jack got up and dug Snake's possibles sack out of her saddlebag, going more by feel than sight. Even without the rain, it would be fully dark now. He fumbled with the drawstrings and fished out a couple of remaining pieces of jerky, shoving one beneath her nose to get her attention. "Might as well eat while we can."

She took the meat and pulled off a chunk with her teeth, chewing without saying a word. They ate and drank fresh water from the creek, which had climbed a few inches higher up the rocks as the storm continued. Fawn noticed the rising water but remembered that it had never gotten high enough during hard rain to overflow the shelter . . . in her lifetime.

Jack watched her settle back and curl into a ball, shivering with cold. He wasn't feeling exactly comfortable himself. After another half hour or so had passed and the storm showed no signs of abating its icy whipping fury, he muttered an oath and slid next to her. "You're freezing and so am I," he yelled over the rain. "Take off your slicker," he instructed, pulling off his own. "We'll use them both for cover."

Fawn knew it was the only way to keep her teeth from breaking. They were chattering like castanets. Grudgingly, she complied. The instant his big body touched hers, she could feel his heat even through their damp clothing. He arranged the slickers like a tent all around them, then curled protectively around her, placing his back to the lashing wind. In moments she was fast asleep.

Sometime in the night the storm passed by. When Fawn awakened, she could see the faint gold light of sunrise reflected against the rocky wall in front of her. To her back, Dillon's body fit against hers like a cocoon. She felt her heartbeat accelerate and knew she had to move, but how?

One of his arms lay across her breasts and his leg pinned hers.

He claimed her. Just as the wolf had done in her painting. She suppressed a shiver. *What have the Powers done?*

Jack knew she was awake but he played possum, waiting to see what she would do. She gently removed his arm and wriggled her hips to slip from under his leg. Her firm little buttocks pressing against his groin made him instantly hard. *Dumb mistake, Dillon!* He quickly rolled away from her before she felt the effect she had on him.

"Morning, Princess," he said, gathering the damp slickers up in his lap while he got his body under control.

"I detest that name," she said through gritted teeth. Damn, even unshaven and damp as a mongrel dog, he looked startlingly handsome in the morning light. She watched him comb his fingers through his mop of thick russet hair, shoving it out of his face while he grinned at her. The discoloration around his eyes had faded now and, thanks to Bright Leaf's skill, his nose was even straight. She practically scrambled to her feet to put distance between them when he stood up.

"I don't have fleas and I don't bite," he said levelly.

But she could see the heat burning in those amber wolf's eyes and knew he desired her. An answering hunger gnawed at her but she quashed it. "I suppose you expect me to thank you for doing what my father's paying you to do." The remark sounded petty. Hating herself, she walked to where the horses stood and gathered up Remy's reins as well as the mare's lead.

"You know . . . Princess," he replied, drawing out the last word, "I doubt even Ruxton has enough money to pay any man to put up with you." He led his bay out into the open air and mounted up.

The rebuke stung. "All right. I deserved that. You were most . . . chivalrous last night. Thank you, Mr. Dillon."

He nodded at her. "You're making progress. It didn't even

choke you to say the words." With that he turned his horse and backtracked toward the trail to Red Wolf Ranch.

"Your incompetence is exceeded only by your arrogance!" The man glared at Josiah Ledbetter, whose red face dripped sweat. With a rumpled suit and thinning hair that hung limply around his big ears, he looked like a fat old bulldog left to roll in the mud after a rainstorm.

"I'd a had them convinced to sell if that damned Injun with the Sundance scars hadn't started talking. Him 'n that girl, doing magic tricks and making the superstitious fools listen like she was some Old Testament prophet."

"And Dillon? The protector you were to eliminate?" his boss snapped. "I suppose he had nothing to do with that dog and pony show they put on."

"His being there was Mordecai Waters's fault," Ledbetter protested. "He let that damned girl shoot him! And he missed Dillon twice." It had been his boss who'd hired Waters but Ledbetter was not impolitic enough to say so.

"You were the one who assured me that you could handle a pack of dumb savages. Convince them to sign over their land for a pittance if my friends slipped through a quick approval of the petitions they signed. Now all you've succeeded in doing is alerting Dillon, and in turn Stanhope, to our attempt to purchase that block of land."

Ledbetter's wrinkled suit had dried to his body after he had ridden through a hellish storm. It had taken him two days to reach Guthrie and he was exhausted. All he wanted was a drink and a bed. "I got those sodbusters to sign over their rights, didn't I?" he asked petulantly.

"By telling Waters to shoot their leader—a brilliant piece of strategy. I explicitly instructed you to maintain a low profile. All you've succeeded in doing is calling attention to our dealings before we have the acquisitions in place."

"At least with that kid in the land office, we have someone who can cover for us," Ledbetter said.

"Some functionary from the Department of the Interior came snooping around a few days ago, wanting to see his records. Claude stalled him, but you must learn who this fellow is."

Ledbetter bobbed his head. "I'll do it."

His boss paced across the thick Turkish carpet in the finest hotel suite in Guthrie. Watching Ledbetter eye the remains of his breakfast tray, he felt a wave of disgust wash over him. "Do not stop for food. You can glut yourself when you've accomplished your assignment."

A large window overlooked the broad street below, lined with red brick and native sandstone buildings as befitted the territorial capital. Although it was early morning, already several thousand people were awake and beginning the day's business. He needed to be about his. Then a thought occurred to him. He fixed the fat man with a hard, dark gaze and asked impatiently, "Why did Waters accompany you back here instead of going after Dillon when that powwow of yours broke up?"

"I couldn't take a chance on him. He might've killed Stanhope's Injun kid—or at least raped her. I think we should get rid of him and hire a new gun."

"I've always found him useful, but you're right, we certainly don't want to involve Ruxton by harming the girl." He glanced impatiently at the clock on the wall. "I have a train to catch, but first I'll clarify his instructions."

Ledbetter pried his bulk from the comfortable chair and scuttled to the door, rubbing his sweaty hand across his face nervously. If his boss knew what he was planning . . . He swallowed for courage. "I'll have the last of the land signed up within a week or two—if Waters just does his job and gets rid of Dillon."

"He'll do his job. I'll see to that. Only do yours or I'll be forced to see to you!"

Outside of the large hotel, Snake paced, cursing at the bigotry that had made it impossible for him to follow Ledbetter. The manager and bellman had eyed him with suspicious anger the moment he walked into the lobby. They had intercepted him before he could reach the stairs. Rather than trying to invoke the Stanhope name, he had left quietly. Creating a scene would only alert the fat man to his presence. Snake hoped Ledbetter would emerge with the man behind Big Oak. Who else would he meet the moment he arrived in Guthrie?

Within twenty minutes, Ledbetter walked out. Unfortunately, he was alone. The half blood cursed in English and Cheyenne, then followed the old thief's buggy down Division Street and around the corner onto Harrison Avenue. They passed five blocks of fancy new brick buildings. Snake hoped Ledbetter would meet others involved in the plot. When the fat man turned onto Second Street and headed for what the locals called Government Acres, Snake had a pretty good idea of his destination.

Sure enough, he stopped his rig in front of the registrar's office. "Gonna pay young Beaurivage a visit, huh?" Snake muttered to himself.

If there had been any doubt that his cousin's St. Louis suitor was involved in this mess, this pretty much eliminated it. When he saw Dillon's man Smitty crossing the street, Snake shrugged. The clever little detective could learn a good deal more about goings-on in the land office than he could.

Unaware of Snake's presence, Smitty followed the fat, disheveled older man who'd stepped inside the registrar's office. As soon as Beaurivage saw the "auditor," he dismissed the fat man who walked quickly toward the door. Smitty made a mental note to find out who the stranger was. He looked as if he had slept in his suit for a month of Sundays.

"Good morning, Mr. Beaurivage. I hope you have your records straightened out now. I have a report to make to Washington, you know," he said officiously.

The Creole frowned at the intruder. Savage Americans! He had not even had time for his morning coffee before two of them importuned him. But he had completed the tedious work necessary to fool this odious little bureaucrat. Crossly, he replied, "The books are quite in order now. See for yourself."

Smitty watched the kid dig out a set of ledgers and plop them on the dusty counter. He turned them around and flipped through the one on top of the pile. Odd, for all the grime in the dingy little office, the ledger's interior pages looked fresh as spring. A niggling suspicion blossomed in his mind, but he scooped up the whole batch and took a seat on a rickety chair in one corner. Doggedly he began to go through the entries, beginning with the preceding year.

When Jack and Fawn arrived back at the ranch that afternoon, the rain-soaked ground was again firm and the sun blazing hot. They had ridden hard, making desultory conversation, speculating about what Snake might learn by following Ledbetter, and what her father might have found. Jack told her he had sent Smitty and Swen to the water station to pursue any leads on the bushwhacker. By now Smitty should have had time to do that and still return to Guthrie to look over Beaurivage's land office records.

As soon as they reached the big house, Fee came dashing out, all too obviously looking for Snake. When she saw only Fawn and Jack, her crestfallen expression was almost comical. Fawn was not amused, however. "Damn that man. He's going to break her heart."

"I think Fee can hold her own," Jack said dryly as they dismounted. "Snake's the one who'd better watch out."

"And where is that red divil then?" Fee asked as a worried frown crinkled her forehead. "He isn't hurt, is he?"

"No, Fee. My rascally cousin is fine," Fawn assured her.

"He's trailing a man who's involved in stealing allotments from the Cheyenne," Jack explained.

"Isn't that dangerous?"

Fawn gave Dillon an exasperated look before soothing Fee. "Snake can take care of himself. All he's doing is following a fat old toad, probably back to Guthrie. He'll return in a day or two. Now, I need a bath and some clean clothes. These feel as if they're glued to my skin."

"I'll see yer bath's set up and lay out a dress," Fee replied, only partially placated.

"I'm going to check for news from your father," Dillon said, striding past the women.

Fee looked from his stiff retreat to Fawn's guarded face. "And what happened while ye were gallivantin' all over creation, then?"

"Nothing. Nothing at all."

Fee snorted in disbelief. "A powerful lot o' stompin' and snappin' goin' on over 'nothing at all.'"

By the time Fawn came downstairs, Jack had taken a quick bath himself and sat at the desk in the small telegraph office at the back of the house. She entered the room while he sent a report to the Stanhopes. When he'd finished, he looked up at her. She was cool and regal as royalty again, with her hair fastened in a gleaming bun at the top of her head. Her dress of sheer lawn was a rich sky blue, with a gently rounded neckline that gave just a hint of the bounty inside.

Damn, the woman would look good in muddy burlap! "You clean up pretty well, Princess."

As his appreciative male gaze raked over her, Fawn felt her body grow wickedly hot. "For a troll, you've managed to make yourself surprisingly presentable also. There must be clean water running beneath your bridge," she said with a sniff. Ignoring her impulse to touch the crisp russet hair peeking indecently through his open shirt collar, she asked, "What has my father found out?"

"Nothing much," he drawled. "Only who owns the Big Oak Land Company."

Chapter Fifteen

"Who is it?" she asked excitedly.

"Curiouser and curiouser, as Alice would say," he murmured, gazing at Max's telegraph message.

"Stop trying to impress me or I'll stuff you down a rabbit hole," she snapped, snatching the wire from his hand. "Etienne Pierre Beaurivage!"

"Do you know if he's any kin to dear, sweet Claude?" Jack arched one eyebrow and studied her as she scanned the rest of the wire.

"I've never heard him mentioned, only Claude's Aunt Cee Cee. But this says the man died in a riverboat crash on the Mississippi over a decade ago. How can his name be on the incorporation papers of the Big Oak Land Company? It was only formed in Missouri two years ago."

Dillon shrugged. "Good question. Your father is trying to find the answer now. What do you know about this Aunt Cee Cee?"

"I've never met her. She's apparently some kind of recluse who shuns society. I always suspected Claude kept my family from meeting her because she wouldn't tolerate Mother or me." Why had she admitted that to Dillon? Until now, she had never allowed herself to believe Claude would accept such bigotry.

Jack nodded sympathetically. "To old-monied French aristocracy from New Orleans or St. Louis, Indian blood would never be socially acceptable. That attitude wouldn't change even if they're now poor as church mice and the Stanhopes are rich as Croesus."

Fawn swallowed an angry retort. Jack was right. Claude had only courted her because she was an heiress. Deep in her heart, had she known that all along—or was she being unfair? Perhaps only his aunt disapproved of Indian women. "Father will have no trouble locating her," she said, deciding to withhold judgment until they had more information.

"Do you think she'll talk to him?" Jack looked doubtful.

Fawn shrugged. "He'll find some way." She suddenly snapped her fingers. "Uncle Steven! Of course. He's charming and accepted in the finest circles of St. Louis society. If she won't talk to Father, I bet she'll talk to him."

"Yeah, that would be good." He considered another idea. "This Big Oak outfit was incorporated in Missouri. Peters might have the connections to dig up some interesting information about it, too."

"If only he weren't in Washington now."

Jack turned back to the telegraph key. "Let's see if your father can reach him."

As he worked intently on his message, Fawn stood behind him, letting herself watch the muscles in his back move beneath the soft tan cloth of his shirt. There were scars on that back. He had scars all over his body, yet they only made him more alluring to her. The marks of a warrior. Her fingers had touched them. She clenched her hands into fists. No! He must not have this control over her.

She was the Chosen Woman. The gift was hers—not his. But Grandfather had said their destinies were entwined. Her visions were so much clearer when she was near him. She needed him and that still frightened her. His skill as a lover only made her long for his touch all the more now that she had tasted the pleasure he could give her. If he knew he possessed such power, what might Jack Dillon do with it—with her?

Taking a deep breath, she quietly let it out, unclenching her hands. Her nails had bitten into her palms. *May the Powers forgive me, I cannot let him own me!*

Snake returned to the ranch late that evening. Sergeant Major Higgins was the only one of the older men still awake. When he saw it was the mistress's cousin, he waved the half blood through to the big house. Hearing the commotion, Jack was the first one to come downstairs. He greeted Snake in the foyer.

"I didn't expect you until tomorrow. Where did Ledbetter go?"

"To Guthrie. Ole Toad hotfooted it directly to one of the fanciest hotels in the capital to report to somebody, but I couldn't get past the lobby to follow him upstairs," Snake said in disgust.

Jack understood his friend's bitterness. "What happened after he left the hotel?" he asked.

"He headed straight to the registrar's office. Yup, thought that'd interest you," he said, grinning when Jack's eyes narrowed. "But once Smitty walked in the door, our fancy Mr. Beaurivage shooed ole Toad away. Maybe the kid was afraid of gettin' warts. Funny thing, though. The fat man waited outside, trying to hide in his buggy."

"Like a whale trying to hide in a minnow pond," Jack said. "I wonder what he was doing?"

"My guess is he intended to follow Smitty."

"Somebody—probably the man he met in the hotel—told him to find out who the auditor is," Dillon speculated. "Now Beaurivage has no doubt given him a name he can check. He'll find out it's false and realize we're on Big Oak's trail."

"That'll take a while. He didn't actually follow Smitty.

Hot spring day for all that blubber to spend in the sun. Grease musta started oozing out. He gave up and took off after an hour or so."

"Did you warn Smitty about him?"

"He'd already noticed ole Toad. Pretty hard to miss."

"Did he or Swen learn anything about our bushwhacker?" Jack asked.

Snake shook his head. "A few cowhands in the saloon by the water tower remembered him gettin' shot, but none of them knew his name. Nobody's seen him since."

Jack cursed. "Another dead end."

"Yeah, but I haven't given up on finding who Ledbetter met at the hotel. I went back and tried my luck with the maids. I convinced a sweet Scots lass to tell me—"

"And just what sweet Scots lass would that be?" Fee inquired dulcetly from the top of the stairs. Her eyes were narrowed and her arms akimbo as she glared down at him jealously.

Snake turned and looked up at her with a besotted grin on his face. "Good evenin', Miss Fee. I was only doing some detective work for Jack."

"The two of you can argue later. Right now I want to know who Ledbetter met." Dillon said impatiently.

Fee stomped down the stairs, with Fawn right behind her. Both women had been preparing for bed when they'd heard Snake's voice downstairs. They had thrown on dresses but had not taken time to unplait their hair. They looked disheveled and excited, Fee with jealousy and Fawn with curiosity.

"Tell me what's going on," Fawn demanded, passing her shorter companion on the steps.

Snake quickly filled them in and then continued. "The Scots maid at the hotel only knew that the man on the third floor had left town. Didn't know where he was going. Couldn't even give me a description. She did tell me an older maid named Jenny Tolliver might know, but she just quit her job and took a train west, to live with a married daughter. Take care of a new grandbaby. That's all I've found out so far."

"Whoever this man is, he must be important," Fawn said.

Fee, who had slipped up to Snake's side, placed her hand on his arm and said innocently, "If they hire sweet Scots lasses, why not a fine Irish colleen? Sure 'n they'll be needin' someone to fill the job o' the woman who quit. I'll find out who yer mystery man is."

"It's too dangerous," Dillon said.

"He's right, Miss Fee. I wouldn't want anything to happen to you," Snake agreed.

"Wouldn't ye, now?" Fee practically purred.

Fawn fought the urge to stamp her foot. She'd witnessed quite enough male arrogance and female flirting for this late hour. "I doubt it'll be dangerous for Fee to work at the hotel for a few days and find out who rented that suite. The worst the manager could do would be to fire her. Besides, I'll be in town to watch out for her."

Now it was Dillon's turn to scowl. "And what do you intend to do while you're in town?" As if he didn't know.

Her smile was cool and stubborn. "Why, visit Mr. Beaurivage and congratulate him on his new position, what else?"

Fee had no trouble getting a maid's job at the Grandham Hotel in Guthrie. The harried manager had had three of "his girls" quit in the past week. Though the "girl" whose place she was taking had been a grandmother, Fee bit her tongue and feigned slavish gratitude for the work. Smirking to herself, Fee rolled up her sleeves and began stripping beds. She would be there only long enough to find out whom Josiah Ledbetter had visited.

The day after they arrived, Fawn had a leisurely bath at the same hotel where Fee was working. Then she dressed in her finest spring suit, a leaf green linen with white lace trim on the collar and cuffs of the jacket. Without Fee to fix her hair, Fawn decided to put it up in a simple coil at her nape, a severe style that accented her high cheekbones and slanted, exotic eyes. The final touch was a tiny wisp of a hat with a peacock feather jutting from it.

She pinned it in place, then stared at her image in the mirror, wondering what men saw when she dressed as a white woman. Dillon had found her desirable even in buckskins and had especially liked the ceremonial tunic she'd worn at the council. His hungry gaze was somehow different from that of other white men. She shook off the thought. It was Claude Beaurivage she had to entice today.

Gallant, elegant, aristocratic Claude . . . who most certainly was involved in a scheme to cheat the People. Even if he did not love or respect her, he did desire her. Had her experience with Dillon taught her that? Her instincts had been sound when she'd invited Jack to make love to her. Now that she understood what transpired between men and women, she was no longer a green girl, infatuated with a callow fortune hunter.

But I didn't invite Jack to make love to me. I was compelled to do it. Fawn quickly quashed that thought.

She checked her appearance one last time. Her skin was still paler than it had been when she'd lived under the relentless great plains sun. But there was no mistaking her Indian blood. She was inches taller than most white women, but Beaurivage was taller than most white men. A bitter smile curled her lips. If he were short and she towered over him, would he have courted her?

Suddenly, the image of the gunman she'd shot, his face all twisted with hate, flashed before her eyes. He had killed that farmer and now he meant to kill Dillon. Jack had been right when he'd told her she should have shot to kill, not wound.

He's here, in Guthrie! The vision came into focus. He was walking up Fifth Street just west of the train tracks, heading north. She had to warn Jack!

She pulled her .45 caliber Deringer from her reticule and checked it again, then carefully placed it in a small satin pocket inside the bag, where it would be within quick reach. Then she dashed out the door and down the hallway to room sixteen, where she pounded on the door. "Jack, it's Fawn. The gunman is here!"

Dillon opened the door and yanked her inside, looking up and down the hall before he closed and locked his door. "Another vision?" he asked with a worried frown.

"I just know," she said tightly. "He intends to kill you." Her mouth went suddenly dry when she realized that he was bare-chested. Faint bits of shaving soap still dotted his face.

He grabbed a towel, wiping it clean, then quickly donned a fresh shirt lying on the rumpled bed. As he buttoned it and tucked it into his trousers, he talked. "You go back to your room and lock the door. I'll find that bastard and see what he can tell me about his bosses. Where did you see him?"

She described her vision, then said, "That part of town is rough, really rough. He might kill you this time if I'm not with you."

He turned and looked at her with a half smile. "Why, Princess, I'm touched."

"In the head, you half-wit." She stood her ground when he stepped closer to her, his gaze locked with hers. He smelled of soap and male musk. "How are you going to convince him to talk?"

"With the barrel of a .38 caliber snub-nosed Colt jammed up his nostril, I think he'll be willing enough," he said dryly. "Now, back to your room. That bastard would shoot you before you could even pull your pop gun out of that little bitty bag."

Fawn bristled. "I won't sit like a mouse in a corner, and you won't tell me what to do. I'm going with you."

Dillon knew there would be no reasoning with her. He also knew if she'd had a vision that told her his bushwhacker was on Fifth Street, then he'd find the bastard there. He snapped his stubby New Navy Colt into its clip shoulder holster, grabbed his suit jacket and unlocked the door. As he put on the coat, he ushered her into the hall. Carrying firearms within city limits was strictly illegal. "After you, Princess."

She gave him what she hoped was a scathing look, then swished quickly past him. As they moved down the hall, they discussed her vision.

"Do you know where he's headed?" Jack asked.

"A livery."

"Any idea about time? Ten minutes ago? Now? Or hasn't it happened yet?"

"I'm not sure. I think he's moving now, headed inside a big stable. A run-down place." She was shocked at the clarity of the vision. And that Dillon so readily accepted her word. This was not like her earlier experiences when she'd felt confused and frustrated.

"That's just a few blocks away. Maybe he's checking his horse before catching some sleep, if he's been out carousing," Dillon speculated.

"No. He didn't look drunk or tired . . . just determined."

Dillon felt his gut tighten. He had to keep her out of the line of fire. The Stanhopes had entrusted him with her safety. He made a quick decision as they passed Smitty's room. "Let's get some help." He knocked. "Smitty, it's me." *Please don't have left for the registrar's office yet.*

He practically sagged with relief when the little man opened the door. "What's up, boss?" Then, seeing Fawn beside Jack, he smiled. "Morning, Miss Stanhope."

Jack quickly shoved her through the door and grabbed

her handbag. He tossed it on the bed as he said to Smitty, "Whatever you do, don't let her out of this room until I come back."

"You can't keep me here! I'll have my father fire you." The two men stood, one on each side of her. Smitty looked pole-axed but Dillon blocked the doorway.

"If you get shot, he'll fire me anyway. Then he'll shoot me. At least this way we both stay alive," Jack said.

"I'll scream the house down!"

She opened her mouth and started to yell but Jack clamped his hand over her lips, pulling her across the small room. "Get your handcuffs." When Smitty hesitated, Jack cursed as Fawn bit his hand and drew blood. "Now, man! She wants to face off with that bushwhacker. He's in town. And she's chewing my damned hand off!"

Smitty practically dashed to the chest and pulled a pair of policeman's handcuffs from the top drawer. Fawn tried to kick him when he came in range but her slim skirt pre-vented her from doing much damage. Dillon was having the devil's own time holding on to her. When she arched her neck and turned her head, the feather in her hat nearly poked him in the eye.

She was a tall, strong woman. If not for the restrictions of her clothing, Smitty doubted even his boss could've held her without hurting her. He was used to cuffing men, and even women, when he arrested them, but this was different. She was a rich lady, their employer's daughter! Ducking under the lethal peacock feather, he sighed in resignation as he reached for one slender arm. He narrowly avoided a punch.

Dillon pressed her tightly against his body, holding on with all his strength as she writhed and kicked. It was like wrestling a pond of eels. Smitty reached for her arm again, clamping his blunt fingers around it. He was short, but bulldog strong. Holding her arm, he clicked the metal link around her wrist, but before he and Jack could complete the task, she suddenly stopped struggling. Her teeth unclenched from Jack's bleeding fingers. When her eyes lost focus, Smitty drew back in consternation.

"What did we do to her? Is she havin' a fit?" he croaked.

"She's having a vision," Dillon replied, still not letting down his guard. It could be a trick. "Finish the job. Cuff her to the bedpost."

Jack pulled her to the heavy wooden bed and Smitty clicked the other cuff around the post. "What now?" he asked, not at all certain he wanted to know.

Before Dillon could reply, Fawn blinked, then said in a flat voice, "He's left Guthrie. He just picked up his horse at the livery and rode out. It's too late." She glared at Jack. "We could've had him and you let him go!"

"I'll take a fast trip over there to be sure. Don't let her talk you into letting her go," he said sternly to Smitty.

Shaking his head in consternation, Smitty looked at Fawn and said, "I'm real sorry about this, Miss Stanhope."

Fawn swung around and sat down on the bed. Other than the tapping of her slipper on the floor, she did not make a sound.

Dillon returned a half hour later, cursing. A man answering the description of the gunman Fawn had winged had stabled his horse overnight in a run-down livery, but left abruptly a quarter hour earlier. The owner had no idea who he was or where he was headed, only that he was leaving Guthrie.

Gingerly, Smitty unlocked the metal bracelet encircling Fawn's wrist, as she glowered at Dillon. She stood up, smoothing her skirt. "May I go now?" she inquired tightly.

"You still intend to bamboozle your Creole gentleman?" he asked.

"After I repair the damage you two 'gentlemen' have done to me," she snapped.

Smitty turned to Jack. "We're in the soup now."

"More like elk stew," Dillon replied cryptically. "Tell me about the registrar's bookkeeping."

"It's fake. Oh, the ledgers are real, but the pages inside are fresh white paper. Everything else in that place is covered with a layer of red dust and cobwebs."

"He switched out the real records and replaced them for you. Nothing in those pages will give us a clue about who's buying the land," Dillon said, pacing in frustration.

Fawn, who stood in front of the wall mirror smoothing her mussed hair and repinning her hat, turned to Smitty. "You said the bindings are old. Do they have the official seal on them?" she asked.

"Looked like it to me," he replied.

As she nodded, Jack said, "I can see the wheels spinning, Princess. What are you thinking?" He knew it would involve Claude and would be dangerous.

"If I can touch those books, I may be able to . . . sense something," she said vaguely.

"You mean locate the real records?" Smitty asked dubiously.

Both men looked at her. Dillon was not pleased. "We'll see what Smitty can find in the registrar's office first."

"Very well. I'll have no trouble getting Claude out of the office, so you can break in." She finished straightening her suit, then scooped up her reticule from the bed. When she walked toward the door, her black eyes shot sparks at both men, daring them to touch her again.

Jack sighed. "All right. Try your wiles on Beaurivage, but I'm going to trail along behind you."

"Make it far behind. Missouri would be nice. Don't interfere and don't let him see you. If he does—"

"I know how to do my job, Princess." He turned to Smitty. "Has Swen found anything more following Ledbetter?"

"No word, so far."

Dillon pulled a battered watch from his pocket and

checked the time. "I'll be back here for dinner. Maybe we'll all have something by then."

"Even Fee," Fawn said. "That is, if Snake will stay away and let her talk to the other maids. He's distracting her."

"Ain't love grand," Smitty murmured with a glint of amusement, as he looked from Miss Stanhope to his boss.

Fee stifled the urge to scream. The woman bent over the scrub board, reddened hands busily rubbing a stained bed sheet in harsh lye soap. The head laundress had been working at the hotel longer than anyone. Several of the other maids said she knew all the regular patrons. But Mrs. Marshall refused to engage in small talk. Fee had tried several times to no avail.

"Here are the sheets from room number twelve. It's that messy the place was," she said, dumping a heavy basket of dirty laundry onto the pile on the floor of the cavernous basement wash room.

Without stopping her scrubbing, Mrs. Marshall replied, "If it's so messy, clean it up, girl. Use your hands more, your mouth less."

As Fee turned to go, she heard the laundress mutter beneath her breath, "Damned lazy Irish." *Well, enough time wasted tryin' to get anything out o' the likes o' her!* None of the other servants would talk about the guests on the third floor. But there was still Naomi Smithers, the woman who worked in the office. She guarded the books as if they were Queen Victoria's diary. If Fee could get a look at them . . .

Deep in thought, she took her empty basket and trudged up the stone steps. She turned the corner to reenter the first floor of the hotel. Suddenly a warm body stepped in front of her. The basket dropped from her hand when she collided with a very solid male chest. Fee looked up into Snake's eyes. "Do ye normally go about knockin' the breath from women?" The moment she said the words, her face flamed.

Every time he looked at her, her breath caught, without so much as a touch—and he knew it, the rascal.

"I'm just watching over you. I slipped in the servants' entrance," he said, his grin fading as he touched her pink cheek with his bronzed hand. "I'm worried about you, Fee."

"Are ye now?" she asked coyly, as a plan took shape in her mind.

Jack watched from across the street, hidden behind a stack of flour barrels just unloaded for the grocery store behind him. He scowled as Claude Beaurivage gallantly assisted Fawn into his fancy rig. They had been inside the registrar's office for nearly an hour while he and Smitty took turns sweating in the hot sun. He slipped into the alley. "They're leaving," he said to Smitty.

"You want me to follow them? Beaurivage knows you," the little detective said reasonably. "You could go over those records as well as me."

Dillon seized the reins of his bay from Smitty's hands. "You get inside and search. I guard Miss Stanhope."

Smitty could only nod as his boss jumped on his horse. Fortunately, the street was crowded with people, horses and wagons. Even in his open landau, Beaurivage would be unlikely to notice his boss, especially if Miss Stanhope continued flirting to distract the Frenchman. Smitty waited until they vanished, then walked across the street. There was a rear door and he was very skilled at picking locks.

Jack gritted his teeth as he watched Fawn batting her lashes at Beaurivage, who was sitting far too close to her for propriety. They made a handsome couple, both tall, slender and dark. They were formally educated, from quality families. Fawn was an heiress and once Beaurivage's family had been rich, too. They were everything he was not. But Claude Beaurivage had a mean streak a mile wide and now that his fine family had lost its money, he'd become a fortune hunter involved in criminal activities.

The rig pulled up in front of a fancy restaurant on West Noble Avenue. When Claude jumped down and turned to assist Fawn, Dillon dismounted and slipped into an alley. *Come on, Smitty. Find those records! I've been skulking in so many alleys lately, I'm growing a tail.*

"I was amazed and delighted to see you walk through that door, my dear," Claude said as he helped Fawn from the rig. "I intended to pay a visit to your ranch as soon as I had the registrar's office set in order. I have missed you more than words can express."

Fawn forced herself to return his heated smile. "Was the office in terrible disarray?" she asked ingenuously as he led her into Le Chanticleer.

"*Mais oui*, it was ghastly. Spiderwebs everywhere—even mice! The man lived like an animal in a stable."

As far as Fawn had noticed, the office still wanted a good cleaning, but she only nodded, then gushed, "This is quite the most splendid place I have seen since leaving St. Louis. If the food is as good as the décor, this will be my favorite restaurant!"

"It is French and passable, but certainly nothing to compare to New Orleans cuisine," he said.

"I've never been to New Orleans. Do you have family there?"

"*Alors*, no longer. Aunt Cee Cee and I are all alone in the world, the last of the Beaurivages. But let us speak of the future, not the past. Come, I have arranged a private table for us," he murmured, snapping his fingers imperiously to bring a waiter scurrying.

They were ushered through the crowded dining area down a carpeted hallway into a small room lined with windows that faced out onto a small garden. An octagonal table in the center was set for two and a huge spray of fresh spring lilacs in a crystal bowl filled the air with sweetness. Fawn made a deliberately wide-eyed inspection of everything, murmuring her delight for Claude. He believed he held her in the palm of his hand. Little did he know . . .

After Claude left Fawn at the door to her room and walked down the hall, she murmured to herself, "I feel as if my face is frozen in a simpering smile." How could she ever have been attracted to such a popinjay? He was vain and self-aggrandizing, just as her parents had tried to warn her. Seeing him out West certainly placed him in a new light. Comparing him to Jack Dillon did, too, but she chose not to dwell on that thought as she unlocked the door and slipped inside. She just hoped she had bought Smitty enough time to search the registrar's office for the real land transfer records.

She removed her hat and tugged off her suit jacket, tossing them on the chair, then began pulling the pins from her heavy hair, massaging her aching scalp with her fingertips. After a moment, she rang the bell pull for a maid. The streets were so dusty, she would require another bath. When the maid had filled a tub with tepid water and departed, Fawn repinned her hair loosely on top of her head to keep it out of the soapy water. She dropped her robe and sank into the big claw-foot tub behind a silk screen in the corner of her room.

The tub was as large as her custom-made one at the ranch. She laid her head back against the rim and fell asleep in a moment, exhausted from the stress of spending the afternoon with Claude Beaurivage. He repelled her. His face swam behind her eyelids, but it twisted bizarrely, now cruel and distorted . . .

Jack knew Beaurivage had escorted Fawn to her room. He waited in the lobby until the dandy left the hotel, then quickly rode to the registrar's office to warn Smitty to clear out. His detective was gone and Beaurivage had not returned. Curious about what both Smitty and Fawn had to report, he returned to the hotel.

Smitty was not in his room. "Probably out checking on Swen to find out about Ledbetter," he muttered to himself. He was continuing down the hall to his room when he heard Fawn scream. Drawing his Colt from its shoulder rig, he raced to her door and tried the knob. Ominously, it swung open, unlocked.

Chapter Sixteen

At first, Jack saw no one in the room. "Fawn!" She gave another incoherent cry from behind the screen in the corner. Expecting to find an intruder, he slid quickly around the flimsy partition, his Colt ready to fire. She was alone, deep in some kind of nightmarish trance . . . and she was naked in a large tub full of water.

Jack holstered the Colt and shucked off his jacket. Tossing it on a chair, he crossed the room and locked the door. When he returned to where she lay, still battling her private demons, he knelt beside her, uncertain what to do. Hesitantly he touched her shoulder. Did he dare awaken her?

Fawn saw only darkness swimming in front of her, as if she were drowning. Claude was pushing her farther beneath the water . . . but then it was not Claude . . . who? His face was shadowed, his voice soothing, familiar, just like Claude's had been this afternoon. But he intended evil. She knew it. "Grandfather, help me!" she cried in Cheyenne.

Then a red wolf materialized and True Dreamer's voice said, "This is your spirit guide. Hold him close to you and together you will stop those who mean harm to the People." The waters parted, the menacing figure was gone, and Jack Dillon's face appeared in its place.

Fawn sat up, blinking, her eyes wide open. She was safe in her hotel room, lying in a tub, and Dillon knelt at her side. His hand on her shoulder was warm and firm, yet oddly gentle. *This is your spirit guide* . . . Suddenly she understood. Her gift would work only with him as her mate. She looked into those strange, hypnotic amber eyes and saw the deep hunger in them. He was as helpless to fight what lay between them as was she. He desired her but he did not understand the grand design of the Powers. Fawn did. She no longer feared his control over her because they shared a gift that went far beyond sexual dominance.

Her voice was husky when she spoke. "It seems you have a penchant for watching me bathe, Jack Dillon."

His hand tingled where it touched her soft shoulder. Yet he did not withdraw it. "You screamed. The door was unlocked. I thought someone was in here attacking you," he said raggedly, unable to tear his gaze from hers. Her eyes glowed like polished ebony. He could drown in their depths.

Fawn blinked and her lashes fanned over her cheeks as she tilted her head and arched her back. She heard his sharp intake of breath as the tips of her breasts lifted above the bubbles on the water. He desired her . . . but she was now willing to admit that she desired him just as much. The thought no longer frightened her. Acting instinctively, she raised her arms and wrapped them around his neck, drawing him to lean over the tub and kiss her.

And kiss her he did. His mouth was voracious, slanting over hers, commanding that her lips open and let his tongue enter. Now she knew this intricate dance. It was breathtaking, robbing her of thought. She surrendered to the hunger and gloried in it. When she twined her tongue around his, he let out a low growl and buried his hands in her hair, pulling out the pins that held it on top of her head. He framed her face, pressing soft, wet kisses on her eyebrows and lids, trailing them across her cheeks and down to the pulse points that thrummed beneath her ears.

When the tip of his tongue rimmed one ear, she moaned low, her wet fingers digging into the hard muscles of his shoulders. His shirt was soaked, the soft cotton clinging to his body. Using her grip on him as leverage, Fawn leaned forward and pressed her bare breasts against his chest. She could feel his heart pounding and knew her own answered in rhythmic cadence.

Jack's hands cupped her breasts, working the nipples between his fingers until they were hard nubs. Then his hands moved lower to her tiny waist, lifting her until she stood in the tub. He suckled each breast. "You taste of lilacs," he murmured as he moved from one to the other.

Her hands dug into his thick russet hair, so like the red wolf's pelt. "My totem, my protector," Fawn whispered. She trembled with pleasure, shivering in his arms. Palms splayed, she slid her hands down his back and began tugging at his shirt, pulling it from his breeches. "You . . . have the . . . advantage," she said breathlessly. "Let me see you naked!"

Jack heard the urgency in her voice and realized how insane this was. Yet he found it impossible to let her go. It was as if a force so powerful it defied imagining had brought them together. Even though he could not form the conscious thought, he knew what he was going to do . . . what he must do.

Fawn felt herself being swung effortlessly into the air, bubbles and droplets of water flying. She wrapped her arms around his neck and nibbled kisses down his throat. He carried her around the screen and walked to the bed, then placed her on it. When he released her she gave a hoarse cry of impatience.

"You wanted me naked," he said as he began to strip; all the while his hungry wolf's eyes raked up and down her glistening body.

Fawn felt a thrill race from her head to her toes, making her dizzy with desire. She watched avidly as he shrugged out of his shoulder holster, then practically tore off his soaked shirt and yanked his feet from his boots, using the jack at the side of the bed. Her fingers kneaded the damp sheets while she watched the play of muscles rippling over his hard, scarred body.

No warrior who had undergone the Sundance ever looked more powerful, more splendid! Yet it was her mystic vision, not his, that bound them together. It was right. It was good, oh, so good. Her eyes traced the subtle patterns of russet hair that ran from his powerful chest, veeing down to where his sex jutted from the dark hair at his groin. She took it in one hand and slid her fingers up and down, gently squeezing as he had taught her. She reveled in the way he threw back his head, the sound of his breath hitching, the sight of his fists clenched at his sides until the tendons in his neck stood out as he gritted his teeth.

He muttered an inaudible oath, then whispered raggedly, "Princess, you'll be the death of me yet."

"Life, my Red Wolf, not death," she whispered in return. "Now, come lie with me." *Yes, he is mine!*

When he sank one knee into the mattress and the heat of his thigh touched her hip, she raised her arms, eager to welcome him. Her thighs parted as he covered her. She raised her legs and scissored his lower body between her thighs. When his heat and hardness probed carefully at the core of her body, Fawn arched up to bid him enter. This time there was no hesitance, no going slowly and waiting for her to accept his fullness.

"Now, please, now," she begged, unaware of the words she uttered.

Feeling her wetness, her beckoning heat, he plunged smoothly, deeply inside her, burying his shaft to the hilt. Jack seated himself, struggling to hold on. Her body fit his like no other ever had. Somehow, he knew deep within him that no other woman ever would. She was his now. Red or white, rich or poor, formally educated or self-taught, nothing mattered but that he keep her.

When she rolled her hips in invitation and dug her nails into his back, he began moving, setting a pounding rhythm that she matched stroke for stroke. But then he surprised her, rolling them over, still joined, until she straddled his hips. He looked up at her startled expression and suddenly felt exuberantly happy. Her breasts stood up, nipples taut and pebbled, her belly sleek and concave, her hips lushly curved.

"I like the view," Jack murmured, reaching up to cup a breast in each hand. He arched his back and drove deep inside her once more.

Fawn quickly realized that she now rode him. A wave of amazed pleasure washed over her as she raised her hips and then impaled herself, catching the new rhythm, glorying in the heady sense of power it gave her . . . that he had freely offered. She threw back her head and let her hair brush his thighs, closing her eyes to concentrate on the buildup of pure sensation.

The soft tingle of her heavy mane of hair touching where they were so intimately joined almost undid him, but he clamped his hands over her hips, slowing her desperate race. "We have time enough. Make it last," he murmured.

If only she could! But Fawn knew what she must have now, and like a starving woman she took it, letting the glorious contractions spill over her in succeeding waves until he followed her over the brink. Feeling him swell even harder and pulse so deep inside of her brought her to a new cataclysm of release.

She screamed out his name before he pulled her to him and covered her mouth with his. As their passion slowly subsided, she could feel his chest rumble with a low, wicked chuckle. She raised herself up and dared to meet his eyes. "What amuses you?" she asked, still too dazed to be angry.

"We would have had half the bellmen and maids in the hotel pounding down the doors if I hadn't stopped your yelling." He looked over at the entry, bemused but not much concerned at the possibility. "Fee would probably lead the charge."

Her eyes opened wide as the haze of passion dissipated. A picture of Fiona Madigan bursting through the door to find them locked together in a tangle of bedcovers took its place. "That isn't the least bit funny," she said crossly, starting to climb off him.

Jack pulled her down into his embrace once more and planted a light kiss on her lips. "Shhh, no one's coming. Listen, you'd hear footfalls down the hall if they were." He did not want to relinquish her or the warm feeling that surrounded him when he held her. When she snuggled against his shoulder, he sighed and caressed her long, silky hair.

Fawn thought she heard him murmur, "What have you done to me, Princess?" just before she fell asleep in his arms. A tiny smile curved her lips.

As darkness fell, Smitty and Swen knocked on Dillon's door, eager to exchange information with him. Hair still wet from a bath, Jack opened the door and let them inside. "Miss Stanhope and Miss Fee are waiting down the hall with Snake," he said, slipping into the sling of his shoulder holster.

"Once we find out who's behind this, are we gonna let the women stay here?" Smitty asked uneasily.

"We would not want ladies in the line of fire," Swen seconded.

"We'll get them safely back to the ranch if we have to hog-tie them to do it," Dillon said grimly. Judging from the look of horror on Smitty's face, he knew the little detective was recalling their battle with Fawn in his room. *If only he knew . . .* "Let's get this palaver done."

Fee opened the door for the trio, who entered Fawn's room. Everyone exchanged greetings, then took their seats around a small table. If any of the men saw water stains on the carpet and floor, none said anything, but Fee's sharp eyes had noted everything when she arrived, including the hastily made-up bed's damp coverlet. After two days as a maid, she was all too aware of the messes people made in hotel rooms . . . and often the reason why, but she kept her speculation to herself.

She took a seat next to Snake and listened as Dillon said, "Let's begin with this." He extracted a telegram from his shirt pocket and laid it on the table. "The baron's old friend Steven Peters has given us a bit of help."

"I thought he was on his way to Washington," Fawn said.

"Your father had him tracked down when dear Aunt Cee Cee refused to speak with anyone, even an English peer. Stevens called in an old debt and wired a friend from Louisiana, a state senator who used to work in Washington. The senator's from a very wealthy Creole family and knew all about the Beaurivage clan."

"Then Claude lied. There are more relatives in New Orleans," Fawn said, her lips thinning.

"Only one. His paternal grandfather's elder sister. She explained to the senator that there were two male cousins left on their decaying family tree."

"Claude told me that he and his aunt came to St. Louis when he was seventeen," Fawn said.

Jack nodded, tapping the wire. "True. But the elder cousin made his way north over a decade earlier. Etienne Beaurivage."

"The fella killed in the riverboat explosion?" Smitty asked.

"Or maybe he's still alive and set up the Big Oak Land Company," Jack replied.

"You mean he faked his own death in an explosion?" Fawn asked, turning over the possibilities in her mind.

Dillon speculated, rubbing his chin. "It's also possible he is dead and someone has assumed his identity."

"Then how did Claude receive his appointment as registrar?" Fawn positively hated herself for falling for the odious dandy's oily charm.

Dillon replied, "According to your father, through a couple of state representatives who're sitting in jail right now on bribery charges."

"Claude has no money to bribe anyone, so it must've been—"

"Our mystery man who's behind Big Oak, whoever he is," Jack said. He looked at Fee hopefully. "Any news about the identity of the man Ledbetter met here?"

"Whoever he is, the fellow might as well be one of the wee people, the way he vanished," Fee replied with a dramatic sigh. "But I just might be able to get his name . . . with a bit of help." She glanced at Snake, giving him a frustrated look. "That is, if I can have some cooperation from a certain 'snake charmer.'"

"I told you it's too dangerous, Miss Fee. You could end up in that fancy new jailhouse." Snake outlined Fee's plan: He would lure the hotel bookkeeper from her office while Fee slipped inside and went through the register. "It could take hours to figure out who checked out just after Ledbetter left the hotel. Besides, I doubt a starchy spinster like Miss Smithers would fall for my charm," he said ironically.

"I've been considering how to get the guest register," Jack said. "Late tonight Smitty and I will pick the lock to her office and take a look."

Swen, who had remained silent until now, spoke. "I have been following Josiah Ledbetter. This morning, he slipped in the back door of a building in what the locals call Government Acres. He appeared very nervous. Once he was inside, I could not tell which office he had entered, so I waited outside the main door until he reappeared. Then I went in and made inquiries. He spent the best part of an hour with the assistant to the territorial secretary, Pierre Despres . . . from Missouri."

"You find anything out about this Despres?" Jack asked.

Swen checked his notes. "He is from a place called Florissant in Missouri. Other than that, I do not have anything yet."

"Florissant is an old French fur trading town just north of St. Louis," Fawn said. "I'm certain my father will be able to find out more about him."

"Good work, Swen. I'll wire the baron. Now," Dillon said, turning to Smitty, "I assume you didn't find the land records in Claude's office."

"Nothing but cobwebs and clutter," the little detective replied with disgust.

"But the bindings on the fake ledgers are genuine?" Fawn looked at Smitty, who nodded. Turning to Jack, she said, "You wire my father about this Pierre Despres and Smitty can take a look at Miss Smithers's register. I'll pay another visit to Claude's office."

"What good will that be doin'?" Fee asked, frustrated to have been cut out of the action. "The Frenchie's not about to tell ye anything."

Fawn's smile was smug. "Who said he would be there?"

"Won't he be calling on you again tonight?" Jack asked.

"I'll arrange to be prostrate with the most terrible headache. Considering that he was raised by vaporing Creole women, he'll never suspect," she replied, arching an eyebrow to indicate how superior she felt to ordinary women.

Dillon grunted in displeasure. "How are you going to get inside—kick down the door?"

Snake grinned. "She might just do it, but I reckon I can force open one of those back windows without too much trouble. Don't worry, I'll keep her out of trouble."

Fawn realized her gift required Dillon's presence. "You go

with Smitty," she said to her cousin. Then grudgingly, she turned to Jack. "You may accompany me if you wish."

Dillon gave a sardonic chuckle. "How magnanimous of you, Princess. Claude may not be the brains of the Beaurivage family, but he's mean. I don't want him to catch you going into a trance holding those ledgers."

Fawn's eyes flashed at him. "Don't be ridiculous. Even without you, I'd be in no danger. Claude would never work at night—he's far too lazy." She resented his implication that she was some carnival fortune teller. Going into a trance, indeed!

"Since I doubt you could jimmy one of those swollen old windows, I know you'll need my help." Jack pulled a lock pick from his shirt pocket and held it up. "Opening a door quietly is a fine art. Ask Smitty." The little detective's face turned red, but Fawn's attention remained on Dillon.

"Why does it not surprise me that you, too, are an expert at sneaking into locked rooms?" she asked dulcetly.

He stared hard at her. Would she like to announce to the assembly what they had done this afternoon? "Not every door is locked," he said. "But the registrar's office will be. I'm going with you. It's settled."

"I'll be Smitty's lookout," Snake said, noticing the sharp exchange between Fawn and Jack. Something was in the wind.

Oiling the waters, Swen interjected, "And I will return to the boardinghouse where Ledbetter stays. Perhaps he will meet this Despres again and I can learn more."

"Good, then we all understand our assignments?" Dillon asked.

Everyone but Fawn nodded agreement. When his eyes fixed on her, she lowered her lashes and said, "Yes."

Fee observed the interchange between Jack and Fawn. It was clear that their mutual antagonism had shifted to another plane. The attraction that had simmered since the day they met had now clearly broken the surface, but the water was still very choppy indeed. Fawn's gaze had repeatedly shifted to Dillon, then quickly darted away whenever he looked at her. She was not flirting. She was trying to conceal her feelings. His for her were obvious—pure male possessiveness.

Fee had been suspicious since they returned from that Indian powwow. After watching them now and seeing that rumpled bed, she was sure. They had become lovers. She felt relieved that Fawn had finally recognized the Frenchie was a shallow fortune hunter. But did this new maturity extend to understanding that a man such as Jack Dillon only gave his heart once?

He was in love with her. What troubled Fee was whether or not Fawn returned that love—or was she using him for some mysterious purpose decreed by her grandfather and those Cheyenne mystical spirits?

Jack sent a wire to the Stanhopes while Fawn dispatched a note to Claude, canceling dinner that evening because of her indisposition. She would meet Jack at the back door of the hotel at midnight. Swen returned to watching Ledbetter, and Smitty went to his room to get some sleep before he and Snake met downstairs when the hotel quieted down.

Fee lay in wait for Snake when he left the hotel, motioning him into a small room filled with mops and pails. Closing the door, she asked, "Have ye given much thought as to how yer gonna keep anyone from seein' the light from Miss Smithers's office after the two of ye sneak inside?"

Snake grinned at her. "You still want to play detective, don't you, Fee?" He bent down and brushed the tip of her nose with a light kiss. "Best if you keep that pretty little thing out of harm's way. If anything happened to you, it'd plumb break my heart."

"Would it now?" she replied, moving closer to him, smiling a saucy grin.

"Yes, it would." The amusement left his face. "I'm not much of a catch—a half-breed who's already had three women leave him, but—"

"Cheyenne women must all be fools if they'd let the likes of ye get away. I'm many things, Snake, but a fool is not among them." She boldly pressed her body against his and rested her hands on his chest, feeling his heartbeat accelerate. That was a good sign. She tiptoed up, wrapping her arms around his neck, pulling him down for a real kiss. "Be warned, I intend to marry ye."

"I stand warned, Fee," Snake murmured just as their lips met. She was so tiny, his delicate Irish rose, but he knew there was an inner core of toughness to Fiona Madigan. It might work out this time.

They kissed with bright passion, his practiced yet tender, hers the earnest bloom of first love. Then Mary McGee, an Irish maid who had befriended Fee, shoved open the door and exclaimed, "Ooh, I'm that sorry, I am. I won't tell a soul!" she whispered, red-faced as she plunked her empty scrub bucket on the floor and backed out of the room.

"You think she's telling the truth?" Snake asked. "I don't want you hurt by gossip."

Fee smiled wickedly and caressed his cheek. "There'll be no harm done to me reputation, but yer sweet to be concerned. After we receive the blessings of the Church, who's to condemn us?"

Snake's face grew harsh. "If you marry a 'breed', plenty will condemn you."

Fee gave a snort of disgust. "As if I'd be concerned with the likes of those. Just ye remember—bein' a stubborn Irishwoman, I'll allow no divorce."

He threw back his head and laughed. "I've never actually been married inside a church before." Then he sobered. "That will make all the difference. That . . . and you."

When he lowered his head for another kiss, she pressed

against his chest. "No more until we've taken our vows and received the blessing," she said sternly.

"You drive a hard bargain, woman," Snake replied, releasing her with a grin on his face.

"That I do, and here's the rest o' it. I'll be with ye tonight when Smitty picks that lock." When he started to protest, she placed her hand over his mouth. "The hotel employs a watchman to make night rounds. I can distract him a wee bit better than ye, can't I now? Or would ye rather cosh the poor old sod on the head?"

She had him there. All Snake could do was give in.

Swen adjusted his position on the roof of the bordello next door to Josiah Ledbetter's boardinghouse on the southwestern edge of town near the train tracks. Even in a young city, this area was already looking seedy. There were no fancy brick or stone buildings here. He thought the sleazy atmosphere fit Ledbetter's character quite well.

He could see both entrances to the building from his vantage point, so the Toad could not slip away unobserved. Ledbetter's buggy was at the livery across the street. Swen's own horse was tethered and ready to ride behind the bordello. He had taken the extra precaution of paying one of the boys who worked there to watch that no drunken thief tried to steal the valuable animal.

The sun had set hours earlier and darkness shrouded him. Once Swen had made certain Ledbetter was taking dinner inside, he'd slipped into the kitchen and asked the boardinghouse owner to wrap up several sandwiches for him. Glad of the extra money, she had even thrown in a thick slice of lemon pound cake. In spite of her run-down establishment, she was a surprisingly good cook. He finished off the last of the food and prepared to wait out the night.

Just as he had become resigned to sleeping on the hard tar and gravel roof, a tall figure walked down the alley and opened the back door of the boardinghouse. Before he stepped inside, he looked up and down the alley. Swen recognized him even before the moonlight struck his face. Claude Beaurivage!

Swen had to find a way to listen to their conversation. Carefully he climbed down the back stairs of the bordello, making a shushing sound to the boy guarding his horse. He followed the Creole in the back door and up the stairs to Ledbetter's room. The hallway was dark and deserted. Everyone was settled in for the night. He hoped for no interruptions, since the narrow hallway offered no place to hide. He could see the light glowing from beneath Ledbetter's door.

By the time Swen reached it and pressed his ear close enough to hear their soft voices, the conversation had already begun.

"He wants to know how your courtship's progressing," Ledbetter said with a snicker.

"She is thrilled that I have come so far into this wretched wilderness for the sake of love," Beaurivage replied with a nasty laugh. "I have only to ask her to be my wife and that ranch will be mine."

"Not yours, Big Oak's. Remember who's in charge," Ledbetter said. "Why aren't you with her tonight?"

"She's indisposed." He muttered an expletive in French. "As if a savage in silk such as that one possessed a lady's delicate constitution. To think I must actually give my name to her!"

"Just be damn sure she'll take it."

Swen waited, hoping to hear more, but just then footsteps echoed on the front stairs and he recognized the cook's voice. She was extolling her boardinghouse's virtues to a new tenant who had arrived late. Cursing silently, Swen moved cat quick for the back stairs before she saw him and sounded an alarm. Should he return to watching Ledbetter from the roof, or would it be a better idea to follow Beaurivage? He debated as he slipped out the back door.

Inside, Claude made an affronted protest at this fat American's audacity. "I told you she would leap at the chance to marry me!"

Ledbetter ignored the dandy's posturing and pulled a thick sheaf of papers from a well-worn leather satchel on the table. "Here are more land transfers to add to the records. Injun brats, old redskins and a whole passel of sodbusters." His chuckle was ugly. "Whites signed off their mineral rights real easy after Mordecai talked to them. As to the Injuns, well, orphans and old crones, they just make their marks for a few dollars, and Big Oak's got a lease for ninety-nine years."

"Convenient that the old ones die and the children can so easily be shunted away in orphanages," Claude said dryly. "Does Mordecai take care of that as well?"

"That's none of your business. Just be sure you got the records in a safe place where that fellow pretending to be an auditor from Washington won't find them."

"*Oui, certainement,*" Beaurivage snapped, irritated to have his judgment questioned. "Has he found out who this vile little American works for?"

"Doubtless the Englishman and his redskin wife," Ledbetter said curtly, still smarting from his tongue-lashing about the failure to kill Dillon. Waters's intimidation had enabled him to complete the last of the land deals. Now it was time the vile little killer dealt with the detective. Focusing on the immediate bane of his existence, he shoved a telegram at Beaurivage. "Read this wire. You're to act on it immediately."

Claude read the telegram, then crumpled it in his fist. "This is preposterous! I would have to stay up the whole night."

"You should've thought of that before you wasted the

evening dallying with those whores next door," Ledbetter snapped. "I sent for you hours ago." He poured himself a stiff glass of whiskey but offered none to the lazy young dandy. "We need another half dozen pages of fictitious entries in your ledgers to keep it looking up to date. Who knows when a real auditor might show up? Stanhope has the power to make that happen."

"I am too tired to do it now. I will begin—"

"You'll begin right now!" Ledbetter hissed, seizing the crumpled telegram from Claude's hand and shoving it in the kid's pretty face. "Get your fancy ass back to that land office and start to work!"

Chapter Seventeen

Dillon jiggled the pick carefully in the lock while Fawn kept watch up and down the alley behind the land office. Somewhere a hound yapped listlessly. The dark and quiet were otherwise unbroken. "You're taking too long," she said.

"Will you be quiet?" he whispered. "I have to concentrate. I'm out of practice."

Fawn glanced nervously up and down the alley. "Good grief! Aren't you any better with that probe than—" Her jaw snapped shut with an almost audible click. "Er, I mean just wiggle it a little and—" She stopped again, horrified.

"That's your job," Jack muttered, intent on his task.

Fawn's cheeks felt like lava now. "You vulgar—"

"Shut up, Princess!" he whispered as the lock snicked. "Ah, got it."

The door creaked when he opened it and entered. Fawn followed, then shut it softly behind her. After Jack's eyes adjusted to the dim moonlight filtering in from a front window, he made his way across the room and closed the curtains. Fawn found a small gaslight near the back of the building and turned it on, adjusting it very low.

"Smitty said the ledgers were on that shelf," Jack said.

She quickly walked over to it and began going down the stacks until she found the most recent dates. Once she removed them, it was apparent that the interior pages were stiff and white, new, while the binding was much older. "Claude has really spent some time reworking these books," she murmured.

"You recognize his handwriting?" he asked, realizing he sounded jealous.

"He has sent me more than a few billets-doux in the past year," she said dryly. "He has good penmanship."

"His only redeeming trait," Jack replied caustically.

To salve her self-esteem at being led on by a fortune hunter, she muttered, "He was an excellent dancer. Make that two good traits."

"Yeah," he snapped. "Well, your sister Della says that in addition to counting, Numbers can still dance like a ballerina. Now forget about Beaurivage. Can you tell anything from the bindings?" He resisted calling her "Princess." No sense in aggravating her further when she needed to concentrate. He watched Fawn kneel and press her palms against the binding of one volume.

Why did she ask me to come with her instead of her cousin? The question niggled at the back of his mind. He thought about that afternoon in her room and a faint smile touched his lips. His princess was prickly as a cactus, but lush as a rose. Both had thorns . . . He was warned.

Claude rode down the alley from Ledbetter's boardinghouse, taking a shortcut to the land office. When he turned the corner he saw two horses and noticed a faint light coming from inside the building. Was it that vile little auditor sneaking back to search for the real records, or was it simply a thief? His face was a grim slash as he pulled a .32 caliber Smith & Wesson from his pocket and dismounted. If the thief was armed, he would slip away and summon the authorities.

When he moved silently to the side window, he was

amazed to see Fawn kneeling with one of the forged volumes in her hands while Dillon stood with his hand on her shoulder. The detective's callused fingers were buried intimately in her loose hair. The look of possession on Dillon's face was unmistakable. Beaurivage cursed savagely to himself. How dare she choose this Irish trash over an aristocrat such as he!

Only with great difficulty did he stifle the impulse to shoot them both. Turning on his heel, he walked stiffly back to his horse, considering how he could gain control of Red Wolf Ranch—and avenge himself on that red bitch. He toyed with an idea that he had been considering for several days already . . . kidnapping her and forcing her to marry him at gunpoint. Then he would have the ranch and a fortune at his disposal.

He mounted up, trying to come up with a plan. Once he had a legal marriage document in hand, she would die in an accident—or perhaps he could arrange for Dillon to take the blame for her murder. Claude smiled grimly, thinking about how he would use the scheming little savage first. He had always intended to get his fill of what she had denied him while he danced attendance on her back in St. Louis.

Of course he would not tell Etienne what he had seen tonight. His cousin had only been using him to obtain Red Wolf Ranch for the advancement of his precious Big Oak Land Company, his empire. Well, dear Etienne could have that damnable empire without Stanhope's land. Claude would hold that briefly until he could find a buyer, preferably in Europe. He could buy time by turning over those incriminating land records to Etienne's minion, the odious Ledbetter. The land transfers no longer had any value for him.

Claude rode directly to the small house he rented at the outskirts of town. A dreary hovel, but it had an overgrown yard with weed-infested flower beds, a perfect place to hide valuables. Without digging up the whole yard, no one would ever find the land records. He reached into a large peony bush and felt an oilskin-wrapped bundle, then dusted it off, all the while keeping watch. Everyone on the quiet street was asleep, all the houses dark.

How could he separate Fawn from her Irish lover? Perhaps he could use these documents to trick Dillon into going after Ledbetter. That could provide a useful distraction while he continued his courtship of Fawn until an opportunity arose to take her captive. But as he walked toward the back of the house where his horse was tethered, he reconsidered. No, Dillon was too dangerous.

Claude required someone to kill the Irishman before he could kidnap the savage. As much as he detested dealing with Mordecai Waters—was in fact afraid of the violent little gunman—he realized that he needed him. Waters would forsake Etienne and Ledbetter if the price were right. Beaurivage smiled at the irony. Waters had been hired by his cousin to kill Dillon. Claude would just make him a better offer to finish the job.

Just as he was mounting up to ride back into town, he saw two riders dismount down the street and steal toward his place, using bushes and outbuildings for cover. Whoever they were, they boded ill for him. Claude hid behind the fallen-down shed at the back of the house, waiting. When he recognized Fawn and Dillon, his heart began to pound. "What in God's name are they doing here!" he muttered to himself.

He watched in disbelief as they moved stealthily to the front of the house. Fawn headed directly toward the overgrown flower bed. It was as if she knew precisely where the package was hidden. Dillon stood guard while she stooped down and rummaged through the peony bushes. Claude dared not chance their catching him with the incriminating documents. Silently he led his horse away. When he was far enough distant, he rode back into town as if the hounds of hell were after him.

From a clump of tall weeds at the front of the house, Fawn and Jack checked the dark place for any signs that Claude was stirring. "I don't think he's here," she said.

"Could be out carousing. This isn't exactly home sweet home for a dude like him," Dillon replied. "But let's be very quiet, just in case he's asleep." He drew his weapon and let her lead the way as he covered her, watching the windows of the shanty while she knelt in front of the peonies.

"They're not here," Fawn said, crestfallen. "But there's a place hollowed out in the center of this bush. Judging from the feel of the soil, it was disturbed recently."

"Somehow Claude must know we're on to him, but how?" Dillon said, scanning the silent street.

Fawn stood up and became suddenly lightheaded. Jack grabbed her. "Hey, Princess, what's wrong?"

She shook her head. "He was here. Just now. Watching us from behind the shed," she whispered hoarsely.

"Are you clearheaded enough to shoot?" he asked. When she nodded and pulled out her gun, he said, "Good. Stay behind the bushes." He slipped silently around the opposite side of the house.

Realizing what he was doing, she followed, watching for Claude as Jack made his way to the shed. She found him kneeling in the dirt, cursing. "You were right. Not much light, but these tracks feel fresh." He stood up and listened, but the only sound he could hear was a hound baying at the full moon. "Where would he take those records?"

"To this Etienne Beaurivage . . . or to Ledbetter," she replied.

"Swen's watching Ledbetter. If Claude shows up this late, he'll know something's wrong."

"But if he goes to our mysterious dead man . . ."

Dillon shrugged. "Nothing we can do now but go back to the hotel and see what Smitty and Snake have found."

"No one on the third floor checked out that day," Snake said to Jack and Fawn as they sat around the table in her large room.

Fee poured glasses of cool water for everyone as the men reported, then lingered behind Snake's chair with her hand on his shoulder when she'd completed her task.

"Whoever was in the room that Ledbetter visited was just borrowing it, apparently," Smitty said, tossing his lock picks on the table angrily.

"And there I was with the night watchman, playing whist for nearly two hours," Fee said, wrinkling her nose with distaste. "Mr. Nevins is not friends with the likes of a bathtub."

"What do we do now, boss?" Smitty asked Dillon.

"Get some sleep. Swen's been out all night watching Ledbetter. He'll need to be spelled in the morning," Jack replied.

Smitty nodded, then asked, "Do you think the Frenchie's left Guthrie with those records?"

"What good would that do him or any of the others?" Jack reasoned. "No, he has to stay here to keep up the pretense of registering legitimate land transfers. But he's moved the real records for some reason we don't know yet." He looked at Fawn, a question in his eyes. Damn, he hated having her around the vicious bastard!

"I'll send him a note in the morning, if he doesn't leave a message for me. He'll be suspicious, but I might still be able to get some information out of him."

Jack reconsidered. "It would be faster—and safer—if I had a talk with him."

"No, that would drive all of the conspirators into hiding. Let me try my luck with Claude again." She drummed her fingernails on the table for a moment, then added, "Maybe my father will wire some news."

After everyone else had slipped from her room, Dillon remained behind. "What's going on behind those big dark eyes?" he asked, tilting her chin to face him.

"I should've sensed Claude watching us. I'm not certain my powers—"

"Your gift is working, Fawn. I'm trained to watch for anyone spying on me and I didn't realize he was there, either," Jack said. "We were just focused on finding the records once you saw the exact place they'd been. You were right about where they were."

Fawn was not willing to accept her mistake. "Yes, but wrong about them still being there. Perhaps Grandfather would be able to guide me."

Jack considered how much he would prefer that she be at the village rather than close to Beaurivage, now that he knew they were on to his duplicity. "True Dreamer knew about Ledbetter's powwow up north. You want to ride out for a visit?"

"No, you misunderstand. Sometimes Grandfather comes to me while I'm asleep."

"Are you saying you want to sleep alone?" he asked, trying to sound neutral when all he wanted to do was carry her over to the bed and make love to her.

She looked into his eyes and smiled. "No, I'm not saying that at all." She wrapped her arms around his neck and began to nibble small kisses at his collar. "Remember? It's my job to wiggle."

Swen had almost decided he'd made the wrong decision, staying to watch Ledbetter rather than following Beaurivage. It was the middle of the night. Then the fat man came out the front door and headed for the livery. In moments his buggy pulled out, heading east down Perkins

Street. Swen stayed well back. Outside of a few saloon patrons staggering their way home, the streets were deserted. Ledbetter had been acting jumpy as a grasshopper ever since he'd fled that abortive council up north.

When he turned his rig north on First and pulled behind a small house, Swen knew who lived there. He smiled grimly, having checked the city directory for the address of Pierre Despres, the assistant to the territorial secretary. "I may just have found our mysterious Etienne Beaurivage," he said triumphantly.

Jack glanced at the wire from Max Stanhope. He'd left Fawn sleeping peacefully around daybreak, returned to his room and cleaned up, then gone to the telegraph office. When Swen caught up to him in the hotel lobby, they moved to a quiet alcove where no one could overhear their conversation. His detective explained the night's events.

"I could not get near enough to overhear what Ledbetter or Despres said, but both men were very uneasy, that much was clear."

Dillon said, "You can bet whatever they talked about, they're up to no good. We may just have found our 'dead' man. According to this wire, Pierre Despres arrived in Florissant, Missouri, a year or so after Etienne Pierre Beaurivage died in that riverboat explosion. Despres is a Creole, but other than some vague rumors about his being originally from Louisiana, his whole life seems to have begun when he arrived in Florissant."

"You believe Despres is using a dead man's name on the land documents?" Swen asked.

"Or Beaurivage didn't die in that explosion. He and Despres are one and the same," Jack replied.

"What do you want me to do now?"

"You're asleep on your feet. Get some rest, then start

searching for our bushwhacker. He may have come back to Guthrie." He explained how they'd narrowly missed catching the gunman, omitting handcuffing Fawn to Smitty's bedpost, a debacle he was certain the little detective would never confess to a living soul.

Swen nodded. "Just give me a couple of hours and I'll start looking. He was a mean one. I doubt carrying a scar from Miss Stanhope's bullet in his right arm has improved his disposition."

"Be careful," Dillon warned. "If you locate him, report to me. I have a personal score to settle with him."

When Jack knocked on Fawn's door an hour later, she was dressed to ride. Scowling, he asked, "Where are *we* going?"

"To the Cook farm. A rider from Grandfather brought me a message just after you left. Some white men are digging up the Cooks' land and showed the widow and her sons a paper saying it was legal."

Jack muttered as he scanned the note. He looked up at her, fixing her with a level gaze. "You *were* going to wait for me." It was not quite a question, but she breezed by it, simply nodding.

"Let's go."

Mordecai Waters stared at the French dandy as if he'd grown two heads. "You want me to kidnap that Injun bitch? On whose orders?"

Claude chafed under the cold gray eyes of the gunman, unnerved yet determined to see his plan through. He had come to the cheap bordello Etienne had mentioned as a favorite lodging place for Waters. The room was as tawdry as the frizzy-haired slattern Waters had dismissed when he knocked on the door.

Ignoring the gunman's questions, he said, "Whatever my cousin is paying you, I'll double it."

Waters gave an ugly laugh, revealing moss green teeth. "You ain't got a pot to piss in, Frenchie. Where you gonna get that kind of cash?"

"If that Injun bitch signs marriage lines, Red Wolf Ranch will be mine to sell as I please, making me one of the wealthiest men in the territory."

"I reckon your courtin' ain't goin' so good, huh?" Waters said with a nasty smirk.

Claude's face heated. He ached to slap that ugly sneer from the gunman's face, but dared not. "She is a savage and has taken up with a man more suited to her own base blood—the detective you were hired to kill." The accusation of failure hung between them.

"So now ya need me to put the fear o' hellfire in the slut—and Dillon? My guess is ya expect me to git him outta the way first."

Claude nodded stiffly. "Just so. My cousin, Ledbetter, the lot of them be damned. I'm offering you a chance to make a good deal of money and leave this ugly wilderness for the white trash and savages to fight over."

Waters rubbed his aching right arm, calculating. "Ya know I got me a score to settle with the squaw."

Beaurivage felt assured. He had been almost certain his offer would entice greedy scum such as this. His old arrogance returned. "Once I have the title to the ranch, it would be my pleasure to turn her over to you. I intend to be a wealthy widower quite quickly," he said with an icy smile. *And I will see that you take the blame for the death of my beloved bride!*

"Jus don't think ya can cheat me," Waters said.

"I would never be so foolish. You kill Dillon. As soon as you've done it, we'll abduct the girl and ride for the Kansas border. I know a judge in Pleasant City who used to work for my cousin until they had . . . ah, a misunderstanding. He will marry us quite legally."

"What about her daddy, that Injun-lover, Stanhope?" Waters asked, as if the thought had just occurred to him.

"You'll have enough money to leave the country if you wish," Claude said. This matter would have been so much simpler if Fawn had remained infatuated with him, but now he was forced to betray Etienne—and use Waters. "This is your only chance to avenge yourself on the Limey's red-skinned daughter," he cajoled.

When Waters grunted agreement, Claude breathed a silent sigh of relief. "Be careful ambushing Dillon. Do not miss this time. When you've finished with him, we will slip into her room and drag her away. Best if all of this is done at night."

Waters scratched his head. "This here judge ya got up Kansas way, what if the bitch won't sign his papers? Once't she does, she's gotta know she's dead."

"I have considered that also." His smile was malevolent. "There are too many people she cares about, a couple of worthless old men, an impertinent Irish serving wench, the savages living on their allotments . . ."

"She signs or I start killin' them," Waters said with an evil grin.

Claude reevaluated the gunman's intellect. Perhaps Waters was not quite as *stupide* as he had first thought. "Just so."

The following day was waning when Fawn and Jack neared the Cook homestead. On the ride they had discussed various reasons why the farmers had been forced to cede mineral rights to Big Oak, for this digging was surely related to it.

"There's been oil discovered in some of the eastern lands, mostly Cherokee," Fawn said. "And there are coal deposits on Choctaw land. But this isn't the right sort of soil for either."

Jack studied her, continually amazed at her intelligence, which matched her striking physical appearance. "And how do you know so much about what kind of land yields oil or coal?"

"While I was being tutored in St. Louis, my favorite science was geology. I want to see where those men Mrs. Cook described are digging."

"If there's something valuable around here, it could help True Dreamer's band," Jack said.

Fawn frowned. "If the whites don't kill them to get it, the way they did poor Mr. Cook."

After a brief conversation with the widow's sons, Fawn and Jack rode about two miles and located the place the Big Oak men had worked. The laborers had abandoned their task and made camp at a stream a few hundred yards away. Carefully skirting them, Jack and Fawn sneaked to the churned-up earth.

She dismounted while he kept watch. Kneeling, she scooped up a fistful of crystalline soil and examined it in the dimming light. "I can't tell anything here, but I'll take some samples back to the ranch where I can look at my textbooks. If I can't figure it out, there's an assayer's office in Guthrie."

He waited while she moved around the wide area where the digging had taken place, putting soil in small canvas sacks. When she was satisfied she had enough, they rode to Red Wolf Ranch, arriving after the dinner hour. Bronc and Clyde were delighted to see them, as was Lula, who set out a feast of cold sliced beef, potato salad and chocolate cake.

After they ate, Jack explained what had transpired in Guthrie, while Fawn went to the large library and pulled down several heavy volumes on earth sciences. After the old folks went to bed, she was still working. Jack brought her a steaming cup of Lula's rich black coffee. "Find anything?"

She took the cup, smiling up at him. "Thank you. I'm about to nod off," she said, taking several sips. "I think I know what Big Oak is after around here. Gypsum."

Dillon looked blank. "Isn't that some kind of soft mineral—used in sculpture, that kind of thing?"

"Hydrated calcium sulfate, to be precise. It's used to make plaster of paris. In its raw form, it's often soft, like in these photographs." She shoved a large book around so he could see the pictures.

"Hardly seems as if it'd be worth killing a man for. It isn't as if it were gold or oil."

"Nothing is worth a human life, but it may become valuable soon. If there's enough of it around this area—and from what I can tell, there is—and if a man named Augustine Sachett receives the patent he's applied for."

"Who the hell is he?" Damn the woman, she was a walking library!

"An inventor of sorts. He's been working on what he calls Sachett Board, hard sheets of building material that could replace the time-consuming process of plastering in houses. The key ingredient is gypsum."

"You mean, he'd have ready-made plaster walls for workmen to put together," Jack said, considering what that might mean in terms of building across the country. "That explains why Big Oak would send killers to get the mineral rights out there."

"My father will want to pursue this."

They walked down the hallway of the silent house to the small telegraph room. Fawn dictated a brief note to Max Stanhope and Jack sent it. When he had finished, he stood up and looked at her. "No one here should know we're lovers, Fawn . . . I mean . . . I . . . aw, hell, I—"

She placed her fingers over his lips, then took his hand, whispering, "Everyone is asleep. If you slip from my room before dawn and muss up your bed, my reputation will remain intact."

"I don't like sneaking around."

"Do you mean you don't want to make love to me tonight?" she asked lightly, testing the water.

His eyes burned in the dim light. "I mean I want to marry you so we don't have to sneak around." He blurted out the words, then felt his face heat. *What a fool, Dillon. Proposing to the boss's daughter and you without a penny to your name!*

Her full lips curved into a delighted smile. "Hardly a romantic proposal, but I just might accept . . . that is, if you can make me as happy tonight as you have before . . ."

Jack grabbed her shoulders and drew her into his arms, kissing her ravenously. "Is this a test, then?" he murmured, too hungry to consider the consequences of his rash proposal.

"One I hope is less painful than the Sun Dance," she replied.

The Limey might kill him, but at the moment, Jack did not give a damn.

She returned the kiss, twining her arms around his neck and rubbing her hips against the decided bulge in his denims, eliciting a growl from him. After several more scorching kisses that left them both breathless, she took his hand in hers and led him from the cramped office. When they reached his room, she paused and whispered, "Your bed makes a larger testing ground."

"Like Custer, is this my last stand?" he asked, feeling uneasy.

"Last stand, white eyes? I certainly hope not." Her voice was husky with desire.

His unplanned proposal had been deadly earnest, but her responses were a little too flippant . . . too in control . . .

Chapter Eighteen

Jack stared transfixed, his earlier unease dissolved. The soft glow of moonlight limed her long, slender body like a caress. She pulled off her moccasins and tossed them aside with incredible grace, then unlaced her shirt and tugged it over her head, letting it drop from her fingers to the floor. He could see the dark shadows of her areolae through the delicate lace of her camisole and his breath hissed out, yet he remained motionless, watching intently.

Fawn could not read his expression, but even with the moonlight at his back she could see the glow of those amber wolf's eyes. Jack's desperate desire emboldened her. This was the way things were fated to be. Her Red Wolf belonged to her . . . and she to him. Her fingers quickly unfastened her buckskin breeches, but then she pulled them slowly over the flare of her hips, giving a subtle twist of her pelvis so they fell to her ankles. When she kicked them away and stood dressed only in knee-length lawn drawers and lace camisole, she lifted her long braid over her shoulder and began to unplait it.

"Let me," Jack finally managed to whisper, stepping closer, his fingers aching to comb through the straight black silk of her hair.

She held out the half-undone braid to him. He reeled her in, tugging gently on it until they faced each other with only inches between them. As he unplaited her hair, he held it up, letting it spill like a black satin curtain around her shoulders. When he had completed the task, he buried his hands in it, holding great fistfuls as he cupped her head and rained soft, wet kisses all over her face. Then his mouth centered on hers and she pressed her body to his, opening her lips for his invasion.

"Your skin is so soft, so smooth and lovely," he breathed against her throat as his hands glided up and down her back, lifting her buttocks with his palms and pressing her lower body against his.

Fawn rolled her hips, glorying in the hardness of his erection straining to be free. She needed to touch his skin, to taste of him as he was tasting of her. She unfastened the buttons of his shirt and pulled it open, nuzzling his chest. When her tongue lashed delicately against a flat male nipple, he expelled an oath of sharp pleasure. She peeled his shirt down, marveling again at the corded muscles of his shoulders and arms. Then she busied her fingers opening his breeches and reaching inside to touch the heat.

Jack almost tore the beautifully sewn camisole as he freed her breasts for his hands to cup and his mouth to suckle. When he felt her hand grip his shaft, he reached between them and stilled her. Raggedly whispering, "I can't wait," he pulled her drawers off, tearing them as they fell to the floor. She kicked them heedlessly aside while he lowered his denims, then lifted her by her bottom until her open legs could wrap around his hips. Backing her against the door, he entered the wet satin of her body in one long, powerful stroke.

Fawn dug her nails into his back and joined the pounding rhythm as he moved in and out of her with increasing swiftness. Her own hunger raged out of control and almost immediately she felt the rippling contractions spiraling through her whole being, leaving her panting and breathless, yet not spent until she felt him tremble and pulse life deeply within her. They stood for a moment, breathing hard, heads resting on each other's shoulders.

Jack murmured indistinct love words and she answered him in a polyglot of Cheyenne and English. Finally, realizing that he was holding her entire weight, she unlocked her legs and slid free, uncertain if her knees would buckle beneath her after their wild exertions. When she felt her feet touch the cool wooden floor, she took a deep breath, not yet daring to release her steadying hold on his shoulders as she leaned against the door for support.

"You're still dressed," she murmured, startled when she realized his denims rode low on his hips and he had not removed his boots.

"It's not because I was planning a quick getaway," he replied, stepping over to the boot jack beside the door. She stood with her camisole bunched around her waist, wearing nothing else, watching him undress with rough precision. "Now, the bed," he said, once he was finished.

Her eyes widened in surprise to see his manroot standing once more at hard, definite attention. He grinned at her, that old familiar, arrogant Jack Dillon grin that she had loved to hate when first they met. "You can do this again?" she asked.

"You were right. No last stand," he replied, closing the distance between them. He watched in approval as she shrugged the camisole over her head, admiring the way her breasts stood proudly erect with dark nipples puckered.

Fawn walked to the bed and stretched out on it, her body languid with invitation. "You look like the Queen of Sheba in storybooks," he murmured in awe.

"Come be my King Solomon," she said, one eyebrow wickedly raised. His powerful horseman's legs covered the distance to the bed. She watched his muscles ripple as his magnificent body reached out to hers.

They fell in a tangle of covers and rolled across the over-sized bed, once again letting the wild impulse of desire over-take them as they kissed and caressed. But this time when he poised to enter her, he stared down into her eyes, willing her to look up at him. "We make it last this time," he whispered, like a sweet promise.

Fawn nodded, desperate to feel their joining yet wanting it to be unending. "Yes," she replied softly as he penetrated her with exquisite slowness, then held them both motionless for several moments.

The savoring was heady, limitless as stars in the night sky, the knowledge of what would inevitably follow all the sweeter because they could defer it and soften the keen edges of de-sire. Fawn let him lead her through the act of love, resting between blinding strokes of ecstasy, the sweet heat coursing through her body like a song.

When they had utterly sated themselves, they both let go and glided over the abyss into a completion that was utterly different from any she had known . . . and every bit as unique for him as for her. On that distant plane, they floated, out of time and space, in a universe that belonged only to the two of them, now become one . . .

Several hours' ride away, the old man sat before the glow-ing coals of his late-night fire and stared into the orange-gold flickering light. "You are complete from this moment on . . . even though you do not yet know it."

True Dreamer smiled serenely when a red prairie wolf howled in the distance.

"Claude's lost his mind. He left the land records with the old crone who runs the boardinghouse where I'm staying," Josiah Ledbetter said nervously to his employer, watching the man's face but unable to read his expression. Ledbetter held up the moldy oilskin pouch. "Don't know what he was thinking."

"Why, if he came to your door in the middle of the night,

were you not there to inquire?" the deceptively dulcet voice inquired.

"It isn't my fault—I'm entitled to a night with a whore, same as any man." Ledbetter tried to sound righteously indignant. "He's your kin, not mine." Daubing sweat from his eyes, he plopped his girth onto a flour barrel. He hated being summoned to the various odd places his employer chose. This time it was the back room of a general store recently purchased by Big Oak.

"Did dear Claude leave any message regarding where he's gone?"

Ledbetter shrugged. "Nothing. Registrar's office is closed. You think he's trying to pull a double-cross?" he asked uneasily.

"That would be unwise . . . most unwise. Tell Mordecai Waters to find him at once."

Ledbetter's sweat was sour now, pouring into his eyes, making them burn as he replied, "I, er, tried to find Waters. He isn't in town either." Ledbetter watched as the implications sunk in.

"I told him to stay where he was." Ledbetter's employer's tone was cold and deliberate. "Now may I suggest that *you* make every effort to find my cousin." It was a command, not a question.

Ledbetter rose so quickly he overturned the barrel. "Yes, sir, I will."

"About last night . . ." Jack paused as Fawn leaped smoothly onto Remy and looked down at him.

"Yes?" she asked, waiting while he mounted his bay. They rode out of the stables, waving good-bye to Clyde and Sergeant Major. By the time they left the ranch, Bronc was already out on the range, overseeing spring roundup. They headed back to Guthrie where Ledbetter, Despres and Beaurivage were under surveillance.

"I asked you to marry me, didn't I?" he asked idiotically, wanting to bite his tongue. How stupid did that sound? Of course he had.

"Do you want to take back the offer?" she asked, her voice quiet as she stared straight ahead.

"No! I mean . . . hell, yes, I want you to be my wife, but you own all this," he gestured around the lush rolling grassland dotted with cattle. "I intend to have a big agency one day, but I'm just getting started. I can't offer you—"

"I was raised on an impoverished reservation when Good Heart—Clyde Campbell—was the agent. He struggled to get the government to give us rations so we didn't starve. I'm used to considerably more deprivation than you." She spoke more sharply than she had intended. Would the money with which she had been blessed come between them because of his foolish male pride?

"You might be surprised," he replied curtly, thinking of Megan and the orphanage.

She studied his profile and the set of his jaw. "You know about Grandfather's band. Tell me about how you grew up."

Her voice was soft but compelling. How could he refuse? How could he resurrect memories that were so painful? Jack swallowed and plunged in. "My father was a Chicago policeman. When I was eight years old and my sister Megan was ten, our parents died in a cholera epidemic. We were set out on the streets by the tenement landlord. I tried to take care of Megan." His breath hitched raggedly.

"You had no family to take you in?" she asked, hearing the pain in his short staccato bursts of narrative.

"Papa and Mama immigrated from Ireland as newlyweds. There was no one in America."

"But you mentioned nuns who taught you," she prompted hesitantly when he volunteered nothing more. She was afraid to ask about his sister.

"That was after . . . after I was caught stealing food for us.

Lucky for me the cop at the precinct house knew my da. He sent us to the Daughters of Charity. They did their best, but Megan . . . I don't want to talk about it."

He looked away but before he did, Fawn saw the raw anguish in his face and remembered the fleeting vision she'd had of a girl being attacked. It must have happened to his sister while they were on the streets. "I think Megan and I have something in common."

"No, you don't. You're alive. She's dead." His voice was brittle.

It was apparent that the subject was closed. Fawn bit her tongue and let it pass. They would have time once these land grabbers had been stopped. They rode in silence for several hours. Finally, discouraged by his stiff, distant manner, she closed her eyes and concentrated, hoping for some insight that would help her heal the pain buried so deeply inside him.

She thought about the vision she had seen of the young white girl who lay cowering in the corner of a filthy room. "Your sister . . . did Megan have carrot red hair?" she asked.

He turned swiftly to face her, his eyes wide with pain. "How could you know that?"

"I saw her—when . . . when we fell to the floor in your car aboard the train . . . you were furious because I'd accused you of being a rapist." She swallowed for courage, then looked at him and said quietly, "Now I understand the reason for your anger. A man attacked her when she was only a child. You restored her honor by killing that man, didn't you? That is the way of the People."

"White society doesn't see it like that," he snapped. "She was damaged goods, soiled, worthless to them. The nuns were kind, but everyone knew. Those people who didn't condemn her pitied her. My sister grew more lost and hopeless every year. By the time she was fifteen, she left the orphanage and went back to the streets. She became a prostitute. One of her customers killed her. I hunted him down and killed him just like the sixteen-year-old boy who'd first raped her."

"When the sixteen-year-old raped her, you couldn't have been more than—what? Eight, nine?" He made no response, only stared straight ahead. "But, he must've been twice your size," she persisted.

"Yeah," was the terse reply.

Fawn felt the awful pain engulfing him. "You were still a boy when you avenged her murder. Your courage and sense of honor are very strong. I understand why the Powers chose you to be my totem, the Red Wolf who has guarded me since childhood." She stared gravely at him, expecting her praise to bring him out of the dark place frozen in his heart. Surely he understood the link between them. After all, it had been ordained by the Powers.

"You saw me in visions when you were a girl?" he asked. A creeping sense of dread snaked up his spine, tightening his gut.

She looked at the peculiar expression hardening his eyes to cold yellow. "You've seen the way you complete me—the way I'm learning to control, to focus my gift now that we—"

The long-suppressed pain and rage caused by Megan's fate, newly awakened, fused with his fearful uncertainty about Fawn's motives for becoming his lover. "Now that you've lured me to your blankets?" he snapped. Unable to think, he lashed out blindly. "Is that what this has been about—using me so you can be the Chosen Woman?"

Fawn jerked back as if he'd slapped her. "No! I never used you. You wanted me as much as I—"

"Oh, yeah, I wanted you, all right. Fool that I was, I thought when you seduced me—and by the way, you're very good at it—that you did it because you loved me."

Fawn brought Remy to a stop, fighting the urge to slash his hard, accusing face with the reins. She concentrated on the growing anger, refusing to feel the pain blossoming inside her heart. "I lured you? You believe I would lie with any man to become leader of my band?"

He reined in beside her, glaring at her. "You said it, I didn't. Not just any man—me. You and True Dreamer have been plotting this ever since I rode into his camp when I was working for Judge Parker. I couldn't understand why you chose a man without formal education or money. Hell, I can't even dance and I sure don't know how to dress like a fancy gentleman. You don't love me, Fawn. You just require my services—only the services aren't quite the ones I thought they were!"

She raised the reins and swung them at his face like a whip. He caught the leather strips with blurring speed, jerking her hand down, but one end cut across his cheek, leaving a thin trickle of blood. Fawn paled, horrified at what she had done. "May the Powers forgive me, I—"

"The Powers be damned! To think I felt guilty, presuming to ask an heiress to marry me. Well, the proposal is off the table, Miss Stanhope. As soon as this job is done, I'm going back to Chicago. Find yourself another stud—or mystical lightning rod or whatever the hell you need!"

Fawn watched him kick his big bay into a gallop and ride away. How had this happened? Tears stung her eyes but she refused to let them fall. "I was going to say that I loved you, Jack Dillon, my Red Wolf," she whispered to his retreating back. Fawn had often thought her gift a burden, but never in her life had it cost her so dearly.

She must go to Grandfather. He would know what had gone wrong, how to make it good again.

Jack slowed his horse after a moment, tamping down the anguish twisting his guts. He was a professional, hired to protect Fawn Stanhope. Leaving her alone was not an option. He owed that much to the baron. But when he turned and looked back, Fawn was riding northwest in the opposite direction. It did not take much of a detective to figure out where she intended to go. He was hardly surprised that she'd seek out the old man who had orchestrated this whole tangle.

With a sigh, he rode to overtake her.

Fawn could hear the hoofbeats pounding behind her. When he caught up, she refused to look at him, just kept on riding, even when he commanded her to stop. He seized Remy's reins from her and pulled them both to a halt.

She sat rigidly in the saddle, like a statue, ignoring him as if he were invisible. "I know you want to see your grandfather, but this isn't a good time. We have work to do in Guthrie. Claude Beaurivage has the records that will incriminate the men behind Big Oak. If you want to stop them, you'll come with me. What's . . . personal between us, well, that'll have to be sorted out later."

What he said was reasonable. How could he be so unreasonable about their relationship, yet so logical about what they needed to do? Her shoulders slumped in resignation. "All right. Let's return to the capital."

When they arrived at the Grandham Hotel, a note was waiting at the front desk. Jack stood by silently while she read it, then asked the clerk for a pen and stationery to send a reply. Dillon followed her when she walked over to the end of the long walnut counter to find room to write and privacy to talk.

"A note from Claude?" he asked politely.

"Unfortunately, no, but it's good news just the same. Uncle Steven has returned from Washington. Father told him I was here." She hated the cool formality of the exchange.

"Has he learned anything new about the Beaurivage family?" Jack asked.

"I'll find out in the morning," she replied tersely.

He could see that she was dusty and exhausted from the

hard ride. There were dark circles beneath her eyes. *Don't let her beguile you again, Dillon.* "Maybe Fee's learned something."

"She should be finished with her shift now. I'll speak to her. You'd better see what your men are doing." It was a dismissal.

"As you wish."

Fawn folded the note. "Please have the clerk send this." He was careful not to touch her hand when he took the paper. She watched as he turned away without a word. *It's as if we're complete strangers.*

During the days Fawn and Dillon had been gone, his men had taken turns following the Toad and Despres, who met frequently. Claude Beaurivage, however, had vanished. Nor had there been any sightings of the bushwhacker around town.

"I think it's time we had a little talk with Josiah Ledbetter and his friend Monsieur Despres," Dillon said to Smitty. The two men sat in the Capital Saloon, directly across the street from the office of the territorial secretary, where a light burned in one window. "Let's see what they're conferring about."

"You think it's a good idea to try facin' them down while they're inside a government office?" Smitty asked.

Jack considered. "If we wait, they'll just split up again. We're spread too thin to keep following them, especially considering we've lost Claude. We've wasted enough time." Jack drummed his fingers impatiently on the table.

Smitty realized how frustrated his boss was. "Well, we could separate them, each of us question one, make the other wonder if they're keepin' their stories straight."

"Let's do it. No one else is in the building. We'll have several rooms all to ourselves." Tossing payment for their beer on the table, Dillon stood up and headed for the door with Smitty behind him.

"Swen hasn't had much luck finding that gunman yet, but he's trying all the cathouses around the worst parts of town," Smitty said as they crossed the street.

Dillon grunted acknowledgement. "Just so he finds the son of a bitch. We need to finish this job."

Smitty nodded. Something had been eating Jack ever since he'd returned to Guthrie that night. His boss looked tired, filthy and as ready to explode as a cocked revolver. Smitty surmised that Dillon and Miss Stanhope must have had a falling-out, but knew better than to ask.

They found the outer door to the office building locked. Opening it quickly proved no problem for Smitty. Once inside, they let their eyes adjust to the dimness, then headed for the lone office door with a bright sliver of light coming from beneath it.

Fee almost collided with Abbie, the sweet Scots lass Snake had mentioned. Both women had just finished for the night and were carrying large loads of dirty linens downstairs to the laundry room. "Ooh, it's that sorry I am. Watch ye don't fall," Fee said, dropping her basket to steady the other woman, who teetered precariously at the edge of the long wooden stairs.

"Och, I'm all right," Abbie replied, rolling her r's broadly, just as Mr. Campbell at the ranch did. "Dinna fash yerself," she replied kindly, stepping back and setting her load on the floor. She helped Fee gather up the napkins and towels that had spilled from her basket.

Fee was certain the young woman knew something about the guest they were looking for but was too frightened to say anything. They chatted about inconsequential things as they walked down the steep steps to the now-deserted basement. "The laundress is a hard 'un, she is. Yesterday she fair dunked me in a tub of bleach when I dropped the hem of a sheet in the dirty water beneath her washboard."

"Aye, that one is bad-tempered as they come. Doesn't like foreigners," Abbie agreed.

"Ye've been here a while. Are there any others, employees 'r guests to be afeard o'?" Fee asked guilelessly. "I don't want to make a mistake and get dismissed."

Abbie ticked off several bellmen and the assistant manager, describing their lecherous tendencies, as well as several ladies who fussed over the tiniest speck of dust in their rooms. But then she described one gentleman who was especially difficult. "The finest suite on the floor and nothing suits his lordship!" Abbie shook her head vehemently.

Fee felt her mouth go suddenly dry. Without realizing it, she had been asking the wrong questions for days! If only Fawn and Jack were safely back from the ranch. She had to find Snake at once. He'd know what to do.

Fawn walked wearily up the stairs to her room, ignoring several well-dressed guests who stared at her filthy buckskins. She was used to shocked expressions and muttered insults. Strangers did not bother her, but what had happened with Jack . . .

She shook her head. The best thing would be to order a hot bath and soak until Fee returned—if she was not already waiting in the room. Just as she unlocked her door and stepped inside, she overheard a word from down the hall. Gypsum! Two men dressed in trail clothes walked down the long hallway, heading to the stairs. She closed her door almost all the way and pressed her ear to the narrow crack so she could hear what they were discussing.

"Hell, I don't need an assay report to know those deposits can make McCreedy Brothers rich," one said.

The second man responded, "Yeah, but I don't like the old man taking fifty-one percent interest when it's our operation. We own the mining company, not Big Oak."

His companion chuckled. "He can't cheat us. Remember,

we know how he got those mineral rights. There'll be plenty of money to go around . . ."

Their voices faded as they descended the steps. Fawn opened her door and debated following them. No, they were just mining engineers. Her father could find out how this McCreedy Brothers outfit connected to Big Oak. He was already investigating who was involved with Big Oak in gypsum mining. Now she had a name to give him! She scrawled a note for Fee and left it on the table, then removed her holster, since carrying firearms inside city limits was illegal. It was only a short walk to send the wire. She expected no trouble.

Pacing in the alley behind the Grandham Hotel, Claude Beaurivage took a swallow of the swill they called brandy in this vile outpost and grimaced. He pulled out his gold watch, one of the few items of value his *grand-père* had left him. Waters was late. He replaced the silver flask in his jacket's inside pocket. He had been watching for an opportunity to kidnap Fawn since formulating his plan and enlisting Waters, but she and Dillon had left town suddenly. Claude had wanted to follow the lovers, kill him and abduct her. But the gunman had refused to go along with his idea, saying it was too risky out in the open.

Instead Waters had insisted they watch the hotel for the return of their quarry. He said he would kill Dillon at night in a back street. With the detective out of the way, they would grab the savage and head for Kansas before anyone knew she was missing. Claude now felt foolish for agreeing. Waters had sent him a message a quarter hour ago, saying their victims had just ridden into the livery. He was to meet the gunman behind the hotel. Waters was nowhere to be seen, but Fawn and Dillon had returned.

Beaurivage had watched Dillon leave the hotel. Was Waters trailing him to finish the detective off? Claude had no idea. But here he was, skulking in this offal-filled back alley, waiting like a stable hand. Glancing up and down the alley impatiently, he still saw no sign of Waters.

Fawn must have gone to her room. Perhaps there was no guard. He decided to kidnap her by himself. Some instinct told him not to trust Waters. He headed to the side of the building, intending to enter by the front door. Just as he rounded the corner, he froze, then jumped back. Fawn, dressed in filthy buckskins that molded shockingly to her body, walked out the front door.

Claude waited for her to turn her back to him, then followed, after making certain no guards accompanied her. She rounded the corner from Division onto Harrison, heading west. He grinned. She was playing right into his hands. He murmured, "*Non*, I do not require the services of Mordecai Waters after all."

Chapter Nineteen

The Western Union office in the Gray Brothers Building had already closed, but Fawn knew there would be a telegrapher on duty all night at the train depot on Oklahoma Avenue. It was only a few blocks along busy city streets to the depot. Leaving the hotel, Fawn walked purposefully down Harrison. She ignored the leering glances from several men as they saw an Indian woman dressed in men's clothing. The cretins probably thought Pawnee Bill's Wild West Show had come to town!

As she turned north, she congratulated herself that no drunks were lingering on the sidewalk outside the Blue Belle Saloon at the corner of Harrison and Second. But when she approached the alley entrance behind the Blue Belle, her luck ran out. She heard stealthy footfalls behind her. She looked over her shoulder and caught the silhouette of a tall, slender man approaching rapidly. The street lights illuminated Claude Beaurivage's face, its handsome planes twisted into an ugly sneer as he raised a pistol and pointed it directly at her.

"Do not make a sound. If you cry out, I will be forced to shoot you and vanish down that alley. You would not wish that, would you, *chérie?*"

His tone was crude and menacing. Fawn cursed her impetuosity as she replied in a calm voice, "No, dear Claude, I would not. Nor would you wish me dead until you hold the deed to Red Wolf Ranch in your greedy hands."

"For a savage, you are surprisingly astute. But you must know that if you deprive me of all hope of procuring that deed, neither do I have the slightest reason to let you live." He cocked the Smith & Wesson.

"I appear to be your prisoner. What do you want me to do now?" Fawn glanced up and down the street. In the distance, a small group of men laughed and talked, unaware of the scene being played out. Would they help an Indian woman if they knew a white man intended to kidnap her? *You're in this alone . . . without Jack's help.* She knew that was why Beaurivage had been able to follow her without her sensing him.

Jack is angry with me . . . somehow that anger diminishes my gift.

"We will proceed down this alley toward the livery where I keep my rig. You should recognize the area, *ma petite.* We are not too far from the registrar's office . . . the one you so recently burglarized."

Fawn did not respond to his accusation. Denial was pointless, but it did explain why he had removed the genuine records from their hiding place—he must have seen them with the false records at his office and realized his "courtship" was over.

"Now, I am going to place this fine weapon beneath my coat. But remember how swiftly I can remove it if you misbehave."

She could smell alcohol on his breath. That worked to her favor. He was desperate. That worked against her. It would make him unpredictable and nervous. She had to remain calm. "I wouldn't dream of misbehaving," she said dryly, as she preceded him into the darkness.

She let him get close by gradually slowing her steps.

Everything depended on being able to reach him. Just as they neared the end of the alley, she swung her left arm backward. Her fist caught him full in the face. He cursed, stumbling as he pulled his pistol out. Fawn dropped and rolled into the shadow of a water barrel, reaching down into the hidden sheath at the back of her waistband for her Deringer. No matter how she dressed, every outfit had a place for her to conceal the small gun. Whether in a ball gown or trail clothes, she had been taught never to go unarmed.

She waited until Claude lunged at her with his revolver raised. He intended to deliver a blow to her temple rather than shoot her. He needed her alive to sign over her ranch. Fawn, however, had no reason to hold her fire. She aimed for the center of his large body and waited. The blunt-nosed little Deringer was only effective at extremely close range. Then he was towering over her, bringing his pistol down with crushing force.

The sharp report of her shot echoed down the quiet streets. He staggered back and crumpled to the ground. Fawn leaped quickly across the space separating them and kicked the pistol from his hand, then knelt beside him as he lay curled on his side. The bullet had lodged in his chest near his heart. The gurgling sounds of death rattled in his lungs as they filled with blood. He gasped out a vicious curse, then went silent.

Across town, Jack and Smitty, guns drawn, faced a quivering Josiah Ledbetter and the man known as Pierre Despres. "Well, now, a late-night meeting. What, I wonder, have you gentlemen been discussing?" Jack asked conversationally, as he swung his leg over one corner of Despres's large oak desk and took a seat.

"Now, see here, whoever you are," Despres protested, "you and your hired gunman can't barge in here and threaten us with drawn guns. Do you have any idea who I am?" he demanded, standing up, all five feet, three inches of him.

Seated on the desk, Dillon's gaze was level with his. "I think you call yourself Pierre Despres, assistant to the territorial secretary . . . or, at least, that's the name you're going by now." He turned to Smitty. "Take old Josiah into the next room. Looks to me like he could use a drink from that fancy liquor cabinet we saw outside."

"You heard the boss," Smitty said, jamming his weapon in Ledbetter's red face.

The fat man looked over to his companion for help, but knew it was useless. Dillon and his henchman had them. All they could do was to say nothing . . . or at least, he prayed it would work out that way. "All right, all right," he said, struggling to get off the low leather sofa. He would stall for time. The cleaning people usually came around midnight. As he rose unsteadily to his feet, he considered whether their arrival would alarm Dillon and Schmitt enough to let them go.

When Smitty closed the door behind him and Ledbetter, Jack pointed his gun at Despres's ample midsection. "What was your name down south, before you arrived in Missouri, hmm?"

Despres blanched and his mouth gaped open, then snapped shut. "I do not have to answer your absurd questions," he replied.

Dillon could see that the bluff had worked. Despres was Claude Beaurivage's dead cousin! "As a matter of fact, you do, considering I'm holding all the aces in this game." He drew back the hammer of his New Navy Colt and pointed it at the politician.

Meanwhile, Smitty was pouring a stiff drink for Ledbetter, to loosen his tongue. The fat man's hand shook when he took the proffered whiskey. He swallowed it down in one gulp and a sour burp sent fire back up his throat. Over his prisoner's coughing, the little detective said, "We know Claude's been fakin' the land transfers and leases. Real stupid, him puttin' spanking new pages inside the old ledgers. Now, you tell me all about your schemes and maybe we can get you out of this with your skin whole. It's your friend outside or you . . . and we know all about him," he bluffed.

"C-can I have another drink?" Ledbetter wheezed. What was going on in the next room? Would his coconspirator talk? Sweat poured like a river down his back, soaking his shirt in spite of the cool night air drifting in from the window behind him. He watched Smitty pour another drink and hand it to him. This time he was careful to swallow slowly as he turned over options in his mind, frantically trying to figure out what to do.

Smitty let his prisoner stew for several minutes while the whiskey did its work. Then he shoved the barrel of his gun directly in Ledbetter's face. "You've had plenty of time. Now, talk."

Ledbetter nodded, his head bobbing like a cork on a choppy river. He'd given the records to Etienne Beaurivage. This whole land-grab was his idea. Let mister high and mighty take care of it. Josiah Ledbetter was going to take care of himself. "All right. I gave the land records to—"

Two shots rang out from the partially open window, splintering the wooden chair on which Ledbetter sat. Both penetrated his back with enough force to send his massive body pitching forward into Smitty, knocking them both against the desk behind him. Shoving Ledbetter down, the little detective leaped to the side of the window and carefully peered out. He could hear footsteps running down the alley. He tried to shove the window the rest of the way open to climb out and pursue the shooter. It was jammed tightly and would not budge.

Dillon heard the shots as well and pushed Despres onto

his hands and knees, ordering him not to move, then yanked open the door and saw Ledbetter lying on the floor. Blood trickled from one sagging cheek. "Someone shot him through here," Smitty said, as he struggled with the window.

They both tried to raise it without success. "Too late," Dillon said. "By the time we get out of this damned mausoleum, we'll never catch him." He knelt beside the fat man but could tell at once that he was dead. "He say anything?"

Smitty shook his head. "I just had him loosened up. Claude musta given him the real land records. He was about to tell me who he passed them along to. Then, bang!" He threw up his hands in frustration. "Any luck with the Frenchman?"

"You aren't going to believe it," Dillon said.

Mordecai Waters smiled grimly as he rode away. That fat old fool would not be blabbing to anyone.

But now he had another job to do. Jack Dillon. How he was going to enjoy finally seeing that damned Injun-lovin' Irishman die. Yessir, Waters had a bullet with Dillon's name on it. He patted the Colt Lightning on his hip and watched his quarry and the little man who worked for him march Despres down the street, probably heading for the jailhouse. He dared not risk trying to take both of them at once. It would be wiser to wait until he caught Dillon alone. Here in town with dark alleyways to hide him, he could kill the detective and melt into the shadows, then ride away clean as a whistle.

Fawn had left Claude and his gun lying in the alley and scaled a fence, landing in some sort of garden. She had hidden there for long minutes, panting, desperately trying to think what she should do next.

The choice had been taken from her when someone found Claude's body and cried out, "It's thet feller from the land office. He musta been robbed and shot!" A hue and cry went up as more men gathered from saloons and various other places, doubtless including drunken patrons of the Blue Belle.

"This here must be his gun. Frenchie was trying to defend hisself."

"Dude never had a chance. Spread out and look for the killer," one man commanded in a voice fortified with whiskey.

Her mind whirling, Fawn had been forced to run or be discovered. But when she'd darted across the brightly lit street, she was spotted. A man had called out, "I see him! This way, fellers!"

As she'd sprinted between two buildings, the sound of the mob seemed to grow louder, the voices more numerous. They were joined by the pounding of horses' hooves. She'd almost pitched headfirst down a steep embankment, but was able to catch herself and slide down the slope on her rump.

Now, like a wild thing, Fawn embraced the darkness, heading for the shantytown that she could barely make out in the distance. Reaching one small frame house, she dashed across its yard. Hearing all the commotion, a short, squat fellow climbed off his porch and peered into the dark. He saw her.

"Hey, what are you doing on my property?" he demanded.

Fawn ignored him and ran faster. When she raced around a large weeping spirea bush, she collided with what felt like a stone wall. It was the chest of a solidly built man. The breath exploded from her lungs on impact. She staggered backward. He, too, grunted and lost his balance, but he was not winded from running.

"I got 'im!" he wheezed, reaching for her with one meaty paw. "Damn, it ain't a feller, hit's a female!" he exclaimed.

Fawn twisted free from his grasp and seized his outstretched arm, pulling him toward her. When he stumbled off balance, she punched him in the solar plexus. He dropped to his knees and she took off again, zigzagging through several darkened yards as the men pursuing her bayed their bloodlust. She was being driven out of the darkness of shantytown, north to the lights of Oklahoma Avenue!

"It's that Injun bitch o' Stanhope's. She's the only one whut dresses in man clothes," yelled one who caught sight of her.

"Let's us teach her what it means to shoot a white man!"

"Yeah, it don't make no difference that rich feriginer wuz fool 'nough ta give her a big, fancy ranch," another chimed in.

When horse hooves closed in behind her, Fawn turned to face the man riding her down. A drunken cowhand lurched to a stop and leaned down to scoop her up. She stepped forward and grabbed hold of his left arm, unseating him. His mount shied when he hit the ground. The horse instinctively tried not to step on the man beneath him. Fawn seized the reins and leaped on the terrified animal's back.

"Hey, she's gettin' away! Stop the murderin' bitch!"

A shot whizzed past her, missing by several feet. Fawn leaned low on the horse's neck and kicked him into a swift gallop. She leaped rickety fences and dodged between dilapidated cabins, out onto brightly lit Oklahoma. If only she knew where Jack or his men were. But she had no idea and there was no time to search with a lynch mob on her tail. *Think, Fawn, think! Who can help you?*

"We've got to find her, Snake." There was a tinge of desperation in Fee's voice as the two of them walked through the hotel lobby.

After leaving Abbie in the washroom, Fee had tracked down Snake. When she'd told him what she'd learned, they had run to the livery stable, praying that Fawn and Jack had made it home safely, hoping to find out where they had gone if they were in Guthrie. If they had not returned yet, Snake would ride toward the ranch to intercept them. When they learned they'd missed their friends by minutes, Snake got his horse. Fee rode double with him, revealing what would have been a delightful bit of leg, under any other circumstances.

The boy at the stable had overheard Jack talking to the "Injun gal," saying that they ought to head to the hotel. When a frantic Fee and Snake returned to the Grandham, they found Fawn's note in her room.

"I can't miss her between here and the telegraph office," he said, trying to soothe Fee, who had reluctantly agreed to stay behind in case either Fawn or Jack returned while he was searching for her.

"But it's late. Sure 'n the office will be closed," she argued.

"No, not Western Union's office. Fawn's heading for the depot," he replied. But when they emerged into the lighted street, the sounds of shots and angry men's voices echoed through the night. "Stay right here!" he commanded Fee, then headed toward the violence.

Fee watched him turn the corner. Fawn was in trouble. The ruckus had to be about her. Had she been shot? Fee knew most of the people in town hated the idea of an Indian woman owning so much land and dressing like a white lady. They also harbored ill will toward the half-breeds who worked at Red Wolf Ranch. She started to run after Snake. What if some mob caught either him or Fawn?

Snake heard the hue and cry and knew his cousin was in serious trouble. From what he could make out, she had shot Claude Beaurivage and then run off on foot. "Hellcat, where are you?" he muttered as he scanned the streets. More men were pouring out of saloons and private residences in the poorer neighborhood, which was only a few blocks from the fancy hotel. The bloodlust of the hunt hung heavy in the air. If only she had a horse, she might stand a chance. Well, hell, he did. He rode beneath a bright street light near an alley where he figured Fawn might hide.

"Hellcat, come on out!" he hissed as loudly as he dared.

"Hey, it's another damned redskin in white men's duds— probably tryin' ta help thet murderin' savage git away," a drunken man cried out, pointing at Snake. A dozen or so men quickly converged, heading toward him.

With an oath, Snake kicked his horse and rode for cover. If nothing else, he could act as a distraction while Fawn made it to safety. He let his pursuers come near, then took off again, but this time shots peppered the air around him. One knocked his hat from his head. Several of the mob were mounted now and closing on him. He circled back down Harrison toward the hotel, hoping most of them would follow, allowing Fawn to escape.

"Don't let 'im get away!"

"I got 'im!" a second rider said, sounding the most sober of the bunch as he drew near and raised a rifle.

Snake felt the sharp punch of the slug at the same instant he heard Fee's scream. He lurched forward in the saddle. A bullet had torn clear through his side. Bad enough, but now his damn fool little gal was running toward him. She'd be mauled by the mob! He held on to the pommel with one blood-slicked hand and reached down to scoop her up with his good arm.

The pain nearly made him black out, but he could see help up the street. Dillon and Swen came running from opposite directions, but now both headed toward the mob. "Hold on, darlin,'" he said, placing her in front of him so his body could protect hers.

"Ye've been shot! Jasus, Mary and Joseph! Yer bleedin'! Bernard Snake, don't ye dare an' die on me before we say our vows."

"Wouldn't dream of it," he said, as everything started to go black in front of his eyes.

Fawn narrowly evaded capture several times but her pursuers seemed to have split up, some heading back in the opposite direction, where she'd heard more shots fired. Luckily, the horse she'd stolen from the cowhand was fresh and strong. The men pursuing her had been drinking and many were on foot. Her buckskin shirt had a rip down one sleeve from a bullet that had burned her skin. But she dared not shoot back, for fear of killing one of them with a lucky shot. That would place her in an even more untenable position. Convincing the local authorities that she'd killed Claude in self-defense would be difficult enough.

She twisted and turned through alleys, heading to the opposite edge of town, the east side. Since she had no way of knowing where Jack or his men were, there was only one place she could go for immediate refuge. Uncle Steven's home was on the southwestern outskirts of Guthrie, near Mineral Springs Park. She would have to make a wide circle all the way around the sprawling town to avoid pursuers. If she could reach her uncle, she knew no one would dare invade his elegant residence—least of all a drunken mob who knew who he was and feared his political power.

"If only he's home," she murmured, praying that he was not working late at his office. After several more brushes with angry men, she galloped to the end of the quiet street where Steven Peters lived. When she saw a light glowing in the big bay window of his home, she let out a ragged sigh of relief.

However, a few of the mob had kept on her trail and caught sight of her as she raced over the last open stretch of road. They turned their horses to give chase. Fawn jumped the white picket fence, ignoring the beautifully tended flower beds as she headed to the front porch. She leaped from the horse's back, flew up the steps and pounded frantically on the door.

"Uncle Steven, it's Fawn! There are men after me, trying to—"

The door opened and the tall older man, wearing a dressing robe and slippers, ushered her inside. "Whatever is going on, my dear? You look frightened to death!" He peered into the darkness where remnants of the mob gathered, muttering among themselves. Finally, their leader dared to open the gate and walk up the flagstone path to the porch.

Peters stepped outdoors, carefully placing Fawn behind him, then demanded, "Who are you, sir, and why are you terrifying this young lady?"

The man pulled off a bowler hat that had seen better days and shuffled nervously as he replied, "She killed the Frenchie—er, the land office clerk. Musta tried to rob him 'n he fought back. She shot him dead in an alley. We seen her runnin' away."

"Claude Beaurivage tried to kidnap me at gunpoint, Uncle Steven," Fawn said, stepping close to her uncle. "If I hadn't shot him, he would've forced me to marry him so he could gain control of Red Wolf Ranch."

Her accuser slapped the bowler across his thigh in disgust. "What white man'd force some squaw to hitch up with him, leastways legal-like?"

"This young lady," Peters stressed the last word angrily, "is the adopted daughter of my very dear friend Maxwell Stanhope, Baron Ruxton, a man well known in this territory. She has been educated by the finest tutors back East and would never rob anyone. Considering she is wealthy beyond your meager imaginings, there is no possible reason for her to have shot the registrar except the one she just gave. Now, I would strongly advise you to disperse this mob and return to your homes before you all end up in serious trouble. I will personally guarantee it!"

Peters stood stubbornly on the porch, Fawn beside him, as Bowler Hat and several of his companions milled around at the foot of the steps. They all knew Peters was wealthy and a close friend of the territorial governor. After another brief spurt of muttering, they left.

Fawn let the breath she'd been holding whistle out. "Thank you, Uncle Steven. I don't know what I would've done if you hadn't sent those men packing."

He smiled at her. "I'm very happy to have been of service, my dear. How on earth would I explain to your father if I had allowed any harm to befall you? Now, please, let me have my housekeeper fetch us some refreshment while you tell me what's happened. I assume this has something to do with Max's investigation."

"Them murderin' divils shot him!" Fee cried, holding on to an unconscious Snake. She was covered with gore. "How can he live, losin' so much blood?" she asked frantically, using her skirt to staunch the flow from his side. "And where are the damned peelers!"

Swen caught Snake as he started to slip from the saddle and steadied his body on the horse. "The police are on the way," he said calmly to Fee. "Hold on to him while I lead the horse out of here." He could see she was terrified. "They are only drunken cowhands. Dillon can handle them."

Dillon faced the angry men with hate-twisted faces. As he stood between the mob and his friends, he slid the Colt from his shoulder holster and cocked it. "Your next step will be through the gates of hell," he said in a clear voice.

The deadly tone stopped the mob. The men looked at his glowing amber eyes and the harsh slash of his mouth. Although the gun dangled from his fist, barrel down, they knew the man was a dangerous professional. No one moved until the drunken cowhand Fawn had pulled from his horse pushed his way to the front of the crowd.

"Thet Injun whore stole my horse. Where I come from, we hang horse thieves," he said, slurring his words.

"What did you do to her?" Jack asked, his chest tightening with dread.

The cowhand stepped forward. "Nothin' she didn't deserve."

Dillon snapped the Colt's barrel hard across the drover's face.

Then a shot rang out.

Chapter Twenty

Jack whirled and fired at the man whose bullet had kicked up a puff of dust directly in front of him. From his hiding place on the rooftop, the shooter dropped his rifle. It fell two stories to the ground. He pitched backward when Jack's slug slammed into his chest. "Very rowdy town," Jack said calmly.

"This ain't Earp's Tombstone, fella!" someone shouted from the back of the crowd.

Eyeing the pack of armed drunks, Dillon said, "Could've fooled me."

"We got laws here, stranger," another man yelled.

Jack stared at the mob. Some would say later that his eyes glowed like "yaller fire." "I have an idea. Why don't you law-abiding citizens do me a favor and go away before I start dropping more bodies and the police cite me for littering?" He cocked the Colt and pointed it at them.

The pack of drunks broke up quickly after that, backing away, heads shaking as many among them became sober for the first time in hours. Once he was certain they would not try anything else, he slid his weapon back into its holster and went after Fee and Swen, who were carrying Snake into the hotel.

Fawn sat at the dining-room table in Steven Peters's elegant home, clutching a cup of hot coffee while his housekeeper,

Mrs. Landers, fussed over her. The woman laid out a plate of ham, cheese and crisp pickles, then sliced sourdough bread from a crusty loaf. "The Mister has spirits, if you'd rather, Miss Stanhope—after what you've been through and all," she clucked.

"No, thank you. I need my wits about me right now. Mr. Dillon will be here just as soon as he gets the message Uncle Steven is sending for me."

The tall, thin, older woman nodded with a frown. "But first you must eat something to keep up your strength. You've been through such an ordeal, poor child."

Fawn had not the slightest appetite, but took a piece of bread and piled ham and cheese on it, then bit into it. The smoky sweet flavors tasted like sawdust to her, although she smiled her thanks. Getting the food to go down her throat was not easy.

"Now you drink that coffee. The Mister will be back as soon as he instructs the hired man to deliver that note of yours."

Fawn smiled. "Thank you. You're most kind."

Mrs. Landers patted Fawn's back clumsily. "I heard the Mister giving the dickens to that ugly mob. You're so fortunate you made it safely here. Taking care with a bit of food is the least I can do. Why don't you lie down now and rest a bit? You'll need your strength."

Fawn shook her head. "I'll go wait for Uncle Steven."

When she left the dining room, Uncle Steven saw her in the foyer. He had just entered his library and picked up some papers, which he shoved aside. "Gracious, young lady, you are indeed heartier than I would have credited. Mrs. Landers assured me you'd want to lie down after your ordeal."

She smiled and shook her head as he approached her. "I'm fine now. I need to speak to Jack Dillon when he gets here."

"I should have known you would feel that way. But you—"

He was interrupted by the sound of rapid hoofbeats from outside. "That must be Jack—Mr. Dillon," she said eagerly.

He patted her hand. "I'll see him inside, my dear."

But before he reached the door, it opened and the gunman who had haunted her nightmares for days walked into the foyer. "Uncle Steven, he's the man who's tried to kill us!" she warned, reaching down for the Deringer hidden in her waistband.

Fee sobbed as they waited in the hotel room for the doctor to arrive. Snake had passed out on the bed and was still bleeding from the gunshot wound in his side.

Swen tried to reassure her by saying, "I have seen men recover from wounds worse than this. The blood is frightening but the bullet went through clean." He looked over at his boss, adding, "Ask him to show you his scars."

Dillon, who had joined them once the mob dispersed, nodded. "He'll live to break your heart, Miss Fee."

"None of it! We're gettin' married—by a priest in the Church," she pronounced, stroking Snake's brow with one bloody hand.

Before either Jack or Swen could react, Smitty burst through the door. "I heard some yahoo shot Snake!" He took in the scene and cursed. "Where the hell are the police in this town—and where's Miss Stanhope?"

Fee looked up, realizing what she had forgotten to tell Dillon and his men. "Dear Lord and the Blessed Virgin! I know who it was in that room with Ledbetter . . ."

Fawn's Uncle Steven looked from Mordecai Waters to her and said patiently, "Mr. Waters, here, was not instructed to kill you, my dear, only your watchdog, Jack Dillon." He smiled at her coldly through stranger's eyes while she clawed at her waistband. "If you're looking for the little pea shooter, it's been removed. Lavinia, er, Mrs. Landers, is most efficient."

"Good. I didn't want ta kill her . . . yet," Waters said with a vicious leer. "She tell ya what she done ta help us out?"

"Yes, my poor dear cousin is out of the way."

"Your cousin! You're Etienne Beaurivage?" Fawn asked incredulously. Then she realized what fools they had all been. "Etienne Pierre Beaurivage—the given names are French for Steven and Peter. You simply Anglicized them to create a whole new identity as Steven Peters. Who died in that steamboat explosion?" she asked, trying to distract this murderous stranger who had pretended for a decade to be a beloved friend of her family. If only Jack would figure out where she had gone for protection. She knew this dangerous man had not sent anyone with her note.

Beaurivage's ugly smile sent a shiver down her spine. "For a benighted savage, you have always been extraordinarily intelligent. The man was Oliver Landers."

"My husband," Lavinia Landers said with a smirk from the doorway. "A drunken, worthless sot who would've gambled away the rest of his family fortune if he hadn't died."

Fawn blinked. "You let this fraud pose as your husband?"

"Only long enough to withdraw what remained of my husband's money from the St. Charles bank, something Ollie had made certain I couldn't do," she replied bitterly.

"I realized that assuming Landers's identity for long enough to gain access to his money would give me the start I required in Missouri. In return, I offered Lavinia financial security."

Left unsaid, Fawn felt certain, was the younger man's becoming her lover, perhaps promising to marry her? Whatever had developed between them had obviously evolved over the past decade into a situation far more beneficial to Etienne than to Lavinia. If only Fawn could devise a way to drive a wedge between them. Her thoughts scattered when the gunman reached out and seized her arm.

Instinctively, Fawn wrenched free and whirled around to

claw his ugly face, eliciting a scream of pain and rage. He knocked her hand away, then punched her in the jaw. Bright lights erupted behind her eyes as she crumpled against the wall.

"Ya filthy redskinned bitch! I'll learn ya how a white man treats yore kind!" He started to kick her, but Etienne Beaurivage stopped him.

"No! Not here. Soon someone from that mob might blurt out where she went. Dillon and his men will figure out quickly enough that she would come to me for help. I have worked out a new plan."

The gunman glared at Fawn while he took a greasy red handkerchief from his pocket and mopped the blood from his scratched face. "I killed Ledbetter—just afore he spilled everthin' to that runty guy what works fer Dillon. They had him 'n that Fr—er, little dude Despres, holdin' 'em in the territorial secretary's office." He looked nervously at his Frenchie boss to see if he had noticed the quickly corrected slur, but Beaurivage was pacing now, considering what to do.

"As I expected, you were not able to dispose of Dillon." Resignation and disgust filled his voice.

"Him 'n that runt, they was together. Took Despres ta the jailhouse. Figgered with Ledbetter 'n Claude dead—"

"Do not 'figger'—ever again. Your mental capacities are not sufficient for it," Beaurivage snapped.

Fawn's dazed mind cleared as she listened to the men. She had to try a bluff. Raising her head, she said, "Jack and his men will know you have me. They'll be here any minute. Let me go—"

"No, I think not. When it became apparent my pitiful baby cousin Claude could not lure you into marriage, I devised another plan to obtain your ranch."

"If you kill me, my father will come after you. Believe me, you don't want to make an enemy of the Limey, Etienne,"

Fawn said coldly, her lips curling around his French name as if it were an oath.

His expression was patronizing. "Do you believe I've amassed the fortune and political power I possess by being stupid, my dear? Of course, I will not kill you . . . Mr. Waters here will do that."

"After I have me some fun learnin' ya yer place," the gunman said with a hate-filled snarl.

"Then you forfeit Red Wolf Ranch," Fawn replied like a poker player. The stakes in this game were her life.

Beaurivage shook his head. "No, I do not think so. After you die such a ghastly death, I will see that justice is brought to your murderer."

When Fawn glanced at the gunman to see how he was taking that announcement, Beaurivage continued smoothly, "Oh, it won't be Mr. Waters but my poor stableman who will be blamed for your rape and murder."

"It's too late for all your scheming. I found out about the gypsum and McCreedy Brothers—I sent word to my father. He'll know everything in a day or two."

"Ah, but as you explained after your narrow escape, you did not have time to send that wire. Max knows nothing. My plan will work. While he and your *maman* are prostrate with grief, I will offer to buy the ranch at a handsome price, with the promise to care for your people, just so the Stanhopes don't have to endure returning to the scene of such tragic events. They will be grateful." He shrugged philosophically. "I had hoped to obtain the land a good deal less dearly, but Claude was always unreliable."

"Father and Mother will never sell Red Wolf, never desert Grandfather and our band!"

"I am quite certain they will. Remember how you trusted me? So will they."

His arrogant self-confidence sent a sliver of doubt to her

heart. Quickly recovering, she said, "The men who chased me know I'm here. If anything happens to me—"

"Yes, inconvenient, I admit, but not beyond remedy." He turned to the housekeeper, who had quietly glided over to a cabinet and taken a length of rope from a drawer. "Lavinia, truss her up securely. After we prepare things, we will require Jed Snopes." He turned to Waters, who waited expectantly . . .

"We should go with you, boss," Smitty protested as Jack checked his Peacemaker and loaded more ammunition into his saddlebags. Swen seconded the opinion, but Jack cut them off with a shake of his head.

"We don't know for certain that Fawn made it to Peters's house, or even if he's really Etienne Beaurivage, only that he owns the hotel and lived in a private suite on the third floor while his fancy big house on Allen Street was being built. The maid told Fee he had a bad temper, but that doesn't make him the man behind Big Oak."

"Accordin' to this Abbie, he still spends time in the hotel. It had to be him Ledbetter went to meet." Smitty's logic was difficult to assail, but Jack could not take the risk.

"Fawn may be hiding somewhere out there in the dark, shot or hurt, maybe even unconscious in some alley. She was on foot and Peters's place is clear across town. Unless she really did steal that drunken cowboy's horse, she could never have made it that far. I need you to light a fire under the police, organize a search party—take this town apart brick by brick if necessary. I'll deal with Peters if she's his prisoner."

Swen had a worried look on his face. "I never found that gunman. He could be with Peters."

"Or here lookin' for her," Smitty admitted grimly.

The thought of Fawn in the hands of that brutal killer

made Jack's blood run cold. "Track down some of those drunks who chased Miss Stanhope," he told Swen.

"I'll get a search party turned out," Smitty said.

While Dillon and his men split up in town, the scene had been carefully set at Etienne Beaurivage's house. He and his housekeeper lay on the floor of the foyer in his mansion. Lavinia's eyes had rolled upward, while blood from a sharp blow to her head seeped through her thinning gray hair and pooled on the spotless hardwood at the foot of the stairs. Her limbs spread out from her emaciated body like those of a broken doll.

Waters had done the job with great zest, much to her shock. The old harridan had been useful to Beaurivage, but her persistent attempts to lure him back into her bed repelled him. He knew sooner or later she would resort to blackmail if he did not marry her. He shuddered at the thought, then winced in pain.

On his orders, Waters had beaten him sufficiently to make the story he would tell quite convincing. His nose was bleeding and one eye blackened. He'd smeared an excess of Lavinia's blood all over his house robe, just for added effect. Now all he need do was wait for Dillon to arrive. After all, "Uncle Steven" was the logical person Fawn would run to under these circumstances. He was counting on a shrewd detective like the Irishman to figure it out, if one of the mob who'd chased Fawn here had not already told him where she was. Without moving his head, which ached abominably, he looked around the area and down the hall. The house had been ransacked and several valuable pieces of jewelry, silver and even his gold watch had been taken. The robbery looked very authentic.

Poor Jed Snopes, the hired man, would hang for killing Lavinia—and for the rape and murder of Fawn Stanhope.

The simpleton had been easily convinced by Waters to carry off the dirty redskin bitch who'd murdered a good white woman like Mrs. Landers. Beaurivage's mouth twisted into a smile as he lay on the floor. Jed's grandfather had been killed by Apaches before the boy had been born. His family had raised him on hate. He was all too willing to help mete out some painful private justice to a murdering redskin . . . even though he did not know the ultimate outcome would be quite different from what he imagined.

Dillon dismounted before Peters's two-story brick mansion and hid his horse in the shadows of an elm tree, then used the cover of outbuildings and bushes to make his way toward the house. Jack peered through the library window and saw open desk drawers and strewn papers littering the carpet. Books had been pulled from shelves and the shade of the lamp illuminating the room sat askew. Colt in hand, he slipped to the front door and tried the knob. Locked. Had Fawn fought her captors?

His heart froze in his chest as he thought of all the gruesome possibilities if Waters was involved. He pulled out a lock pick and quickly opened the door. Once inside, he could make out two bodies lying on the floor, motionless. One was a woman. For an instant in the dim light he thought it was Fawn. His heart stopped beating until he realized it was an old white woman. The other figure was Peters. Both appeared to be either unconscious or dead.

Without taking time to check, he moved silently down the hall, listening for any sound of an intruder. Had Waters done this? Where was Fawn? As he walked toward the kitchen, he checked all the rooms downstairs but found nothing. Then, seeing the back servants' steps leading to the second floor, he climbed them silently.

A complete search of the house yielded only more vandalism, but Jack's heart skipped a beat when he saw something glinting on one bedroom floor. He cautiously walked over and picked up Fawn's little pearl-handled Deringer. She kept a hideout gun with her always. Smelling the barrel, he knew it had been fired recently. "Probably the gun she used on Claude," he muttered, shoving it into his pocket.

Dillon quickly descended the front stairway when he heard a faint groan. Either Peters or his housekeeper was still alive! He knelt beside the woman and felt for a pulse. She was dead. Then Peters moved. He looked as if he'd been beaten pretty badly. Jack quickly fetched a glass of water and a cool cloth from the kitchen. Propping up the older man's head, he applied the cloth, eliciting another moan. Peters's eyes remained closed.

Jack resisted the urge to slap his face to bring him around. The old man was covered with blood and his nose might have been broken. One eye was swollen shut but the other's lid fluttered faintly. "Where is Fawn Stanhope?" he demanded.

Peters only groaned again, but then his right eyelid opened.

Jack took the water and put it to Peters's cracked lips. He took a sip, then coughed. As light from the rising sun crept into the foyer, the injured man blinked and tried to sit up, then fell back against Dillon's knee with a whoosh of breath.

"What happened to Fawn?" Jack asked again.

"We were . . . all sleeping . . . when I heard a scream." Peters coughed again but seized the glass with a shaking hand and took a long swallow.

Taking a deep breath for patience, Jack asked, "Was Fawn here?"

"Yes, poor child. She'd been . . . through an ordeal . . . asleep . . . we were all asleep. Mrs. Landers . . ." His voice faded as he turned his head and looked at the woman's body, then shivered. "My housekeeper. She must have heard him down here and come to investigate . . ."

"Who? Who did she hear?"

"Jed. Jed Snopes, my hired hand. He has quarters in the stables. When I heard her scream, I awakened and rushed down the steps. I saw him strike her with the butt of his rifle. I tried to stop him and we fought."

Obviously Peters had lost. Jack asked, "Where was Fawn while this was happening?"

"Mrs. Landers had given her a sleeping potion so she could rest in one of the guest bedrooms upstairs. Poor Mrs. Landers gave her one of her own night rails and helped her undress. She is . . . she is not here?" he asked, bewildered.

"Why would your hired hand try to kill you?" Dillon asked.

"He had a sack stuffed with jewelry, my gold watch . . . other things. He dropped it when poor Mrs. Landers accosted him."

"So he wanted to rob you, and you and your housekeeper interrupted. That doesn't explain why he'd take Fawn," Jack said suspiciously.

"Jed . . . he hates Indians." Peters haltingly explained Snopes's background.

"I need to check the stables," Jack said, not at all certain he believed Peters, in light of what Fee had uncovered. Still, there had been what looked like a robbery, and Peters and his housekeeper had been brutally attacked. "Can you stand up?"

"I . . . don't believe so." The old man clutched his stomach. "He struck me with his fist. He's a large man, well over my height."

"Don't move. I'll fetch help." Jack ran down the hall for the back door. He could hear Peters imploring him to find Fawn.

As he reached the stables behind the house, Jack struck a match. Terrified that his love's broken body might be inside, he stepped quickly through the open door and flattened himself against a wall. He scanned the dim interior and saw no trace of her, a good and a bad sign. A matched pair of black carriage horses stabled in the rear nickered in welcome. He recognized them from Peters's visit to the ranch. But two other stalls were empty.

The hired man's room was off to one side. Jack approached cautiously, his gut clenched for fear of what he might find. It was empty. The squalid area held only a bunk covered with filthy sheets and a rickety chair. The pegs on the wall held no tack or articles of clothing. Whatever Jed Snopes had owned, he'd taken with him when he lit out.

Jack retraced his steps to the stable entrance and quickly fired two shots in the air, yelling for attention until the rear door of the nearest house opened. A burly man clutching a shotgun stepped onto the porch. "Mr. Peters has been beaten and robbed by his hired hand," Jack called out. "Fetch a doctor."

As soon as the man nodded, Dillon knelt down and examined the ground. In the soft dust, he could make out hoofprints.

"Two horses," he murmured. That meant Fawn was alive . . . the prisoner of a cold-blooded murderer.

A man who, according to Peters, had a pathological hatred of Indians.

Chapter Twenty-one

$\mathcal{B}$ertie Valence was a man of precise habits. Every morning, with the exception of Sunday, he arrived at the telegraph office precisely at seven. That gave him half an hour to read the *State Leader* before opening his doors for business. He sat down at his station and opened his key. Almost immediately, it began its metallic chatter. He picked up a pencil and started decoding.

When he had completed his task, he sat staring at the message with disbelief. Valence's finger quickly started tapping the key. Before he delivered this wire, he had to make certain there was no mistake. Several minutes later the old man jammed his arms back into his suit jacket, seized two copies of the telegram and methodically locked the door behind him.

First he had spent a sleepless night at his boardinghouse, listening to the noisy uproar sweeping through Guthrie. Now this. What was the world coming to? he wondered. Valence scuttled as fast as his short legs would carry him toward police headquarters.

"Have you seen Jack?" Smitty asked Swen, when the two men accidentally collided on the street. Both had spent the fruitless hours of the night searching through the city, aided by Guthrie police officers.

"I thought he was with you," Swen replied. "You mean he never came back from Steven Peters's house?"

Smitty's forehead creased in a worried frown. "Whole town's in an uproar. He could be searching someplace around the area, but I don't like it that neither of us seen him."

"You think Miss Fee was right about Peters?" Swen shifted uneasily.

"I think we pay Mr. Steven Peters a little social call and see. The coppers will keep on searching here," Smitty replied.

They headed for the livery stable. A short bookish little man with a precisely manicured moustache came trundling down the street, directly in their path.

"Looks like that piece of paper in his hand's just caught fire, way he's wavin' it around," Smitty said. "Say, ain't that the telegraph operator?"

"If it is, he is very upset over the message he is carrying," Swen said. "We should ask if it concerns Miss Stanhope."

Bertie Valence slowed down when the two strangers, one quite large, the other nearly his size, intercepted him. "Who are you?" he asked nervously, when it became apparent they were not going to let him pass.

"We work for Jack Dillon, who works for Max Stanhope. That message wouldn't happen to concern him or his daughter, would it?" Smitty asked, reaching for the telegram.

Valence's indrawn breath gave them the answer. As he gaped at Smitty, Swen seized the paper from his grasp.

"See here, you have no right to—"

"If it concerns the Stanhope family, we do," Smitty said, glancing down at the message his partner handed him. He cursed, shoving one sheet back into Valence's hand. "Hightail it to the police chief with this copy. Tell him Schmitt and Swensen are on their way to Steven Peters's house!"

Fawn had spent long brutal hours thrown over Waters's saddle, her head bouncing against the toe of his boot as they rode madly through the darkness. Just before dawn they'd neared the small cow town of Hammerston, where the gunman paused long enough to stuff a filthy rag in her mouth and threatened to cut her throat if she made a sound. Then he took the bedroll from his saddle and covered her with it before they rode in. When Waters removed the blanket, they had stopped at the back entrance to a large frame building.

The giant Jed Snopes roughly pulled her from the horse's back before Waters dismounted. Snopes hoisted her over one beefy shoulder as if she were a sack of potatoes, while Waters unlocked the door and said with a leer, "Nice 'n quiet in here. Private, too."

"Yew shore it's safe?" Snopes asked, looking around the big, crowded storeroom. "I don't see why we couldn'ta jest taken keer o' the redskin out in the open, left her body fer the buzzards when we's finished with 'er."

Waters glared at the much bigger man. "Open country's no good for an ambush. Remember, she's got her lover boy comin' after her. What the hell ya think we left easy-to-read tracks for? Now put her over there." He pointed to a dark corner where a large pile of crates were stacked helter-skelter.

Snopes dumped her on the dirty wooden floor and shoved her back between two crates so she could not move. "We shoot thet feller, won't the sheriff—"

"Mr. Peters is a real powerful man. Town marshal here owes him a favor. That's why he told me to take care o' her here. No one'll ask questions. I'm gonna go look around, figure where Dillon's likely ta ride in. Watch our prisoner."

Snopes's moon face had creased with a nasty grin. "Oh, I kin watch this murderin' bitch, right 'nough."

"Remember what Mr. Peters told you. Ya gotta listen to me and I want her first. I'll be back soon's I can."

That had been an hour ago, and Fawn had been desperately trying to devise a means of escape ever since. She knew what Waters was doing—what Beaurivage had instructed him to do before he awakened Snopes and brought him into the house for the carefully staged performance. The gunman had probably already removed the stolen goods hidden in his saddlebags and placed them in Snopes's saddlebags. The hired man would be hanged as a rapist, thief and murderer while Waters continued working for Etienne Pierre Beaurivage, alias Steven Peters.

And Jack Dillon would die along with her!

Under Snopes's hateful stare, Fawn knew reasoning with him would be useless. Even if she were not gagged, this man would never believe a word she said. She had to find a way to outsmart both of them before they ambushed Jack. For the hundredth time, she looked around the storage room. Many of the old packing crates had rusty metal braces on the corners.

Abruptly, she realized that being wedged uncomfortably between two of them might be a godsend. Fawn felt behind her. If she could loosen one edge of an L-shaped brace, it might be sharp enough to cut the rope binding her hands.

After a minute she felt the sharp edge of a brace. But just then Waters returned to the storeroom. He explained to Snopes how they would ambush Dillon. She used the distraction to tug at one edge of the brace. Her fingers stung when the metal sliced through flesh. She kept her face impassive, using the pain to strengthen her resolve, the way Grandfather had taught her. She had survived Johnny Deuce. She would survive this.

You and the Red Wolf will face much danger, great evil. Only face it together and you will triumph. True Dreamer's voice floated through her mind and Fawn suddenly saw Jack riding toward the dusty little town. He would be here soon! She redoubled her efforts, freeing one metal edge. It was wickedly sharp. When she angled the rope to saw it apart, the metal cut her wrist. Fawn ignored the pain. As she worked on the rope, she concentrated on Jack, her Red Wolf, bringing his face into sharp focus in her mind. Then she stared at Jed Snopes and Mordecai Waters.

I am here, my love, but so are these men who want to kill us. Use my powers to see as I have used yours. Please listen to your heart, Red Wolf. She held her eyes closed and concentrated on the image of Jack as he rode closer to town.

"I figure we got us time fer some fun," Waters said, grinning at her. "Untie her legs so's she kin spread 'em. Ya lookin' forward ta whorin' some more, bitch?"

Snopes knelt on one knee and took a Bowie knife from his belt. Fawn had managed to sever the ropes binding her wrists. Now she let Snopes cut her legs free and drag her clear of the boxes. Then she lunged forward and jabbed the sharp metal shard from the crate into his eye. He dropped the knife with a shriek of agony.

"Bitch done blinded me! Oh Gawd, oh Gawd—" He held both hands to his face as blood poured through his fingers.

Waters cursed and tried to shove the larger man out of the way but was too late to save Snopes for a hangman's noose. Fawn slashed the hired hand's own knife cleanly across his throat.

"Ya filthy redskinned bitch! Ya done spoilt the boss's plans!" Waters yelled as he kicked the knife from her hand, sending it skittering across the floor.

He drew his revolver and leveled it at her while Snopes gurgled his last. "Now, start peelin' off them pants, an' be quick 'bout it! Leastways, I'm gonna have me some fun 'fore I kill ya—and yore squaw man."

Jack had been tracking the horses over dry, windswept plains for what seemed like forever. Images of Fawn in Snopes's power blended with those of Megan and Paddy O'Roarke. He had killed the older boy for raping his sister, but he had been too late. Her life had been over after that. He could not fail Fawn as he had Megan!

When the town appeared on the horizon, he figured this was where Snopes had chosen to hide out. How long had he and Fawn been there? Was he too late? Suddenly he heard Fawn's voice, low and calm, imploring him, *Please listen to your heart, Red Wolf.* Then the image of a big man he knew must be Snopes flashed before his eyes, followed by a second hate-filled face that turned his blood to ice—the gunman! *I am here, my love, but so are these men who want to kill us.*

He kicked his bay into a gallop while the images whirled through his mind. He could see a terrifying struggle between his love and two vicious brutal men intent on raping and killing her. Where had they taken her in this town filled with strangers? *Use my powers to see as I have used yours.* Then a two-story frame building of faded red clapboard came into focus. He rode faster.

Frightened women in drab calico and hard-eyed suspicious cowmen watched the heavily armed stranger whip his lathered horse down the main street and stop in front of Bremer's old store. He studied it for a moment, seeing the boarded-up front. Then, without a word, the gunman disappeared behind the freestanding old building. Nervous whispers moved like bees in clover up and down the street, as everyone waited to see what was going to happen.

When Jack reached the back of the building, he saw a door. Jumping from his horse, he drew his gun and approached. As he touched the knob, he heard the sounds of a struggle going on inside. He silently opened the door and stepped into the dim, crowded interior, nearly tripping over the body of Jed Snopes. Nearby, Fawn's moccasins and pants lay in a heap.

She was fighting the gunman with single-minded determination as he tried to knock her down. Fawn clawed his face with bloody hands. He slapped her viciously, then seized her braid and twisted it around his fist until he had her head immobilized. They turned back and forth so quickly that Jack dared not shoot. Holstering his gun, he approached the combatants silently from behind.

Jack sensed that Fawn knew he was there. He grabbed the killer's shoulder and spun him around. "Try fighting a man instead of a woman, you rutting bastard!" He raised his fist, but the gunman sidestepped, his hold on Fawn's hair still tight as he pulled her in front of him and dragged her back.

"Don't move or I'll snap her goddamned redskinned neck!"

Jack stayed just out of reach, waiting.

Fawn could feel her eyes tear as Waters yanked harder on her braid. She tried to kick him, but her bare feet did little damage. His good arm tightened around her neck but then the excruciating pain on her scalp eased. She could feel him reaching for something in the back pocket of his breeches. "Jack—"

His arm clamped across her throat, cutting off her warning. *He has a hideout gun!*

Just as Waters brought the little Zig-Zag Deringer up to fire at Jack, she twisted enough to elbow him in the ribs and break free. He swung the little gun up and fired but Dillon drew his Peacemaker with lethal speed. Two shots erupted a split second apart. Dillon's slug tore into Waters's chest, knocking him backward.

A look of black rage twisted Waters's face as he crumpled to his knees, rocking back and forth. His bullet had gone wild, hitting the ceiling. The little gun dropped from his hand and he pitched forward, gasping for breath. Jack raised his gun to fire again. His face was cold, the weapon aimed point blank at Waters's head.

"No, Jack!" she cried, then lowered her voice as she placed her hand on his arm. "You don't have to kill him—not this way! You were in time. You didn't fail me. He didn't rape me. Please, listen to your heart, Red Wolf." He stood perfectly still for a long time, but finally, he lowered his weapon and holstered it. The unholy light glowing in his eyes dimmed.

"I thought I'd lost you," he murmured, wrapping his arms around her. "Fawn, Fawn, my love . . . I heard your voice and I saw . . ."

"You saw through me, just as I've seen through you. This gift from the Powers is for both of us together, Jack," she said, holding on to him as tightly as he held her.

"You led me here," he whispered in wonder, realizing for the first time just how deeply their lives were intertwined. "You called me Red Wolf and I knew . . . I knew." He looked into her luminous black eyes and saw the glitter of tears. "Can you forgive me for all the cruel, foolish things I said, Chosen Woman?"

She could tell he was holding his breath, waiting for her to speak. Her heart overflowed with joy. "Only if you tell me you love me as much as I love you," she replied as tears trickled down her cheeks.

"I've loved you probably from the first time we met when you called me a troll," he said with a lopsided grin. "I just didn't know it for a while, and you didn't exactly make it easy at first. I'll always love you, Princess."

She tilted her head and smiled. "It wasn't easy for me at first, either. A princess isn't supposed to love a troll, but I love you so much I'll even live under your bridge."

They laughed the way young lovers do, but when he took his thumb and wiped the trickle of blood from her cut lip, the reality of their situation intruded into the brief idyll.

"I could've lost you to that drunken mob—or Claude could've killed you. What on earth made you leave the hotel alone at night?"

She quickly outlined what she'd overheard when she'd gone to her room and her need to inform her father. "I should've found Snake and Fee before I went dashing off, but I wasn't thinking straight after the way we parted."

"I was a fool to let my pride come between us. Forgive me?" he asked, brushing a soft kiss on her bloody lip.

"I should have explained things better, but I was afraid of sharing what I foolishly thought of as my gift. It's our gift, Jack," she said, returning his kiss.

When he saw the cuts on her hand and wrist, he pulled a handkerchief from his pocket, tore it in half and bound the wounds. As he worked, she explained how her "uncle" had arranged to have her killed. When she'd finished her story, he said, "I had a gut feeling Peters was lying, but all I could do was go after you first."

"I knew you'd come," she said simply.

"Grandfather, again?" he asked, knowing the answer. "He understood how all this would work out."

She could read the wonder—and the love—in his eyes. "Considering the gunfire, some local lawman will probably show up soon. I'll get dressed while you take care of Waters."

She quickly slipped into her breeches and moccasins while Jack used Snopes's shirt as packing to staunch the bleeding from Waters's wound. "He won't be going anywhere soon, but I think he'll live."

"Good, he can hang with Etienne Beaurivage," she said, as a tall, gaunt man with a drooping handlebar moustache hesitantly opened the door.

He wore a badge but made no attempt to draw his gun as he said, "I'm the marshal here. You kill them fellers?" he asked Dillon.

"That one isn't dead—yet," he replied, gesturing to Waters. "Both of them are wanted in Guthrie for murder and kidnapping. They took this woman and brought her here after killing another woman there," Jack said, carefully extracting papers from his shirt pocket that identified him as a detective working for Max Stanhope.

Once Marshal Crawford learned that Steven Peters was involved in kidnapping and murder, he agreed to fetch a doctor for Waters and to hold him until the authorities from Guthrie arrived.

As Fawn and Jack rode back to the capital, she explained in detail everything that had happened since they had parted. Jack told her that Snake had been shot during the night's mob frenzy while she was being chased all over town.

"Is he going to be all right?" Fawn asked, biting her already painful lip in apprehension.

"With Fee threatening him if he doesn't live to marry her in church, I don't think your cousin will dare die," Jack replied.

She closed her eyes and then smiled. "Yes, he will recover . . . but as to making Fee happy, that's not clear."

"You just might be surprised. I think he loves her and an Irishwoman's not one to take lightly."

"Neither is an Irishman," she said, then asked, "What are Smitty and Swen doing?"

He sketched what had happened between Pierre Despres and Ledbetter. "They were partners in a scheme to steal several thousand acres of land during the rush this fall. We thought Despres was Etienne Beaurivage, but he was only a petty criminal who'd fled to Missouri after selling a riverboat he didn't own in Louisiana. He just happened to show up around the time Beaurivage supposedly died."

"So Ledbetter was double-crossing Peters," she said.

Dillon shrugged. "Ledbetter thought he could get away with it and Peters would be none the wiser."

"A costly mistake. Why didn't my gift tell me who Steven Peters really was?" she wondered aloud.

"Maybe because I broke the link between us?" His expression was grim. "You could've died because of my bloody pride!"

"Enough regrets. It's all ended the way it was supposed to end." She shook her head, still amazed about "Uncle Steven." "I've known that man since I was thirteen years old!"

"And when did you start to understand your visions?"

"After I met you."

"After we first made love, Fawn," Jack said gently, receiving a warm smile from her that suddenly made the horror of the day evaporate like mist at sunrise.

Halfway back to Guthrie, Smitty caught up to them, much relieved to see that his boss and the lady were safe. "I expected to find you were buzzard bait. Damn—er, pardon, Miss Stanhope," he said, ducking his head in apology. "I sure am happy to see you're both safe."

"Waters is pretty badly wounded, being treated in the town jail. The man Peters sent with him is dead," Jack said.

"I killed him with his own knife." Fawn's tone was level, but her hands whitened on the pommel of her saddle when she spoke.

Smitty gave her a nod of reassurance. "Should've known you'd take care of them swine with a little help from Dillon here. Swen's gettin' some county sheriff's deputies to follow me. Oughta catch up pretty soon."

"Then you already knew about Peters?" she asked.

"Big Oak Land Company, McCreedy Brothers. The baron, he figgered out the whole thing and wired it to you 'n Jack. Steven Peters ain't the governor's assistant anymore. He's nursing his black eye and bloody nose in the jailhouse with that little worm Despres for company. Miss Fee was right about Peters bein' Etienne Beaurivage. Police found the real land office records in his office. Big Oak bought up mineral rights and land allotments all over the place. Wanted somethin' called gyp—somethin' er other."

"Gypsum. It's going to be worth a lot of money one day," Fawn said, then asked, "How is my cousin?"

"Shot a little bit but it ain't as bad as Miss Fee takes on, Miss Stanhope. Jack and me, we both had worse." He fished out a wrinkled copy of the telegram and handed it to Jack. "Here's the report from the baron."

Jack quickly read it, then gave it to Fawn, saying, "Max Stanhope tried to gather more information from that Louisiana congressman and found out Peters had never wired him, just made up a story to keep us from checking further. After that, the whole fabric of Peters's fictional life started to unravel."

"The Beaurivage family plantation lost by Claude and Etienne's grandfather was named Grand Chêne, Big Oak in English," she said, rereading the lengthy wire a second time. "For a man so clever, he made some very stupid mistakes."

"Yeah, like trying to deceive your father," Jack said dryly.

She gave him an arch look. "Remember that when he's your father-in-law," she replied with a smirk.

Smitty smothered a chuckle with a cough. "You think I oughta see about helpin' that town marshal holdin' Waters?" he asked Dillon, the glee in his eyes clearly visible to his red-faced boss and the smiling Miss Stanhope.

"Since Waters went there expecting to kill me and walk away, I imagine that would be a wise idea, even considering that he's wounded."

"I'll save 'im for the hangman's rope. He can dance on air with his boss!" Smitty said, turning his horse back toward Hammerston.

They reached the capital late that afternoon and Fawn went directly to the hotel to see how Snake was doing, while Jack stopped by the jail to report on Waters and Snopes.

When Fawn entered Fiona Madigan's room, she found Fee sitting up on the bed, asleep, her back against the headboard while one hand lay possessively on Snake's shoulder. He lay stretched out beneath the covers with a large white bandage wrapped around his midsection—and a big grin on his face.

"I see you're alive," Fawn said, immensely relieved.

"Did you doubt it? Everyone was plenty worried when you disappeared."

"Jack saved me. We're going to be married," she said, as her eyes moved from her cousin to Fee's drooping head.

The implication was clear. "Yep, so are we—in a church."

"The altar will probably explode."

"Be nice, Hellcat. You gonna let Grandfather do the honors, you being the Chosen Woman for the People?"

Fee's head jerked up. "Her mither's Church of England. She'll want her eldest to have all the propers, see if she doesn't."

Fawn sighed. "I haven't spoken with Jack about it yet. I do want Grandfather's blessing . . . but you're right," she added, looking at Fee. "Mother will insist on a big church wedding."

"Might know talk 'bout weddin's would wake you up," Snake said with a chuckle, patting Fee's hand just as Jack walked into the room.

"Who's getting married?" he asked guilelessly.

Fee swung her legs off the bed and sat primly on the edge. "We are!"

Fawn linked her arm through Jack's and gave it a tug. "We are, too! Twice!"

"I reckon our days of freedom are numbered, partner," Snake said to Dillon as he squeezed Fee's hand.

Fawn looked expectantly at Jack. In spite of his declaration of love hours ago, he had not reiterated the rash proposal he'd made before their terrible fight. Did he still feel she was too rich and he too poor?

Jack could see the doubt in her eyes. "For a princess, you've set your sights pretty low, but if you'll have me . . ."

He waited a beat, seeing the glow in her ebony eyes. "Will you marry me . . . Princess?"

"You are a troll—but yes! Yes! Yes, Jack Dillon, I will," she exclaimed, throwing her arms around his neck and kissing him until he staggered back against the wall.

When Jack wrapped his arms around her and returned the kiss fiercely, Snake said plaintively to Fee, "And here I am, all bandaged up and too sore to move. Some fellows have all the luck!"

"Just think of all the tender care ye'll be receivin' until ye can move," Fee purred.

Chapter Twenty-two

The sun hung like a brilliant orange ball on the western horizon when the Red Wolf crested the hill, leading a string of horses down to True Dreamer's lodge. He sat tall on his big bay, riding with only a blanket, in the way of the high plains horse Indians. As he neared the lodge where Grandfather stood, Fawn could not tear her eyes from Jack . . . her Red Wolf.

How barbarically splendid he looked in beautifully soft buckskin leggings and high moccasins that were fringed and beaded. The breastplate covering his chest was quilled with eagle feathers. A beaded headband held back unbarbered russet hair the color of his namesake. He made a magnificent Cheyenne warrior!

She was decked out in the beautiful white tunic and leggings she had worn to the council. Had some part of her known even then that these would be her wedding garments? Had he not asked her that very question? she remembered with a smile. She could feel Bright Leaf and Talks Much beaming as they stood behind her. The feast they had prepared would begin after the marriage exchange was complete. Her heart hammered in her breast when Jack slid from his horse and approached Grandfather.

Holding out the tie line to a dozen splendid bay horses, each the equal of his own mount, he placed it in True

Dreamer's hand, then bowed respectfully and stepped back, waiting for Grandfather to speak.

The old medicine man nodded in approval. "You have offered a handsome bride price for my granddaughter. I accept it with pride. You have honored Chosen Woman and the way of the People in doing this." He turned and handed the rope to Snake, who led the horses around the side of the lodge and tied the line.

Grandfather motioned Jack forward, then gravely extended his right hand to Fawn. When she grasped it, he placed her hand in Jack's. "Together you will lead the People on a difficult journey between red and white worlds." He raised his hands over them and said, "I give you my blessing, and I ask the Powers to continue to guide you through the future as they have in the past."

Fee, still feeling a bit overwhelmed by the alien environment and the vast open prairie, squeezed Snake's hand when he returned to stand by her side. His presence reassured her, as did the simple gold band she wore on the third finger of her left hand.

Snake looked down at her. "This seem right and proper to you, darlin'?" he whispered as Fawn and Jack walked down to the riverbanks.

"Sure and why wouldn't it, for the Chosen Woman herself?" she answered with a wide smile.

"Seems to me like they're hitched," Smitty said to Swen.

"Aye, laddie, they are," Clyde Campbell interjected, lighting his pipe.

"I ain't never seen a Cheyenne weddin' afore, but this here wuz real purty," Bronc averred.

"Shore wuz," Lula agreed, wiping a tear from her eye.

Sergeant Major harrumphed. "This is well and good, but nothing takes the place of a marriage in the Church of England."

Swen slapped the sturdy Englishman on the back, laughing as he said, "The Stanhopes are planning one of those in St. Louis. Jack and his lady will be the most married folks you ever did see. Come, it is time to eat and they have roasted elk."

The friends followed the bride and groom to the feasting fires where everyone joyously celebrated, giving congratulations and best wishes for a long life filled with many children.

As quickly as was seemly, Jack and Fawn slipped away to a small lodge that she and her aunts had built with help from other women of the band. She led him inside where a flame flickered in the fire pit, casting a soft, golden glow that would be welcome in the cool night to come. A feast of roasted elk, vegetable stew, an assortment of fresh berries and a pot of coffee was set out beside the fire. Off to the other side, their wedding blankets lay, soft and inviting.

"Shall I serve you the way I did at our last feast here?" Fawn asked with a mischievous smile as she knelt beside the fire.

Jack raised one eyebrow. "Not on your life! I don't intend to end up wearing my supper this time."

"Would I be so ungrateful, considering the splendid bride price you gave for me?"

"Yes, you would, but you're still worth every pony in the territory."

"For a troll, you do know how to flatter a woman," she replied as she poured two cups of fragrant coffee and added sugar to his. "Ah, this is heavenly. Good Heart knows how much our people love the sweet water."

Accepting his cup, he said, "All your friends from the ranch brought handsome gifts. Let's feed each other." He stabbed a slab of roasted meat with the knife on the carving board and sliced a piece, holding it out for her, his hand cupping it so the juices would not spill on her finery.

"Umm, delicious. The savory from Sergeant Major's herb garden adds a wonderful flavor." She selected the fattest strawberry and popped it into his mouth.

"Hard to believe an old martinet like him would make a hobby of growing herbs," Jack said.

"It's a fine old English tradition . . . speaking of which, do you mind awfully having to go through a big church wedding at the Episcopal Cathedral in St. Louis?"

Jack smiled and touched her cheek. "Your mother has her heart set on it. Besides, I know how much it'll mean for your father to give the bride away, since they couldn't be here for this ceremony."

"Then . . . then you do feel married now?" she asked hesitantly.

"About as married as a man can be. Want me to show you?" His voice was thick with desire.

"Please do," she replied, setting her cup aside and sliding over to the blankets.

He knelt before her and ran his fingers through her long straight hair, which fell like a curtain of black silk around her white tunic. She looked just as she had in the painting she'd done before even meeting Jack. He had been stunned when she'd shown it to him.

"I've never seen so much beautiful hair," he whispered, burying his hands in it and framing her face for a kiss that lasted long, delicious moments.

When they broke apart, they were breathless with the magic of it. "Raise your arms," he commanded her as he lifted the hem of her tunic and slowly pulled it over her head. Beneath it she wore only a heavy medallion of beaten copper that glistened against the burnished satin of her skin. It nestled in the deep vale between her breasts. "I like the Cheyenne custom of no undergarments."

His eyes glowed like molten amber as he admired the slim, straight perfection of her body. He ran his hands up her arms and held her shoulders while lowering his head to place soft, wet kisses on her neck, moving down, feeling the pulse at her throat accelerate.

Fawn held on to his biceps, her head tilted back as she felt the fire of his lips, whisper-soft on her skin. When he took a nipple in his mouth and suckled it she arched her back, offering her body to him while she murmured, "Oh my, I'm feeling more and more married myself." He worshipped at her breasts, cupping them in his callused hands, teasing the nipples into hard dark buds with his tongue.

When she could stand no more, she glided her hands around his neck and lifted the leather band holding his breastplate in place. "I would see your battle scars, my brave warrior." She set aside the breastplate and began kissing the old wounds on his chest and side, the newer one on his arm. Her hands splayed on his chest, her nails raking through the russet hair that arrowed downward. "You are the Red Wolf in every part of your body," she whispered, reaching for the leather ties to unfasten his breechclout.

"Not so fast. I want to see all of you." He gently pushed her backward onto the blankets, then knelt between her legs and quickly undid the thongs that secured her calf-high moccasins, flinging them aside. He let his fingers glide over the smooth curves of her hips and legs, lingering on her slender ankles. "You are so incredibly lovely." When he kissed her toes they curled in pleasure.

Fawn looked up at him, her heavy-lidded eyes devouring the hard ripple of his muscles in the firelight. His amber wolf's eyes, once so disturbing, now appeared warm like the sun, the sharp planes of his face softened by love. How broad his chest and powerful his shoulders. He could carry her as if she were indeed a princess! But now she wanted their bodies close in a different way.

She reached up for his arm and pulled him to her. As he lay beside her, she sat up and said, "I will perform wifely duties now." She loved his wicked grin when he raised an eyebrow and said raggedly, "I'm at your disposal, Princess."

She removed the moccasins from his feet and pulled the leggings off his muscular legs, marveling at their power. Then she unfastened his breechclout and freed his straining sex. Her fingers traced a long jagged scar down his thigh. When she pressed her mouth to it and kissed it, he hissed out a breath. She moved her lips slowly higher, nearing the apex of his legs and her ultimate destination.

"Fawn." He breathed her name like a prayer as she wrapped her hand around him and lowered her mouth to taste of him. Her tongue was hot and daring, curling in scalding delight up and down his shaft. His hips bucked involuntarily when she cupped his sac with her hand. Jack withstood her delicious ministrations as long as he could before whispering raggedly, "I can't wait to have you!"

"I hope not," she said simply, lying on her back as his big body covered hers. But instead of entering her, he kissed her throat, then moved lower to her breasts and belly, dipping his tongue in her navel. His hands cupped her hips and his mouth brushed her mound. Then he laved her, tasting the sweet creamy flesh that wept for his touch. When the tip of his tongue circled the hard little bud at the core of her, she cried out his name.

Jack reveled in her surrender and the sharp little contractions that told him she was beginning to crest. Then he rose up and plunged deep inside her, glorying at the wet satin clenching him. She wrapped her legs around his hips and arched, begging him to stroke. He began slowly, building ever higher, then holding off when she climaxed, before starting over . . . and over. He watched her head thrash from side to side in ecstasy until his own body felt near to bursting. Then he rode hard and heedless, all restraint gone until he, too, plunged over the edge and felt as one with his wife.

They lay locked together for many moments as the

flickering firelight bronzed their bodies. The quiet satiation was bliss in and of itself. She held fast to him, feeling the steady beating of his heart. And knew his soul. Closing her eyes, she could see him as a small boy grinning happily at his older sister, then as the furious avenger beating a far larger youth who had attacked her. That was when his nose had been broken . . . but now it was miraculously straight once more . . . as if his whole life could begin anew.

Jack saw Fawn as a little girl playing in a field of wildflowers, singing to herself, until a small, evil man rode out of nowhere and seized her, carrying her on a long and bitter journey. His heart ached for the pain she'd endured but swelled with pride for the strength of her spirit that sustained her until Max Stanhope had killed her tormenter and her grandfather's medicine had healed her body. He blinked and murmured in her ear, "I just had the strangest dream."

Fawn opened her eyes and said, "We are one now and always will be. It was no dream but my life before you came into it."

He looked at her as he realized what this meant. "I could see it."

"Yes, as I could see your life. I told you that we belong to each other. Neither one controls the other."

"But we need each other."

She nodded. "Now we begin together."

He caressed her cheek and murmured, "Chosen Woman, I'm very grateful that the Powers have chosen me for your husband. Let us begin together."

"Forever . . ."

At the feasting fire by the river, the old medicine man sat with his friends. Everyone laughed and talked but he just smiled serenely. The Powers had chosen wisely, as they always did. Now everything had come full circle in their Grand Design.

Discover Great Native American Romance

If you crave the turbulent clash of cultures and the heat of forbidden love, don't miss these exciting Native American Romances:

Comanche Moon Rising by Constance O'Banyon
Coming August 2009

Struggling to make a new life for herself and her young brother on a rugged ranch in Texas, Shiloh finds an unlikely protector in the chief of a nearby band of Comanches. But when he kidnaps them, she is torn between outrage and the powerful attraction she feels for the virile warrior.

Black Horse by Veronica Blake
Coming October 2009

Adopted by the Sioux as a young child, Meadow thinks of herself as one of the People, until a white visitor to their camp notices her pale coloring and begins questioning her background. When torn from the only home she's ever known, a virile young chief must risk his freedom to rescue her.

More Great Native American Romance!

Chase the Lightning by Madeline Baker
Chase the Wind by Cindy Holby
Shadow Walker by Connie Mason
Half-Breed's Lady by Bobbi Smith

Award-winning Author

CAROLINE FYFFE

"The love that unfolds in this tender and emotional story will touch your heart. Don't miss this breathtaking debut."
—Patti Berg, *USA Today* Bestselling Author

Chase Logan liked being a loner, a drifter, free and clear as a mountain stream. But one look into Jessie Strong's sky blue eyes and in the span of a heartbeat, he found himself agreeing to be her husband—and a father!

Jessie knew it was all pretend. And only temporary. Just until the adoption went through for three-year-old Sarah. But the longer Chase stayed, the less she could imagine a long, lonely Wyoming winter without him.

Times may be tough—supplies short and danger just outside the doorstep—but with the strength of the pioneer spirit and the warm glow of love in their hearts, Chase and Jessie are determined to have a true family at last, no matter

Where the
Wind Blows

ISBN 13: 978-0-8439-6284-0

To order a book or to request a catalog call:
1-800-481-9191
Our books are also available at your local bookstore, or you can check out our Web site **www.dorchesterpub.com** where you can look up your favorite authors, read excerpts, glance at our discussion forum, and check out our digital content. Many of our books are now available as e-books!

☐ **YES!**

Sign me up for the Historical Romance Book Club and send my FREE BOOKS! If I choose to stay in the club, I will pay only $8.50* each month, a savings of $6.48!

NAME: _____

ADDRESS: _____

TELEPHONE: _____

EMAIL: _____

☐ I want to pay by credit card.

☐ **VISA**　　☐ **MasterCard.**　　☐ **DISCOVER**

ACCOUNT #: _____

EXPIRATION DATE: _____

SIGNATURE: _____

Mail this page along with $2.00 shipping and handling to:
Historical Romance Book Club
PO Box 6640
Wayne, PA 19087
Or fax (must include credit card information) to:
610-995-9274
You can also sign up online at **www.dorchesterpub.com**.
*Plus $2.00 for shipping. Offer open to residents of the U.S. and Canada only.
Canadian residents please call 1-800-481-9191 for pricing information.
If under 18, a parent or guardian must sign. Terms, prices and conditions subject to change. Subscription subject to acceptance. Dorchester Publishing reserves the right to reject any order or cancel any subscription.